'Don't you feel the chemistry between us as well?'

'I don't know what you're talking about,' Sophie whispered, and Matias raised his eyebrows in an expression of frank incredulity.

'Of course you do,' he corrected her casually. 'Although,' he continued, 'I understand that you might want to deny it. After all, it's not exactly something either of us bargained for, is it?'

No truer words spoken, Matias thought wryly. All things considered, he would have placed greater odds on him catching a rocket to the red planet.

He shrugged eloquently. 'But there you are. These things happen.'

Sophie's brain finally cranked into gear and anger began building inside her with the force of suppressed molten lava. He was a rich, powerful man who had her on the run, and because of that he figured he could come on to her because he happened to find her attractive.

'I'm sorry,' she said coldly, 'but I'm not interested.'

Matias laughed as though sh[...] hilarious joke. 'A[...] don't feel that ele[...] noted the blush tha[...] yes. Of course you[...] Why deny it?'

Cathy Williams can remember reading Mills & Boon books as a teenager, and now that she is writing them she remains an avid fan. For her, there is nothing like creating romantic stories and engaging plots, and each and every book is a new adventure. Cathy lives in London. Her three daughters—Charlotte, Olivia and Emma—have always been, and continue to be, the greatest inspirations in her life.

Books by Cathy Williams

Mills & Boon Modern Romance

Cipriani's Innocent Captive
The Secret Sanchez Heir
Bought to Wear the Billionaire's Ring
Snowbound with His Innocent Temptation
A Virgin for Vasquez
Seduced into Her Boss's Service
The Wedding Night Debt
A Pawn in the Playboy's Game
At Her Boss's Pleasure
The Real Romero
The Uncompromising Italian
The Argentinian's Demand
Secrets of a Ruthless Tycoon

The Italian Titans

Wearing the De Angelis Ring
The Surprise De Angelis Baby

One Night With Consequences

Bound by the Billionaire's Baby

Seven Sexy Sins

To Sin with the Tycoon

Visit the Author Profile page
at millsandboon.co.uk for more titles.

LEGACY OF
HIS REVENGE

BY
CATHY WILLIAMS

First Published in Great Britain 2017
By Mills & Boon, an imprint of HarperCollins*Publishers*
1 London Bridge Street, London, SE1 9GF

© 2017 Cathy Williams

ISBN: 978-0-263-92549-4

Our policy is to use papers that are natural, renewable and recyclable
products and made from wood grown in sustainable forests. The logging
and manufacturing processes conform to the legal environmental
regulations of the country of origin.

Printed and bound in Spain
by CPI, Barcelona

LEGACY OF
HIS REVENGE

CHAPTER ONE

'THERE'S A DAUGHTER.'

In receipt of this revelation, Matias Rivero looked at his friend and trusted associate, Art Delgado. Like Matias, Art was thirty-two. They had gone to school together and had formed an unlikely friendship with Matias the protector, the one who always had his friend's back. Small, asthmatic and bespectacled, Art had always been an easy target for bullies until Matias had joined his class and, like a dangerous, cruising shark, had ensured that no one came near the boy who had spent the past two years dreading the daily onslaught of beatings.

Now, all these years later, Matias was Art's boss and in return Art was his most loyal employee. There was no one Matias trusted more. He motioned for Art to sit and leaned forward to take the mobile phone handed to him.

He scrolled down the three pictures capturing a small, homely, plump little creature leaving Carney's mansion in an old car that looked as though its only wish was to breathe its last breath and depart for the great automobile parking lot in the sky.

Matias vaguely wondered why she wasn't in a car befitting a man who had always made social climbing his priority.

But more than that he wondered who the hell the woman was and why he hadn't heard of her before.

'How is it that I am only now finding out that the man has a child?' Matias murmured, returning the mobile phone to his friend and relaxing back in the chair. 'In fact, how do you know for sure that the woman is his daughter?'

At a little after seven, his office was empty. It was still summertime hot, it was Friday and everyone else had better things to do than work. There was nothing pressing to hold his attention. His last lover had been dispatched a few weeks ago. Right now, Matias had all the time in the world to think about this development in his campaign.

'She said so,' Art told him, pushing his wire-rimmed spectacles up his nose and looking at his friend with some concern. 'But I don't suppose,' he added uneasily, 'it makes any difference, Matias. Does it?'

Matias pushed his chair back and stood up. Seated, he was formidable. Standing, he towered. He was six feet three of solid, packed muscle. Black-haired and black-eyed, the product of an Argentinian father and a dainty Irish mother, Matias had resoundingly come up trumps in the genetic lottery. He was sinfully beautiful, the hard lines of his lean face wonderfully chiselled into absolute perfection. Right at this moment, he was frowning thoughtfully as he strolled towards the floor-to-ceiling bank of glass that overlooked the busy London streets in the heart of the city.

From this high up, the figures down below were matchstick small and the cars and taxis resembled kids' toys.

He ignored the latter part of his friend's remark and

instead asked, 'What do you mean "she said so"? Surely I would have known if the man had offspring. He was married and it was a childless union.' But in truth, Matias had been uninterested in the personal details of James Carney's life.

Why would he care one way or another if the man had kids or not?

For years, indeed for as long as he could remember, he had been focused on bringing the man to his knees through his company. The company that should never have been Carney's in the first place. The company that had been founded on lies, deceit and Carney's outright theft of Matias's father's invention.

Making money and having the power associated with it within his grasp was so entwined with his driving need to place himself in a position to reach out and wrench Carney's company from under his feet, that it would have been impossible to separate the two. Matias's march towards wealth had also been his march towards satisfying his thirst for revenge. He had gained his first-class degree, had bided his time in an investment bank for two years, making the money he needed to propel himself forward, and then he had quit with money under his belt and a black book stuffed with valuable connections. And he had begun his remorseless rise to the top via mergers and acquisitions of ailing companies, getting richer and richer and more and more powerful in the process.

Throughout it all, he had watched patiently for Carney's company to ail and so it had.

For the past few years, Matias had been circling the company, a predator waiting for exactly the right time. Should he begin the process of buying shares, then flooding the market with them so that he could plunge the company into a premature meltdown? Should he wait until the company's health deteriorated beyond repair so that he could instigate his hostile takeover? Choices, choices.

He had thought about revenge for so long that there was almost no hurry but the time had finally come. The letters he had recovered from his mother's possessions, before she had been admitted to hospital three weeks previously, had propelled him towards the inevitable.

'Well?' he prompted, returning to his chair although he was suddenly restless, itching now to start the process of retribution. 'You had a convivial conversation with the woman? Tell me how you came to your conclusion. I'm curious.'

Matias looked at Art, waiting for clarification.

'Pure coincidence,' Art admitted. 'I was about to turn into Carney's drive when she came speeding out, swerved round the corner, and banged into the car.'

'The woman crashed into my car? Which one?'

'The Maserati,' Art admitted. 'Nasty dent but her car, sadly, was more or less a write-off. No worries. It'll be sorted.'

'So she banged into my Maserati,' Matias hurried the story along, planning on returning to this little episode later down the line, 'told you who she was and then…what?'

'You sound suspicious, Matias, but that's exactly what happened. I asked her if that was the Carney residence and she said yes, that her dad lived there and she had just seen him. She was in a bit of a state because of the accident. She mentioned that he was in a foul mood and that it might be a good idea to rearrange whatever plans I had with him.'

'So there's a daughter,' Matias said thoughtfully. 'Interesting.'

'A nice girl, Matias, or so it would seem.'

'Impossible.' That single word was a flat denial. 'Carney is a nasty piece of work. It would be downright impossible for him to have sired anything remotely *nice*.' The harsh lines of his face softened. For all his friend's days of being bullied, Art had an instinctive trust in the goodness of human nature that he, Matias, lacked.

Matias had no idea why that was because they were both mixed race, in Art's case of Spanish descent on his mother's side. They had both started at the bottom of the pecking order and had had to toughen up to defend themselves against casual racism and snobbery.

But then, Matias mused not for the first time, he and he alone had witnessed first-hand the way criminal behaviour could affect the direction of someone's life. His father had met James Carney at university. Tomas Rivero had been an extraordinarily clever man with a gift for all things mathematical. He had also been so lacking in business acumen that when, at the age of twenty-four, he invented a computer program that facilitated the analysis of experimental drugs, he was a sitting duck for a man who had very quickly seen where the program could be taken and the money that could be made out of it.

James Carney had been a rich, young thing with a tribe of followers and an eye to the main chance. He had befriended Tomas, persuaded him into a position of absolute trust and, when the time was right, had accumulated all the right signatures in all the right places that ensured that the royalties and dividends from the software went to him.

In return, Tomas had been sidelined with a third-rate job in a managerial position in the already ailing family business Carney had inherited from his father. He had never recovered mentally.

This was a story that had unfolded over the years, although, in fairness to both his parents, nothing had ever been said with spite and certainly there had never been any talk of revenge on the part of either of them.

Matias's father had died over a decade previously and Rose Rivero, from the very start, had not countenanced thoughts of those wheels turning full circle.

What was done, was done, as far as she was concerned. The past was something to be relinquished.

Not so for Matias, who had seen his father in those quieter moments, seen the sadness that had become a humiliating burden. You didn't have to be a genius to work out that being shoved in some dingy back office while you saw money and glory heaped on undeserving shoulders had damaged his father irreparably.

As far as Matias was concerned, his father had never fully recovered from Carney's theft. He had worked at the company in the pitiful job condescendingly given to him for a couple of years and then moved on to another company, but by then his health was failing and Rose Rivero had had to go out to work to help make ends meet.

If his mother had cautioned against revenge, then he had had enough of a taste for it for the both of them.

But he knew that over the years the fires had burned a little less brightly because he had become so intensely consumed in his own meteoric rise to the top. It had been propelled by his desire for revenge but along the way had gathered a momentum of its own, taken on its own vibrant life force...distracted him from the goal he had long ago set himself.

Until he had come upon those letters.

'She must have produced her insurance certificate,' Matias mused, eyes narrowing. 'What's the woman's name?'

'I'll email you the details.' Art sighed, knowing without having to be told the direction of his friend's thoughts. 'I haven't had a chance to look at it but I took a picture of the document.'

'Good,' Matias said with some satisfaction. 'Do that immediately, Art. And there will be no need for you to deal with this matter. I will handle it myself.'

'Why?' Art was the only person who would ever have dared ask such a forthright question. Especially when the question was framed in a tone of voice that carried a warning.

'Let's just say that I might want to get to know her better. Knowledge is power, Art, and I now regret that I didn't dig a little deeper into Carney's private life. But don't look so worried! I'm not the big bad wolf. I don't make a habit of eating innocent young girls. So if she's as *nice* as you imply, then she should be as safe as houses.'

'Your mother wouldn't like this,' Art warned bluntly.

'My mother is far too kind for her own good.' For a few seconds, Matias thought of Rose Rivero, who was recuperating from a near fatal stroke at one of the top hospitals in London. If his father had never recovered from Carney's treachery, then his mother had never recovered from his father's premature death. When you looked at it, Carney had not only been responsible for his family's unjust state of penury, but beyond that for the stress that had killed his father and for the ill health and unhappiness that had dogged his mother's life. Revenge had been a long time coming but, if only James Carney knew it, it was now a juggernaut rolling with unstoppable speed towards him...

Sophie Watts stared up at the soaring glass tower in front of her and visibly quailed.

The lovely man whose car she had accidentally *bruised* three days previously had been very accommodating when she had phoned the number he had given her when they had exchanged details. She had explained the situation with her insurance policy and he had been sympathetic. He had told her in a friendly enough voice that she would have to come and discuss the matter personally but he was sure that something could be sorted out.

Unfortunately, the building in front of her did not look like the sort of user-friendly place in which cheerful and accommodating people worked, sorting out thorny situations in a cordial and sympathetic manner.

She clutched her capacious bag tightly and continued staring. Her head told her that she had no option but to move forward with the crowd while her feet begged to be allowed to turn tail and flee back to her low-key corner of East London and her little house in which she did her small-scale catering and baking for anyone who needed her services.

She didn't belong here and the clothes she had carefully chosen to meet Art Delgado now felt ridiculous and out of place.

The young women sweeping past her with their leather computer bags and clicking high heels were all dressed in sharp black suits. They weren't dithering. They were striding with purpose into the aggressive glass tower.

A small, plump girl with flyaway hair wearing a summery flowered dress and sandals didn't belong here.

Sophie propelled herself forward, eyes firmly ahead. It had been a mistake to come here *first thing* so that she could *get it over with*. That idea had been great in theory but she hadn't banked on the early rush-hour stampede of city workers. However, it was too late now to start chastising herself.

Inside, the foyer was a wondrous and cruel blend of marble, glass and metal.

Arrangements of sofas were scattered here and there in circular formations. The sofas were all very attractive and looked enormously uncomfortable. Clearly management didn't want to encourage too much lounging around. Ahead of her, a bank of receptionists was busily directing people while streams of smartly dressed worker bees headed for the gleaming lifts opening and closing just beyond an array of stunted palm trees in huge ceramic pots.

Sophie felt a pang of physical longing for her kitchen, where she and Julie, her co-worker, chatted and baked and cooked and made big plans for the upmarket bakery they would jointly open one day. She craved the feel of her apron, the smell of freshly baked cake and the pleasant playing around of ideas for meals they had booked in for catering jobs. Even though she was now talking

to one of the receptionists, explaining who she wanted
to see, confirming that an appointment had been made
and stuttering over her own name, she was unhappily
longing to be somewhere else.

Frayed nerves made her miss what the snappily
dressed girl in front of her had just said but then she
blinked and registered that a mistake had been made.

'I don't know a Mr... River,' she said politely.

'*Rivero.*' Eyebrows arched up, lips tightened, eyes
cooled.

'I'm here to see a Mr Delgado.'

'Your meeting is with Mr Rivero.' The receptionist
swivelled the computer towards her. 'You are to sign
in. Anywhere on the screen will do and just use your
finger. Mr Rivero's secretary will be waiting for you
on the tenth floor. Here's a clip-on pass. Make sure you
don't remove it because if you do you'll be immediately
escorted out of the building.'

In a fluster, Sophie did as she was told but her heart
was hammering inside her as she obeyed instructions,
allowing herself to be swept along in a group towards
the nearest lift and then staring fixedly at nothing in
particular as she was whooshed up to the tenth floor,
as directed.

Who was Mr Rivero? She had banked on the comfort of explaining her awkward situation to the very nice
Mr Delgado. What sort of hearing was she going to get
from a complete stranger? She was as tense as a bow
string when, disgorged into the plushest surroundings
she had ever seen, she was taken in hand by a very tall,
middle-aged woman whose expression of sympathy did
nothing to quell her escalating nerves.

And then she was being shown into an office, faced

with a closed door, ushered through it and deposited like an unwanted parcel in a room that was simply breathtaking.

For a few seconds, eyes as round as saucers, Sophie looked around her. She hadn't budged from where she had been placed just inside the door of a gigantic office. She cravenly recoiled from actually being bold enough to walk forward. Bag clutched tightly in front of her, she gradually became aware of the man sitting behind the desk. It was as if, suddenly, she focused, and on focusing felt the thudding impact of shock because the guy she was staring at was the most stunningly drop-dead gorgeous specimen she had ever seen in her entire life.

Her breathing slowed and even though she knew she was staring, she couldn't help herself. His hair was raven black, his eyes the colour of the darkest, richest chocolate, his features lovingly and perfectly chiselled. He oozed the sort of stupendous sex appeal that made heads swing round for a second and third look.

The silence stretched and stretched between them and then it dawned on her that she was making an absolute fool of herself.

'Miss Watts.' Matias was the first to speak. 'Do you intend to hover by the door for the duration of this meeting?' He didn't get up to shake her hand. He didn't smile. He did nothing to put her at ease. Instead he nodded at the chair in front of his desk. 'Sit down.'

Sophie shuffled forward, not knowing whether she was expected to shake his hand as a formality, but his expression was so forbidding that she decided against it and instead sank into the leather chair. She almost immediately leaned forward and rushed headlong into the little speech she had earlier rehearsed.

'I'm really sorry about the car, Mr...er... Rivero. I honestly had no idea that your friend was turning into the drive. It's so difficult to see round that bend, especially in summer. I admit I may have been driving a little faster than usual but I want to impress upon you that it was *unintentional*.' What she could have added but didn't was that her vision had been blurred because she had been doing her utmost not to cry after a stormy and upsetting meeting with James Carney.

Matias was watching her intently, his dark eyes narrowed on her flushed and surprisingly pretty face. He was a man who went for catwalk models, with long, angular bodies and striking, photogenic faces, yet there was something alluring about the woman sitting in front of him. Something about the softness of her face, the pale, vanilla shade of her unruly hair, the perfect clarity of her aquamarine eyes, held his attention and he could only assume that it was because of her connection to James Carney.

He hadn't known the woman existed but the minute he had found out he had recognised the gift that had landed in his lap for what it was.

He thought back to those letters he had unearthed, and his jaw tightened. That soft, wide-eyed, innocent look wasn't going to fool him. He didn't know the full story of the woman's relationship to Carney but he certainly intended to find out, just as he intended to exploit the situation he had been handed to discover if there were any other secrets the man might have been hiding. The broader the net was cast, the wider the catch.

'Employee,' Matias replied. This just in case she got

it into her head that special favours were going to be granted because of Art's personal connection with him.

'I beg your pardon?'

'Art Delgado is my employee. He was driving my Maserati. Miss Watts, do you have any idea how much one costs?'

'No, I don't,' Sophie said faintly. He was having the most peculiar effect on her. It was as though the power of his presence had sucked the oxygen out of the air, making it difficult to breathe.

'In that case, allow me to enlighten you.' He named a sum that was sufficiently staggering to make her gasp. 'And I have been told that your insurance policy is invalid.'

'I didn't know,' Sophie whispered. 'I'm usually so good at dealing with all that stuff but things have been a bit hectic recently. I know I cancelled my old policy and I had planned on renewing with somewhere cheaper but...'

Matias held up one imperious hand to stop her in mid flow. 'I'm not interested in the back story,' he informed her coolly. 'To cut to the chase, the damage you have done to my car will run to many, many thousands.'

Sophie's mouth dropped open. 'Thousands?' she parroted.

'Literally. I'm afraid it won't be a simple case of sorting out the dent. The entire left wing of the car will have to be replaced. High-performance cars charge high-performance prices.'

'I... I had no idea. I haven't got that sort of money. I...when I spoke to your friend...sorry, your employee Mr Delgado on the phone, he said that we would be able to work something out.'

'Sadly working something out really isn't in his remit.' Matias thought that his old friend would raise a sardonic eyebrow at that sweeping statement.

'I could pay you back over time.' Sophie wondered what sort of time line would be acceptable to the unforgiving man staring coldly at her as though she were an undesirable alien that had suddenly invaded his personal space. She somehow didn't imagine that his time line was going to coincide with hers. 'I run a little catering business with a friend,' she hurtled on, desperate to bring this uncomfortable meeting to an end and even more desperate to find some sort of solution that wouldn't involve bankruptcy for her and Julie's fledgling start-up company. 'We only opened up a year and a half ago. Before that we were both primary school teachers. It's taken an awful lot of borrowing to get everything in order and to get my kitchen up to the required standard for producing food commercially, and right at this moment, well...there isn't a great deal of spare change flying about.'

'In other words you're broke.'

'We're really making a go of things, Mr Rivero!' Heat flared in her cheeks. 'And I'm sure we can work something out when it comes to a repayment schedule for your car...'

'I gather you're James Carney's daughter.' Matias lowered his eyes, then he pushed back his chair and stood up to stroll across to the impressive bank of windows, in front of which was a tidy sitting area complete with a low table fashioned in chrome and glass.

Sophie was riveted at the sight of him. The way he moved, the unconscious flex of muscle under the expensive suit, the lean length of his body, the casual strength he exuded that was frankly spellbinding. He turned to look at her and it took a big effort not to look away.

His throwaway remark had frozen her to the spot.

'Well?' Matias prodded. 'Art was on his way to pay a little visit to James Carney on business,' he expanded, 'when you came speeding out of his drive like a bat out of hell and crashed into my car. I had no idea that the man even had a family.' He was watching her very carefully as he spoke and was mildly surprised that she didn't see to ask him a very fundamental question, which was why the heck should Carney's private life have anything to do with him?

Whatever she was, she clearly didn't have a suspicious nature.

Sophie was lost for words. She had been shaken by the accident, upset after the visit to her father, and Art Delgado, so different from this flint-eyed guy assessing her, had encouraged her into a confidence she rarely shared with anyone.

'Of course…' Matias shrugged, curiosity spiking at her continued silence '… I am not primarily concerned with the man's private life but my understanding was that he was a widower.'

'He is,' Sophie whispered, ashamed all over again at a birthright she hadn't asked for, the consequences of which she had been forced, however, to live with.

'So tell me where you fit in,' Matias encouraged. 'Unless, of course, that was a little white lie you told my employee on the spur of the moment.' He appeared to give this a little thought. 'Maybe you were embarrassed to tell the truth…?'

'Sorry?' That garnered her attention and she looked at him with a puzzled frown.

'Young girl having an affair with an old man? I can
see that you might have been embarrassed enough to
have said the first thing that came to your head, anything that sounded a little less unsavoury than what you
really are to Carney.'

'How dare you?' Sophie gasped, half standing.
'That's disgusting!'

'I'm just trying to do the maths.' Matias frowned and
tilted his head to one side. 'If you're not his lover, the
man must have had a mistress while he was married.
Am I right? Are you Carney's love child?'

Sophie laughed bitterly because nothing could have
been further from the truth. Love had never come into
the equation. Before her untimely death, her mother,
Angela Watts, had been an aspiring actress whose great
misfortune had been her Marilyn Monroe blonde-bomb-
shell looks. Prey to men's flattery and pursued for her
body, she had made the fatal error of throwing her net
too wide. James Carney, young, rich and arrogant, had
met her at a club and, like all the others, had pursued
her, but he had had no intention of ever settling down
with someone he considered a two-bit tart with a pretty
face. Those details had been drummed into Sophie from
as soon as she was old enough to understand. He had
had fun with Angela and she had foolishly thought that
the fun would actually go somewhere, but even when
she had contrived to trap him with a pregnancy he had
stood firm, only later marrying a woman he considered
of the right class and social position.

'He met my mother before he was married,' Sophie
confessed, belatedly adding, 'not that it has anything to
do with…well, *anything*. Mr Rivero, I would be more
than happy for you to draw up a schedule for repayment.

I will sign it right here and right now and you have my word that you will have every penny I owe you back. With interest if that's what you want.'

Matias burst out laughing. 'That's very obliging of you,' he drawled lazily. 'Believe it or not, I haven't become a successful businessman by putting my faith in the impossible. I have no idea what you owe the bank but I suspect you're probably barely making ends meet. Am I right?'

He tilted his head to one side and Sophie looked at him with loathing. He might be sinfully handsome but she had never met anyone she hated more on the spot. She wasn't stupid. He had all the money in the world, from the looks of it, but he wasn't going to be lenient when it came to getting back every penny she owed him and she knew that he wouldn't give a hoot if he drove her little company into the ground to do it.

Right now, he was toying with her like a cat playing with a mouse.

'We could work out a schedule,' he mused, 'but I would be on my walking frame before you made the final payment.' She really had the most wonderfully transparent face, he thought. Impossible though it was, she looked as pure as the driven snow.

But perhaps she wasn't fashioned in the same mould as the father. Certainly, she wouldn't have had the example set by him on a daily basis if she was the product of a youthful affair. He was surprised, in fact, that she had any contact with the man at all and he wondered how that had worked when Carney's socially acceptable wife had been alive.

Matias wasn't going to waste time pondering stuff like that, however. Right now, he was working out how best to use her to his advantage. When he pulled the plug on Carney, he intended to hit him on all fronts and he wondered whether she could be of use to him in that.

What other secrets was the man hiding? Matias knew that the company was beset with financial problems but, in the ether, there had been rumours of foul play... Sometimes skeletons were hard to find, however hard you dug, and Carney was a man who was sly and smart enough to cover his tracks. Wouldn't it be satisfying if all his dark secrets were to be exposed to the cruel glare of light...?

Could this fresh-faced girl be the key to unlock more doors? And what if there were personal skeletons? An attack on all fronts was certainly worth considering. He was honest enough to acknowledge that this level of revenge was probably beneath him, but those letters he'd found...they had made this personal...

'You could always ask Daddy for the money,' he ventured smoothly, knowing what the answer would be.

'No!' This time she did stand up. Her full mouth was drawn into a thin, obstinate line. 'I won't have... my father involved in this. Bankrupt me if you want.' She reached into her bag, pulled out one of the business cards, remembering how filled with optimism she and Julie had been when they had had them printed. 'Here's my business card. You can come and see the premises. It's just in my kitchen but the equipment must be worth something. I have a number of big jobs lined up, so if you're patient I can do those and you can have the money. As for the rest... I will sell my house and I should be able to sort out the rest of the debt with money left over after the mortgage has been covered.'

Matias looked at her, every line of his powerful body

indicating a man totally relaxed, totally unfazed by her emotional outburst.

Dark eyes roamed over her. She had tried to do something businesslike with her hair but somewhere along the line it had rebelled and tangled, white-blonde strands already curling around her cheeks. Her eyes were wide and a curious shade of turquoise and fringed, he noted, with thick dark lashes, which was at odds with the colour of her hair. And her body...

He shifted in his chair, astonished that he was even bothering to notice that she had curves in all the right places and luscious breasts that were prominent against the truly appalling flowered dress she was wearing.

She lacked sophistication and clearly had no style gene whatsoever, so what, he wondered, with a certain amount of irritation, was it about her that captured his attention so completely?

'You're overreacting,' he told her as she remained standing, her blue eyes dark with worry, anger and distress.

'You've just told me that you're not willing to come to any kind of arrangement with me about the money I owe you for your stupid car!' Easy-tempered by nature, Sophie was shocked at the stridency of her voice and the fact that she *was yelling at him*! 'I can't go to my bank and draw out the kind of money I would need to make good the damage. So, *of course I'm going to be upset*.'

'Sit down.'

'No. I'm going. You can get in touch with me on the number on the card! I'm going to have to talk this through with Julie. I don't know what she's going to say. She's put in most of her savings to try and get this business of ours going, as have I, so I'm going to have to find the money to pay her back too and make sure she doesn't have to pay for my mistake.' Her voice was wobbling and she stared off into the distance in an attempt to stop herself from crying.

Matias squashed all feelings of guilt. Why should he feel guilty? He was staring at a woman whose father had destroyed his family. In that scenario, guilt didn't exist. After all, all was fair in love and war, wasn't it?

'You could do that,' he murmured, 'or you could sit back down and listen to the proposition I have for you.'

CHAPTER TWO

'GO EASY ON THE GIRL,' Art had urged his friend the previous day. 'Because Carney's her father, doesn't mean that she has been cut from the same cloth.'

Matias hadn't argued the point with his friend, but he had privately held the view that the apple never fell far from the tree and an innocent smile and fluttering eyelashes, which he was guessing had been the stunt the woman had pulled on Art, didn't mean she had a pure soul.

Now, however, he was questioning the judgement call he had made before he had even met her. He was seldom, if ever, wrong when it came to summing people up, but in this instance his friend might have had a point. Matias wasn't going to concede that the woman spent all her spare time helping the poor and unfortunate or that she was the sort who wouldn't have recognised an uncharitable thought if it did a salsa in front of her. What he *did* recognise was that he would be better served in his quest for revenge by getting to know her.

She was an unexpected piece of a puzzle he had thought was already complete and he would have to check her out.

He had waited years for retribution. Waiting a couple

of weeks longer wasn't going to kill him and it might put him in an even stronger position than he already was.

He looked at her anxious face and smiled slowly. 'There's no need to look so worried,' he soothed. 'I'm not a man who beats about the bush, Miss…it *is* Miss, isn't it?'

Sophie nodded and automatically touched her ring-free finger. Once upon a time, she had had a boyfriend. Once upon a time, she had had dreams of marriage and kids and a happy-ever-after life, but reality had had something different to say about that.

'Boyfriend?' Matias hadn't missed that unconscious gesture. No ring on her finger. Had there been one? Once? Was she divorced? She looked far too young, but who knew? It wasn't his business but it paid to know your quarry.

Sophie sat on her hands. 'I don't see what that has to do with…your car, Mr… Rivers…'

'Rivero.' Matias frowned because it wasn't often that anyone forgot his name. In fact, never. 'And in point of fact, it has. You owe me money but if you're telling the truth, then it would seem that you have little to no hope of repaying me.'

'Why wouldn't I be telling the truth?'

Matias debated whether he should point out that her father would surely not be keen to see his child slaving in front of a hot oven cooking food for other people, so how likely was it that catering was her full-time occupation? Or maybe she was the sort who rebelled against their parents by pretending to reject money and everything it stood for? When you came from money and had comfort and security as a blanket to fall back on, it was easy to play at enjoying poverty. From what he knew of the man, keeping up appearances ran to a full-time occupation and surely his offspring would have been dragged into that little game too?

However, he had no intention of laying any of his cards on any tables any time soon. At any rate, it would be a matter of seconds to check her story and he was pretty sure she was telling the truth. Her car, for one thing, did not suggest someone with an enviable bank balance and the oversight with the insurance added to the impression.

He shrugged. 'Maybe you imagine that pleading poverty will touch some kind of chord in me.'

'That never crossed my mind,' Sophie said honestly. 'I can't think that anyone would be mad enough to try and appeal to your better nature.'

'Come again?' Momentarily distracted, Matias stared at her with outright incredulity.

The woman was here on the back foot, staring bankruptcy in the face if he decided to go after her, and yet she had the cheek to *criticise him*? He almost couldn't believe his ears.

Sophie didn't back down. She loathed arguments and avoided confrontation like the plague, but she was honest and forthright and could be as stubborn as a mule. She had had to be because she had had to take up where her mother had left off when it came to breathing in deep and pursuing what she felt James Carney owed her.

Right now, she had no idea where Matias was going with some of his remarks. He had mentioned a solution to the problem staring her in the face, but she couldn't help noticing that he hadn't actually said what that solution might be.

If he was stringing her along only to pull the rug

from under her feet, then she wasn't going to sit back and allow him to bully her in the process.

'If you had a better nature,' she pointed out, 'then you would try and understand what it's like for me. You probably don't have a clue about what it's like to struggle, because if you did then you would be able to put yourself in my shoes, and if you did that you might try and find a solution to the problem instead. If you give me a chance, then I will pay you back, but first you have to give me a chance.'

'Is this your idea of buttering me up?' Matias said coldly. 'Because if it is, then you're heading in the wrong direction. Let's not forget that you're here with a begging bowl.' He would come back to her father and exactly how hard he'd made Matias's family *struggle* in due course.

Sophie's soft mouth tightened. She had a lot of experience when it came to begging bowls and she had learned the hard way that buckling under threat never got anyone anywhere.

'You said that you had a proposition for me,' she reminded him, clinging to that lifebelt and already willing to snatch at it whatever the cost. Perhaps if she had had only herself to think about, she might have backed off, but there were more people at stake here than just her.

Matias was already pleased that he had decided to go with the flow and exploit the opportunity presented to him. Soft and yielding she might look, but it had quickly become apparent that she was anything but.

He felt the kick of an unexpected challenge. So much of his life was predictable. He had reached the pinnacle of his success and he was still in his early thirties. People kowtowed to him, sought his advice, hung onto his every word, did their utmost to please him. Bearing in mind that financial security and the power that came with it had been his ambition for as long as he could remember, he was now disappointed to acknowledge that there was something missing from his life, something that not even the glowing fires of revenge had been able to fulfil.

He had become jaded over time. When he thought back to the hungry young man he had once been, his whole body alive for the task he had set himself, he felt as if he were staring backwards at a stranger. Certainly, on a personal level, the fact that he could have any woman he wanted was something that had long lost its novelty value. Now, for the first time in ages, he was facing a challenge he could sink his teeth into and he liked the feeling.

'In two weeks' time...' Matias had returned to his desk and now he pushed back his leather chair and relaxed with his hands folded behind his head '... I am due to host a long weekend party at one of my houses. Around eighty people will be descending and they will be expecting the highest standard of catering. I will provide the food. You will handle everything else. Naturally, you won't be paid. Succeed and we can carry on from there. I have no intention of exercising my right to frankly bankrupt you because, for a start, driving without being insured is illegal. If I went the whole way, you'd be in prison by dusk. Instead, I will play it by ear.'

'In other words,' Sophie said stiffly, 'you'll own me until you consider the debt to be paid off.'

Matias tilted his head to one side and smiled coolly. 'That's one way of putting it...' Okay, so it was the only way of putting it. He would be able to take his time finding out about her and thereby finding other ways back to her father. Were those rumours of foul play in the company vaults true? Was that something the man had confessed to his offspring? If so, if that level of information could somehow be accessed, then he would have the most powerful weapon for revenge within his grasp. He couldn't care less about the damage to his car. He could take it to the nearest scrapyard and buy a replacement without even noticing any dent in his limitless income.

'And when you think about the alternatives,' he mused, 'you'll conclude, pretty fast, that it's a sweet deal for you.' He gave a gesture that was as exotically foreign as he was. 'You might even be able to...' he flicked out the business card she had earlier given him '...distribute these discreetly during the weekend.'

'And will I be able to bring my business partner?'

'I don't think so. Too many cooks and all that. I will ensure that you have sufficient staff to help but essentially this will be your baby.' He glanced at his watch but didn't stand, leaving it to Sophie to deduce that he was done with her. She stood up awkwardly and looked at him.

How could someone so effortlessly beautiful be so utterly cold-hearted?

Although, she had to acknowledge, at least he hadn't done what he had every right to do and contacted the police. She could have kicked herself for that little window during which she had forgotten to renew her insurance with a different company. So unlike her but then she had had so much on her mind.

'Will there be something...er...in writing?'

'Something in writing?'

'Just so that I know how much of the debt will be covered when I handle the catering for you that weekend…'

'You don't trust me?'

Sophie gazed off and thought of her father. She'd had to learn fast how to manage him. Trust had never been in plentiful supply in their relationship and she thought that it would be prudent not to rely on it in this situation either.

'I don't trust many people,' she said quietly and Matias's ears pricked up.

He looked at her carefully. 'No?' he murmured. 'I don't trust many people either but then, as you've pointed out, I don't have a better nature whereas I expect you probably do. Am I right?'

'I've found that people inevitably let you down,' Sophie told him painfully, then she blinked and wondered what on earth had induced her to say that. 'So it would work if I could have something in writing as I go along…'

'I'll get my secretary to draw something up.' All business now, Matias stood up, signalling that her time was up. 'Rest assured, you won't be required to become my personal slave in return for a debt.'

His dark eyes flicked to her as she shuffled to her feet. She gave the impression of someone whose eyes were always downcast and he could see how Art had been knocked sideways by her meek persona, but he wasn't so easily fooled. He had seen the fire burning just below the surface. She blushed like a virgin but those aquamarine eyes flashed like a siren call and he couldn't wait to get to the bottom of her…and discover in the process what she could contribute to the picture he had already compiled of her father.

* * *

'But I just think that there must have been *some other way* of sorting this situation out! I'm going to be left here for *several days* on my own and I just don't know whether I can manage the Rosses' cocktail party on my own!'

Sophie's heart went out to Julie and she looked at her friend sympathetically. Sympathy was about all she could offer. She had signed up to a deal with the devil and it was a better deal than she might have hoped for. Even though she hated it.

She had been over all the pros and cons of the situation, and had apologised profusely to her friend, who was not as confident in the kitchen as she was.

'But on the bright side,' she said in an upbeat voice, 'think of all the possible connections we could make! And,' she felt compelled to repeat because fair was fair, 'he could have just taken everything from us to sort out the damage to his car. I honestly had no idea *that a car* could cost that much to repair! It's mad.'

He was sending a car for her and Sophie looked at her watch with a sense of impending doom. A fortnight ago, his secretary had emailed her with an extensive list of things she 'should bring, should know and should be prepared to undertake'.

There was to be no veering off from the menu and she would have to ensure that every single dish for every single day was prepared to the highest possible specification.

She was told how many helpers she would have and how they should behave. Reading between the lines, that meant *no fraternising with the guests*.

She was informed of the dress code for all members of staff, including herself. The dress code did not include jeans or anything that might be interpreted as casual.

She gathered that she was being thrown in at the deep end and this detailed information was his way of being kind to her. She assumed that he had diverted his original catering firm to some other do specifically so that he could put her through her paces and she had spent the past two nights worrying about what would happen if she failed. Matias Rivero wasn't, she thought, callous enough to take the shirt off her back, but he intended to get his money's worth by hook or by crook. He might be unwilling to throw her to the sharks, but he wasn't going to let her get off lightly by agreeing to monthly payments that would take her decades to deliver what was owed.

This was the biggest and most high-profile job she had ever got close to doing and the fact that he would be looking at her efforts with a view to criticism filled her with terror. She wondered whether he hadn't set her an impossible task just so he could do his worst with a clear conscience when she failed. He struck her as the sort of man who saw ruthlessness as a virtue.

His car arrived just as she was giving some final tips to Julie about the catering job she would be handling on her own, and Sophie took a deep breath and reached for her pull-along case.

There would be a uniform waiting for her at his country house, which was in the Lake District. However, his instructions had been so detailed that she had decided against wearing her usual garb of jeans and a tee shirt to travel there and, instead, was in an uncomfortable grey skirt and a white blouse with a short linen jacket. At a little after ten in the morning, with the sun climbing in the sky, the outfit was already making her perspire.

She hung onto the hopeful thought that she would probably find herself stuck in the kitchen for the entire time. With any luck, she wouldn't glimpse Matias or any of his guests and she knew that, if that were the case, then she would be all right because she was an excellent chef and more than capable of producing the menu that had been emailed to her.

She wouldn't even have to bother about sourcing the ingredients, because all of that would already have been taken care of.

Her high hopes lasted for as long as the very smooth car journey took. Then nerves kicked in with a vengeance as the car turned between imposing wrought-iron gates to glide soundlessly up a tree-lined avenue on either side of which perfectly manicured lawns stretched towards distant horizons of open fields, shaded with copses. It was a lush landscape and very secluded.

The house that eventually climbed into view was perched atop a hill. She had expected something traditional, perhaps a Victorian manor house with faded red brick and chimneys.

She gasped at the modern marvel that greeted her. The architect had designed the house to be an organic extension of the hill and it appeared to be embedded into the side so that glass and lead projected as naturally from rock and foliage as a tree might grow upwards from the ground.

The drive curved around the back, skirting a small lake, and then they were approaching the house from the side where a sprawling courtyard was large enough to house all those important guests she had been expecting to find. Except the courtyard was empty aside from three high-performance cars parked haphazardly.

All at once, a quiver of nervous tension rippled through her. She could have become lost in a crowd of people. In an empty mansion, and it certainly looked empty, getting lost wasn't going to be that easy.

And for reasons she couldn't quite understand, reasons that extended well beyond the uncomfortable circumstances that surrounded her presence here, Matias made her feel…awkward. Too *aware of herself*, uncomfortable in her own skin and on edge in a way she had never felt before.

Her bag was whipped away from her before she had time to offer to take it herself and then she was being led through a most marvellous building towards the kitchen by a soft-spoken middle-aged woman who introduced herself as Debbie.

It was a cavernous space of pale marble and pale walls on which were hung vast abstract canvasses. She could have been walking through the centre of a fabulous ice castle and she actually shivered because never had she felt so removed from her comfort zone.

It had been hot outside but in here it was cool and quite silent. When she finally turned her attention away from her impressive surroundings, it was to find that Debbie had disappeared and instead Matias was lounging in the doorway of the kitchen.

'You're here,' he commented, taking in the prissy outfit and the flat black pumps and the neat handbag, which had apparently replaced the Santa's sack she had been carrying the last time he had seen her. He straightened and headed straight back in the direction of the kitchen, expecting her to follow him, which she did.

Sophie was tempted to retort where else would she be when she'd had no choice, but instead, she said politely to his back, 'I expected it to have been a bit busier.'

'The first of the guests don't arrive until tomorrow.' Matias didn't bother to turn around. 'I thought you might find it helpful to acquaint yourself with the kitchen, get to know where everything is.'

They had ended up in a kitchen that was the size of a football field and equipped to the highest possible standard. Sophie felt her fingers itch as she stared around her, dumbstruck.

'Wow.' She turned a full circle, eyes as wide as saucers, then when she was once again looking at him, she asked, 'So are you going to show me where everything is?'

Matias looked blankly around him and Sophie's eyebrows shot up.

'You don't know your way around this kitchen at all, do you?'

'I'm not a cook so it's true to say that I've never had much time for kitchens. I'm seldom in one place for very long and I tend to eat out a great deal. I'm a great believer in the theory that if someone else can do something better than you, then it would be cruel to deny them the opportunity.'

Sophie laughed and was surprised that he had managed to make her laugh at all. Her cheeks warmed and she looked away from those piercing dark eyes. Her heart was beating fast and she was confused because once again she could feel the pull of an attraction that went totally against the grain.

For starters, he had proven himself to have all the characteristics she despised in a man. He was arrogant, he was ruthless and he had the sort of self-assurance that came from knowing that he could do what he wanted and no one would object. He had power, he had money and he had looks and those added up to a killer combination that might have been a turn-on for other women but was a complete turn-off for her.

She knew that because he was just an extreme version of the type of men her mother had always been attracted to. Like a moth to an open flame, Angela Watts had been drawn to rich, good-looking men who had always been very, very bad for her. She had had the misfortune to have collided with the pinnacle of unsuitable men in James Carney, but even when that relationship had died a death she had still continued to be pointlessly drawn to self-serving, vain and inappropriate guys who had been happy to take her for a ride and then ditch her when she started to bore them.

Sophie had loved her mother but she had recognised her failings long before she had hit her formative teens. She had sworn to herself that, when it came to men, she would make informed choices and not be guided into falling for the wrong type. She would not be like her mother.

It helped that, as far as Sophie was concerned, she lacked her mother's dramatic bleached-blonde sex appeal.

And if she had made a mistake with Alan, then it hadn't been because she had chosen someone out of her league. It had just been...one of those things, a learning curve.

So why was she finding it so hard to tear her eyes away from Matias? Why was she so aware of him here in the kitchen with her, lean, indolent and darkly, dangerously sexy?

'Why don't you look around?' he encouraged, sitting at the kitchen table, content to watch her while he worked out how he was going to engineer the conversation into waters he wanted to explore.

She was very watchable. Even in clothes that were better suited to a shop assistant in a cheap retail outlet.

He was struck again by how little sense that made considering who her father was, but he would find out in due course and in the meanwhile…

He looked at her with lazy male appreciation. She had curves in all the right places. The hazy picture he had seen on Art's phone had not done justice to her at all. His eyes drifted a little south of her face to her breasts pushing against the buttons of the prissy, short-sleeved shirt. At least the jacket had come off. She was reaching up to one of the cupboards, checking the supply of dishes, he presumed, and the shirt ruched up to reveal a sliver of pale, smooth skin at her waist, and a dormant libido that should have had better things to do than start wanting to play with a woman who was firmly off the cards kicked into gear.

'Everything looks brand new.' Sophie turned to him, still on tiptoes, and he could see that indeed the crockery and the glasses in the cupboards could have come straight out of their expensive packaging. 'How often has this kitchen been used?'

'Not often,' Matias admitted, adjusting position to control his insurgent body. He glanced away for a few moments and was more in charge of his responses when he looked at her once more. Her hair was extraordinarily fair and he could tell it was naturally so. Fine and flyaway—with her heart-shaped face it gave her the look of an angel. A sexy little angel.

'In summer, I try and get up here for a weekend or so, but it's not often possible. Taking time out isn't always a viable option for me.'

'Because you're a workaholic?' Not looking at him, Sophie stooped down to expertly assess what the situation was with pots and pans and, as expected, there was no lack of every possible cooking utensil she might need. Next, she would examine the contents of the fridge.

With her catering hat firmly in place, it was easy to forget Matias's presence on the kitchen chair and the dark eyes lazily following her as she moved about the kitchen.

'I've discovered that work is the one thing in life on which you can depend,' Matias said, somewhat to his astonishment. 'Which, incidentally, is how I know your father.'

Sophie stilled and turned slowly round to look at him. 'You know my father? You actually *know* him?'

'I know *of* him,' Matias admitted, his dark eyes veiled. 'I can't say I've ever met the man personally. In fact, I was contemplating a business venture with him, which accounts for Art heading towards the house when you came racing out of the drive and crashed into my Maserati.' The delicate bones of her face were taut with tension and his curiosity spiked a little more.

'You had an appointment with my father?'

'Not as such,' Matias told her smoothly. 'Art was going to…let's just say…lay the groundwork for future trade…' In other words, he had sent Art to do the preliminary work of letting Carney know that his time was drawing to a close. He, Matias, would step in only when the net was ready to be tightened.

'Poor Art,' Sophie sighed, and Matias looked at her with a frown.

'Why do you say that?'

'I don't think he would have got very far with James even if he'd managed to gain entry to the house.'

'*James?* You call your father *James*?'

'He prefers that to being called Dad.' Sophie blushed. 'I think he thinks that the word *dad* is a little ageing. Also…'

'Also,' Matias intuited, 'you were an illegitimate child, weren't you? I expect he was not in the sort of zone where he would have been comfortable playing happy families with you and your mother. Not with a legitimate wife on the scene.'

Sophie went redder. What to say and how much? He was being perfectly polite. He wasn't to know the sort of man her father was and, more importantly, the reasons that had driven her mother to maintain contact with him, a legacy she had passed on to her daughter. Nor was she going to fill him in on her private business.

But the lengthening silence stretched her nerves to breaking point, and eventually she offered, reluctantly, 'No. My mother was a youthful indiscretion and he didn't like to be reminded of it.'

'He got your mother pregnant and he refused to marry her…' Matias encouraged.

Sophie stiffened because she could see the man in front of her was busy building a picture in his head, a picture that was spot on, but should she allow him to complete that picture?

The conversation she had had with her father just before she had blindly ended up crashing into Matias's car had been a disturbing one. He was broke, he had told her.

'And don't stand there with your hand stretched out staring gormlessly at me!' he had roared, pacing the magnificent but dated living room that was dark and claustrophobic and never failed to make Sophie shudder. 'You can take some of the blame for that! Showing up here month in month out with bills to settle! Now, there's *nothing left*. Do you understand me? *Nothing!*'

Cringing back against the stone mantelpiece, truly fearful that he would physically lash out at her, Sophie had said nothing. Instead, she had listened to him rant and rave and threaten and had finally left the house with far less than she had needed.

What if he was telling the truth? What if he *was* going broke? Where would that leave her…? *And more importantly, where would that leave Eric?*

As always, thinking of her brother made her heart constrict. For all her faults and her foolish misjudgements, her mother had been fiercely protective of her damaged son and had determined from early on that she wasn't going to be fobbed off by a man who had been happy enough to sleep with her for four years before abandoning her as soon as the right woman had finally appeared on the scene. She had used the only tool in her armoury to get the money she had needed for Eric to be looked after in the very expensive home where his needs were catered for.

Blackmail.

How would those fancy people James mixed with like him if they knew that he refused to support his disabled son and the family he had carelessly conceived, thinking that they would all do him a favour and vanish when it suited him?

James had paid up and he had continued paying up

because he valued the opinion of other people more than anything else in the world, not because he felt any affection for either the son he had never seen or the daughter he loathed because she was just an extension of the woman who, as far as he was concerned, had helped send him to the poorhouse.

If there was no money left, Eric would be the one to pay the ultimate price and Sophie refused to let that happen.

If Matias was interested in doing a deal with her father, a deal that might actually get him solvent once again, then how could it be in her interests to scupper that by letting him know just how awful James was? If her father had money then Eric would be safe.

'That's life.' She shrugged, masking her expression. 'There aren't many men who would have found it easy to introduce an outside family to their current one.' She took a deep breath and said, playing with the truth like modelling clay, 'But he's always been there for my mother... And now...er...for me...financially...'

Matias wondered whether they were talking about the same person. 'So you would recommend him as someone I should have dealings with?'

Fingers crossed behind her back, Sophie thought of her brother, lost in his world in the home where she visited him at least once a week, her brother who would certainly find life very, very different without all that care provided, care that only money could buy. 'Yes. Of course. Of course, I would.' She forced a smile. 'I'm sure he would love to have you contact him...'

CHAPTER THREE

MATIAS LOWERED HIS stunning dark eyes. So she either had no idea what kind of man her father was or she knew perfectly well enough and was tainted with the very same streak of greed, hence her enthusiasm for him to plough money into the man.

He wondered whether, over time and with her father's finances going down the drain faster than water running down a plughole, she had found herself an accidental victim of his limited resources. She had just declared that her father had supported her and her mother and Matias had struggled to contain a roar of derisive laughter at that. But she could have been telling the truth. Perhaps the dilapidated car and the debt owed to the bank were the result of diminishing handouts. She might have been an illegitimate child but it was possible that Carney had privately doted on her, bearing in mind that his own marriage had failed to yield any issue. Advertising a child outside marriage might have been no big deal for many men, but a man like Carney would have been too conscious of his social standing to have been comfortable acknowledging her publicly.

For a moment and just a moment, he wondered whether he could notch up some extra retribution and publicly shame the man by exposing a hidden illegitimate child, but he almost immediately dismissed it because it was…somehow unsavoury. Especially, he thought, shielding the expression in his dark eyes, when the woman sitting in front of him emanated innocence in waves. There was such a thing as a plan backfiring and, were a picture of her to be printed in any halfway decent rag, a sympathetic public would surely take one look at that disingenuous, sensationally sincere face and cast *him* in the role of the bad guy. Besides, Carney's close friends doubtless knew of the woman's existence already.

'I will certainly think about contacting your father,' Matias intoned smoothly, watching her like a hawk. He became more and more convinced that she was playing him for a sap because she was suddenly finding it seemingly impossible to meet his eyes. 'Now, you've looked at the menu. Tell me whether you think you're up to handling it.'

Sophie breathed a sigh of relief at the change of subject. She hated the little white lie she had told, even though she was surely justified in telling it. Matias might be disgustingly rich and arrogant but he still didn't deserve to be deceived into believing her father was an honourable guy. On the other hand, if the choice was between her brother's future safety and well-being and Matias investing some money he wouldn't ever miss, then her brother was going to win hands down every time.

But that didn't mean that she'd liked telling Matias that fib.

She jumped onto the change of topic with alacrity. 'Absolutely.' She looked around her at the expensive gadgets, the speckled white counters, the vast cooking range. 'And it helps that your kitchen is so well equipped. Did you plan on doing lots of entertaining here when you bought the house?'

'Actually, I didn't buy the house. I had it built for me.' He went to the fridge, extracted a bottle of chilled white wine and poured her a glass. It seemed wildly extravagant to be consuming alcohol at this hour of the afternoon but she needed to steady her nerves, which were all over the place. 'And I had no particular plans to use the space for entertaining. I simply happen to enjoy having a lot of open space around me.'

'Lucky you,' Sophie sighed. After two sips of wine, she was already feeling a little less strung out. 'Julie and I would have a field day if we had this sort of kitchen. I've done the best with what I've got, but getting all the right equipment to fit into my kitchen has been a squeeze and if the business really takes off, then we're definitely going to have to move to bigger premises.'

Matias wondered whether that was why she had encouraged him to contact her father and put some work his way. Was it because she would be the happy beneficiary of such an arrangement?

Suspicious by nature and always alert to the threat of someone trying it on, he found it very easy to assume the worst of her, in defiance of the disingenuous manner she had. Judge a book by its cover and you almost always ended up being taken for a ride.

Not only did he have the example of his father to go on, who had paid the ultimate price for judging a book by its cover, but he, Matias, had made one and only one catastrophic misjudgement in his heady youth. On the road to the vast riches that would later be his and caught up in the novel situation of being sought after by men far older than himself who wanted to tap his financial acumen, he had fallen for a girl who had seemed to be grounded in the sort of normality he had fast been leaving behind. Next to the savvy beauties who had begun forming a queue for him, she had seemed the epitome of innocence. She had turned down presents, encouraged him to sideline the sort of fancy venues that were opening up on his horizon and professed a burning desire to go to the movies and share a bag of popcorn. No boring Michelin restaurants for her!

She had played the long game and he had been thoroughly taken in until she had sprung a pregnancy scare on him. Talk had turned to marriage pretty quickly after that and God knew he might just have ended up making the biggest mistake of his life and tying the knot had he not discovered the half-used packet of contraceptive pills in her handbag. Quite by accident. Only then, when he had confronted her, had her true colours emerged.

That narrow escape had been a turning point for him. A momentary lapse, he had discovered, was all it took for your life to derail. Momentary lapses would never again occur and they hadn't. Matias ruled his own life with a rod of steel and emotions were never allowed free rein. He took what he needed out of life and discarded what ceased to be of use to him.

Art was the only person on earth who knew about that brief but shameful episode and so it would remain. Matias had had little time for the perils of emotional roller-coaster rides, having grown up as witness to the way his father's emotional and trusting nature had led him down a blind alley, and his disastrous love affair had been the final nail in the coffin, after which he had entombed his heart in ice and that was exactly the way he liked it.

'You said you've only been in the catering business for a year and a half. What prompted the change of career?'

'We both enjoyed cooking.' Sophie realised that her glass of wine was empty and he appeared to have topped it up. She moved to sit at the wonderful kitchen table fashioned from black granite and metal. 'We became accustomed to friends asking us to cater for them and bit by bit we came to the conclusion that, in the long run, we might very well be better off doing something we both loved and were good at. Julie was fed up with her teaching job and I guess I just wanted a change of career.'

'It must have been a leap of faith for you. Changing career that dramatically takes guts.' Had she embarked on that career change with the mistaken impression that her father was still wealthy enough to fund her? Had she had to resort to borrowing from the bank when she found herself out of a job and unable to turn to her parent for a handout? Was that why she was struggling financially?

Lucas knew that James Carney's financial position had been poor for a few years.

'Maybe. Haven't *you* ever had to change career or were you born with a silver spoon in your mouth?' she asked.

'You say that as though you're not familiar with that situation yourself.'

'I'm not,' Sophie said flatly and Matias looked at her through narrowed eyes.

'I confess I find that hard to believe, given your father's elevated lifestyle.'

'I'd really rather not talk about him,' Sophie hedged warily.

'You don't like talking about your father? Why is that? I grant you, it must have been a nuisance living in the shadows, if indeed that was the case, but surely if, as you say, he helped you and your mother through the years…well, he must be quite a character because many men in a similar situation would have walked away from their responsibility.'

Sophie muttered something inaudible that might have been agreement or dissent.

'Of course, life must be altogether easier for you now,' Matias continued conversationally. 'I gather his wife died some years ago, so presumably he has taken you under his wing…'

'We don't have that sort of relationship,' Sophie admitted stiffly and Matias's ears pricked up.

'No?' he encouraged. 'Tell me about him. The reason I ask is simple. If I'm to have any financial dealings with him, it would be useful to try and understand the sort of person he is.'

'Do you take this close an interest in *all* your…er… clients?' This more to divert the conversation than anything else. Sophie had no real idea how people in the business world operated.

'I have slightly more elaborate plans for your father's company,' which wasn't exactly a lie, then he shrugged.

'Is that what you do?'

Matias frowned. 'Explain.'

'Well, do you…er…invest in companies? The truth is I honestly don't know the ins and outs of how companies operate. I've never had much interest in that sort of thing.'

'I see…so you don't care about money…'

'Not enough to have gone into a career where I might have made a fortune. Life would have been a lot easier if I had.' For starters, she thought, she wouldn't have had to endure the monthly humiliation of picking up where her mother had left off, and going to her father with cap in hand because Eric's home was costly and there was no other choice. 'I don't suppose I'm ruthless enough.'

'Is that a criticism of me?' Matias asked wryly, amused because it was rare for anyone to venture any opinion in his presence that might have been interpreted as critical. But then, as she had pointed out, whatever better nature he had was seldom in evidence and things weren't going to change on that front any time soon.

Sophie was caught between being truthful and toeing the diplomatic line. Talking about her father was out of bounds because sooner or later she would trip up and reveal exactly the sort of man he was. Telling Matias Rivero what she thought of him was also pretty questionable because he had thrown her a lifeline and he could whip it back whenever it suited him. If she succeeded in this task, a good proportion of her debt to him would be wiped out. As agreed, she had received a detailed financial breakdown of what she could expect from her weekend's work.

Getting on the wrong side of him wasn't a good idea. But he *had* asked…

And something about the man seemed to get her firing on cylinders she didn't know she possessed.

'Well, I *am* here,' she pointed out and Matias frowned.

'Where are you going with that?'

'You intend to get your pound of flesh from me by

whatever means necessary and if that's not ruthless, then I don't know what is.'

'It's not ruthless,' Matias informed her, without a hint of an apology. 'It's good, old-fashioned business sense.' On more levels than she could ever begin to suspect, he thought, dispelling a fleeting twinge of guilt because all that mattered was getting her despicable father to pay for what he had done all those years ago.

Matias thought back to the slim stash of letters he had found shoved at the back of his mother's chest of drawers. He would never have come across those letters if she hadn't been rushed to hospital, because he had had to pack a bag without warning for her. Her housekeeper had had the day off and Matias had had no idea what sort of things his mother might need. He had opened drawers and scooped out what seemed to be appropriate clothing and in doing so had scooped out those unopened letters bound with an elastic band.

His mother's writing. He had recognised that instantly just as he had noted the date on the stamps. They had all been sent over a period of a few weeks at a time when his father had been taking what were to be his last breaths before the cancer that had attacked him two years previously had resurfaced to finish what it had begun.

Curiosity had got the better of him because all those letters had been addressed to the same man. James Carney.

In actual fact, he need only have opened one of the letters because they had all contained the same message.

A plea for help. A request for money for an experimental treatment being carried out in America for precisely the sort of rare cancer his father had contracted.

None of the letters had been opened—they had just been returned to sender. It was plain to see that the man who had defrauded Matias's family and reaped the financial rewards that should have, at the very least, been shared with his father, had not had the slightest interest in what his mother had wanted to say to him.

Carney had been too busy living it up on his ill-gotten gains to give a damn about the fate of the family who had paid the price at his hands.

There and then, Matias had realised that retribution was no longer going to be on the back burner. It was going to happen hard and fast. The time for dragging his feet was over.

If Carney's illegitimate daughter now found herself caught in the crossfire then so be it. He wasn't going to lose his focus and the woman sitting opposite him was all part of his bigger plan. He could bring the man down the routine way, by bankrupting him, but he was getting a feeling…that there was more to the saga of his hidden daughter than met the eye. What could she tell him? Any whiff of a financial scandal, any hint that the health of his ailing company was tied up with fraud, would be the icing on the cake. Not only would such public revelations hit Carney where it hurt most, but a long prison sentence would loom on the horizon for him. All in all, a thoroughly satisfying outcome.

'Julie, my partner, wouldn't agree with you.' Sophie stuck her chin out at a mutinous angle. 'I've left her barely coping with one of the biggest contracts we've managed to secure since we started our catering company. We could really harm our business if she doesn't succeed because one poor job has a knock-on effect in the catering world.'

'You don't have my sympathy on that score,' Matias told her bluntly. He was unwillingly fascinated by the way she coloured up when she spoke and the way her aquamarine eyes, fringed by the lushest lashes possible, glittered and sparkled like precious gems.

Her skin was as smooth as satin and she didn't appear to be wearing a speck of make-up. She oozed *natural* and if he wasn't the cynical guy that he was, he would be sorely tempted to take her at face value because that face appeared so very, very open and honest.

Step up the memory of the ex who had almost got his ring on her finger on the back of appearing open and honest! Good job he wasn't the sort of idiot who ignored valuable learning curves.

'Here's a free piece of advice…never go into business with anyone. However, considering you've passed that point, you should have made sure that you weren't going into business with dead wood. Have you got anything signed allowing you to disentangle yourself from a ruinous partnership without feeling the backlash?'

Two bright patches of colour stained her cheeks and she glared at Matias without bothering to conceal a temper that was rarely in evidence. She looked at him, furiously frowning, all the more irate because he returned her glare with a lazy, amused smile. Her skin tingled as he held her gaze and kept on holding it, sucking the breath out of her and making her agonisingly aware of her body in ways that were confusing and incomprehensible.

Her breasts felt heavy and *full*, her nipples were suddenly sensitised, their tips pebble hard and scratchy against her bra, and there was a tingling between her legs that made her want to touch herself.

Sophie was so shocked that she looked away, heart hammering hard, barely able to breathe normally.

What on earth was going on with her? It was true that she hadn't had any interest in men since she had broken up with Alan, but surely that wouldn't make her susceptible to a man like Matias Rivero? He epitomised everything she disliked and if he was, physically, an attractive guy then surely she was sensible enough to be able to get past outward appearances?

'Julie is *not* dead wood,' she denied in a voice she barely recognised.

'If she's panicking because you're not there to hold her hand, then she's incompetent.'

'Thank you for your advice,' she said with sugary sarcasm, 'although I won't be paying much attention to it because I actually haven't asked for it in the first place.'

Matias burst out laughing. Against all odds, he was enjoying himself with the one person on the planet he should have wanted to have as little to do with as possible. Yes, he was on a fact-finding mission but he hadn't anticipated having fun as he tried to plumb her depths for some useful information on her father.

'Would it shock you to know that I can't think of anyone who would dare say something like that to me?'

'No,' Sophie told him with complete honesty and Matias laughed again.

'No?'

'Men with money always surround themselves with people who suck up to them and, even if they don't, people are so awed by money that they change when they're around rich people. They behave differently.'

'But you're different from them?' Matias inserted

silkily. 'Or are you just someone who can afford to make penury their career choice because there has always been a comfort blanket on which to rely should push actually come to shove?'

'I don't expect you to believe me,' Sophie muttered. 'James supported us because he had to. I was grateful for that, but there was never any question about there being any comfort blanket for the...for us...'

Matias looked at her narrowly, picking up *something* although he couldn't quite be sure what.

'Because he had to...' he murmured. 'You're not exactly singing his praises with that statement.'

'But like you said,' Sophie pointed out quickly, 'he could have just walked away from his responsibility.'

'Unless...' Matias let that single word hang tantalisingly in the air between them.

'Unless?' Sophie gazed at him helplessly and thought that this was what it must feel like to be a rabbit caught in the headlights. There was something powerful and *inexorable* about him. His head was tilted to one side and his midnight-dark eyes were resting lazily on her, sending little arrows of apprehension racing through her body like tiny electrical charges.

'Unless he felt he had no choice...'

Sophie stilled. She was caught between the devil and the deep blue sea. Tell him everything and he would have nothing to do with her father, who would probably have to declare bankruptcy if everything he said was true, and where would that leave Eric? Yet say nothing and who knew where this conversation would end up?

She remained resolutely silent and thought frantically about a suitable change of subject. Something innocuous. Perhaps the weather, although that alert expression in Matias's dark, brooding eyes didn't augur well for some inconsequential chit-chat at this juncture.

He looked very much like a dog in possession of a large, juicy bone, keen to take the first bite.

'Is that it?' he pressed softly. 'Did your mother apply a little undue pressure to make sure she was taken care of? Is that the relationship you have with your father now? I expect a man like him, in a reasonably prominent position, might have found it awkward to have had the mother of his illegitimate child making a nuisance of herself.'

Lost for words, Sophie could only stare at him in absolute silence.

How on earth had he managed to arrive at this extremely accurate conclusion? And more to the point, how had the conversation meandered to this point in the first place?

'I thought you might have been the secret child he spoiled, bearing in mind his marriage failed to produce a suitable heir.' Matias was shamelessly fishing and not at all bothered at Sophie's obvious discomfort.

'I really don't want to talk about James,' Sophie eventually said, when the silence had become too much to bear. 'I know you're interested in finding out what you can before you sink money into…er…his company, but you're really asking the wrong person when it comes to business details and I don't feel comfortable discussing him behind his back.' Something her father had said, in the rush of anger, rose to the surface of her addled brain…something about *where* all the money he had given them over the years had come from, a paper trail that should have been brushed under the carpet but was threatening to re-emerge under the eagle eyes of independent auditors. She shivered.

Matias debated whether to press the issue or fall back on this occasion and he decided that, with time on his hands, there was no point trying to force her into revealing secrets that might be lurking just below the surface.

For sure, something wasn't quite right but he'd discover what that was sooner or later.

In the meanwhile…

'Is there anything you need to know about the job?' he asked briskly, finally changing the subject to her obvious relief. The details could very well be left to his head housekeeper, who was busy with preparations in the vast house somewhere, but Matias was drawn to continuing the conversation with her.

His life had become very predictable when it came to women. He had made one youthful mistake, had learnt from it and ever since his relationships had all had two things in common. One was that they followed exactly the same pattern and the second was that they were all short-lived.

The pattern involved mutual attraction with the expected lavishing of expensive presents, in something of a brief courtship ritual, followed by a few weeks of satisfying sex before he began getting bored and restless.

It didn't matter who he dated or what sort of woman happened to catch his eye. From barrister to catwalk model, his interest never seemed to stay the course.

Was Sophie right? People behaved differently in the presence of the powerful, influential and wealthy. Were the women he dated so awed by what he brought to the table that they were unable to relate to him with any kind of honesty?

Unaccustomed to introspection, Matias, for once, found himself querying how it was that he was still so resolutely single at his age and so jaded with the re-volving door of relationships he enjoyed. When had no-strings-attached fun turned into liaisons that seemed to get shorter and shorter and become less and less satisfying?

He frowned, disconcerted by this *breach of protocol* and refocused on the woman in front of him.

'Would you be able to help me if I had any ques-tions?' Sophie quipped and he dealt her a smile that was so sudden and so devastating that she had a mo-ment of sheer giddiness.

She blinked, owl-like, mouth parted, her cheeks tinged with delightful colour.

She wasn't angry…she wasn't defensive…she wasn't on the attack…

She was *aware*.

Matias felt that kick of his libido again, forbidden, dangerous but, oh, so pleasurable.

It had been a little while since he had had a woman. His most recent girlfriend had lasted a mere two months, at the end of which he had been mightily re-lieved to see the back of her because she had gone from compliant to demanding in record time.

Was his brief sexual drought generating a reaction that was as thrilling as it was unexpected?

There was certainly something undeniably sexy about Sophie and he couldn't put his finger on it. Maybe it was because he knew that he shouldn't go anywhere near her.

A thought entered his head like quicksilver. Why not? She was attractive. Indeed, it was a while since he had had his interest sparked by a woman who appeared to be uninterested in the usual game playing. There had been no coy looks, fluttering lashes or suggestive remarks. Admittedly, she was here under duress because he had placed her in an impossible situation, but even so she was doing a good job of keeping him at arm's length.

Matias watched her with brooding interest. If he wanted information on the Carney man, then surely pillow talk would yield everything he wanted to know?

Just like that, his imagination took flight and he pictured her in his super-king-sized bed, her tangle of long white-blonde hair spread across his pillow, her voluptuous pale nakedness there for his enjoyment. He wondered what her abundant breasts might look like and he imagined suckling at them.

An erection as solid as steel made him twinge in discomfort and he did his utmost to drag his mind away from imagining salacious, tawdry details about her.

'You're right,' he drawled, settling further into the chair, his big body relaxed, his hands loosely linked on his lap, his long legs extended to one side. 'If you want help, you're going to have to talk to my housekeeper. I have next to no interest in the workings of a kitchen, as I've already mentioned.'

'How lovely for you to be in a position like that,' Sophie said politely, still reeling from the way he *got to her* and made her whole body vibrate and rev up and behave almost as though it didn't belong to her at all.

'In case you're thinking that I was born with a silver spoon in my mouth, you're wrong.' He frowned because it wasn't in his nature to tell anyone anything about him that wasn't strictly essential. He didn't do confiding, especially not in women who could take one small slip-up and celebrate it as a signpost to the nearest bridal shop.

'I never said that,' but Sophie had the grace to blush because she'd certainly been thinking it. Rich, arrogant and privileged from birth had been her assumption.

'You have a very transparent face,' Matias told her wryly. 'You don't have to spell it out. It's there in your expression of disapproval. You think I'm an arrogant, ruthless tycoon who has it all and has never suffered a day's hardship in his entire life.'

Sophie didn't say anything. She was busy trying to get her body to behave and to look past Matias's devastating and unwelcome sex appeal. However, no matter how hard she tried to tell herself that she was only responding the way any normal, healthy young female would respond to a guy who would have been able to turn the head of a ninety-year-old woman with failing eyesight, she still could scarcely believe that he was capable of having that huge an impact on her.

To combat the drag of her disobedient senses, she even did the unthinkable and disinterred the mental image of her ex, Alan Pace. On paper, he had been the perfect life partner. Sandy-haired, blue-eyed and with just the sort of even, friendly disposition that had made her feel safe and comfortable. Sophie had really begun to nurture high hopes that they were destined for the long run.

She was always careful to vet the people she introduced to her brother; when, after three months, she'd filled Alan in on Eric, he had been surprised that she hadn't said anything sooner and had been happy to meet him.

Unfortunately, meeting Eric had marked the beginning of the end for them. Alan had not been prepared for the extent of her brother's disabilities and he had been quietly horrified at the thought that taking Eric out was a very regular activity and one which Sophie enjoyed and did without complaint. He had envisaged the possibility of him having to become a joint carer at some indeterminate point in the future, and although Sophie had squashed that suggestion because Eric was very, very happy where he was, she had not been able, in all good conscience, to rule it out altogether. After that, it had just been a matter of time before Alan had begun heading for the nearest exit.

Yet harking back to Alan, she had to admit to herself that not even *he* had affected her the way Matias seemed capable of doing. And before it all went belly up, Alan had been the perfect boyfriend! So what the heck was going on with her?

Not only was the man gazing at her with dark-eyed intensity very much *not* the perfect *anything*, but the last thing she felt in his presence was *safe and comfortable*.

Privately Sophie was appalled that she might bear any resemblance to her wayward mother, who had spent a lifetime making all the wrong choices and going for men just like the one sitting opposite Sophie, men who had *Danger, health hazard* stamped all over their foreheads in bright neon lettering.

'It doesn't matter what I think of you,' she said quickly, because this was the only way she could think of to bring their interaction to an end and she desperately wanted to do just that. 'I'm here to do my duty and now, if you'll excuse me, might I go and freshen up? And then perhaps I could talk to the person I will be working alongside? Also someone who can show me how everything works here?'

He was being dismissed! Matias didn't know whether to be amused or outraged.

He stood up, as sleek and graceful as a panther, and shoved his hands in the pockets of his trousers.

Sophie looked away. She knew that her face was bright red and that she was perched on the edge of her chair, rigid with tension and so aware of him that she could hardly breathe. He was just so staggeringly good-looking that she had to consciously *not* look at him and even *not* looking at him was making her go all hot and cold.

'Excellent idea,' Matias drawled, his keen eyes taking in every sign of her discomfort and also the way she was pointedly avoiding his eyes. He felt the thrill of a challenge and was already circling it, playing with thoughts of what happened next in this little scenario. 'Wait here. I will ensure that you are shown the workings of the kitchen and then to your quarters, which I trust you will find satisfactory.'

And then he smiled, slowly and lazily, and Sophie gave a jerky nod of her head, but he was already turning and striding out of the kitchen.

CHAPTER FOUR

Sophie had only dimly speculated on what a long week-end party might be like. She had mostly thought along the lines of one of those upper-class country affairs where a dozen people wafted around in flowing robes, smoking cigarettes in long cigarette holders and talking in low, restrained, cut-glass accents. She had seen stuff like that in period dramas on television. Generally speaking, there was always an unfortunate death at some point.

Matias's party, she could tell as soon as guest number one had arrived, was not going to be quite like that.

Through the kitchen windows, which overlooked the spread of lawns at the back of the house and the long avenue and courtyard where the cars would be parked, the first guests arrived in a roaring vintage car, which disgorged a couple who could have stepped straight out of a celebrity magazine.

Debbie, the lovely housekeeper in her fifties who had, the day before, showed Sophie the ropes, had been standing next to her and she had said, without batting an eyelid, that everyone in the village had been waiting for this party with bated breath because the guest list was stuffed full of celebrities.

And so Sophie had discovered as the day had continued and the guests had begun piling up. All told, there would have been getting on for eighty people. Many would be staying in three sumptuous hotels in the vicinity, where chauffeurs were on standby to take them there at the end of the evening and return them to the house in time for breakfast and whatever activities had been laid on.

Through a process of clever guesswork, Sophie deduced that this wasn't so much a weekend of fun and frolic with Matias's nearest and dearest, but something of a business arrangement. The scattering of A-list celebrities from the world of media and sport was interspersed with a healthy assortment of very rich, middle-aged men who oozed wealth and power.

Sophie guessed that this was how the fabulously wealthy did their networking.

The supply of food was constant, as was the champagne. Having had a brief respite the day before, when Matias had done as asked and introduced Sophie to the people she would be working with, Sophie had been hard at it since six that morning.

Brunch was the first thing on the menu. An elaborate buffet spread, then tea before supper made an appearance at seven-thirty in the evening.

Sophie had no idea what these people did when they weren't eating and she didn't have time to think about it because she was rushed off her feet cooking and giving orders and hoping and praying that nothing went wrong.

She didn't glimpse Matias, even in passing. Why would he venture into the bowels of the kitchen where the lowly staff were taking care of his needs when he had the movers and shakers there to occupy him?

Strangely Art, Matias's employee, *had* put in an appearance in the kitchen and he had been as lovely as she recalled. Kind, gentle, almost making her think that there might be a purpose to his surprise visit, even though he had just briefly passed the time of day with her. And she wasn't quite sure why Matias had made sure to make the distinction that Art was only his *employee*, because it was clear, reading between the lines, that the two had a close bond, which, in turn, made her feel, stupidly and disturbingly, that Matias couldn't possibly be the cruel ogre she thought him to be. Didn't people's choice of friends often tell a story about *themselves*? Crazy.

Nose to the grindstone, she nevertheless still found herself keeping an eye out for Matias just in case he put in an appearance and when, at a little after eleven that evening, she made her way up to her quarters, she was foolishly disappointed not to have seen him at all.

Because she needed to make sure that everything was on target for her repaying some of the stupid debt she owed him, she reasoned sensibly. She had worked her butt off and she wanted to know that it hadn't been in vain, that day one had definitely wiped out the amount that had been agreed on paper.

The last thing she needed was to be told, when it was all over and done with and she'd shed a couple of stone through sheer stress, that he wasn't satisfied or that he'd had complaints about her or that the food had given his guests food poisoning and so she would have to cough up the money she owed him even if it meant her going bust.

She, herself, had no idea what the reaction to all her hard work was because she didn't emerge from the bowels of the wonderfully well-equipped kitchen for the entire day and night.

Waiters and waitresses came and went and an assortment of hired help made sure that dirty crockery was washed and returned for immediate use.

In addition to that plethora of staff on tap, Sophie also had a dedicated sous chef who was invaluable and did all the running around at her command.

But it was still exhausting and she had two more days of this before the first of the guests would start departing!

Surely, she thought, she would see Matias *at some point*! Surely he wouldn't just leave her to get on with it without poking his nose into the kitchen to see whether he was getting his pound of flesh!

It was simply her anxiety given the circumstances that resulted in Matias being on her mind so much.

She was cross with herself for letting him get under her skin. She recalled the way her body had reacted to his with a shudder of impatience. He'd given her the full brunt of his personality in all its overpowering glory when there had been no one else around, but now that he was surrounded by his cronies he couldn't even be bothered to check up on her and make sure he was getting value for money.

It infuriated her that, instead of being relieved that he wasn't hovering over her shoulder or popping up unexpectedly like a bad penny, she was disappointed.

By the time the festivities were coming to an end and the end of the long menu was in sight, she had reconciled herself to the fact that she would leave without seeing Matias at all and would probably find out the outcome of this exercise in repaying the money she owed him via his secretary.

He'd made his appearance and he wasn't going to be making another one.

She hadn't even had a chance, with everything happening, to have a look around the house! Not that she'd wanted to mingle with the guests. She knew her place, after all, but she'd hoped that she might have had a chance, last thing at night, to peep into some of the splendid rooms. No such luck because there had always been someone around or else the sound of voices from one of the rooms had alerted her to the presence of people who seemed to think nothing of staying up until the early hours of the morning.

The guests finally departed during the course of Monday in a convoy of expensive cars. The sound of laughter and chatter filtered down to the kitchen where most of the hired help had tidied, cleaned and left to go back to the village, where they would no doubt regale their family and friends with excited tales about what and who they'd seen.

Had Matias gone? By five-thirty, with just Sophie and Debbie left on the premises doing the final bits of tidying, she knew that he had. Without telling her how she had performed.

For some reason, she was booked to remain in the sprawling mansion until the following morning, and she had naturally assumed that there would be guests to cook breakfast for on that morning, but now she realised that she had been kept on to do cleaning duties after the guests had left.

He'd bought her lock, stock and barrel. She hadn't been asked to simply prepare meals, which was her speciality, but he had also kept her on to do basic skivvy work and he knew that she had no choice but to comply.

'You take the left wing of the house,' Debbie told her kindly. 'I've checked and all the guests have gone. There shouldn't be anything much to do at all because the rooms have all been cleaned on a daily basis. This is just a last-minute check to make sure nothing's been forgotten…and you've been saying that you wanted to have a peep at some of the rooms. It's worth a look. Mr Rivero doesn't come here very often but it's always a treat for us when he does because it's such a grand house.'

Finally back in her comfortable jeans and tee shirt, Sophie decided to do just that. Having not stuck her head over the parapet for the past three days, she took her time exploring the various rooms she had been allocated.

Debbie had been right: there was hardly any tidying to be done at all. Rooms had already been cleared of debris and vacuumed. She wound her way up the marble and glass staircase, admiring the canvasses on the walls as she began checking the bedrooms on the first floor.

The house looked untouched, having been completely tidied by a small army of staff.

Her mind was a complete blank as she pushed open the final door at the end of a long corridor that offered spectacular views of the lake from behind vast floor-to-ceiling panes of reinforced glass.

The first thing she noticed was the feel of pale, thick carpet under her feet as most of the house was a mixture of marble, wood and pale, endless silk rugs. Automatically, she kicked off her sandals and then stepped forwards.

Her eyes travelled to the huge bed…the white walls… the chrome and glass built-in wardrobes…the window that was just one massive pane of glass, uninterrupted by curtains or even shutters, through which Nature in all its lush green glory stretched towards the still black waters of the lake.

Then, to the left, a door she hadn't even noticed because it so cleverly blended into the pale paint opened and she was staring at Matias.

In pure shock, she took a few seconds to appreciate that he was semi naked. Obviously, he had just had a shower. His dark hair was still damp and a white towel was loosely draped around his lean hips. Apart from that scant covering…nothing. Bare chest, bare legs, bare *everything else*.

Sophie wanted to look away but she couldn't. Her mouth fell open and her eyes widened as she took in the broad muscularity of his shoulders, the width of his hard chest, the arrowing of dark hair down towards that low-slung towel. He was so absurdly, intensely *masculine* that all the breath left her in a whoosh.

She knew that she was staring and she couldn't do a thing about it. When she finally looked him in the face, it was to find him staring back at her, eyebrows raised. 'Inspection over?'

Matias had made a point of steering clear of her for the past few days. He'd regrouped and realised that what he had viewed as an interesting challenge that could lead to a number of pleasurable destinations with Sophie was in fact a poorly thought-out plan generated by a temporary lapse in his self-control.

She might be intensely attractive and he might very well be able to rationalise his visceral response to her, but taking her to his bed could only be a bad idea. Yes, pillow talk might result in him hitting the jackpot when it came to finding out more about Carney but there had been no point kidding himself that that had been the overriding reason for his sudden desire to act like a caveman and get her between the sheets. She'd done something to him, cast some spell over him that had made him lose his formidable self-control and that wasn't going to justify whatever jackpot it might or might not lead to.

So he'd kept away. He'd even considered sleeping with one of the single women who had been at the party, a model he had known briefly several months previously, but in the end had ditched the idea.

Because having entered his head, Sophie had stubbornly lodged there like an irritating burr and he'd found he didn't want anyone else.

And now here she was. His dark eyes roved over her flushed face and then did a quick tour of her body. These were obviously the clothes she was most comfortable in and she looked sexy as hell in them. The faded jeans clung to her curves like a second skin and the tee shirt revealed breasts that were gloriously abundant.

The kick of his libido demolished every single shred of common sense. Matias had no idea what it felt like to operate without self-imposed boundaries. He was finding out now as he looked at her and surrendered to a surge of lust that could not be forced into abeyance.

The thrill of a challenge waiting to be met was one that wasn't going to go away until it was dealt with.

He padded across to the bedroom door and quietly shut it and Sophie's head swung round in alarm.

'What are you d-doing?' she stammered, frozen to the spot.

'I'm closing the door,' Matias told her gently. 'In case you hadn't noticed, I'm not exactly dressed for visitors.'

'I was going to leave…' Sophie shuffled a couple of paces back but it was laborious, like swimming against a strong current. 'I had no idea that you were still here.'

'Where else would I have been?'

'I thought you'd left with all the other guests.'

'And not had a talk to you about your performance?'

'Have I done something wrong?' Sophie asked in a rush, red as a beetroot, torn between wanting to flee and needing to stay to hear whatever criticisms of her work that he had.

Matias didn't answer. He turned around and headed towards his wardrobe and Sophie broke out in a film of nervous perspiration.

'I'd rather talk to you…s-somewhere else,' she stuttered. 'If I'd known you were in here, I would never have entered.'

'I make you uncomfortable,' Matias said flatly, spinning round to look at her and at the same time throwing on a snowy white shirt without yet removing the towel. He didn't button it up but left it hanging open over his fabulous chest and Sophie's mouth went dry.

'You're barely clothed,' she pointed out breathlessly. 'Of course I feel *uncomfortable* and I certainly don't imagine I'll be able to have a conversation about my duties in your bedroom!' She went a shade redder. 'What I *mean*…is that this is…*isn't* the place for a serious conversation. If I've failed in the task you set me, then… then…' She looked in horror as he hooked one finger over his towel.

She turned away and Matias laughed softly. Okay, so the woman had somehow reduced him to a level of dithering unheard of. Normally, he approached women and relationships with just exactly the same assured directness with which he approached work. Both were a known quantity and neither induced anything in him other than complete certainty of the outcome.

But with *her*...his taste for revenge had been diluted by desire. What should have been clear-cut had become cloudy. He had vacillated like a hapless teenager between pursuit and withdrawal and had tried to reclaim the loss of his prized self-control only to find it now slipping out of his grasp.

He'd acted out of character and that disturbed him because it never happened.

'You haven't failed,' he said quietly. 'If you give me five minutes, I'll meet you downstairs in the kitchen and we can debrief.'

He headed towards the en-suite bathroom and Sophie fled back down the stairs to the kitchen where she had to take a few seconds to regain her self-control. She was sipping a glass of water when the kitchen door slid open and there he was, drop-dead gorgeous in a white shirt cuffed to the elbows and a pair of black jeans that showed his powerful body off to perfection.

'Have something a bit more exciting than water.' He headed straight for the oversized wine cooler and extracted a bottle of wine and then two glasses. 'You must feel as though you need it. I've thrown you in at the deep end and you've risen to the occasion.' He poured them both a glass of wine, sipped his and then, eyes on her face, tilted his head in a salute.

Sophie cleared her throat. 'Were you expecting me to fail?'

'I thought you would pull through. I didn't think that you would handle the situation with such efficiency. Everyone raved about the food and I was impressed with the way the timetable was adhered to.'

'Thank you.' She blushed and drank some of the wine.

'Naturally, the past few days only cover a proportion of the debt but you've made a start.'

'Will you be in touch about…er…another arrangement so that I can try and schedule my jobs accordingly? Julie did very well handling the cocktail party on her own but she was very nervous and I would rather not put her through that. If I know when you need me, then I can make sure I'm only missing food preparation on the premises rather than in situ at a client's house.'

'No. I can't tailor my timetable to suit your partner, I'm afraid.' He paused, gazed at her, again felt the fierce kick of desire and wondered how he could have been sufficiently short-sighted to have imagined that he could make it disappear on command. It would disappear but only after he'd had her, only when he'd sated a craving that made no sense and had sprung from nowhere. 'Did you enjoy the long weekend?'

'I was under a great deal of pressure,' Sophie confessed stiffly. 'But it was challenging catering for that amount of people. It was the largest party I've ever done.'

'I didn't see you put in an appearance.'

'I was busy overseeing the food. Besides…'

'Besides?'

'What would I have done out there? Asked everyone if they were enjoying the food?'

'You could have circulated, handed out your business cards.'

'I would have felt awkward,' Sophie admitted truthfully. 'Those sort of big bashes aren't my thing. I wouldn't have fitted in.'

'You underestimate your...charms,' Matias said softly. 'I imagine you would have fitted in a great deal better than you think.'

Sophie looked at him and wondered whether she was imagining *something* in his voice, something low and speculative that was sending a shiver down her spine and ratcheting up her painful awareness of him and her heightened reaction to his proximity. Was he actually *flirting* with her? Surely not.

Confused, she stared at him in silence and he stared right back at her, holding her gaze and making no effort to look away. He sipped his wine, gazed at her over the rim of the glass and the effect was devastating.

She was utterly defenceless. She didn't know what he was playing at. This made no sense at all. She was lower than the hired help! She was the hired help plus some!

'I sh-should head upstairs,' she stuttered, half standing on wobbly legs. 'If it's all the same to you, there's nothing left here for me to do. Er...and...if you're satisfied with...with my efforts...then maybe your secretary...can contact me...'

She ran her fingers through her tangled hair and licked her lips because *he was still looking at her with that brooding, veiled expression and it was doing crazy things to her nervous system.*

'And if...if it's okay with you, then I shall get a cab to

the station tonight. I was under the impression that there would be some guests here until tomorrow morning, which is why I was…ah…booked to stay for one final night…' She took a deep breath and exhaled slowly. 'I wish you wouldn't stare at me like that,' she said, licking dry lips.

'Why?'

'Because it makes me feel uncomfortable.'

'Funny, I've never had any complaints from a woman because I haven't been able to keep my eyes off her. On the contrary, they're usually at great pains to make sure that they position themselves directly in my line of vision in the hope that I'll notice them. This is the first time I can genuinely say that I've found myself in the presence of a woman I can't seem to stop looking at.'

Shocked, Sophie literally could find nothing to say. Her vocal cords had dried up. All she could do was stare. He was so ridiculously beautiful that it seemed utterly mad for him to be saying this sort of stuff to her. Even more crazy was the fact that her whole body was surging into overdrive and melting like wax before an open flame.

She wasn't this person! She was level-headed and practical and she knew when and where to draw lines. Not that she had had to draw any since her break-up with Alan. Since then, and that had been over three years ago, men had been put firmly on the back burner and she hadn't once been tempted to dip her toes back into the dating pool. Not once. So why was her body on fire now? Because a guy with too much money, too much charm and too much in the looks department was coming on to her?

'Don't you feel the chemistry between us as well?'

'I don't know what you're talking about,' Sophie whispered and Matias raised his eyebrows in an expression of frank incredulity.

'Of course you do,' he corrected her casually. 'Although,' he continued, 'I understand that you might want to deny it. After all, it's not exactly something either of us bargained on, is it?' No truer words spoken, Matias thought wryly. All things considered, he would have placed greater odds on him catching a rocket to the red planet.

He shrugged eloquently. 'But there you are. These things happen.'

So he fancied her and wanted to have sex with her. Sophie's brain finally cranked into gear and anger began building inside her with the force of suppressed molten lava. He was a rich, powerful man who had her on the run and, because of that, he figured he could come onto her because he happened to find her attractive.

And the worst thing was that he had picked up vibes from her, vibes that had informed him that the pull was mutual. But if he thought that she was now going to fall into bed with him then he had another think coming!

'I'm sorry,' she said coldly, 'but I'm not interested.'

Matias laughed as though she'd cracked a hilarious joke. 'Telling me that you don't feel that electric charge between us?' He noted the blush that crept into her cheeks. 'Ah, yes. Of course you do. You're feeling it now. Why deny it?'

'I won't be…doing anything with you.' She wanted to walk through that door, head held high with contempt and hauteur, because he could buy her services but he *couldn't buy her*, but her feet were nailed to the ground and she found herself standing up but going nowhere.

'You're mistaking me for one of those women who *plant themselves in your line of vision*,' she continued, voice shaking with anger and mortification, 'but I'm not. Yes, I'm here because there's no other way I can pay off the money I owe you, and I can't let my colleague down because she would stand to lose out financially, just as I would if you called the debt in, but that doesn't give you the right to sit there and make a pass at me!'

Her feet finally remembered what they were there for and she stalked towards the door.

The sound of his voice saying her name brought her to an immediate stop. As noiseless as a predator stalking prey, he was right behind her when she spun round and she stumbled backwards a couple of steps, heart beating wildly behind her ribcage, her every sense alert to his commanding presence.

Her nostrils flared, an automatic reaction to the clean, woody scent of whatever aftershave he was wearing.

'Do you honestly think,' Matias asked in a voice that managed to be measured and yet icily condemnatory at the same time, 'that I might actually believe your body comes as part of the repayment schedule for the damage you did to my car?'

Sophie went bright red. Put like that, she could see what an idiot she'd been because when it came to women he certainly didn't need to use any unnecessary leverage. The guy could have whomever he wanted, whenever he wanted.

And he'd wanted her.

That treacherous thought slithered into her head, firing her up against her will.

'I suppose not,' she grudgingly conceded, 'but I

feel vulnerable being here, singing for my supper.' She looked away and then raised her bright blue eyes to his. 'I'm not anything like those women who were here this weekend…'

Matias's eyebrows shot up. 'I didn't think you'd noticed who was here and who wasn't.'

'I saw them coming and going through the kitchen window and some of the guests came on kitchen inspection a few times over the weekend.'

'And?'

'And what? They were all clones of one another. Tall and skinny and glamorous. I assumed that one of them might have been your…er…girlfriend.'

'If I had a girlfriend, we wouldn't be having this conversation.'

'We don't even like one another,' Sophie breathed, 'and *that's* why we shouldn't be having this conversation!'

'Do you have a boyfriend?'

'What if I had? Would it make a difference?'

'Possibly.' He tilted his head to one side. 'Possibly not. Why do you compare yourself to other women?'

'I'm just saying that I'd imagine those women you asked to your house here were exactly the sort of women you normally dated…and so what would you see in someone like me except *easy availability*?' She was playing with fire but the sizzling danger of this treading-on-thin-ice conversation was weirdly and intensely seductive. It was the sort of conversation she had never in her life had before with any man.

'Want me to spell it out for you?' Matias husked. 'Because I will, although I'd rather do that when you're lying naked in my bed.' He vaguely recalled when he had originally played with the notion of getting her between the sheets because pillow talk might reveal secrets he could use to his advantage. Standing here now, with a fierce erection that was demanding release, the only talking he wanted to do in bed was of the dirty variety. In fact, just thinking about it was driving him completely nuts.

He didn't know what it was about this woman but she made him lose his cool.

'And that won't be happening,' Sophie informed him prissily, edging back, away from the suffocating radius of his powerful personality. 'Ever!'

'Sure about that?' Matias laughed softly, fired up on every possible cylinder. 'Because that's not a concept I recognise.'

'Too bad,' Sophie muttered, and then she turned tail and fled before she could get even more sucked into a conversation that was dangerously explosive and *dangerously, dangerously exciting.*

Not even the luxury of her accommodation, which still made her gasp after four nights, or the calming, long bath she had could clear her head.

Matias's dark, brooding, insanely sexy face swam in her head, stirring her up and making it impossible for her to fall asleep and when, finally, she did, it was a restless, broken sleep until eventually, lying in the darkened room at nearly two in the morning, she decided that counting sheep wasn't getting her anywhere.

She made her way as quietly as she could towards the kitchen. Aside from the security lights outside, the house was shrouded in darkness, which should have been spooky but was strangely reassuring.

She already knew her way round the kitchen like the

back of her hand and there was no need for her to switch
on any lights as she padded unhesitatingly towards the
fridge to get some milk so that she could make herself
a mug of hot chocolate. Time to find out whether it was
true that hot chocolate encouraged sleep.

Stooping and reaching to the back of the shelf for
the milk, Sophie was unaware of footsteps behind her
and certainly, with only the light from the fridge, there
were no helpful warning shadows cast so the sound of
Matias's voice behind her came as a shock.

She straightened, slammed her head against the
fridge shelf, sent various jars and bottles flying and
stood up as red as a beetroot to confront a highly amused
Matias staring down at her with his arms folded.

CHAPTER FIVE

BROKEN GLASS LAY around her. One of the jars had contained home-made raspberry jam. Sophie had remarked on how delicious it was when she had first had it on a slice of toast a few mornings ago and had been told that Mrs Porter, who lived in the village, made it and sold it in one of the local shops.

Sophie didn't think that Mrs Porter would have been impressed to see her hard work spilled all over the tiled kitchen floor like blobs of gelatinous blood. It joined several gherkins and streaks of expensive balsamic vinegar.

'Don't move,' Matias commanded.

'What are you doing here?' Sophie said accusingly, remaining stock-still because she was barefoot, but horribly aware of her state of undress. She hadn't dressed for company. It was a mild night and she had forsaken her towelling dressing gown and tiptoed downstairs in the little skimpy vest she wore on warm nights and the tiny pair of soft cotton pyjama shorts that left an indecent amount of thigh and leg on display.

Indecent, that was, if you happened to be in a kitchen with the man who had been haunting your dreams kneeling at your feet carefully picking up bits of glass.

He didn't look up at her. He seemed to be one hundred per cent focused on the spray of broken glass around her. Looks, however, could be deceiving for Matias was acutely aware of her standing there in a lack of clothing that was sending his blood pressure through the roof.

'I own the house,' he pointed out with infuriating, irrefutable logic as he continued with his glass retrieval while trying to divert his avid gaze from her fabulously sexy legs, pale and shapely in the shadowy darkness of the kitchen. 'I find that seems to give me the right to come and go as I please.'

'Very funny,' Sophie said tightly.

'I'm here for the same reason you are.' He sat back on his haunches to cast a satisfied look at his cleaning efforts, then he raised his eyes to hers and took his time looking at her. 'I couldn't sleep.'

'Actually, I was sleeping just fine.'

'Which is why you're here at a little after two in the morning?'

'I was thirsty.'

'Stay put. There are probably fine shards of glass on the ground still and I suppose I should clear up all this mess.' He seemed to give that a little thought. 'No. Scratch that. I'll leave the mess but I meant what I said about staying put and the shards of glass. Get a sliver of glass in your foot and you'll probably end up having to be taken to hospital.'

'Don't be ridiculous!' But she daren't move. Bleeding in his kitchen wasn't going to do. Coping with her embarrassing state of semi-nudity was definitely the better option. She would just have to stand here while he took his time removing every piece of glass from the floor.

She could have kicked herself for being so stupid but bumping into him was the last thing she had expected.

Meanwhile, she could barely look down at herself because all she could see was her pale skin, her braless breasts, which were unfashionably big, and her nipples poking against the fine ribbing of her vest.

And all she could do was to make unhelpful comparisons in her head. Comparisons between herself and the women who had been at his party. Next to most of the women there, she was the equivalent of a walking, talking dumpling, and while none of them had been his girlfriend Sophie had no doubt that those were exactly the sort of women he went for. Long and thin with poker-straight hair and faces that seemed to resent the business of occasionally having to smile.

'This could take for ever,' Matias gritted, standing up and peering down at the floor. 'I don't have for ever.' He stepped forward and before she had time to even open her mouth in protest he was scooping her up as though she weighed nothing.

'Good job I was sensible enough to come down here wearing shoes,' he murmured, grinning as he looked down at her.

'Put me down!'

'Not until you're safe and sound and not until I make sure that those very pretty feet of yours are free from any slivers of glass…'

'I'd know if I'd stepped on glass,' Sophie all but sobbed, acutely aware of the way her scraps of clothing were rucking up everywhere. One of her breasts was practically popping out of her vest. She couldn't bear to look. She wasn't wearing underwear and she could feel the petal softness of her womanhood scraping against the side of the pyjama shorts.

And worst of all was what her disobedient body was doing. Turned on by the strength of his arms and the iron-hard broadness of his muscular chest, her nipples were tight and pinched, the rosebud tips straining against the vest, and she was so wet between her legs.

She could only hope that he didn't notice any of that on the way to her room.

She squeezed her eyes shut and didn't open them when she felt him push open a bedroom door.

'Ostrich.' Matias was fully aware of her body, every succulent inch of it, soft and warm in his arms. He could just about see the rosy blush of a nipple peeping out. 'Why have you got your eyes shut?'

Sophie duly opened her eyes, glared at him and then, slowly but surely, it dawned on her that they weren't in her bedroom. He had taken her to a bedroom that was unapologetically male, from the chrome and glass of the fitted wardrobes to the walnut and steel of the bed, over which hung an abstract painting that was instantly recognisable, the bedroom she had frantically backed out of a few hours ago.

'Your bedroom.' She gulped, when her vocal cords finally decided to play ball.

'Let me check your feet.'

'Please, Matias…'

'Please, Matias…*what*?' He deposited her very gently on his bed, as though she were as fragile as a piece of porcelain, but he wasn't looking at her. Instead, he was once again kneeling in front of her and he then proceeded to take one foot in his big hand, to inspect it closely for wayward glass.

It was ludicrous!

But the feel of his hands on her…wreaked havoc with her senses and also felt just so…*sexy*.

Something that sounded very much like a whimper emerged from her throat and their eyes met.

Understanding passed between them, as loud and clear as the clanging of church bells on a still Sunday morning.

Desire. Loud and thick and electric and definitely mutual.

'We can't,' was what Sophie heard herself whimper, breaking the silence between them. She didn't even bother to pretend that she didn't know what was going on any more than he pretended not to recognise the capitulation behind that ragged, half-hearted protest.

'Why not?' Matias had thought about sleeping with her for his own purposes but now he couldn't remember what those purposes were because cold self-control had been replaced with a raging urgency to take her to bed whatever the cost.

'Because this isn't a normal situation.'

'Define normal.'

'Two people who want to have a relationship.'

'I won't deny that I don't do relationships, but sex doesn't always have to lead to a once-in-a-lifetime relationship.'

'Not for you,' Sophie whispered as her resolve seeped away the longer he looked at her with those dark, sinfully sexy eyes. 'But for me…' She turned away and swallowed painfully.

Matias joined her on the bed and gently tilted her head back to his. 'For you?'

'My mother wasn't careful when it came to men,' she

told him bluntly. 'She was very attractive…she had that *something* that men seem to find irresistible…'

'You talk as though that *something* is something you don't possess.'

'I don't,' she said simply, raising her eyes to his and holding his gaze with unwavering sincerity. 'Men have never walked into lampposts when I sauntered past, they've never begged or pleaded or shown up with armfuls of roses in the hope that I might climb into bed with them.'

'And they did all those things for your mother?'

'She had that effect on them.'

'If that were the case, why didn't she and your father marry…considering he fathered a child with her?'

Sophie opened her mouth to tell him that James Carney had fathered more than one child but something held her back. What? Was it her fierce protectiveness over Eric? A need, born of habit, to save him from the curiosity of other people, even though he wouldn't have cared less?

Or was it a hangover from the way Alan had ended up reacting to her disabled brother?

Sophie told herself that she didn't care one way or another what a perfect stranger thought of her situation, least of all someone like Matias. She told herself that if he planned on doing business with her father, then the presence of her disabled brother wouldn't matter a jot, and yet she pulled back from the brink and swallowed down the brief temptation to spill her guts. She was a little startled that she had even been tempted to tell him at all.

'James always thought that he was too good for my mother.' Sophie hid the hurt behind that crisply delivered statement of fact. 'He was rich and he was posh and he didn't think that my mother was the right sort of woman for him.'

Matias's jaw clenched because this came as no surprise at all to him, and Sophie saw his instinctive reaction with a trace of alarm as she remembered how important it was for him to inject money into her father's nearly bankrupt company.

'It happens.' She shrugged and moved on quickly. 'You might fancy me, but you can't pretend that you don't feel the same way about me as he did about my mother. You're rich and powerful and it doesn't matter who my father is or isn't—the fact is that I have never grown up in the sort of circles you would have moved in.'

'You don't know what sort of circles I moved in as a child,' Matias heard himself say. He was uneasily aware that this was a deviation from his normal handling of any sort of *situation* with a woman. Since when had he turned into the sort of touchy-feely person who wanted to waste time talking when a perfectly good bed beckoned?

'I can guess. I'm not stupid.'

'You're anything but stupid. Although it *was* fairly stupid of you to be driving without insurance.'

'Please don't remind me.'

'My parents had no money,' Matias said abruptly. 'They should have but they didn't. I grew up as the kid on the wrong side of the tracks. I went to a tough comprehensive where I learned that the only way to get out in one piece was to be tougher than everyone else, so I was.'

Sophie's mouth fell open, partly because this was so

unexpected but mostly because he was confiding in her and everything was telling her that this was a proud, arrogant man who never confided in anyone.

She felt a little thrill and her heart turned over because the unexpected confidence marked something more between them than *lust*. You didn't confide like that in someone you just wanted to take to bed and throw away afterwards.

Sophie didn't work that out in any way that was coherent or analytical. It was more of a *feeling* that swept through her and in the wake of that *feeling* she softened. *This was how barriers got broken down; this was how defences were surmounted.*

Except she wasn't thinking any of that right now, she was just ensnared by a desire to know more about him.

'Enough talking,' Matias said gruffly, meaning it. 'Because I'm rich and powerful now doesn't mean that I don't fancy you for all the right reasons.'

'Which are what?' Sophie whispered, and Matias dealt her a slow, slashing smile that sent every nerve in her body quivering in high excitement.

'You have a body I would walk over broken glass to touch,' he expanded, not touching her but wanting to with every pore in his body.

'Don't be silly.' She laughed shakily, driven to bring this whole crazy situation down to a prosaic, pedestrian place because she just couldn't quite believe that she was impressionable enough to be swept off her feet by a man like him. 'I'm short and I'm...well covered. The world is full of short, plump women like me. We're a dime a dozen.'

'You're doing it again, running yourself down. You shouldn't, because what you have is more than just a body I could find anywhere.' He laughed. 'You might think that your dear mama failed to pass on that special *something* but you'd be wrong because you definitely have it in bucketloads.'

Don't say that, something in Sophie wanted to yell, but over and above that was a hot yearning at the soft, lazy timbre of his voice and a melting feeling at the way he was looking at her. This was the sort of textbook situation she had always cautioned herself against and yet here she was, blossoming like a flower in the sunshine and wanting this inappropriate man more than she could have ever believed possible.

Belatedly, she realised that her clothes were still askew, her vest tugged down, her shorts scrunched up at the crotch. She shifted and just like that words melted away, replaced by the delicious frisson of burning desire.

Matias straightened. A full moon streamed through the floor-to-ceiling panes of glass, casting a silvery glow through the room. She was so beautiful that he could barely contain himself. And *still* he wasn't sure what she would do if he touched her.

Or what *he* would do if he touched her and she turned away. A cold bath wouldn't begin to sort it out.

He didn't have long to ponder the problem because she took the decision right out of his hands. She reached up and stroked the side of his face, her huge eyes wide, her full mouth softly parted.

Matias caught her hand and drew her finger into his mouth. His gaze didn't leave hers as he sucked it, sucked it so that she knew that that was just how he was going to suck her nipple and, without even realising it, she responded by pushing her breasts out. Her nipples were tingling. Eyes half closed, she gasped when he slid his hand under the vest and cupped her breast.

He still had her finger in his mouth and was still sucking it, and still holding her gaze, his dark eyes lazy and hypnotic as he rolled his finger over the stiffened bud of her nipple. That was all he did and it was enough for her body to shriek into a response that was a hair's breadth away from orgasmic.

It was electrifying.

Sophie moaned. 'I want you.'

Matias held her hand, playing with the wet tip of her finger. 'Your wish is my command. You want me? Rest assured that you will have me, as hard and as often as you want.'

She'd expected him to drive into her without further ado. She could see the hunger in his dark eyes and it matched hers. He didn't. Instead, he arranged her on the bed, straddled her for a few seconds and then slowly pulled down her shorts.

She was so soft, so silky smooth, her skin so pale in the moonlight. He had to stare and even as he stared he did his damnedest to control his breathing, but he was so turned on that he had to make an effort to remember that breathing involved sucking air in and releasing it out.

In one swift movement, he stood up, holding her riveted attention, and stripped off.

Sophie had never seen anything so magnificent in her entire life. No artist would have been able to do justice to the sheer perfection of his body. A broad chest tapered down to a washboard-flat stomach and then lower, to an erection that was impressively huge, a thick, long shaft of steel that made her want to pass out because she was so turned on.

She'd had one serious boyfriend. Her level of experience was very definitely on the lower end of the spectrum and nothing had prepared her for the impact of being in the grip of true, shameless, wanton desire. Desire shorn of everything but a need to live for the moment and take what was on offer. Desire that was looking for nothing beyond the next sixty seconds and the sixty seconds after that.

Sophie would never have believed herself capable of actually *being here and being this person* because it contravened all her principles. But now that she *was* here, she felt wildly, wickedly decadent.

Naked, Matias spread apart her legs and then lowered himself to do something that felt so intimate that she froze for a few seconds.

'Problem?' he purred and she blushed madly.

'I've never had anyone do…that…'

'Then relax and enjoy. Trust me, you'll be begging for more.' With which, he flattened her thighs wide open, hands placed squarely on them, and he lowered his dark head between her legs. His tongue was delicate between her wet folds and then, delving deeper, he found and teased her clitoris until he could feel it throbbing. Her whimpers became cries mixed with moans. Her fingers dived into his dark hair. One minute, she was pushing him down to suck her harder, the next she was tugging him up and squirming in a futile attempt to control her reaction.

Sophie had never, ever felt anything like this before. She hadn't known that this level of pleasure even existed. She half opened her eyes and his dark head moving between her legs made her shudder and gasp. She bucked against his mouth as the rush of building pleasure began to consume her, began to take over her body, then she was coming and she could no more stop the crescendo of her orgasm than she could have stopped a runaway train with the palm of her outstretched hand.

She cried out and then panted and arched and cried out again as she spasmed against his mouth.

It seemed to last for ever.

'Matias…' this when she was finally back down on planet earth '…you shouldn't have…'

'Shouldn't have what?' He had moved up to lie alongside her and he tugged her so that their bodies were pressed so closely against one another that they could have been joined. 'Pleasured you? I wanted to. I wanted to taste you in my mouth when you came.'

'It's not just about me.'

'Kiss me and hold me. You're so beautiful. I want to feel your mouth on me…but first I need to taste your breasts. I've been fantasising about them for so long. I want to see if they taste the way I imagined they do.'

'You've been fantasising about my breasts?'

'It's hardly my fault that they're so damned gloriously big.'

'Too big.'

Matias propped himself up on one elbow to examine them. He circled one nipple with his finger, watched it pinch and stiffen. She had generous full breasts and her nipples were boldly defined circular discs. He leant down and delicately darted his tongue over one and then he suckled on it. It tasted better than his wildest imaginings. Sweet as nectar, yet with the tang of salt.

It throbbed in his mouth as he drew it in and the touch of her hand at the nape of his neck and then curled into his hair was the most powerful aphrodisiac imaginable.

She was so headily responsive and yet she wasn't doing the usual gymnastics that so many of the women he bedded performed, gymnastics they always hoped would impress him enough to cement their staying power in his life.

Sophie was honest in all her responses and her little whimpers of pleasure carried a note that was almost of surprise, as if every touch was new and pretty sensational.

Good God, he thought, hanging on to restraint by a thread, a man could get addicted to this sort of thing. It was just as well that he was cool-headed enough to recognise this for what it was and to recognise himself for what *he* was. He was immune to being snared even by a woman who was driving him crazy.

He guided her mouth to his erection and knew, in the way she hesitated at first, that this was probably new to her as well, and that gave him a kick as powerful as a rocket launcher.

Sophie licked his shaft and enjoyed the way he shuddered. It made her feel more comfortable about coming into his mouth the way she had, with such wild abandon. Then she took him in her mouth and built up a rhythm of sucking that had him groaning out loud as his fingers tangled in her silver-blonde hair.

Her experience ran to the very basic when it came to sex. Her innocent fumblings with Alan, the guy she had thought she might end up marrying, were a thousand light years away from…*this*.

Her body was aching and yearning and tingling all

over again. She released him and lay down again, her back arched, her hair fanning out on the pillow, her eyes closed. He was watching her. She could feel it and it thrilled her.

When she sneaked a peek, she blushed shyly and was tempted to cover her breasts with her hands but she didn't.

'I want you,' Matias groaned heavily and she sighed and smiled at the same time, not quite believing what they were doing but wanting more of it and wanting it *now*.

'Then take me,' she whispered.

The seconds it took for him to fetch a condom and put it on felt like hours because she was so hot for him.

She parted her legs and then the joy and pleasure of him entering her made her heart swell and turned her on in every corner of her body. He thrust long and deep and hard and built a rhythm that started slow, getting firmer and stronger until their bodies were moving as one.

She was so tuned into him...it felt as though they had been lovers for ever. She knew when he was going to come as surely as she knew when *she* was, and when he groaned and arched back, his big, powerful body shuddering, she, too, felt her own body ascending to a climax, coming along with him, moving to the same primitive beat.

Spent, Sophie lay in his arms. His breathing was still a shallow rasp and she could feel the perspiration binding their bodies, making them hot and slippery. It felt so good and she wriggled and nestled into him, enjoying the way his arms clasped around her.

Did she fall asleep? She must have done although when she drowsily opened her eyes she was still wrapped in his arms, his thigh between her legs, her breasts squashed against his chest.

Half asleep, she reached down to touch him and felt the immediate stir of his body as he came to life in her hands. He was no more awake than she was. He was warm and half asleep and so was she, and the merging of their bodies was as natural and instinctive as the rising and setting of the sun or the changing of the tides.

When she woke the following morning, the sun was creeping into the room, weak and grey. There was a fine drizzle of rain. Where was Matias? Not lying next to her. Sophie yawned and shifted, turning onto her side to find him working at the desk by the window.

Matias heard the sound of her stirring and immediately stiffened because this whole situation had unnerved him. The sex had been amazing but afterwards...

Hell, they had fallen asleep together, wrapped around one another like clambering vines. Sleeping was something he did on his own. Women lay in his bed for sex but retreated to another bed for sleep or, better still, cleared off. Yet he had thought nothing of falling asleep with her in his arms, and then, in the middle of the night, they had made love again, and without protection. He'd barely been awake and it had been the most mind-blowing experience of his life, almost dreamlike and yet at the same time so exquisitely *real*. Their bodies had joined together and fused and he'd come explosively.

And now...

'We didn't use contraception.' He swivelled to face her, his body already responding to her warm, flushed face and the peep of her soft, generous breasts. He wanted to have her again immediately and that unnerved him as well.

'Huh?'

'Last night. You woke me up and we made love without protection.'

Sophie shot up into a sitting position, pulling her knees towards her. 'I—I didn't think…' she stammered. She wouldn't be pregnant. She *couldn't* be pregnant. Alarm and dismay flooded her face. 'There's no way there could be an accident,' she shot back, eyes huge. 'It's the wrong time of the month for me…'

Was it? She was too fraught to do the maths.

'And I couldn't be *that* unlucky.'

Disconcerted, Matias frowned. 'Unlucky?'

Sophie leapt out of the bed, belatedly remembered that she was buck naked and dragged the duvet out to cover her. Having sex with no protection had catapulted him right back to the conniving girlfriend who had almost booked herself a trip down the aisle on the back of a fake pregnancy scare, but the horror writ large on Sophie's expressive face was telling a different story and as she scuttled away from him his instinct wasn't to pursue his accusations. His instinct was to chase her right back into his bed.

'Do you honestly think I would *want* to find myself pregnant by *you*?' Her voice was high and unsteady.

Matias stood up, as sleek and graceful as a panther, and as dangerous to her state of mind. 'Why are you bothering to try and cover yourself? I've seen you in your birthday suit and, besides, your left breast is out.'

Sophie looked down and was confronted by the sight of her pink nipple perkily defying her attempts at concealment. When she raised her eyes again it was to find Matias standing right in front of her. He had slipped on his boxers to work but aside from that he was gloriously naked and she almost fainted at the surge of desire that swept through her like a tidal wave.

'You don't mean it when you say that you'd be unlucky if you discovered you were pregnant by me,' he grated and Sophie glared at him.

'You're *so* arrogant.'

'You like it.'

'You're *so* not my type.'

'You like that too. It's boring when you're with someone who's just like you. Where's the excitement in that?'

'I don't want exciting. I've *never* wanted exciting. My mother wasted most of her life *wanting exciting.*'

'You're not your mother,' Matias returned without skipping a beat, settling his hands on her soft shoulders and gently massaging them. 'And you may not want *exciting* but that doesn't mean that your goal in life should be to settle for *deadly dull.* I'm taking it,' he continued, the low, lazy drawl of his voice sending shivers up and down her spine, 'that you're putting me in the *exciting* category.'

'This isn't funny, Matias!'

'It's anything but,' he agreed. 'Especially,' he surprised himself by adding, 'considering I had a narrow escape with a woman who claimed to be pregnant so that she could get me to put a wedding band on her finger.'

'What?' Sophie tried to recapture some of the anger she had felt but his fingers were doing things to her body and she was relaxing and unbending and turning into a rag doll at his touch.

She was also, she discovered, heading back to the bed, a fact she only realised when she toppled back onto the mattress, with the duvet flying off her, leaving him in no doubt that, for all her protests, she was most definitely turned on by him. The tips of her nipples were stiff peaks and the rub of wetness between her legs was practically audible.

Matias didn't give her time to think. He'd never considered himself the sort of guy who could fall prey to the mindless demands of his body, but he was discovering that that was just the sort of guy she turned him into. It wasn't going to last longer than a heartbeat so why, he thought, shouldn't he just yield and enjoy the once-in-a-lifetime experience?

He shoved her over so that he could take up position lying next to her and before she could start protesting he slipped his hands between her legs and edged his finger into her, feeling her wetness with a soft moan of satisfaction.

'Stop doing that,' Sophie protested, squirming half-heartedly to distance herself from his exploring fingers. 'I can't think when you do that. You're arrogant and you have a nerve implying that I would be the sort of girl who would engineer a pregnancy to try and get you up the aisle!'

'Did I imply that?'

'Yes, you did! What girlfriend?'

Matias lay back and stared up at the ceiling. 'I was young and cocky and on my way up. I thought I knew it all and could take on anything. Turned out I was no match for a woman who wanted to start at ground zero with me. She'd spotted my potential. I was already a massive earner by then and driving around like a strutting bull in a red Ferrari.'

'Obnoxious, in other words,' Sophie muttered darkly, but she was secretly won over by the way he could mock himself.

'Very,' Matias confirmed drily. 'She told me she was pregnant. Turned out she wasn't but that was something I only discovered by accident.'

'You told me I'm not my mother,' Sophie ventured, still on the defence and still smarting but wanting him so badly it hurt, 'and I'm not your ex-girlfriend.' She wasn't going to curl into him, which was what she wanted to do, but she wasn't turning away either. She couldn't.

'And now that we've established that...' he moved his hand away from the dampness between her legs to her breast and the teasing pink nipple begging to be licked '...why don't we skip breakfast and carry on with our magical mystery tour of one another?'

'I have to get back to London,' Sophie said raggedly, her body already quivering in acquiescence.

'No, you don't. Have you forgotten that you have a debt to settle?'

'Not like this!'

'No,' Matias agreed seriously, 'not like this, but I *would* like to commission you to cook me breakfast and I'm not hungry yet, at least not for food.'

'Matias...'

'I want you in my bed, Sophie, and then, when we've made love and I've pleasured you in every way I know how, I would like to employ you to prepare breakfast for me because there's still the matter of that pesky debt to be paid off. Will you do that?'

'I'll do that.' Sophie frowned. 'But when we leave here...'

Matias raised his eyebrows and teased the fluff between her legs until he could see her thoughts getting all tangled up in her head. 'Hmm...?'

'When we leave here,' she panted, giving in as he

knew she would, 'none of this happened. Okay? I go back to being the caterer you employ so that I can pay off the money I owe you. It's back to business.'

'Sure,' he agreed smoothly, wanting her even more now that she was setting just the sort of rules and regulations that should, in theory, appeal to him, because they were exactly the ones he would set himself. 'But enough talking…'

CHAPTER SIX

FOR THE FIRST time since she had arrived, Sophie was
able to appreciate Matias's sprawling mansion at leisure
because she stayed to cook him breakfast the following
morning and the morning after that.

'But I thought all the guests had gone,' Julie had
proffered in a puzzled voice, when Sophie had phoned
and told her the situation.

Sophie had muttered something and nothing about
not all the guests having gone just yet, and what choice
did she have considering she was indebted to the man
and so had to do as he commanded or else face having
their business dismantled like a house of Lego bricks
in the hands of a hyperactive toddler.

She could just about extrapolate sufficient truth from
what she had said to paper over her guilt at playing tru-
ant, because that was what it felt like.

She was preparing breakfast for Matias but that was
just a nonsense excuse for what she was really doing.
She was his lover and she was enjoying every second
of it. Having curled up into herself after her experience
with Alan, she was feeling liberated in a way she had
never hoped to be. She was, she felt, on a journey of
self-discovery and she had stopped asking herself how

that was possible when Matias was so unsuitable. She just knew that he gave something to her, added some crazy dimension to her life that made her forget all the principles she had spent her life nurturing.

She was being reckless for the first time in her life and she was liking it.

You're not your mother, Matias had told her and she had actually listened and allowed herself to unbend and live a little without beating herself up about it. Okay, so Matias wasn't going to be around for ever but that didn't mean that she was going to suddenly develop a taste for inappropriate men. No, Matias was her walk on the wild side and why shouldn't she enjoy him while she had the chance?

He was rich, he was powerful, he was arrogant and he was self-assured to the point of ridiculous, but he was also, she had discovered, an extremely thoughtful lover, a good laugh, was weirdly tuned into her thoughts and just so, so unbelievably clever.

Hovering on the fringes of her enjoyment, however, was the looming certainty that he wouldn't be around for much longer, although when she thought about that a guilty little voice whispered in her head, *But won't he be...? After all, you'll still have to pay off the rest of your debt...maybe there'll be more breakfasts to be prepared...*

Breakfast this morning had been an elaborate concoction of eggs, spinach, ham and a hollandaise sauce on freshly baked bread.

The smell of the bread still lingered in the kitchen as Sophie tidied away the dishes while Matias reclined at the kitchen table like a lord and master, replete after having his appetite sated.

She turned around and he beckoned her across and patted his lap.

'Sit,' he commanded with a grin, watching as she sashayed towards him, fresh as a flower without make-up and sexy as hell in some cut-off faded jeans and a baggy tee shirt.

She wasn't wearing a bra. He liked her without one. He liked being able to reach out and touch her without having to go through the bother of unclasping boring fastenings.

They'd been larking around for two days like teenagers and Matias still couldn't get enough of her. He hadn't steered the conversation towards her father again. Hadn't even thought about it. The only thing on his mind had been her fabulous body and what it did to him.

'Nice breakfast,' he murmured as she settled obediently on his lap. He slipped his hand under the tee shirt, found the generous swell of her breast and the tight bud of her nipple, then he lifted the shirt and angled her so that she was straddling him and began suckling at her breast.

He had no idea what she possessed that could make him act like a horny teenager but she had it. In his saner moments, he remembered who she was and what his original plan had been in getting her to repay her debt by working for him. Unfortunately, those saner moments had been rarer than hen's teeth.

Watching her bustle about his kitchen, in a parody of domesticity that should have sent him running for the hills, had kick-started a nice little erection and sucking her nipple now was intensifying it to the point of painful.

He shifted under her and felt her smile as she reached

down and found his hard shaft, holding it firmly but getting little traction because of his jeans.

Too little traction. He adjusted his big body and, reading him and responding instinctively, Sophie slid off his lap, discarding her tee shirt along the way, and then she eased off his trousers with a little help from him.

He was so beautiful he took her breath away. She couldn't believe that in a space of just a few days she had moved from novice to wanton, had blossomed under his touch like a plant given life-saving nutrients. He'd encouraged her to touch, to experiment, to wallow in his open adoration of her body. He'd been a masterful teacher. He'd lavished attention on every inch of her body and taught her just how to touch him and where to make him feel good.

Now, with his trousers and boxers in a heap on the ground, she took his thick shaft between her hands and played with him, absolutely enjoying the way he slid a little further down the chair and loving the guttural moan that escaped his lips. His hand cupped the crown of her head as she took him into her mouth and his fingers curled into her hair as she began to suck.

They were in their private paradise, a delicious bubble where they had been able to indulge their appetite for one another without interruption, a bubble in which thoughts and conjectures and *reality*, at least *for her*, had not been allowed to intrude.

She stood up, noting that his eyes were closed, those thick, lush lashes casting shadows on his razor-sharp cheekbones. His nostrils were flared. He knew what she was going to do and was lazily waiting to be pleasured.

Sophie couldn't get her jeans and underwear off fast

enough. He did that to her, made her whole body agitate with an urgency to be satisfied. She was wet between her legs, dripping, aching to have him inside her.

She knew where he kept his condoms and quickly fetched one from the wallet in his trousers on the ground. They had made love without protection that one single time and never again. Now, she slipped a condom out of its foil and took him between her hands so that she could put it on him.

His eyes were slumberous on her, hotly working her up to a peak of excitement, and she groaned out loud as she lowered herself onto him, her every nerve ending tingling as he circled her waist with his big hands, then she was moving on him, pressing down to feel him deep inside her, letting him take her to places only he could.

He levered her head towards him and kissed her as she moved on him, a deep, hungry, urgent kiss that made her moan and then she was coming, hurtling towards that peak of satisfaction, her body moving in perfect rhythm with his until the world exploded and all she could feel was the intense pleasure of her climax that went on and on, subsiding eventually in little, erotic waves that left her shaking and trembling.

She sagged against him, head against his chest, listening to his slow, ragged breathing that very gradually returned to normal. They were both practically slipping off the chair and she reluctantly climbed off him and began sticking back on her clothes.

He looked so peaceful there, his big body relaxed, his eyes half closed as he watched her scramble to put on her tee shirt and then hop into her underwear.

He wasn't at all self-conscious about his body. Where, even now that they had made love what felt like a thousand times, she still needed to put on her clothes rather than parade her nudity, he couldn't care less.

He stood up, flexed his muscles and looked at her sideways with a satisfied smile.

'Work is beginning to call,' he drawled, eyeing the puddle of clothes on the ground and deigning to put on his jeans but nothing else. 'She's an extremely demanding mistress.'

'Yes, I have to get back as well.' Sophie's heart sank but she smiled brightly at him. 'Julie's beginning to tear her hair out because we've just landed a pretty big order and it's hard planning a menu together over text or on the phone.'

'You still owe me for my car...' He swerved round her and, standing behind, wrapped his arms around her waist and leant down so that he was talking into her hair, his voice a little muffled.

Sophie literally thrilled. She couldn't help grinning from ear to ear. She knew that this situation wasn't going to last and was probably the least sensible thing she could be doing but the pull of having fun was irresistible. She couldn't think beyond it.

'But,' Matias continued gravely, 'you're paying off the debt quickly. That said... I might still need you to do some catering for me and I rather enjoy the private catering you've been providing, by which I mean those excellent breakfast options you've presented to me.'

Sophie swivelled round so that they were facing one another and she looked up at him. 'I like cooking you breakfast,' she told him. 'Do we...er...put a date in the diary? How does this work?' She sighed and reached up to link her fingers behind his neck. 'I mean, Matias, how does this *really* work? Is there a time frame? And if I choose to stop…*this*…then what happens? I feel vulnerable thinking that we've entered new territory.'

'Do you think I'm going to penalise you if you decide you want to stop being my lover? I won't. I'm not that kind of guy. You're free to make your choice. I still want you, Sophie, but there's no way I want you to feel that you're somehow committed to pleasing me for fear of what I might do if you change your mind.'

The bubble was beginning to burst. They weren't going to be in one another's company twenty-four-seven, making love, talking, making love again. True, Matias had taken himself off for brief periods to work, during which time she had video called Julie so that she, too, could remember that real life was going on outside his glasshouse mansion, but most of their time had been spent in one another's company.

Living in the moment had been easy. She had been able to turn a blind eye to real life because real life was located somewhere outside the glass and concrete of his house. Real life was back in London. Well, they were returning to London soon and although she had told him that, once they left, what they had would come to an end, she didn't want it to end and that frightened her.

They hadn't mentioned actual numbers at all in terms of the money she still owed him for the damage to his car. She didn't care about that because she had discovered that, despite the fact that he could be stunningly arrogant, he was also incredibly fair and incredibly honourable.

What did concern her was the deal he was considering making with her father. That, too, was a subject that hadn't been raised, but it would be just as soon as they drove away from their little bubble and the real world started to intrude. She had promoted James Carney as someone he *should* deal with, had sidestepped most of the truth about her father because what was at stake was the fate of her beloved brother.

Suddenly it was vitally important that she tell him about Eric. She didn't have to compromise any deal Matias wanted to do with her father, but at least when the deal was done and should her father show his true colours, *which wasn't inevitable because he would be on the back foot*, Matias would put two and two together and understand why she had done what she had, why she hadn't warned him off.

Not that, Sophie feverishly told herself, there would be any problems. Her father was broke. He needed Matias. He would be on best behaviour.

'Good,' she said vaguely, wondering how to send the conversation in the direction in which she wanted it to go and finally deciding to just say what she had to say. 'And about my father...'

'Yes?' Matias's ears pricked up. He marvelled that this was the first time Carney had been mentioned in their couple of days alone together when the original purpose of her being here was to provide information that he could use. It irked him that he had been so side-tracked by her that he had taken his eye off the ball.

'Will you still...er...be interested in investing money in his company?' Sophie had the whole back story about Eric prepared for Matias and was a little taken aback at the sudden deathly silence that greeted her question.

'Ah. We haven't discussed that, have we?'

'I guess there have been a few distractions.' She laughed nervously.

'So there have.' Matias looked at her coolly, his quick

brain putting two and two together and not liking what he was coming up with.

'What's wrong?'

'What makes you think that something's wrong, Sophie?'

'I don't know. What have I said? I just thought that… we're going to be leaving here and I wanted to talk about what happens next.'

'Why would that lead to a discussion of my plans for your father? But now that we're on the subject…you've, apparently, no idea about the ugly business of making money, but did you know your father is…shall we say… battling one or two financial problems…?' Matias was watching her intently and he was as still as a statue.

She knew. It was there, written plainly on her face. She'd played the clueless card, but she'd known all along that her old man was broke. She wasn't even trying to deny it.

'And,' Matias continued, testing the ground as the steady burn of rage began to build inside him, 'of course, if any deal is to go through, then there will have to be certain background checks…'

'Background checks?' she squeaked.

Matias shrugged but he was picking up everything he wanted to know and more from her reaction. 'The business community is a small world. There have been certain rumours of shady dealings…'

Sophie's face drained of colour. Her legs felt shaky. Her brain was in meltdown as she thought of what would be revealed in *background checks*. She knew nothing for sure, but she suspected…

'Surely that wouldn't be necessary,' she whispered.

'Oh, dear.' Used. He'd been used. She'd slept with

him to facilitate a deal with her father whom she knew to be penniless and crooked. She was clearly running scared from background checks that she must know could open up a can of worms. He'd got the information he'd wanted after all, but the fury of finding himself played once again was volcanic in its intensity. 'You seem apprehensive. Did you think that you could *distract* me into putting money into your bank account without doing my homework thoroughly?'

Sophie's face drained of colour as she tried to make sense of what he was saying but the dots weren't joining up. What was he implying?

Some part of her was desperate to give him the benefit of the doubt and to find a reasonable explanation for the cold, veiled expression on his handsome face but a chill was growing inside her and it make her feel sick and giddy.

'I d-don't know what you're talking about,' she stammered.

'Don't you?' Not even his duplicitous ex-girlfriend from long ago had managed to produce a rage like this. He'd learned *nothing* because he'd been conned again. If he'd smashed his fist against the wall, he would have driven it right through the brickwork, so powerful was the torrent of emotion coursing through his body. 'I don't know why I didn't stop to question your sudden departure from shy and blushing to hot and ready for sex.'

'That's an awful thing to say!'

'If memory serves me right, you had your claws out when we first met...'

'Because you were horrible to me! Because you threatened to shut down my business to pay off a debt!'

'But then we came to a satisfactory conclusion, didn't we? But when did you decide to hop in the sack with me? Was it when you found out that I might decide to have business dealings with your father? Did you think that you were clever in trying to withhold the true state of your father's coffers and the fact that he's a crook? Did you think that your sexy body would seal the deal for me regardless of that?'

Sophie stared at him round-eyed. She was looking at a stranger. Gone was the teasing, seductive guy who could turn her off and on like a light switch.

'No! I would never do something like that! The only reason I mentioned my father and…well…is because I wanted to tell you something that…'

Matias held up one imperious hand. 'Not interested. The fact is there's something you should know.' He killed the tight knot in the pit of his stomach. Sex was sex but business was business and this was the business of retribution and he'd been a fool to have ever been distracted by her gorgeous body and beautiful, duplicitous face.

Sophie was spellbound, filled with creeping dread and apprehension. He was pacing the kitchen, restless and somehow vaguely menacing in the soft prowl of his movements.

'Regrettably, you've got hold of the wrong end of the stick. The fact is, the only interest I have in your father won't be leading to any lucrative deals that might result in more money lining your pockets.' He looked at her flushed face narrowly and it got on his nerves that he half wanted her to deny that she had any interest in any of her father's money that might come her way, but she remained silent and he could tell from the expression on her face that money trickling down into her grasping little hands had been exactly what she had hoped for.

She'd turned into his compliant lover because sex was a most persuasive tool. His mouth tightened and cold hostility settled like glacial ice in his veins.

'You don't understand,' Sophie protested weakly, but everything seemed to be moving at bewildering speed and her brain couldn't keep up.

'I think I understand very well indeed. But here's what *you* don't understand. Not only will I *not* be putting money into your father's business, but my intention couldn't be more different. I won't be the making of your bankrupt, disreputable scumbag of a father. I will be the ruination of him.' He clenched his jaw as her mouth fell open and the colour drained away from her face. 'You may not remember but I mentioned in passing to you that my parents should have had money and all the little luxuries that go with the sort of well-oiled lifestyle your daddy dearest enjoyed, but sadly they didn't.'

'I remember… I meant to ask you about that…but…'

'Distractions…ah, yes, they got in the way.' Matias smiled coldly. 'Let me fill in the gaps. Your father stole my father's invention and used it to prop up the sad sack company he had inherited that was already on its last legs, and in the process made himself rich beyond most people's wildest dreams. My father was naïve and trusting, a simple emigrant who believed the rubbish your father told him about them going in as partners, jointly reaping the financial rewards of something my father invented. I know, because I've seen the proof of those conversations with my own eyes in letters that were kept in a folder. It never occurred to my parents that they could have taken the man through the courts and got what they deserved.'

'No.' But she already believed every word that was being said because that was very much the sort of thing her father would have done.

'My father never recovered from the betrayal of his trust. What your father did infected every area of my family's life. My father died prematurely from a rare cancer and do you want to hear the worst of it? I recently found more letters, hidden away amongst my mother's things, begging letters from my mother to your father, pleading for some money to send my father to America where groundbreaking work was being done in that area, clinical trials that were beyond my parents' meagre means.'

'I'm so sorry,' Sophie whispered brokenly.

'So,' Matias rammed home, every syllable filled with icy condemnation made all the more biting because he knew that he had allowed himself to drift into territory he should never have occupied, 'my intention was always to make your father pay for what he did.'

'What are you saying?'

'I think you know. I knew about Carney's penury. I wanted more information and I got it. A stint in jail seems appropriate considering what he did, wouldn't you agree? So thank you for corroborating what I suspected. Now I know exactly which rocks to turn over when I have your daddy's company in my hands.'

A wave of sickness swept through her. She had accepted that they were ships passing in the night and had justified her extraordinary response to him on all sorts of grounds about lust and desire, but now that the extent of his deception was unravelling in front of her she knew that she had felt a great deal more for him than lust or desire.

He had managed in drawing out a side of her that she hadn't known existed. He had made her laugh and forget all the worries that plagued her. When she had been with him, she had stopped being the girl who had been let down by an ex, the girl who had to grovel for handouts, the girl with the disabled brother whom she fiercely protected, the girl whose career could crash and burn at any moment, leaving her nowhere. When she'd been with Matias, unlikely as it was, she had been carefree and sexy and *young*.

But that had been an illusion because he had used her to get information about her father out of her, and the depth of her hurt was suffocating.

'I played right into your hands with that accident, didn't I?' Her voice was stilted but despair, as toxic as acid, was filling every corner of her. 'You don't care a jot that *I* never hurt your family.' She wasn't going to try and explain anything about Eric to him now, nothing at all, and she hated herself for allowing him to get so close, close enough for her to have been tempted to open up about her beloved brother. This ruthless, unfeeling man in front of her wouldn't even care. 'Did you even fancy me?' Tears stung the backs of her eyes. She was asking questions and she didn't want to know the answers but she couldn't help herself.

Matias flushed darkly. It pained him to see the wounded hurt in her eyes but he wasn't going to be sidetracked by that. This time he was going to stick to the brief. No way was he going to let her swing the tables round and cast him in the role of the criminal.

She'd been after money and that was the long and short of it, end of story.

'I should have stopped to ask myself why a man like you would have looked twice at me,' Sophie continued bitterly.

'Can you deny,' Matias intoned coldly, 'that you wanted me to pour money into your father's company because you knew that, if I did, some of it would inevitably come your way?'

Sophie closed her eyes.

She had needed that money but she would die before she explained it to him now. Instead she had to accept that she had been a tool to be exploited by him in his search for revenge. They hadn't been getting closer. That had all been in her stupid mind because he hated her for a crime she hadn't committed.

Matias noted that she couldn't even meet his eyes and he bunched his fists, resisting the urge to punch something very, very hard. He was uncomfortable in his own skin and that enraged him. He moved to the door, remained there for a few seconds, his body deathly still and yet seeming to exude a savage, restless energy.

'Our return to London will mark the end of any relationship between us.'

'But what about the money I still owe you?' Panicked, she licked her lips nervously.

'Do you honestly think that I would want to set eyes on you ever again, Sophie?'

Tears gathered at the backs of her eyes and she swallowed painfully, not wanting to cry in front of him but fearing that she would. Her heart was thundering inside her and her head was beginning to hurt.

'You're going to take my company away from me,'

she said flatly. 'You don't care who you hurt in your desire for revenge. It doesn't matter that I had nothing to do with whatever my father did to your father.'

Matias's jaw clenched. His eyes drifted down from her defiant heart-shaped face to the body he had so recently taken and he was furious that, in defiance of the hostile atmosphere simmering between them, his body was still insisting on responding to hers with unbridled gusto.

He harshly reminded himself that whatever she trotted out, nothing could excuse the fact that she had tried to encourage him to open dealings with her father because she'd wanted his money. Whatever guise it took, the apple never fell far from the tree. Greed was in her blood and nothing else mattered.

'Consider the debt to me paid in full,' he gritted. 'I won't be going after your company so you can breathe a sigh of relief. I walk through this door and all dealings between us, as I've said, come to an end. I will instruct my secretary to email you confirming that you no longer owe me anything for the damage to my car and you should consider yourself fortunate, because there are no limits for me when it comes to getting justice for what your father did to mine. In life, there is always collateral damage.'

Being referred to as *collateral damage* just about said it all, Sophie thought, devastated. Thank goodness, she hadn't confided in him about Eric. Thank goodness she hadn't allowed him even further into her heart.

'I shall go and pack my stuff up and then I think I'll get a taxi to the station and take the first train back to London.'

'My driver will deliver you to your house. In the

meantime, I have ignored work demands because of certain *distractions.*' His mouth curled into a sardonic smile. 'It's time for me to return to normality and not a moment too soon.'

Every word that passed his beautiful mouth was a dagger deep into the core of her but, no, she wasn't going to break down in front of him. She wasn't going to let him see how far he had already burrowed into her.

She nodded curtly and remained where she was as he turned his back on her and walked out of the kitchen.

Then and only then did her whole body sag, like a puppet whose strings had been abruptly cut.

But only for a few minutes, a few minutes during which she breathed deeply and did her best to find the silver lining in the cloud. It was what she had spent a lifetime doing. She'd done it every time she visited her brother and reminded herself that life with him in it, however damaged he was, was so much better than life without him in it. She'd done it every time she'd gone to her father, cap in hand, to beg for the money needed to keep Eric safe and happy, and left with the cash.

She would do it again now, and she would thank her lucky stars that she hadn't had the opportunity to emotionally invest even further in a guy who'd used her. And she'd thank her lucky stars that her debt to him was repaid in full.

But, as she got ready to leave, flinging her possessions in the case she had brought with her, her heart was still telling her that life was never going to be the same again.

CHAPTER SEVEN

SOPHIE LOOKED AT the innocuous white stick with the two bright blue lines and felt a wave of nausea surge through her all over again.

This was the third pregnancy test she had done and still her mind refused to compute the enormity of what was staring her in the face. She was sorely tempted to use the last one in the box but she knew that she had to accept the horrible, terrifying truth that she was pregnant. One reckless mistake had resulted in the baby growing inside her. She could do a hundred more tests and nothing was going to change that inalterable fact.

She was having Matias's baby.

A guy who had played her, used her and then discarded her without a backward glance. It had been a little over five weeks since she had last seen him, disappearing through the kitchen door of his over-the-top hillside mansion. Since then she had received a formal email from his secretary informing her that all monies owing to him had been cancelled. Since then, her father's company had gone into liquidation and was now in the process of being eaten up by Matias's sprawling empire. Sophie knew that because it had been on the news. Her father, needless to say, wanted no more to do with her because of the situation he was in. He had no more money to give her and the last time she had seen him, he had angrily accused her of helping to send him to the poorhouse. He'd conveniently overlooked the fact that the failure of his company had been down to his own incompetence and she had not reminded him, choosing instead to walk away and deal with the problems the bankruptcy presented to her brother's future.

Had Matias put the final nail in the coffin and sent the police after her father as well? She didn't know. If so, that was a further public humiliation to come.

Released from having to maintain appearances for the sake of his peers, she and Eric had been cut loose and Sophie had spent every night for the past fortnight trying to find a solution to the problem of how to keep her brother in the safe home he had grown accustomed to.

She was stressed beyond belief and now this had happened.

'You'll have to tell him,' was the first thing Julie said to her later that morning when she showed up at the house.

Sophie looked at her friend, utterly defeated and without a silver lining in sight. 'How can I?' she asked, remembering how they had parted company and feeling the stamp of pride settle in her like a stone. 'You know what happened, you know…' her voice cracked and she took a deep breath and continued in a rush '…what his motives were for getting involved with me.'

'But this is no longer about your father, Soph, or whatever revenge Matias Rivero was after. This is about a new life growing inside you that can't be made to take the blame for a situation he or she had nothing to do with.'

Sophie knew that in her heart of hearts. How could she withhold the baby's existence from his own flesh and blood? Matias would have to know but only because she could see no other way around it. She would have to make sure he knew that she *wanted nothing from him*. She didn't care how much money he had. As far as she was concerned, she would do the right thing and tell him about the baby, but after that she would walk away.

And he would be able to breathe a sigh of relief because she knew that the last person he would want to see show up at his office, again, would be her.

First time, she had shown up having crashed into his car. Now, she would be showing up with a baby-shaped wrecking ball solidly aimed at his life.

She could remember just how she had felt that first time she had shown up at his impressively scary office headquarters and spoken to the receptionist. Sick with nerves at an uncertain outcome, and yet with just enough hope that everything would be okay because although she wasn't going to be seeing the very empathetic Art Delgado, deep down she had clung to the belief that the guy she *would* be seeing might be cut from the same cloth.

One day later, as Sophie yet again stood outside the impressive building that housed Matias's legendary empire headquarters, hope was nowhere in existence.

She had had several hours to get her head round her situation and yet she was no nearer to locating any silver linings.

She strode into the glass building with a great deal more confidence than she was feeling and asked for Matias with the sort of assurance that implied an audience would be granted without argument.

'It's a personal matter,' she added to a frowning young blonde girl, just in case. 'I think Matias… *Mr Rivero*…would be quite upset if you don't inform him that I'm here. Sophie Watts. He'll know who I am and it's urgent.'

Would he see her? Why should he? His parting shot had been that he never wanted to set eyes on her again, even if that involved kissing sweet goodbye to the thousands of pounds she still owed him.

About to go to the boardroom to close a multimillion-pound deal, Matias was interrupted by his secretary and told that Sophie was in the foyer several stories below.

For approximately two seconds, he debated delivering a message back that he was unavailable.

He didn't. He'd walked away from her weeks ago but hadn't managed to escape whatever malign influence she had over him. She'd lodged under his skin like a burr, appearing like a guilty conscience just when he least needed it and haunting his dreams with infuriating regularity.

Everything was going nicely when it came to dismantling her father's company, ensuring that the man was left standing out in the cold with no shelter in sight. Behind the scenes, further revelations would come when he moved to phase two, which would involve the long arm of the law. An eye for an eye.

It should have given him an additional sense of satisfaction that his daughter, whose greed had matched her father's, would also be standing in the same cold spot, without any shelter on the horizon. Unfortunately, every time he tried to muster the appropriate levels of satisfaction at a job well done, the image of her soft heart-shaped face popped into his head, giving him pause for thought.

Revenge had been served cold, but it was not as sweet as it should have been.

It didn't help that his mother had read all about the takeover in the newspapers and had summoned him to the hospital where she was recovering nicely. She'd never agreed with his thirst for retribution and nothing had changed on that front.

All in all, he was pleased that he had done what he had done, because as far as he was concerned those wheels of justice had to turn full circle, but he was surprised at how dissatisfied he remained at what should have been a stunning victory of the present over the past. And he knew it was all down to Sophie.

'Show her up,' he told his secretary in a clipped voice, instantly deciding to put his meeting on hold, regardless of the value of the deal. 'And tell Jefferies and his team that Bill Hodgson will be handling the initial closing stages.' He ignored the startled look on her face because such an about-face was unheard of.

His mind was already zooming ahead to what Sophie might want from him.

Money was the first and only thing that came to mind. She had encouraged a deal with her father so that she could benefit from the financial injection. No deal meant no financial injection, which meant that she still wanted money, except it wasn't going to come from her dear papa.

He was outraged that she would try her luck with him. He knew that he certainly shouldn't be allowing her any chink through which she might try and slip. But he couldn't resist the opportunity to see her and he was, he acknowledged, curious to see what approach she would take to try and wheedle cash out of him.

Would she shoot him one of those sweet, innocent, butter-wouldn't-melt-in-her-mouth smiles? The kind of smile that instantly went to his groin and induced all manner of erotic, dirty, sexy scenarios in his head? He got a kick imagining her sashaying into his office, hot for sex. He'd send her on her way, but he still experienced a massive surge of desire playing with the thought.

The single knock on his door found him relaxing in his chair, his hands loosely linked on his washboard-flat stomach, his expression one of mild curiosity.

'Yes.' The door opened, his secretary stood to one side and there she was, tentatively walking into his office, blushing in the way that would send any normal, red-blooded man's pulse through the roof. She was wearing a pair of grey trousers and a white blouse and his eyes immediately dropped to the soft swell of her breasts and, right on cue, his brain lurched off at a predictable tangent, remembering exactly what those luscious breasts had felt like, had tasted like. 'What have you come for?' he asked abruptly, putting paid to the raunchy turn of his thoughts. He pushed himself away from the desk but did nothing to make her feel comfortable. Why should he?

'Can I sit down?'

Matias nodded to the chair. 'I wouldn't make myself too comfortable if I were you,' he drawled. 'Time is money, after all. On the subject of which, I'm taking a stab in the dark here at the reason for your sudden, unexpected visit. Because this isn't a social call, is it?'

'No.' Her voice was steady and Sophie was proud of

that, although that, in fairness, was the only part of her that felt remotely controlled. She hadn't laid eyes on him for weeks but she hadn't stopped thinking about him, and, seeing him in the flesh now, she was shocked that she could have so massively underestimated the impact of his physical presence.

His lean, dark face was even more stunningly beautiful than she recalled, his mouth more cruel, more sensuous, his body…

Sophie didn't want to think about his body. She just wanted to say what she had come to say and leave before her steady voice went the way of the rest of her. She reminded herself of the man he had turned out to be, vengeful and ruthless, and a lump of ice settled inside her, the cold knot of hatred, which she welcomed.

'Didn't think so.' Matias's lips thinned. He was recalling in vivid detail the mind-blowing sex they had shared… He was also recalling the reason she had slept with him. 'I expect you read all about your father's downfall in the financial pages.'

'You must be pretty pleased with yourself.'

Matias flushed darkly, nettled by the cool disdain in her voice. 'Your father got what he deserved.' He shrugged. 'And yes, I'm quietly pleased with myself, although I have to say that had he not let his company run aground, my job would have been considerably less easy. He was a thief, a conman and eventually an idiot who let go of the reins and never thought that the horse might bolt. A great deal of highly suspect financial dealings is being uncovered, but that won't come as any surprise to you. In due course, your father and Her Majesty will be more than nodding acquaintances, but not in the way he would doubtless like. But you haven't

come here for a chat. I'm a busy man so why don't we
just cut to the chase, Sophie? No deal with your father
means no rescue of his terminally ill company, which
means no cash in hand for you. So I'm guessing that
you're here to see whether there isn't another way to
elicit money out of me.'

'I wouldn't accept a penny from you if my life depended on it,' she snapped. Every word that had passed
his beautiful lips stung, every word was a reminder of
exactly what he thought of her.

If she could have turned tail and run for the hills,
she would have, but Julie had been right. A father deserved to know about the existence of his child, even
if he chose to do nothing with the knowledge. However
much she hated him for how he had treated her, she was
fair enough to recognise that simple fact.

'We're going round the houses here, *querida*. In one
sentence, why don't you just tell me what the hell you're
doing in my office?'

'We had unprotected sex, Matias. Do you remember?'

Two sentences that dropped into the still silence between them with the power of an unexploded bomb.

Usually quick on the uptake, Matias could literally
feel his brain slowing down, skidding to a halt in the
face of what she had said and what she hadn't.

'I remember…' he said slowly. It was strange but
that languorous bout of lovemaking, in that quiet sur-
real lull between sleeping and waking, had stayed right
there, between the sheets, trapped in a moment in time.
Had he subconsciously shoved it to the back of his mind
rather than face the possibility that taking her without protection might have had consequences? Or had

it just seemed unreal in the light of day and therefore easily forgotten?

He was remembering now, remembering the way their bodies had fused, warm and lazy and barely awake.

'I'm pregnant, Matias,' Sophie told him flatly.

She'd not envisaged what sort of reaction she would get from her announcement. In her head, she said what she had to and then walked away. Now, as she watched the vibrant bronze of his face slowly pale, she found herself riveted to the chair into which she had sunk.

'You can't be,' he denied hoarsely.

'I've done three tests. I didn't even think about it until I started feeling nauseous every morning and re-alised that my period hadn't come.'

'It's impossible.' Matias raked his fingers through his hair and realised that his hand was shaking. Pregnant. She was having his baby. Just like that, his eyes darted to her still-flat stomach, then to her breasts, which now, suddenly, seemed bigger and lusher than he remembered. 'And if this is your attempt to try and get money out of me, then you're barking up the wrong tree. You seem to forget that I've had ample experience of a woman who will use a so-called pregnancy to worm her way into my bank balance.'

Sophie rose on shaking legs. 'I'm going now, Matias. I know you had a poor experience in the past and I'm very sorry that I've had to come here and spring this on you, but I'm not your ex-girlfriend, I'm not lying and I certainly don't want a penny from you. After what you did to me, do you honestly think that I could ever want anything from you? *Ever?* I'm here because I felt you should know about your baby.'

Matias watched as she began walking towards his office door. Everything seemed to be happening in slow motion or maybe it was just that his brain had now totally seized up, unable to deal with a situation for which he had not, in any way, shape or form, prepared himself. He didn't move as she opened the office door but then he did, suddenly galvanised into action.

He caught her as she was barrelling along the corridor towards the bank of lifts and he placed his hand on her arm, forcing her to a stop.

Who cared whether his bizarre behaviour was being observed?

'Where do you think you're going?' he gritted.

Sophie's eyes flashed. 'Back home! Where do you think? I can't believe you would have the nerve to accuse me of faking a pregnancy to try and extort money out of you. What sort of person do you think I am? No. Don't bother answering that! I know already!' She yanked her arm out of his grasp and hit the button on one of the lifts, which obligingly opened at her command. She stepped in, eyes firmly averted from Matias, but she was all too aware of him stepping into the lift with her and slamming his fist on one of the buttons, which instantly brought it to a shuddering stop between floors.

'What are you doing?' Alarmed, Sophie finally looked him squarely in the eyes and then blinked and made a huge effort to drag her eyes away because, even when she was seething with hatred, she still couldn't help finding him so impossibly attractive. It wasn't fair!

'We need to talk about this and if this is the only way to get you to talk to me, then I'll take it.'

'You can't just *do that*.' Sophie was shocked because

wasn't that breaking the law? Normal people didn't just *stop a lift to have a conversation*! But then since when was Matias Rivero a *normal human being*?

'Why not?'

'Because…because…'

'Are you going to have a conversation with me about this or are you going to put on your running shoes the second we're out of this lift? Because you can't drop a bombshell like that in my lap and then try and dodge the bullet.'

'I don't want anything from you,' Sophie repeated fiercely. 'I hate you!'

'Message received loud and clear.'

'And I didn't engineer getting pregnant to try and get money out of you! That's a vile thing to say even from you, but why should I be surprised?'

'Let's not waste time going down that road. It's not going to solve anything.'

'And I have no intention of getting rid of this baby, if that's what you're thinking!'

'Did I insinuate that that was what I wanted?' Matias raked frustrated fingers through his hair. Her colour was high, her eyes were glittering like aquamarines, and she was the very essence of bristling feminine fury. He set the lift back on its way down. 'We're going to go to a small wine bar five minutes' walk from this office. I know the guy who owns it. I'll make sure we get a good seat at the back somewhere and we can have a civilised conversation about this problem. Agreed?'

Sophie scowled. 'You used me just to get dirt on my father.' She looked at him narrowly and with hostility. 'We can talk about this if you like but I don't want you to forget how much I detest you for doing what you did.'

Matias hung onto his temper. He had no doubt that she was telling the truth and, with the dust settling, the grim reality of what had happened was beginning to take shape. He was going to be a father. When it came to his bucket list, having a kid had never been on it and yet here he was, with only a few months left of sweet independent singledom because of one crazy mistake.

Life as he knew it was about to undergo a seismic change and getting wrapped up in blame and counter-blame wasn't going to alter that.

The wine bar was half empty and they were, indeed, afforded utter privacy at the very back, where they were tucked away from the other tables. Matias ordered a coffee for them both and then looked at her directly.

'When did you find out?' he asked quietly, shunning anything that might lead to another emotive outburst.

'Yesterday.' Sophie glared bitterly at him and fiddled with the handle of her cup before taking a sip and grimacing because her taste buds were no longer quite the same. 'And don't think that it wasn't as big a shock for me as well! Don't think that I haven't thought about how Fate could have been so cruel!'

'Whatever has happened in the past, we have to put behind us or else we'll be stuck on a treadmill of never moving forward and the only way we can deal with this problem is to move forward towards a mutually agreeable solution.'

Sophie stared coldly at him because every word he said, while making perfect sense, left her feeling angry and defensive. Problem? Mutually agreeable solution? She rested her hand protectively on her stomach, a gesture that Matias keenly noted, just as he understood that treading on eggshells about summed up where he was right at this moment. She had come to his office under duress and was not inclined to give him the benefit of any doubts, but she was hardly the saint she made herself out to be, he thought. She talked a lot about him using her but hadn't she been after his money? No, she wouldn't be in line for a halo any time soon, but, like it or not, he had to listen to his own words of advice and approach the situation dispassionately.

'That's easier said than done,' Sophie said tonelessly and Matias heaved an impatient sigh.

'You wanted me to engineer a deal with your father because you thought he might be able to help you financially if he wasn't in financial trouble himself. Am I right?' His voice was level and cool. 'So when you rant and rave about what a bastard I am, take a long look at yourself and try and put things into perspective.'

He hadn't wanted to raise this thorny issue because he didn't see what the point of raising it might be, considering it wouldn't advance any sort of solution to their problem, but raise it he had and he was disconcerted by the absolute lack of suitable apology on her face. Clearly a sense of guilt didn't feature in her repertoire.

And yet that seemed strangely at odds with the person she came across as being. Surely his judgement couldn't be that skewed?

'You *are* a bastard.' But she flushed because he'd never given her the chance to explain about Eric and it was understandable that he had somehow ended up with the wrong end of the stick. She looked at him, her bright eyes filled with unspoken challenge. 'And how very lucky you are that I won't be hanging around and making a nuisance of myself by demanding anything from you. I'm not the nasty gold-digger you seemed to think I am and I wouldn't touch a penny from you if my life depended on it!'

'You're telling me that you weren't after money from me by trying to encourage me to do a deal with your father? Even though you knew that his company was on the brink of collapse? Even though you knew that he was probably criminally involved in skimming cash from the till?' Matias laughed shortly. 'Let's have your definition of a gold-digger, then, Sophie...'

'I don't care what you think of me,' Sophie said tightly. She'd had her tale to tell, had been ready to spill the beans about Eric because she had been seduced by Matias on an emotional level, had taken him for being someone he had not been. She'd had a narrow escape— so should she spill the beans *now*?

No way, she decided grimly. He was still after her father and there was no way she would allow Eric's privacy to be invaded by the press, which was exactly what could happen should Matias choose to publicise her brother's existence. Her darling, fragile brother was not going to be part of Matias's retribution or even unintentional *collateral damage*.

Matias instantly realised that that simple statement held the distinct possibility of opening up another quagmire and so he opted for silence.

'So what is your explanation for your behaviour?' he eventually demanded, grudgingly curious to find out what she would be able to come up with that didn't begin and end with her need to have money injected into her company.

'I don't have to provide you with an explanation,' Sophie retorted quickly, cringing back from a vision of reporters banging on the window of her brother's bedroom, terrifying him because he would be hopelessly confused and panicked.

'I just need to take everything you say at face value and believe you. Is that it?'

'You don't have to do anything you don't want to do. I haven't come here because I want anything from you and there's no *we* in this situation. I came here because I felt it was the right thing to do but this isn't a problem that I'm forcing you to face. I don't trust you, Matias, but you deserved to know about the pregnancy so here I am.'

'We're back to this again. Let's move away from that and focus on the present and the future. And just for your reference, there very much *is* a *we* in this situation because half of my chromosomes, whether you like it or not, happen to be inside you right now in the form of a baby neither of us expected but which both of us have to deal with.' His instinct was to qualify what he had to say by telling her that everything depended on whether she was telling the truth, but he decided that silence on that subject was definitely going to be the diplomatic course. 'You're having my baby...' For a few seconds he was stunned again by the impact that had on him. Matias Rivero, a father. He still couldn't quite get his head round that. 'If you thought that you could just pass on that information and then walk away, job done, then you were sorely mistaken. I won't be walking away from my responsibility, Sophie.'

'I don't want to be your responsibility.'

'You're not but my unborn child is, whether you like it or not. I didn't sign up to this but it's happened and we have to deal with it. You have an unhappy family background so maybe that's led you to imagine that stability is overrated, but I haven't and I am a firm believer in the importance of having parents in a child's life. Both parents.'

'I happen to believe very strongly in stability,' Sophie corrected him tightly, '*because* I've had an unhappy family background. I didn't know how you would react when I came to see you, bearing in mind the way we parted company, but you can rest assured that I won't stand in the way of your seeing your child.' She hated the way he made her feel. She didn't want to be here, and yet, in his presence, she felt so *different*, as though she were living on a plane of heightened sensation. She felt *alive*. She wanted to walk out but felt compelled to stay. She wanted to ignore his staggering, unwelcome impact on her senses but was drawn to him by invisible strings that she couldn't seem to sever. She loathed him for what he had done and loathed herself almost as much for knowing that somewhere inside her he still stirred something…something only he could somehow manage to reach.

'That's not good enough, *querida*.' Matias had never contemplated marriage and now here he was, facing marriage as the final frontier, and not simply marriage, but marriage to the woman who was the daughter of his sworn enemy. And yet what other solution was there? He had no intention of being a bit player in his child's life, forking out maintenance payments while having his visiting rights restricted and curtailed by a vengeful mother. Sophie wouldn't forget the circumstances that had brought him into her life and she would have the perfect opportunity, should she so choose, to wreak a little healthy revenge of her own by dictating how much or how little influence he had over his own flesh and blood.

He thought of his mother, recovering in a private hospital in London. She would be so upset if she ended up as only a part-time grandparent, snatching moments here and there with a grandchild caught in a tug of war between two warring parents. Matias might have been put off emotional commitment thanks to a conniving ex and the lessons learnt from his own emotional father and where it had got him in the long run. That said, he hadn't been lying when he'd told Sophie that his childhood had consisted of a strong and supportive family unit and now, in the face of this unexpected development, that strong family bond locked into place to override everything else.

'Twenty minutes ago, you were telling me that time was money, so I'd better go now.'

'Things change. Twenty minutes ago I didn't realise that you were carrying my baby.' His sharp eyes were glued to her face while he programmed his brain to accept the news she had broken to him, to start thinking outside the box. 'You're now set to be a permanent feature in my life. I want to be there for my child twenty-four-seven and the only way that can be achieved is if we marry.'

Deathly silence greeted this extraordinary statement and Sophie's mouth inelegantly fell open in shock.

'You've got to be kidding.'

'You might have come here out of a sense of duty but I have no intention of going away like an unpleasant smell because you refuse to accept that the past is over and done with.'

'I will never forget how you used me in your quest for revenge. You used me once and who's to say that you won't use me again?' She thought of Eric, the secret that Matias could not be allowed to uncover because what if his desire for revenge hadn't been sated? She looked at him from under lowered lashes and shivered. So beautiful, so powerful and so incredibly ruthless.

'Sophie, that story has ended. We are travelling down a different road now.' But Matias was genuinely puzzled by her statement. What else could he possibly use her for? For better or for worse, he had uncovered everything there was to uncover about her father.

He continued to look at her and noted the way her cheeks slowly coloured, arrowed in on the soft tremble of her full lips. The air between them was suddenly filled with a charge he recognised all too well, a sexual charge that made him immediately harden for her. He vividly recalled the silky wetness that always greeted his exploring fingers, his questing mouth, and he clenched his jaw.

He motioned, without looking around, for the bill and wondered whether she was conscious of the signals she was sending out under all the hostility and mistrust, signals that were as powerful as a deep sea-depth charge, signals that advertised a connection between them that was founded on the oldest thing in the world...sexual attraction.

'Think about it, Sophie, and I will call you tomorrow so that we can pick up this conversation.' He smiled slowly and watched intently as a little shiver went through her. 'I think we both need to do a little private reflection, don't you?'

CHAPTER EIGHT

SHE'D TURNED DOWN his extraordinary marriage proposal and she'd done the right thing.

Of course there were pros and there were cons. Every decision was always laced with pros and cons! But she had done the right thing. She'd been to see Eric, sat in his soothing presence, watched his contentment in his peaceful surroundings. Somehow she'd find the money to pay for him carrying on living there, but she would never expose him to the cruel glare of a curious and judgemental public.

Was she being selfish? Was she failing to consider the reality, which was that a child would always be better off with two parents as opposed to one and that was something that should override every other concern?

No. How could you hitch your wagon to a man you didn't trust? A man you felt might betray you again? And anyway, trust issues aside, two parents only worked if the glue that bound them together wasn't a child, but love. Matias didn't love her and he had never pretended that he did. He felt responsible for her, responsible for the child he had sired, and was admirably willing to step up to the plate and do his duty, but duty was a far cry from love.

Duty would wear very thin at the edges as time marched on. Duty would be the very thing he would come to resent when he found himself harnessed to a woman he would never have voluntarily chosen to spend his life with.

But three weeks had gone by and Matias just seemed to *be around so much*.

He hadn't said it in so many words, but there had been no need because every look he gave her and every word that passed his lips said *don't fight me*.

She'd turned him down but, like a predator waiting for the right moment to strike, he was simply biding his time.

He didn't realise, she thought, that he would never wear away her defences because there was more than just her and their baby at stake. At stake was a brother he knew nothing about and never would and that bolstered all her resolve when his presence just felt *too overwhelming*.

Nothing he could say, no logic he could use, could ever make her do anything that might jeopardise her brother's privacy and happiness.

She was congratulating herself on being strong as she sat, the first to arrive, at the posh restaurant where Matias had arranged to meet her for lunch. He had been away for the past three days and her stomach was already tightening in nervous knots as she braced herself for that first glimpse of him. On the one hand, she had been relieved that, although he had been scrupulous about maintaining contact with her by phone, he hadn't imposed his presence on her on a daily basis. On the other hand, she wondered whether she might have become more blasé about his physical presence if he were around more, if she had a chance to get accustomed to him. She didn't like the way he still made her feel and she hated the memories of him touching her that refused to go away. They weren't on that page any longer! Things had changed and they were never going to be on that page together again.

Lost in thought, she looked up to find that he had arrived and he wasn't alone.

Art was with him. She hadn't seen him since the weekend party in the Lake District and she rose to her feet, already smiling as he walked towards her. Behind him, Matias towered, unbearably sexy in his work clothes, one hand in his trouser pocket, the other hooked to his jacket, which was slung over his shoulder.

Seeing that warm, genuine smile on her face as she looked at Art, Matias sourly thought that it was something *he* hadn't seen for a while. She'd repeatedly thrown his marriage proposals back in his face and he'd been sharp enough to realise that the harder he pushed, the faster she would back away.

There was no way he was going to let her run out of his life because it suited her. Pride refused to let him forget that she had slept with him as a ruse to get him to invest in her father's company, but common sense dictated that he get her onside because he was never going to be persuaded into the role of part-time father.

He watched, his expression shuttered, as she and Art chatted away like the old friends they weren't and something hit him hard, something so unexpected that it was like a punch to the gut.

He didn't like seeing her relaxed interaction with his friend. He didn't like the way she was so at ease in his company. He didn't care for the tinkling of her laughter as they found God only knew what to talk about, considering they'd known each other all of five seconds.

Jealousy and possessiveness rammed into him with the weight of a sledgehammer and he interrupted their conversation to coolly inform her that Art wasn't going to be joining them for lunch.

'That's a shame.' Sophie sighed with genuine disappointment, which got on Matias's nerves even more.

He scowled, met Art's curious eyes and scowled even more. 'Don't let us keep you,' he said abruptly, and Art grinned broadly but stood up, moving to drop a kiss on Sophie's cheek before heading out.

'That was *so* rude,' she said. 'It was lovely seeing Art again! I had no idea you two were so close. You never said! I can't believe you *grew up together*!' They were like brothers and it had brought her up short to acknowledge that Art adored Matias. Even in the space of half an hour, she had been able to glean that from their interaction and seeing them together had unwillingly reminded her of just why she had been seduced by him. There was a side to Matias that wasn't a bastard, a side that could elicit a depth of affection from a loyal friend who was clearly a wonderful human being. It was suddenly confusing to admit that he was also many other things, a complex guy with so many dimensions, it made her head swim.

Not that she was going to let that deflect her from the path she had decided to take.

'I had no idea I had a duty to tell you every detail of my life just because you're carrying my baby,' Matias drawled lazily, sitting back as menus were placed in front of them. Her cheeks were still flushed and she looked so damned sexy that the jealousy that had attacked him from nowhere five minutes ago staged another onslaught. He knew he was being irrational but he couldn't help it.

'You never said that you were going to visit your mother...'

'I could hardly let her find out about us via the grapevine.'

'She must have been disappointed,' Sophie said quietly. 'No mother likes to think that her child has... well...is going to have a family...you know...so unexpectedly...and without the usual build-up...'

Matias allowed her to run aground. Seeing his mother had reinforced his belief that the only solution was to marry the woman blushing opposite him. If she was going to dig her heels in, then he would have to work along the lines that there was more than one way to skin a cat. He'd seen the way she still looked at him. 'Naturally,' he murmured smoothly, 'she would have preferred the love and marriage scenario...'

'But you told her how it was? That this isn't that sort of situation?'

Matias didn't say anything because he had told his mother no such thing. 'Pregnancy becomes you, Sophie,' he said instead, relaxing into the chair and staring at her until the faint colour in her cheeks deepened and he saw the latent *awareness* of him that she was always so careful to try and conceal. 'Your body's changing. You're wearing looser clothes. Are your breasts getting bigger?'

'Matias!' Sophie was shocked because he hadn't been direct like this before.

Heat blossomed inside her. Her breasts ached and she felt the tingle of awareness stickily making its presence felt between her legs. *That* was what those casual words were doing to her!

'It doesn't get more intimate than having my baby…' he shrugged, his fabulous eyes not leaving her face '… so why are you so surprised that I am curious about the physical changes occurring to you? It's natural. I'm fifty per cent responsible for those physical changes.'

'This conversation is not appropriate! We no longer have that kind of relationship!'

'You think that we are more like…*what*?'

'Well, *friends*. At least, that's what we should be aspiring to become! We've talked about this and we both agree that it would be best for our child if we remain on good terms.' She cleared her throat and tried to ignore the suffocating effect his intense gaze was having on her nervous system. 'Remember we agreed that you would be able to see him or her any time you wanted?'

'So we did…'

'We may not have expected this…' she dug deep to repeat the mantra she had told herself '…but we're both adults and um…in this day and age, marriage isn't the inevitable solution to dealing with an unexpected pregnancy… We discussed this.'

'Indeed…'

'There's too much water under the bridge between us.'

'I won't deny that.' She had deferred, for once, and he had ordered for both of them, a sharing platter that was now placed between them. 'But I'm curious. What do you suggest we do with the mutual desire that's still putting in an unwelcome appearance?'

Sophie's mouth fell open. He had brought out into the open the one thing she had desperately tried to shove into a locked box. 'I don't know what you're talking about!'

'Liar,' Matias said softly. 'I could reach out and touch you right now and you'd go up in flames.'

'You couldn't be further from the truth,' Sophie denied weakly. 'I could never be attracted to someone who used me like you did. Never!'

'*Never* is a word that has no place in my vocabulary.'

'Matias…' She thought of Eric and the importance of hanging onto her resolve, but seeing Matias with Art had weakened that resolve, had reminded her of those sides to him that could be so wonderfully seductive, so thoughtful and unexpectedly kind.

'I'm listening.'

'I know you find it funny to make me uncomfortable.'

'I think about you all the time. I wonder what your changing body looks like under those clothes.'

'Don't say things like that! We don't have that kind of relationship! We talked about that.' She sought refuge in the platter in front of her but she could feel him staring lazily at her, sending her into heady meltdown. Her whole body was throbbing with the very awareness he was casually dragging out into the open and forcing her to acknowledge.

'I don't like to stick to the script. It makes for a boring life.' Matias sat back. He let his eyes drift at a leisurely pace down her curvaceous body and felt his mouth twitch because she was as rigid as a plank of wood, as if her posture were fooling him. 'In fact,' he drawled, 'I'm taking the afternoon off.'

'Why?'

'Do I have to provide a reason? And stop looking at

me like that. You should be thrilled at the prospect of spending time in my company. And do me a favour and refrain from telling me that we *don't have that kind of relationship.*'

'I can't leave Julie in the lurch.'

'She's going to have to get used to you no longer holding her hand when you finally decide to listen to me and quit working. She's a big girl. She'll cope.'

'I can't *quit working*, Matias.'

'Let's not go there. You don't need the money.'

Sophie thought of Eric and her mouth firmed. The irony was that Matias wanted to throw money at her. Once upon a time not all that long ago he had turned his back on her and tossed her to the kerb but now that she was pregnant, everything had changed. They had not discussed money in any great depth yet, but he had already made it clear that his child, and her by extension, would want for nothing.

And yet, how could she allow herself to ever become financially dependent on him? Her pride would never allow it and, more than that, what if she began to trust again only to find that she had once more made a mistake? What if, by then, she was totally reliant on the money he was so keen for her to have because she'd stopped working? No, there was no way she could give up her job. Maternity leave was one thing. Resignation was quite another.

Another roadblock, Matias thought with frustration. He impatiently wondered why she couldn't just recognise that his solution was the best and only way to move forward. What woman wouldn't want a life of luxury? What woman wouldn't want to be able to snap her fingers and get whatever she wanted? It wasn't as though they didn't have an electric connection still thrumming between them like a live charge. What more advantages did he have to bring to the table for her to accept his proposal? Why, he thought, did she have to be so *damned stubborn*?

'I've taken the afternoon off, *querida*, because I have a surprise for you.'

'I hate surprises,' Sophie confessed.

'I know. I'm not a big fan of them myself but I am hoping you'll like this one. It's a house.'

'A house?'

'For you,' he said bluntly and her eyes widened in surprise.

'You've gone and bought a house *for me*?' She bristled. 'Why would you do that?'

Matias sat back, taking his own sweet time, and looked at her evenly. 'Because,' he said calmly, 'you won't be bringing up our child in that tiny box of yours with its converted kitchen.'

'There's nothing wrong with *that box*,' Sophie cried hotly as pride kicked in and lodged inside her.

'Don't argue with me on this.' Matias's voice was forbidding. 'You've turned down my marriage proposal, in defiance of common sense. You've dug your heels in and dismissed all financial help I've offered as unnecessary handouts. You've insisted on working long hours even though you're unnecessarily putting our child at risk. You are *not* going to wage war with me on this.'

'How have I been putting the baby at risk?' Sophie asked furiously.

'You don't have to work until midnight baking cakes for anyone's anniversary party.'

'*Once*. I've done that *once*!'

'Or,' Matias ploughed on remorselessly, 'waste three hours in traffic delivering a four-course meal for a dinner party.'

'That's my job!'

'You're overexerting yourself. You need to take it easy.'

Sophie released a long sigh but… *Had anyone ever really looked out for her? Ever really cared whether she was taking on too much or not?* Of course, this wasn't about *her*, but about the precious cargo in her stomach, and it would be downright foolhardy to start thinking otherwise *but still…*

'I know you're not a gold-digger, Sophie. You don't have to keep trying to prove it to me over and over again.'

'That's not what I'm doing.'

'No? Then what is it?'

'I won't rely on you financially. I can't. I need to have my own financial independence.' Suddenly she felt small and helpless. She wished she were able to lean on him and just accept what was on offer. He made it sound so easy. Clean break from what had happened between them in the past and onward bound to the future he wanted her and his child to have, but there was so much more to the story than he knew.

'Well, you're going to have to compromise on this, whether you like it or not, *cara*.' His voice was cool and unyielding.

Their eyes tangled. He reached out and brushed a speck of something from the side of her mouth, then left his finger there for a few seconds to stroke it over her lips. 'A little bread,' he said roughly, his big body firing up immediately because it was the first time he'd touched her in weeks.

Sophie's eyes widened. For a minute there she had leaned towards him and her whole body had burned from the inside out, as though molten lava were running through her veins. *The way he was looking at her, with those deep, dark, sexy eyes...*

Yearning made her weak and it was a struggle to pull away from the magnetic drag on her senses.

'You have no idea what my taste is like. In houses.' Which was as good as accepting whatever over-the-top house he had flung money at, in defiance of the fact that he must have known that she would have kicked up a fuss about it. Her heart was still hammering and she lowered her eyes and took a few deep breaths before looking at him once again. She could still feel the burning of her skin where he had touched her. 'Don't get me wrong, Matias.' Her tone crisped up but her body, awakened by his touch, *wanted more.* 'You have a lovely place in the Lake District but I couldn't imagine living in a massive greenhouse like that. I don't know what your apartment's like but I'm guessing it's along the same lines...'

'Damned by faint praise,' Matias murmured, wanting her more than he had ever wanted anything or anyone in his life before and damn well determined to have her because he could *smell* the same want radiating from her in waves.

'What I'm saying is you and I obviously don't have the same taste in houses so it's unlikely I'm going to like whatever it is you've bought.'

'I haven't bought it yet,' he drawled. 'I may be arrogant but I thought you might actually like to have a say in the house you want to live in.' Eyes on her, he signalled for the bill and then stood up.

He dominated the space around him and she was helplessly drawn towards him, like a moth to a bright light. She couldn't quite understand how it was that he could continue to exercise this powerful effect on her after what he had done, or how common sense and logic hadn't prevailed when it came to stepping back from him. She wondered whether pregnancy hormones had taken over and were controlling all her responses, heightening her emotional state and making her vulnerable to him when she should have been as detached from him as he was from her and getting down to the business of building a friendship for the sake of the child she was carrying.

Outside, his chauffeur was waiting for them, but instead of accompanying them he drove them to his office where they switched cars, and Matias took the wheel.

'Where is this house?' Sophie asked because she had expected something in Chelsea or Mayfair or one of those frighteningly expensive postcodes close to where he had his own apartment.

'I'm going to disappoint you…' he slid his eyes sideways to glance at her and smiled '…by keeping it a surprise. Now, talk to me, *querida*. Don't argue with me. Tell me about that client of yours…'

'Which client?' Because stupidly, even though she had so many defences erected when it came to Matias you could construct a small town behind them, she *still* found it frighteningly easy to talk to him when he turned on that charm of his.

'The vegan with the wart on her face.'

'I didn't think I'd mentioned her to you.'

'When we're not fighting,' Matias murmured softly, 'we're getting along a hell of a lot better than you give us credit for. There's so much more we could be doing, *querida*, instead of making war...'

Sophie only realised that they had been driving for longer than she thought when the crowded streets and houses fell away to open space and parks and they pulled up outside a picture-perfect house shaped like a chocolate box with an extension to one side. Wisteria clambered over the front wall and, set right back from the lane, the front garden was dilapidated and overgrown.

'It needs work,' Matias told her, reaching into the pocket of his jacket, which he had flung in the back seat, and extracting some keys, which he jangled on one finger as he opened his car door. 'And it hasn't been lived in for several months, hence the exuberance of the weeds.'

'I hadn't expected anything like this.' Sophie followed him up to the front door, head swinging left to right as she looked around her. The house stood in its own small plot, which was hedged in on three sides. He opened the door, stood aside and she brushed past him and then stood and stared.

There were rooms to the right and left of the hallway. Lovely square rooms, all perfectly proportioned. A sitting room, a more formal living room, a study, a snug and then along to the kitchen and conservatory, which opened out at the back to a garden that was full of trees and shrubs and plants that had taken advantage of absentee owners and decided to run rampant.

The paint was faded. In the sitting room, the gently flowered wallpaper seemed to speak of a different era.

'The house was owned by an elderly lady who lived

here for most of her life, it would seem,' Matias was murmuring as he led her from room to room. 'She didn't have any children, or perhaps they might have persuaded her that the house was far too big as she got older, but it would seem that she was too attached to it to sell up and leave and as a consequence the latter part of her life was spent in only a handful of rooms. The rest were left in a state of gradual decline. When she died a little over a year ago, it was inherited by a distant relative abroad and the probate took some time, hence it's only just come onto the market.'

She walked from room to room. Her silence spoke volumes. She wasn't bristling; she wasn't complaining. In the matter of the house, he had clearly won hands down.

Matias intended to win hands down in every other area as well.

He was waiting for her in the hallway, leaning against the wall, when she completed her third tour of the house, and he didn't budge as she walked towards him, her eyes still wide as saucers.

'Okay.' Sophie smiled crookedly. 'You win.'

'I know.'

'Don't be arrogant, Matias,' but she was still smiling and she wasn't trying to shuffle more distance between them. The silence stretched until she licked her lips nervously.

But she hadn't taken flight.

'I don't just want to win when it comes to finding a house for...you,' he said gruffly.

'Matias, don't.' But her voice was high and unsteady, and against her will her body was straining with desperate longing towards him, liquid pooling between her legs, the swollen tips of her nipples tightening into sensitive buds.

'Why do you insist on fighting this thing that's still here between us?'

'Because we can't give in to...to lust...'

'So you finally admit it.'

'That doesn't mean anything. It doesn't mean I'm going to do anything about it.' She looked at him and couldn't look away. His dark eyes pinned her to the spot with ruthless efficiency. She couldn't move, couldn't think, could scarcely breathe.

Her head screamed that this was *just not going to do*. She couldn't afford to lose sight of what was sensible but her body was singing from a different song sheet and when he lowered his head to hers, her hands reached out. To push him away? Maybe. Yet they didn't. They curled into his shirt and she melted helplessly as he kissed her, softly and teasingly at first and then with a hunger that matched her own.

His tongue found hers. His hands, on her shoulders, moved to her arms then cupped the full weight of her breasts.

He played with her nipples through her top but then, frustrated, pushed open the buttons and groaned as he felt the naked skin of her chest and then, burrowing beneath the lacy bra, finally got to the silky fullness of her breasts and the ripe protrusion of a nipple.

'You're definitely bigger.' His voice was shaking.

'Matias...'

'Touch me.' He guided her hand to his erection, which was a hard, prominent bulge against the zipper of his trousers.

'We can't make love here!'

Wrenched back to the reality of what she was saying, Matias struggled not to explode in his trousers. He breathed deeply, cupped the nape of her neck and drew her to him so that their foreheads were touching.

Her breath was minty fresh, her skin as soft as satin and he ached for her. 'We talk, Sophie,' he breathed in a driven undertone. 'Don't tell me we're at one another's throats all of the time. And we want one another.'

Sophie knew what he was saying and she longed to capitulate but she was only in this place because she was pregnant. Had she not been, they would be enemies on opposite sides of the fence. Were it just a question of her, then would she think about his offer? Maybe. She could cope if it turned out that she couldn't trust him. Again. But she couldn't trust him with Eric. Could she?

Confusion tore through her.

'Come back to my place with me,' he urged.

'I won't marry you,' she said weakly.

Matias all but groaned in frustration but he didn't. Instead, he smoothed his hands over her shoulders and kissed her very gently, very persuasively on her mouth and felt her move from hesitation to abandon. He kept kissing her. He kissed her until she was breathless. He kissed her until he knew for certain that there was nothing and no one left in her head but him, then he broke apart and said, in a barely restrained voice,

'Let's go.'

CHAPTER NINE

HER HOUSE.

In her head, to go to Matias's house would have been a complete declaration of defeat. Within the confines of her own four walls, however, she could kid herself that she was still in control, even though she had lost it in his arms and even though *she wanted to carry on losing it*.

If I sleep with him, she thought, then it would be *a conscious decision*. It wouldn't mean that she had lost all control and it certainly didn't mean that she would marry him. She would never trust him again. How could she? She would never jeopardise Eric's privacy because she'd made another mistake, but…

She wanted Matias so badly. He was in her system like a virus and she wanted to be cleared of that virus because it was driving her round the bend.

He reached out to link his fingers lightly through hers in the car. They barely spoke but the electricity between them could have set a forest ablaze. His mobile phone rang several times. He ignored it. Looking at his strong, sharp profile, the lean contours of his beautiful face, Sophie wondered what was going through his head. He didn't love her but he still fancied her. He'd told her that there was no need for her to keep trying to prove to him that she was no gold-digger, but deep down she knew that he would always believe her culpable of trying to get him to sink money into her father's dying company and invest in a man who had turned out to be a thief. He had no idea that Eric existed and so would never understand why she had done what she had, and she could never tell him about her brother because family loyalty was more powerful than anything else.

But whatever the situation, he was right. A fire burned between them and what were they to do about it?

Having never invested in the crazy notion that lust was something that couldn't be tamed, Sophie was realising just how far off the mark she'd been with her orderly, smug little homilies.

It was after four-thirty by the time they made it to her house. Sophie thought it was serendipity that Julie was out on a job, setting up with an assistant they had hired, for a lavish dinner party in Dulwich.

Compared to the glorious setting of the house they had just seen, her two up, two down, squashed in the middle of an uninspiring row of terraced lookalikes, was a shock to the system. She'd vigorously defended her little place but now she felt that she could see it through Matias's eyes. Poky, cramped, unsatisfactory.

She turned to find him looking at her with a veiled expression as he quietly shut the door behind them. Shivers of anticipation raced up and down her spine.

'Empty house?' he asked, walking very slowly towards her, and Sophie nodded.

'Julie's on a job. She won't be back until tomorrow afternoon. Matias... I'm glad about the house... This place would really not have been suitable for a baby. I mean, of course, it would have worked if there were no other option but...'

'Shh.' He placed one finger over her lips and her heart sped up. 'Don't talk.' He was directly in front of her now and he bent his head and kissed her. A long, lingering, gentle kiss that made her weak at the knees. 'Much as I enjoy the sound of you telling me that I was right, there's more, a lot more, I want to enjoy right now.' He cupped the back of her neck and carried on kissing her, taking it long and slow and feeling a kick of satisfaction as her body yielded to his, moulding bit by bit to his hard length until they were pressed together, entwined.

Without warning, he lifted her off her feet and Sophie gasped and clung to him as he made his way up the narrow staircase.

He'd seen enough of her place to know that finding her bedroom wasn't going to require in-depth navigation skills. The place was tiny. He doubted there were more than two bedrooms and he was proved right, finding hers with no trouble at all as it was at the top of the stairs.

Cheerful colours tried to make the most of a space that could barely contain the bed, the chest of drawers and the wardrobe that were crammed into it. Two posters tried to attract the eye away from the view outside of other terraced houses and beyond that a railway line.

He set her down on the bed and she promptly pushed herself up onto her elbows to look at him as he drew the curtains together, shutting out the weak sunlight and plunging the room into subdued tones of grey and sepia.

'It's been too long,' he intoned with a slow, possessive smile that ratcheted up her spiralling excitement.

He was standing with his back to the window and he remained there for a few seconds, just staring at her, before walking towards the bed, ridding himself of clothes on the way.

He was sheer masculine, powerful beauty in motion and he took her breath away.

She was frankly amazed that she had been able to withstand his potent sex appeal for as long as she had, but then today was the first time he had yanked that monster out of the cupboard and forced her to confront it.

She half closed her eyes, watching as, down to his boxers, he stood by the side of the bed and gazed down at her.

Tentatively, she reached out and ran the tips of her fingers across the washboard hardness of his flat stomach.

He was wired for her. His erection was prominent under the boxers, which didn't remain on for longer than necessary.

'I don't have to tell you how much I want this,' Matias said gruffly. 'The evidence is right in front of you.'

Sophie gave a soft little whimper and sat up straighter, angling her body so that she could lick the shaft of his pulsing erection.

She tasted him like someone savouring an exquisite delicacy. Her tongue flicked and touched, her mouth closed over him and she sucked while, with her hand, she enjoyed the familiar feel of his hardness. His taste was an aphrodisiac.

She felt as if somewhere, in the back of her mind, she had stored the memory of the noises he made when she did this, his deep, guttural grunts. His fingers clasped in her hair were familiar. She wanted him so badly she

was melting for him and wanted nothing more than to
fling off all her clothes so that he could take her.

Reading her mind and knowing that if he didn't
watch it, he would come right now, in her mouth, Matias
reluctantly separated her from him. When he glanced
down, his shaft was slick and wet and he had to clench
his fists to control the urge to put her right back there,
have her take him across the finishing line with her
hands and her mouth.

No. He'd fantasised about this for far too long to blow
it on a horny, teenage urge to grab and take.

But hell, he was on fire as he sank onto the mattress
so that he could remove her clothes.

She was wearing far too much and he was way too
fired up to do justice to the striptease scenario. He
needed to get under the layers of fabric as quickly as
possible so that he could feel her.

Her clothes hit the deck in record time and she
helped, squirming out of her cumbersome bra and wriggling free of the lacy underwear, which, he noted in
passing satisfaction, was of the sexy thong variety, a
choice of lingerie he knew he had encouraged her to
wear.

It was almost a shame that he was so hot and hard because he would have liked to have taken his time teasing
her with his tongue through the lace of her underwear.

'Matias…' Sophie fell back against the pillow and
arched a little so that her full breasts were pushed out
invitingly to him.

He was kneeling over her and, on cue, he took her
breasts in his big hands and massaged them gently until
his thumbs were grazing her nipples and sending shivers of racing pleasure straight downwards.

She circled him with her hand and played with him, knowing just how fast and firm he liked the rhythmic motion of her hand.

'Matias…what?' he encouraged with a wicked smile and she looked back at him with wry understanding because she knew just what he wanted.

'You know…' she blushed furiously '…what I like…'

'Oh, I know…' He bent to suckle her nipple, drawing it into his mouth and taking his time to lave it with his tongue, circling the aching tip until she was writhing under him.

He knew her so well. It felt as though they had been making love for ever. Knew that she liked him to be just a little rough, to nip her big, pouting nipples until she became even wetter and more restless. He knew what else she loved, and he explored lower down her glorious body, taking time to appreciate all the small changes he had wondered about.

Her breasts were at least a cup size bigger and her nipples were more pronounced in colour, no longer a rosy blush but a deeper hue. Her belly was just a bit more rounded. Having never thought about babies or becoming a father, at least not since the hapless incident a thousand years ago with the ex-girlfriend who had tried it on, he had never looked twice at pregnant women, but this woman, with his baby inside her, was beyond sexy.

Her roundness thrilled him, made him even harder than he already was.

Working his way down her body, he slipped his hand between her legs and played with the soft down between them. Then he slipped his finger into her and she moaned softly and squirmed until his finger was deeper inside her, finding her softness and working a path to the tiny bud that was begging for attention.

He knew that if he dawdled too long there, she would come. She was the most responsive woman he had ever known. So he played with the tingling bud, then stopped, then played with it again, until she was begging him to take her.

'Not just yet,' he whispered. Hands on her waist, he dropped down between her legs and nuzzled, breathing in her honeyed sweetness.

He flicked his tongue along the slit of her womanhood, then began exploring her wetness.

His finger had already teased her and now his tongue did the teasing, until she was moaning and wriggling, pushing him down hard one minute, jerking him up the next, her fingers curled into his hair.

She bucked against his mouth, rising up with jerky movements, and he cupped her buttocks, holding her still and torturing her with the insistent push of his tongue inside her.

'I'm going to come,' she gasped as her body began moving quicker to capture every small sensation of him between her legs. 'I don't want to come like this, Matías... I want to *feel you inside me.*'

Matías rose up. He automatically reached down to find his wallet but then he remembered that there was no need for protection and he dealt her a slashing smile.

'The horse has already bolted...' he grinned '...so no need to do anything about locking the stable door.'

Sophie drowsily returned his smile. Her body was hot and flushed and the waves of pleasure that had almost but not quite taken her over the edge were still there, making her want to wriggle and touch herself.

'You're so hot for me, *querida*...'

'I can't help it,' Sophie half groaned. 'It's a physical thing.'

'Now, now, don't go spoiling the mood. I want to ride you and take you to the outer reaches of the universe.' He prodded her with the blunt head of his shaft and she parted her legs, unable to contain her eagerness to have him deep inside her.

He slid in and the sensation was beyond belief. She was slick and wet and tight and her softness welcomed him in ways that he couldn't define but just knew made him feel better than good.

He wanted her so badly. This was going to have to be fast and hard. He couldn't hang around any longer, he couldn't devote any more time to foreplay or else he risked the unthinkable.

He drove into her, thrusting long and deep, and she wrapped her legs around his waist and, yes, he rode her until she was bucking and crying out with pleasure, until the breathing hitched in her throat. Until, cresting a wave, she came just as he did, with a rush of sensation that flowed over her and around her like a tsunami.

She arched up and stiffened as his powerful body shuddered against her and she panted and rocked beneath him until at last...she was spent.

Matias levered himself off her. It was a downright miracle of circumstance that he now found himself here, with her. The number of *what ifs* between them could have stocked a library.

What if...she hadn't crashed into his car?

What if...he hadn't lived a life hell-bent on revenge?

What if...he hadn't seen fit to weave her into his revenge agenda?

What if…she hadn't spent time under his roof at his place in the Lake District?

What if, what if, what if…?

But here they were, having made the most satisfying love imaginable. In no way, shape or form was he tiring of her. On the contrary, he desired her with an urgency that none of his other relationships had ever had. He felt a possessiveness towards her that defied belief.

He had accepted the shock to his system that impending and unforeseen fatherhood would confer.

He had risen above the challenge of playing a blame game that would get neither of them anywhere.

But had he really believed that this unforeseeable passion and downright *insatiable craving* would form a part of the picture? Was it the evidence of his own virility and the fact that she was carrying his baby that made his feelings towards her so…*ferociously powerful*?

She had stuck to her guns about not marrying him, frustrating his natural urge to get what he wanted. His powerful need to *never* back down until he had what should be his within his grasp had hit a roadblock with her. He refused to contemplate any situation that involved him losing control over his child, and by extension, he told himself, *her*.

Seeing his mother as she recuperated in hospital, as he had now done several times, had only reinforced his determination to take her as his wife.

Thus far, the inevitable meeting between his mother and Sophie had been avoided, but sooner or later his mother would want to meet the woman who was carrying her grandchild and when that time arrived Matias was determined that marriage would be on the cards. There would be no difficult conversation in which his mother would be forced to concede that the grandchild she had always longed for would be a fleeting presence in her life.

'Was that as good for you as it was for me, *querida*?' He shifted onto his side and manoeuvred her so that they were facing one another. He brushed a strand of hair away from her face and then kissed her very gently on her mouth, tracing the outline of her lips with his tongue.

Sophie struggled to think straight. She had done what she had spent weeks resolving not to do. She had climbed back into bed with him and where did that leave the *friendship* angle she had been working so hard at since she had turned down his marriage proposal?

What disturbed and alarmed her was the fact that it had felt *right*.

Because…because…

Because she loved him. Because he'd swept into her life, inappropriate and infuriatingly arrogant, and stolen her heart, and even though he had used her and couldn't be trusted, because who knew whether he would use her again, she still couldn't help but love him. She'd made love to him and it had been as wonderful and as satisfying as walking through the front door of the house you adored and finding safety within its four walls. Which was a joke, of course, but then so were all the stupid assumptions she had made about love being something she would have been able to control. She could no more have controlled what she felt for Matias than she could have controlled the direction of a hurricane.

'Well?' Matias prompted, curving a hand possessively around her waist, challenging her to deny what was glaringly obvious.

'It was nice,' Sophie said faintly, still wrapped in the revelation that had been lurking there, just below the surface, for longer than she cared to think.

'Nice? *Nice?*' Matias was tempted to explode with outrage but ended up bursting out laughing. 'You certainly know how to shoot a man down in flames.'

'Okay.' She blushed. 'It was pretty good.'

'Getting better,' he mused, 'but I still prefer *amazing.*'

'It was amazing.'

'When you showed up at my office,' Matias said softly, 'it was a shock, but I really want this baby, *querida*. You tell me you don't want to marry me. You tell me the ingredients for a successful marriage aren't in place, but we talk. Yes, we fight as well, but *we talk*. And we still have this thing between us. We still want one another passionately. Isn't that glue enough? You say you're not prepared to make sacrifices yet *I* am, because I truly feel that any sacrifice I make for the sake of our child will, in the end, be worth it. Don't we both want what, ultimately, will be best for our baby? Can you deny that? We can't change the past but we can move on from it. We can stop it from altering the course of the future.'

Sophie could feel the pulse in her neck beating, matching the steady beat of her heart, the heart that belonged to him, to a man who would never, *could* never return the favour.

He talked about sacrifices, though, and surely, *surely* he would never use her again? Not when they shared a child? Could she trust him or had the past damaged that irreparably?

'Maybe you're right,' she said, meeting his eyes

steadily. 'Of course I want what's best for our baby. Of course I know that two parents are always going to be better than one.' And maybe, she dared to hope, in time she would trust him enough to confide in him about her brother, despite what had happened between them. Alan had turned away from what he had perceived as a challenge too far in Eric and she had locked herself away after that. Of course, she had never consciously decided that remaining on her own was the preferred option, but how could any relationship ever have blossomed in the bitterness that had grown over the hope and trust she had invested in her ex-boyfriend? Alan had not deserved the faith she had put in him. Compared to Matias, what she'd felt for Alan was a pale shadow of the real thing. But however strong her love, she still couldn't guarantee that Matias, a guy who had been motivated by revenge when he had decided to *cultivate her*, would live up to her expectations.

But they were having a baby together and she *wanted and needed him*.

In due course, he might even jump through all the hoops and prove to be worthy of her trust, but that was something she would never find out unless she gave him a fighting chance.

Matias looked at her and wished that he could see what she was thinking so seriously about. She was staring back at him but her thoughts were somewhere else. Where? Never had the urge been so strong to *know* someone, completely, utterly and inside out. He had never delved into what the women he dated thought about anything. He had wined and dined them and enjoyed them but digging deep hadn't been part of the equation. Sophie made him want to dig deep.

'So...?' he murmured, with a shuttered expression.

'So we don't have to get married...' Sophie breathed in deep and prayed that she was doing the right thing '...but we can live together...' That was called giving him a chance, giving him an opportunity to prove that he could once more be trusted before she opened up that part of her he knew nothing about.

Matias greeted this with a lot more equanimity than he felt. Live together? It wasn't the solution he was after, but it would have to do. For now...

Matias got the call as he was about to leave work.

'I'm sorry.' Sophie was obviously moving in a rush. Her voice was tight and panicked. 'I'm going to have to cancel our dinner date tonight. Something's come up, I'm afraid.'

'What's come up?' Already heading to his jacket, which was slung over the back of the cream sofa that occupied the adjoining mini suite in his glasshouse office, Matias paused, returned to the desk and grabbed the little box containing the diamond bracelet he had ordered three days previously and had collected that day as a surprise for her.

He had taken to surprising her every so often with something little, something he had seen somewhere that had reminded him of her.

Once, it had been an antique book on culinary art in Victorian times, which he had quite accidentally found while walking to his car after a meeting on the South Bank. The bookshop had been tucked away next to a small art gallery and he had paused to glance at the offerings in painted crates on trestle tables outside.

She had smiled when he'd given it to her and that

smile of genuine pleasure had been worth its weight in gold.

Then he had bought her a set of saucepans specially made for the stove in the new house, because he had found one of her house magazines lying on the sofa with the page creased with an advertisement on their lifetime guarantee and special heat-conducting values. Whatever that was supposed to mean.

And again, that had hit the spot.

The diamond bracelet was the most expensive item he had bought thus far and he sincerely hoped that she wouldn't refuse to accept it. She could dig her heels in and be mulishly stubborn about things that were beyond his comprehension and for reasons he found difficult to fathom.

Matias knew that he was shamelessly directing all his energies into getting what he wanted because the longer he was with her, the more unthinkable it was that she might eventually want to cut short their *living together to see how it goes* status and return to the freedom of singledom, free to find her soul mate.

He shoved the box into the inside pocket of his jacket, which he had stuck on without breaking the phone connection.

Her voice, the strained tenor of it, was sending alarm bells ringing in his head. She had been fine when he had seen her the day before. They had met for breakfast because she had gone to help Julie and he had wanted to see her before he headed off to Edinburgh, where he was taking a chance on a small pharmaceutical company that was up for grabs.

'Where are you, *querida*?' he asked, doing his utmost to keep his voice calm and composed.

'Matias, I really have to go. The taxi is going to be here any minute and I have to get a few things together before I leave. In fact…wait…the taxi's here.'

'Taxi? Don't you dare hang up on me in the middle of this conversation, Sophie! What taxi? Why are you taking a taxi somewhere? What's wrong with the car? Is it giving you trouble? And where are you going, anyway?'

'The car is fine. I just thought that, in this instance…'

Her voice faded, as though she had dumped the phone on a table because she needed to do something.

What?

Matias was finding it impossible to hang onto his self-control. She sounded as though she was on the verge of tears and Sophie never cried. She had once told him that when things got tough, and there had been plenty of times in her life when they had, then blubbing never solved anything.

It had been just one more thing he had lodged at the back of his mind, something else that slotted into the complex puzzle that comprised her personality.

And now she was on the verge of tears for reasons she would not identify and she didn't want to talk to him about it. He had done his damnedest to prove to her that she had been right to take a punt on him. He had not batted an eyelid at the very clear nesting instincts that had emerged when she had begun decorating the house. He had also gone light on her creep of a father in the wake of the company takeover, allowing him to salvage some measure of self-respect by not sending him to prison for being trigger-happy with the pension pot, although Carney was much diminished by the end of proceedings, which had afforded Matias a great deal of satisfaction.

He had even deflected an immediate visit to see his mother, because, while she was recovering nicely, much spurred on by news of a grandchild on the way, he had wanted to protect Sophie from the inevitable pressing questions about marriage. The last thing he'd wanted was to have her take fright at his very forthright mother's insistence on tradition and start backing away from the arrangement they had in place.

But even with all of this, it was now perfectly clear that there were parts of her that still bore a lasting resentment because of the way their relationship had originally started.

Why else would she be on the verge of tears and yet not want to tell him why?

'What do you mean by "in this instance"?' he demanded, striding towards the door and heading fast to the bank of lifts.

Most of his employees had already left. The hardcore workaholics barely glanced up as he headed down to the underground car park where his Ferrari was waiting.

'I have to go.'

'Tell me where. Unless it's some kind of big secret?'

'Goodness, Matias!' Hesitation on the other end of the phone. 'Okay, I'm heading to Charing Cross hospital.'

Matias froze by his car, sickened at the thought that something was wrong with her or the baby. 'I will meet you there.'

'No!'

He stilled, unwilling to deal with what her stricken response was saying to him. 'Okay...'

'Matias, I'll see you back at the house. Later. I don't know what time but I'll text or I'll try to. You know what they can be like at hospitals.'

'This is my baby as well, Sophie. I want to be by your side if there's any kind of problem.'

'There's no problem there. Don't worry.'

Naturally, Matias didn't believe her. Her voice was telling a different story. She was frantic with worry but when it came to the crunch, she didn't want him by her side to help her deal with it.

She would show up the following morning and would be bright and cheery and would downplay his concern and they would paper over the unsettling reality that in a time of crisis she would simply not allow him to be there for her.

There was no point driving to the hospital—the parking would be hellish—but Matias was going to be there. He was not going to let her endure anything she might find distressing on her own, and, he grimly acknowledged, it wasn't simply because it was a question of *their* child.

He didn't think twice. His driver was on standby. He would hit the hospital running before she even got there. Playing the long game was at an end. Like it or not, there was going to be a pivotal change in their relationship and if he had to force her hand, then so be it.

Rushing into the hospital after too many hold-ups and traffic jams to count, Sophie raced through the revolving doors and there he was, right in front of her.

He towered, a dark, brooding presence restlessly pacing, hand shoved deep in his trouser pocket. A billionaire out of his comfort zone and yet still managing to dominate his surroundings in a way that brought her to an immediate skidding halt. The cast of his beautiful face was forbidding. People were making sure not to get too close because he emanated all kinds of danger signals that made her tense up.

'Matias…'

Eyes off the entrance for five seconds, her voice brought him swinging round to look at her. 'I'm coming with you,' he said grimly. 'You're not going to push me out this time.'

'I haven't got time to do this right now,' but her heart was beating wildly as she began walking quickly towards the bank of lifts, weaving through the crowds.

'Sophie!' He stopped her, his hand on her arm, and she swung to face him. *'Talk to me.'*

Their eyes tangled and she sighed and said quietly, 'Okay. It's time we had a talk. It's time you knew…'

CHAPTER TEN

MATIAS EXPECTED HER to head straight to the maternity ward. However, she ignored the signs, moving fast towards the lift and punching a floor number while he kept damn close to her, willing her to talk and yet chilled by her remoteness. She barely seemed aware of his presence as she walked quickly up to one of the nurses at a desk and whispered something urgently to her, before, finally, turning around and registering that he was still there.

Matias looked at her carefully, eyes narrowed. They hadn't yet exchanged as much as a sentence. He was a guy who had always made it his duty to keep his finger on the pulse and know what was going on around him, because if you knew the lay of the land you were never in for unpleasant surprises, but right now he didn't have a clue what was going on and he hated that, just as he hated the distance between them.

Was this the point when everything began to fall apart? A sick chill filtered through his veins like poison.

'What's going on?' he asked tightly and Sophie sighed.

'You'll find out soon enough and then we'll need to talk.' She spun round and he followed as she walked straight towards one of the rooms to gently push open the door.

Matias had no idea what to expect and the last thing he was expecting to see was a young man on the bed, obviously sedated because his movements were sluggish as he turned in the direction of the door, but as soon as he saw Sophie he smiled with real love and tenderness.

Matias hovered in complete confusion. He felt like an intruder. He wasn't introduced. He was barely noticed by the man in the bed. He was there to watch, he realised, and so he did for the ten minutes she gently spoke to the boy, holding his hand, squeezing it and whispering in soft, soothing, barely audible tones.

She stroked his forehead and then kissed him before standing up and gazing down at the reclining figure. The boy had closed his eyes and was breathing evenly, already falling into sleep.

She glanced at Matias, nodded as she raised one finger to her lips, and only when they were outside the room did she turn to him.

'You're wondering,' she said without preamble. He was so shockingly beautiful and she loved him so much and yet Sophie felt as though they had now reached a turning point from which there would be no going back. She hadn't considered when the time would be *right* for him to meet Eric. Fear of an eventual negative outcome had held her back but Fate had taken matters into her own hand and now here they were.

'Can you blame me?' Matias responded tersely, raking his fingers through his hair, his whole body restless with unanswered questions.

'We need to talk but I don't think the hospital is quite the right place, Matias.'

Matias was gripped by that chill of apprehension again because there was something final in her voice. 'My place. It'll be quicker than trying to get back to the cottage.' On this one, single matter he could take charge and he did. Within ten minutes they were sitting in the back of his car, heading to his penthouse apartment, to which she had been only a handful of times.

The silence between them was killing him but he instinctively knew that the back seat of a car was not the place to start demanding answers any more than the environs of a hospital would have been.

He glanced at her a couple of times, at her averted profile, but she was mentally a million miles away and he found that incredibly frustrating. He wanted to reach out and yank her back to him. He found that he just couldn't bear the remoteness.

Caught up wondering how she was going to broach the taboo subject she had successfully managed to avoid so far, Sophie was barely aware of the car purring to a stop outside the magnificent Georgian building that housed his state-of-the-art modern penthouse apartment.

It was an eye-wateringly expensive place, now seldom used because he had become so accustomed to spending time at the cottage. They had fallen into a pattern of behaviour and it was only now, when the possibility of it disappearing was on the horizon, that she could really appreciate just how happy she had been.

Even though she knew that he didn't love her, he was perfect in so many ways. He just didn't feel about her the way she felt about him.

The cool, minimalist elegance of his apartment never failed to impress her, although, for her, it was a space she could never have happily lived in.

Now, though, with so much on her mind, she barely noticed the large abstract canvasses, the pale marble flooring, the pale furniture, the subtle, iconic sculptures dotted here and there.

She went directly to the cream leather sofa and sat down, immediately leaning forward in nervous silence and watching as he sat down opposite her, his body language mirroring hers.

'So?' Matias asked, his beautiful eyes shuttered and tension making his voice cooler than intended. 'Are you going to tell me who that guy was?' He saw the way she was struggling to find the right words and he added, tersely, 'An ex-boyfriend?'

'I beg your pardon?'

'Is he an ex-boyfriend, Sophie?' Matias demanded icily. 'The love of your life who may have been involved in an accident? I watched the interaction between the two of you. You love the guy.' Something inside him ripped. 'How long has he been disabled? Motorbike accident?' Every word was wrenched out of him but he had to know the truth.

'I do love him,' Sophie concurred truthfully. 'I've always loved him.'

Matias's jaw clenched as the knot in his stomach tightened. He wasn't going to lose it but he wanted to hit something hard.

'And he wasn't involved in an accident, at least not in the way you mean. Eric has been like that since he was born.'

Matias stilled, eyes keen, every pulse in his body frozen as he tried to grapple with what she was saying.

'Eric is my brother, Matias,' Sophie said quietly.

'Your brother...'

'He lives in a home just outside London, but something spooked him and he had a panic attack and went a little berserk. Hence why he's in hospital. He hurt himself while he was thrashing around. Nothing serious but they couldn't deal with it at the home.'

'You have a brother and you never told me…'

'I have no idea where to begin, Matias. If you just sit and listen, I'll try and make sense. My father only had contact with our family because he was left without a choice. When Eric was born, my mother knew that the only way she would ever be able to afford to take care of him would be with financial help from James. She had a lot of faults but a lack of devotion to Eric wasn't one of them. She made sure James paid for Eric's home, which is very expensive, and when she died it was up to me to make sure he carried on paying. It sounds callous, Matias, but it was the only way.'

'You wanted me to invest in your father's business because you wanted to make sure he could carry on paying for your brother's care.'

Sophie nodded, relieved but not terribly surprised that he had picked it up so quickly. For better or worse, it was a relief to be explaining this to him. If he chose to walk away, then so be it. She would be able to deal with the consequences, even though she knew that she would never be the same again without him in her life.

'I've always managed to put aside a nest egg and I've been dipping into it to cover the costs of Eric's home since James's business went to the wall, but, yes, I encouraged you to think that investing in James would be a good idea, not because I wanted the money for myself, but because I would have done anything, I'm afraid, to make sure my brother is safe and happy.'

'Why didn't you tell me?'

'How could I, Matias?' Sophie tilted her chin at a mutinous angle, defensive and challenging. 'You used me to confirm your suspicions about James and even when you came back into my life, it was because you felt you had no choice.'

'Sophie...'

'No, let me finish!' Her eyes glistened because if the end was coming then she would have to be strong and she didn't feel strong when she was here, looking at him and loving him with every bone in her body. 'I didn't tell you about Eric because there was no way I wanted you to think that you could exact more revenge by going public with what my father had done, shaming him by telling the world that he had fathered a disabled child he had never met and only supported because he had no choice.'

And just like that, Matias knew the depth of her distrust of him. Just like that he saw, in a blinding flash, how much he had hurt her. She had bowed her head and listened to him accuse her of things she had never been guilty of, and she had closed herself off to him. She clearly didn't trust him and she never would.

'I wish you had told me,' he said bleakly.

'How could I?' Sophie returned sadly. 'How could I take the risk that you might have been tempted to involve Eric in your revenge scheme, when the press would have turned it into a story that would have ended up hurting him, destroying both his privacy and his dignity? And also...'

Matias was processing everything she said, knowing that he had no one but himself and his blind drive for vengeance to blame for where he was right now. 'Also?' He looked at her.

'Eric is fragile. When Alan, my ex-boyfriend, walked out of my life, having met him just the once, Eric was heartbroken and felt responsible. I thought Alan was the one for me and I just didn't think that he would walk away because the duty of caretaking Eric was too much.'

'Any creep who would walk away from you because of that was never the one for you,' Matias grated harshly. 'You should count your lucky stars you didn't end up with him.'

'You're right. What I felt for Alan wasn't love. I liked him. I thought he was safe, and safe was good after my mother's experiences with men. But yes, I had a lucky escape. Don't think I don't know that.'

'I was driven by revenge.' Matias breathed in deeply and looked at her with utter gravity. 'It was always there, at the back of my mind. I was always going to be ambitious, I guess. I was always going to be fuelled to make money because I knew what it was like to have none, but I also knew what it was like to know that *I should have*. Your father was to blame and that became the mantra that energised a lot of my decisions. For a while, the chase for financial security became a goal in itself but then, like I told you, my mother fell ill and I discovered those letters. At the point when you entered my life, my desire to even the score with your father was at its height and…you became entangled in that desire. You didn't deserve it.'

Sophie looked at him questioningly, urging him to carry on and weak with relief that he seemed to have taken the situation with her brother in his stride.

'I thought you wanted to push me into investing into someone you knew was on the verge of bankruptcy and probably crooked as well because you wanted to carry on receiving an allowance from him.'

'I understand,' Sophie conceded, 'that you would have thought that because you knew nothing about Eric… You didn't know that there were other reasons for my doing what I did.'

'I saw red,' Matias admitted. 'I felt I'd been used and I reacted accordingly, but the truth was that deep down I knew you weren't that kind of person. *Querida*, you didn't trust me enough to tell me about your brother and I can't begin to tell you how gutted I am by that, even though I know that I have no one but myself to blame. I expected you to wipe away the past as though it had never existed, and I couldn't appreciate that I hurt you way too much for you to find that easy to do.'

This was the first time Matias had ever opened up and she knew from the halting progress of his words that it was something he found difficult, which made her love him even more. He was apologising and it took a big man to do that.

'I never want to hurt you again, my darling. And I will always make sure that your brother is protected and cared for in the way he deserves. Just give me the chance to prove to you how much I love you and how deeply sorry I am for putting you in the position of not thinking you could trust me with the most important secret in your life.'

Sophie's eyes widened and her heart stopped beating before speeding up until she felt it burst through her ribcage.

'Did I just hear you say…?'

'I love you,' Matias told her simply. 'I never thought that I would fall in love. I was never interested in falling in love, but you came along and you got under my skin and before I knew it you had become an indispensable part of my life. When we went our separate ways, it was weird but I felt as though part of me had been ripped away. I didn't understand what that was about, but now I realise you were already beginning to occupy an important position in my life.'

'You never said,' Sophie breathed. 'Why didn't you say?'

'How could I?' Matias smiled wryly at her. He stood up and went to sit on the sofa next to her but he didn't try and pull her towards him, instead choosing to reach out and link her slender fingers through his. He absently played with her ring finger, giving no thought to what that said about the road his subconscious mind was travelling down. 'I was barely aware of it myself. We never expect the things that take us by surprise. Love took me by surprise.'

'As it did me,' Sophie confessed, so happy that she wanted to laugh and cry at the same time. 'When I first met you, I hated you.'

Matias's eyebrows shot up and he shot her a wolfish smile. 'Yet you still managed to find me incredibly sexy...'

'Don't be so egotistical, Matias.' But Sophie couldn't resist smiling back at him because he could be incredibly endearing in his puffed-up self-assurance. 'I thought I was going to see Art and instead I was shown into the lion's den.'

'It's a good job you *didn't* see Art,' Matias said drily. 'You would have walked all over him. He would probably have ended up giving *you* a new car and forgetting all about the damage you did to mine. You charmed the socks off him.'

Sophie blushed. 'We would never have met, though…'

'We would have,' Matias asserted. 'Our paths were destined to cross, even if you *did* hate me on sight.'

'Well, you *were* threatening to pull the plug on my business because I'd bumped into your car…'

Matias acknowledged that with a rueful tilt of his head. 'And so the rest is history. But,' he mused thoughtfully, 'I *should* have suspected that the ease with which I became accustomed to the notion of being a father was a pointer as to how I felt about you. If I hadn't been so completely crazy about you, I would have never slipped into marriage proposal mode so seamlessly.'

'And then I turned you down…'

'You did. Repeatedly. You have no idea how much I've wanted to prove to you that you could take a chance on me.'

'And you have no idea how much I've wanted to take that chance, but I was just too scared. I think, to start with, it really was because I was suspicious and unsure as to what you might do if you found out about Eric. My gut told me that I could trust you, despite all the water under the bridge, but my gut had lied once and I dug my heels in and refused to listen to it a second time. And then, later, I was scared to think about how you might react to Eric. Alan had been a dreadful learning curve for me. I'd been hurt and bewildered at the man he turned out to be and Eric had been terribly upset. He doesn't have the wherewithal to cope with upsets like that. Whatever happened, it was very important to me that he not become collateral damage. I could cope with that but he would never be able to.'

'I'm glad I met him,' Matias said seriously. 'Now can we stop talking? Although, there *is* one thing I still have to say…'

'What's that?' Sophie whispered, on cloud nine.

'Will you stop sitting on the fence and marry me?'

'Hmm…' Sophie laughed and pulled him towards her and kissed him long and hard, and then she brushed his nose with hers and grinned. 'Okay. And by that I mean…yes, yes, yes!'

A handful of months later, another trip had been made to the hospital. Sophie's labour had started at three in the morning and had moved quickly so that by the time they made it to the maternity ward baby Luciana had been just about ready to say hello to her doting and very much loved-up parents.

She had been born without fuss at a little after nine the following morning.

'She has your hair.' Sophie had smiled drowsily at Matias, who had been sitting next to her, cradling his seven-pound-eight-ounce, chubby, dark-haired baby daughter.

'And my eyes.' He had grinned and looked lovingly at the woman without whom life meant nothing. His life had gone from grey to Technicolor. Once upon a time, he had seen the accumulation of wealth and power as an end unto itself. He had thought that lessons learnt about love and the vulnerable places it took you were enough to put any sensible guy off the whole Happy Ever After scenario for good. He had sworn that a life controlled was the only life worth living. He'd been wrong. The only life worth living was a life with the woman he adored at his side.

'And let's hope that's where the similarities end,' Sophie had teased, still smiling. 'I don't need someone else in my life who looks bewildered at the prospect of boiling an egg.'

And now, with their beloved baby daughter nearly six months old, they were finally getting married.

Sophie gazed at her reflection in the mirror of the country hotel where she and her various friends, along with Matias's mother, had opted to stay the night.

Rose Rivero was back on her feet and, as she had confided in her daughter-in-law-to-be some time previously, with so much to live for that there was no question of her being ill again any time soon.

'You look stunning,' Julie said and Matias's mother nodded. The three of them were putting the final touches to Sophie's outfit, making sure that every small rosebud on her hairpiece was just right. 'You're having the fairy-tale wedding you've always longed for.'

Sophie laughed and thought back to the journey that had brought her to this point. 'It's not exactly been straightforward,' she murmured truthfully.

'I could have told you that my son is anything but straightforward,' Rose quipped. 'But you've calmed him down and grounded him in ways I could never have imagined possible.'

'You wouldn't say that if you could see him storming through the house looking for his car keys, which he seems to misplace every other day.' Sophie laughed and walked to the door, while the other two followed, to be met by the rest of the bridal party in the reception downstairs, where cars were waiting to take them to the quaint church, perched on a hillside with a spectacular view of the sea beneath.

Never in her wildest dreams had she imagined a life as perfect as this.

She still had an interest in the catering firm and frequently went there to help out, but it was largely left to Julie and her three helpers, who now ran the profitable business with a tight rein. Their beautiful new premises had been up and running for some months and they were even thinking of expanding and opening a restaurant where they would be able to showcase their talent on a larger scale and to a wider audience.

James Carney had avoided the harsh punishment originally planned by a vengeful Matias, but life had changed considerably for him. With the company no longer in his hands, he had been paid off and dispatched down to Cornwall where he would be able to lead a relatively quiet life, without the trappings of glamour that had been gained from his underhand dealings with Tomas Rivero. Occasionally he dropped Sophie an email and occasionally she answered, but she had no affection for the man who had made her mother's life and her own a nightmare of having to beg for handouts and always with the threat that those handouts could stop at any given moment.

Matias was in possession of the company, which his father should have jointly owned, and it was now a thriving concern, another strand in his hugely successful empire.

But it was with Eric where Sophie felt the greatest flush of pleasure, for her brother could not have been made more welcome by Matias and he was developing skills that still continued to amaze her. He was no longer living in his own little world, really only able to communicate with her, his carers and a handful of other patients. Now, he was making strides in communicating with the outside world, without the fear and panic that had previously dogged him, and she could only think that Matias's patience and little innocent Luciana were partly responsible for that progress. And maybe, she occasionally thought, he was intuitive enough to re-alise that the sister who came to visit him was no lon-ger stressed out. He was safe for ever. He had begun a specially adapted computer course and was showing all sorts of talents hitherto untapped.

Sophie thought of her daughter as she was driven to the church. Luciana would be there, with her nanny, and although the ceremony would mean nothing to her she would enjoy the photos when she got older.

Sophie breathed in deeply as she stepped out of the chauffeur-driven Bentley and then she was in the church, as nervous as a kitten to be marrying the man who meant everything to her.

Matias turned as everyone did, as the music began to play. This was the final piece of the jigsaw. He was marrying the woman he loved and he could not have been prouder.

The breath hitched in his throat as he looked at her walk slowly up the aisle towards him. The cream dress fitted her body like a glove. She had returned to her former weight and all those luscious curves were back, tempting him every single time he looked at her. She was holding a modest bouquet of pale pink flowers and her veil was secured by a tiara of rosebuds that mim-icked the flowers in her hand.

She was radiant. She was his. Possessiveness flared inside him, warming him.

He'd never contemplated marriage but now he knew he wouldn't have been complete without it, without her having his ring on her finger. And the wedding could not have been more to his taste. He might be a billionaire, but this simple affair was perfect.

'You look stunning, *querida*,' he murmured, when she was finally standing beside him and before they both turned to the priest.

'So do you.' Sophie gazed up at Matias. He did this to her, even though she saw him daily, even though he was as much a part of her life as the air she breathed. He made her breathing ragged and he made her heart skip a beat.

The special girl in my life, Matias thought with a swell of pride. Well…one of them.

He looked to the back of the church and there was the other one, being cradled by the nanny, fast asleep.

Matias smiled and knew that this was exactly where he was meant to be, and much later, when all the revelry had died down and the last of the guests had departed, he felt it again, that flare of hot possession as he gazed at the woman who was now his wife.

The following morning, they would be off on their honeymoon. Luciana would be there, as would her nanny and his mother.

'Why are you grinning?' Sophie asked, reaching to undo the pearl buttons of the lavender dress she had slipped into after the wedding ceremony had finished.

Sprawled on the four-poster bed in the hotel where they would be spending the night before flying by private jet to one of Matias's villas in Italy, he was a vision of magnificent male splendour. He had undone the buttons of his white shirt and it hung open, exposing a sliver of bronzed, hard chest.

'I'm grinning,' he drawled, 'because not many newly-weds take the groom's mother with them on their honeymoon.' He beckoned her to him with a lazy curl of his finger and watched, incredibly turned on, as she sashayed towards him, ridding herself of her clothes as she got nearer to his prone figure.

By the time she was standing next to the bed, she was wearing only the lacy bra that worked hard to contain her generous breasts and the matching, peach-coloured lacy pants.

Whatever he had to say to her flew through the window because he couldn't resist rolling to his side and then sliding his finger under the lacy pants so that he could press his face against her musky, honeyed wetness, flicking an exploring tongue along the crease of her womanhood and settling to enjoy her for a few moments as she opened her legs a fraction to allow his tongue entry.

Then he lay back and sighed with pure pleasure when, naked, she lay next to him and slipped her hand under his shirt.

'You and Luciana mean the world to her,' Matias said softly, 'and I want to thank you for that, for taking the sadness out of my mother's life and…' he stroked her hair and kissed her gently on her full mouth '… I want to thank you for being my wife. You put the sound and colour into my world and I would be nothing without you.'

Sophie pushed aside his shirt and licked his flat brown nipple until he was groaning and urging her down as he unzipped his trousers.

'I love you so much,' she whispered. 'Now you're going to have to keep quiet, husband of mine, because it's our honeymoon and there are a lot of things I want to do with you before the night is over...'

* * * * *

*If you enjoyed LEGACY OF HIS REVENGE,
why not explore these other stories
by Cathy Williams?*

*CIPRIANI'S INNOCENT CAPTIVE
THE SECRET SANCHEZ HEIR
BOUGHT TO WEAR THE BILLIONAIRE'S RING*

Available now!

'After such a *"lovely evening…"'* Cesare's amusement was deeper now, his accented English doing even more to make her breathless '…there is only one way to end it, no?'

For an instant he held Carla's gaze in the dim light, daring her to accept, to concede, to do what he wanted her to do—what he'd wanted from the first moment he'd set eyes on her.

'Like this,' he said.

He stretched his hand out, long fingers tilting up her face to his as his mouth lowered to hers. Slowly, sensuously, savouring. With skill, with expertise, with a lifetime of experience in how to let his lips glide over hers, to let his mouth open hers to his, to taste the sweetness within. As soft, as sensual as silk velvet.

She drowned in it. A thousand nerve-endings fired as he made free with her mouth, his long fingers still holding her. And when he had done he released her, drew back his hand, let it curve around the driving wheel.

He smiled. *'Buone notte,'* he said softly.

From Mistress to Wife

From the bedroom—to the altar!

Eloise and Carla have never expected irresistible
passion—until they meet the powerful alpha
billionaires who will steal their innocence. But nights
of passion can have unexpected consequences…

When Eloise Dean falls at Vito Viscari's feet,
they are both overcome with a desire
they can neither resist nor deny!

Claiming His Scandalous Love-Child

Carla Charteris knows falling for the enigmatic
Count of Mantegna will only bring heartache, but
what will happen when temptation proves irresistible?

Carrying His Scandalous Heir

Available now!

You won't want to miss this passionately sexy duet
from Julia James!

CARRYING HIS SCANDALOUS HEIR

BY
JULIA JAMES

MILLS & BOON

First Published in Great Britain 2017
By Mills & Boon, an imprint of HarperCollins*Publishers*
1 London Bridge Street, London, SE1 9GF

© 2017 Julia James

ISBN: 978-0-263-92549-4

Printed and bound in Spain
by CPI, Barcelona

Julia James lives in England and adores the peaceful verdant countryside and the wild shores of Cornwall. She also loves the Mediterranean—so rich in myth and history, with its sunbaked landscapes and olive groves, ancient ruins and azure seas. 'The perfect setting for romance!' she says. 'Rivalled only by the lush tropical heat of the Caribbean—palms swaying by a silver sand beach lapped by turquoise waters… What more could lovers want?'

Visit the Author Profile page at millsandboon.co.uk for more titles.

For Kathryn—thank you for all your hard work!

CHAPTER ONE

CARLA LOOKED AT her watch for the umpteenth time, glancing out across the crowded restaurant towards the entrance. Where *was* he? Anxiety bit at her, and an emotion more powerful than that—one she had never felt before. Had never thought to feel about the man she was waiting for.

She had thought only to feel what she had felt the first time she had set eyes on him. And she so desperately wanted to set eyes on him again now—walking in, striding with his effortlessly assured gait, tall and commanding, with that inbuilt assumption that he could go wherever he liked, that there would always be a place for him, that people would move aside to let him through, that no one would ever dream of turning him down or saying no to him—not about anything at all.

She had not turned him down. She had denied him nothing—granted him everything. Everything he'd ever wanted of her...

Memory, hot and fervid, scorched within her. From the very first moment those hooded night-dark eyes had rested on her, assessing her, desiring her, she had been lost. Utterly lost! She had yielded to him with the absolute conviction that he was the only man who could ever have such an impact on her. That moment was imprinted on her—on her memory, on her suddenly heating body... on her heart.

Memory scorched again now, burning through her veins...

The art gallery was crowded with Rome's wealthy, fashionable set, and champagne and canapés were circling as Carla threaded her way among them, murmuring words of greeting here and there.

Reaching for a glass of gently foaming champagne, Carla knew that she herself could be counted as one of them. Oh, not by birth or breeding, but as the stepdaughter of multi-millionaire Guido Viscari she could move in circles such as these and hold her own and look the part.

Her cocktail dress in a deep blue raw silk had come from one of the currently favoured fashion houses, and it hugged a figure that easily passed muster amongst all the couture-clad females there. Her face, too, as she well knew, also passed muster. Her features veered towards the dramatic, with eyes that could flash with fire and full lips that gave a hint of inner sensuousness.

It was a face that drew male eyes, and she could sense them now—especially since she was there on her own. Unlike many of the other guests, she had a genuine reason for attending this private viewing other than simply being there to while away an hour or so before dining.

But she'd long got used to the constant perusal that Italian men habitually bestowed upon females. It had shocked and discomfited her ten years ago, when she'd been a raw English teenager new to Italian life, but since then she'd grown inured to it. Now she hardly ever noticed the looks that came her way.

Except— She stilled suddenly, the champagne glass halfway to her lips. *Someone was looking at her.* Someone whose gaze she could feel on her like a physical touch. Her eyes shifted their line of sight. Someone who was making her the centre of his observations.

And then, as her gaze moved, she saw him.

He'd just come into the gallery. The receptionist at the welcome desk was still smiling up at him, but he was ignoring her, instead glancing out across the room. Carla felt a little thrill go through her, as though somewhere deep inside her a seismic shock were taking place, and she noticed his gaze was focussing on *her*.

She felt her breath catch, seize in her throat. She felt a sudden flush of heat go through her. For the man making her the object of his scrutiny was the most devastating male she had ever seen.

He was tall, powerfully built with broad shoulders, his features strong…compelling. With a blade of a nose, night-dark hair, night-dark eyes, and a mobile mouth with a twist to it that did strange things to her.

Unknown things…

Things she had never experienced before.

The flush of heat in her body intensified. She felt pinned—as though movement were impossible, as though she had just been caught in a noose—captured.

Captivated.

For how long he went on subjecting her to that measuring, assessing scrutiny she could not tell—knew only that it seemed to be timeless.

She felt her lungs grow parched of oxygen… Then, suddenly, she was released. Someone had come up to him—another man, greeting him effusively—and his eyes relinquished hers, his face turning away from her.

She took a lungful of air, feeling shaken.

What had just happened?

The question seared within her…and burned. How could a single glance do that to her? Have such an effect on her?

Jerkily, she took a mouthful of champagne, needing its chill to cool the heat flushing through her. She stepped away, averting her body, making herself do what she had come there to do—study the portraits that were the subject of the exhibition.

Her eyes lifted to the one opposite her.

And as they did so another shock went through her. She was staring—yet again—into a pair of night-dark eyes. The same eyes…the *very* same.

Night-dark, hooded, sensuous…

That little thrill went through her again, that flush of heat moved in her body. The portrait's eyes seemed to be subjecting her to the same kind of measuring scrutiny that the man by the door had focussed on her.

She tore her eyes away from the face that looked out at her from the portrait. Moved them down to the brass plate at the side of the frame. She hardly needed to read it—she knew perfectly well who the artist was.

Andrea Luciezo, who, along with Titian, was one of the great masters of the High Renaissance. His ability to capture the essence of those who had sat for him—the rich, the powerful, the men who had controlled the Italy of the sixteenth century, the women who had adorned them—had brought them vividly, vibrantly, to life. Luciezo—whose dark, glowing oils, lustrous and lambent, infused each subject with a richly potent glamour.

Her eyes went from the name of the artist to that of his subject. She gave a slow, accepting nod. *Yes, of course.*

Her gaze went back to the man in the portrait. He looked out at all those who gazed at him with dark, hooded, assessing eyes. She looked at the powerful features, the raven hair, worn long to the nape of the strong neck, his jaw bearded in the fashion of the time, yet leaving unhidden the sensuous line of his mouth, the unbearably rich velvet of his black doublet, the stark pleated white of his deep collar, the glint of precious gold at his broad, powerful chest.

He was a man whom the artist knew considered his own worth high, whose portrait told all who gazed upon it that here was no ordinary mortal, cut from the common herd. Arrogance was in that hooded gaze, in the angle of his head, the set of his shoulders. He was a man for whom the world would do his bidding—whatever he bade them do...

A voice spoke behind her. Deep, resonant. With a timbre to it that set off yet again that low, internal seismic tremor.

'So,' he said, as she stood immobile in front of the portrait, 'what do you think of my ancestor, Count Alessandro?'

She turned, lifted her face, let her eyes meet the living version of the dark, hooded gaze that had transfixed her across the centuries—the living version that had transfixed her only moments ago and was now transfixing her again.

Cesare di Mondave, Conte di Mantegna.

The owner of this priceless Luciezo portrait of his ancestor, and of vast wealth besides. A man whose reputation went before him—a reputation for living in the same fashion as his illustrious forebears: as if the whole world belonged to him. To whom no one would say no—and to whom any woman upon whom he looked with favour would want to say only one thing.

Yes.

And as Carla met his gaze, felt its impact, its power and potency, she knew with a hollow sense of fatalism that it was the only word *she* would ever want to use.

'Well?'

The deep voice came again and Carla realised that she needed to speak—had been commanded to answer him. For this was a man who was obeyed.

But she would not obey immediately. She would defy him in that, at least.

Deliberately she looked back at the Luciezo, making him wait. 'A man of his time,' she answered finally.

As you are not a man of your time.

The words formed in her head silently, powerfully. No, the current Conte di Mantegna was *not* a man of the twenty-first century! She could see it in every austere line of his body. He carried his own ancient ancestry in the unconscious lift of his chin at her reply, in his dark brows drawing together.

'What do you mean by that?'

Again, the question demanded an immediate answer.

Carla looked back at the portrait, gathering her reasons for the reply she had made him.

'His hand is on the pommel of his sword,' she essayed. 'He will slay any man who offers him insult. He subjects himself to the scrutiny of one who can never be his equal, however much genius Luciezo possesses, simply in order that his illustrious image can be displayed. His arrogance is in every line, every stroke of the brush.'

She turned back to the man who had commanded her

to speak. Her answer had displeased him, as she had known it would.

There was a dark flash in his eyes, as he riposted, 'You mistake arrogance for pride. Pride not in himself but in his family, his lineage, his honour. An honour he would defend with his life, with his sword, —that he *must* defend because he has no choice but to do so. The artist's scrutiny is to be endured because he must be ever mindful of what he owes his house—which is to protect it and preserve it. His portrait will be his persona in his own absence—it will persist for posterity when he himself is dust.'

The night-dark eyes went to those in the portrait. As if, Carla thought, the two men were communing with each other.

Her brow furrowed for an instant. How strange to think that a man of the present could look into the eyes of his own ancestor… That, in itself, made *il Conte* entirely different from all those who—like herself—were simply cut from the common herd of humanity…who had no knowledge of their ancestors from so many centuries ago.

Her expression changed, becoming drawn for a moment. She didn't even know of her own more immediate forebears. Her father was little more than a name to her—a name reluctantly bestowed upon her when her mother's pregnancy had required that he marry her, only for him to be killed in a car crash when she was a small child. His widow had been unwelcome to her in-laws, and Carla had been raised by her mother alone until her remarriage to Guido Viscari when Carla was a young teenager.

I know more about my stepfather's family than I do about my own father's!

To a man like *il Conte* that very ignorance about her paternal forebears must seem incomprehensible, for he would know the identity of every one of his entire collection of ancestors for centuries—each of them doubtless from families as aristocratic as his own.

With such a heritage she could not be surprised by his immediate retort. Yet she had one of her own.

'Then it is entirely to the credit of Luciezo's mastery that he can convey all that with his portrait,' she replied, making her voice even. 'Without his genius to record it your ancestor *is* merely dust.'

There was defiance in her voice—and an open assertion that, however many heraldic quarterings the illustrious Conte di Mantegna was possessed of, none could compare with the incomparable genius of a great master such as Luciezo.

That dark flash came again in the depths of the Conte's eyes. 'Will we not all be dust in years to come?' he murmured. 'But until that time comes…'

Something changed in his voice—something that suddenly made the heat flush in her blood once more, as it had done when she had realised his gaze was upon her.

'Should we not *carpe diem*?'

'Seize the day?' Carla heard her voice answering. But inside her head she was registering that sudden change in the Count's voice, the smoothing of that low timbre. She could see, now, the change in his eyes. He was looking at her. Approving of what he saw. Sending that flush of heat through her again.

'Or, indeed, seize the evening,' he murmured again, with the slightest husk in his voice.

And now there was no mistaking the message in his voice. None at all. Those dark, long-lashed hooded eyes were resting on her, and the message in them was as old as time.

She pleased him. Her appearance, at any rate, even if her words did not. But their exchange had merely been the mechanism by which he had approached her—had given him the opening he desired, by which he would obtain the end he sought.

The end he now stated openly.

'Have dinner with me tonight.'

It was as simple as that. As straightforward. His dark, expressive eyes were resting on her, and Carla felt their impact—knew their message. Knew what reply she should make to this powerful, sensual man, who was displaying every obvious sign of his intent.

Her habit had always been to say no—the few relationships she'd had over the years had never been with Italians, nor conducted in Rome under the avidly speculative glare of the circles in which she moved. And never had she fancied herself to be deeply emotionally involved. It had been only friendship and compatibility that attracted her—no more than that. It was safer that way. Safer than yielding to any overriding sensual attraction that might ignite a passion that would be hard to quench.

After all, no one knew better than she what *that* might lead to. Hadn't it happened to her own mother? Falling for a man who, when he'd been faced with unintended pregnancy, had not wished to commit to her?

Although his father had cracked the financial whip and forced a marriage, there had been no happy ending. Her father had chafed at marriage, chafed at fatherhood—and had been on the point of leaving her mother when he was killed. Was it any wonder, Carla asked herself, that she was wary of making such a mistake herself?

So, for every reason of good sense, there was only one reply for her to make to this arrogant, sensual man who possessed the power to disturb her senses.

Yet she could not say the words. Could only find the means to give a slight, fleeting, demurring half-smile, and a self-protective sweeping down of her eyelashes to hide the all too revealing response in her eyes as she made an evasive reply.

'So…have you loaned any other paintings to the exhibition?' she asked.

Her voice sounded abrupt, even breathless, but she did not care. She met his gaze head-on, keeping hers quite limpid, though the effort was great—the more so since in his eyes was a look of knowingness that told her he had understood immediately why she had not answered him.

But to her relief he followed her diversion.

'Indeed,' he murmured, still with that semi-amused look in his eyes that was so disturbing to her. 'The Luciezo is, in fact, part of a triptych. The other two portraits are on display across the gallery.'

There was a discernible tinge of annoyance in his voice at the curator's decision as he indicated across the width of the gallery, towards an alcove in which Carla could make out two portraits.

'Shall we?'

The cool voice held assumption, and Carla found herself being guided forward. He halted, lifting his hand to the portraits they were now in front of.

'What do you make of them?'

Carla's trained eyes went to the portraits, immediately seeing the skill and artistry in them, seeing in them all the hallmarks of a master. Her eyes narrowed very slightly. But not Luciezo.

'Caradino?' she ventured.

She felt rather than saw the glance the Count threw at her. Surprise—and approval.

'Caradino,' he confirmed. He paused. 'Many attribute his few surviving works to Luciezo.'

She gave a slight shake of her head. 'No,' she said. 'There is a discernible difference.'

Her eyes ran over the portraits, taking in the brush-work, the lighting, the shadows. Her gaze went from appraising the technicalities of the portraits to the subjects themselves. And then, for the first time, her eyes widened as her gaze rested on their faces.

So unalike. So very, *very* unalike.

One so fair and pale. A married woman, clearly, as illustrated by the tokens in the painting—her pearl earring, the sprig of myrtle in her lap, the dish of quinces on the little table at her side—and yet there was about her, Carla could see, an air almost of virginity…as if with different garments and accoutrements she might have modelled for a painting of the Virgin Mary.

A crucifix was in her hands, glinting between her long, pale fingers. Carla looked at the woman's eyes.

Sadness. As if, like the Virgin Mary, she had in her gaze a foretelling of the great sorrows that were to come.

She pulled her gaze away. Let it rest on the other woman's face.

Another young woman. In this portrait the subject's hair was a lush chestnut-brown, lavishly unbound and snaking down over one bare shoulder. Her gown was a sumptuous red, not a celestial blue, and cut low across her generous bosom to reveal an expansive amount of soft, creamy skin. She held red roses in her hands, rubies gleamed at her throat and on her fingers, and her hands rested on her abdomen—its slight swell discreet, but undeniable.

Carla drew her eyes away from the telltale curve of the young woman's figure, moved them back up to scrutinise her face. Beautiful, in a sensuous way, framed by her rich tresses, her cheeks flushed, lips full and with a sensual cast to them. Carla's eyes went to the woman's eyes and held them for a long moment—held the unseeing gaze that looked out over the centuries between the two of them.

'Who *are* they?'

Her own voice cut short her perusal, and she drew her gaze away to look back at *il Conte*, standing at her side.

'Can you not tell?' he asked. He glanced back to the portrait of his ancestor, across the room, then back to Carla. 'His wife—and his mistress. He had them painted at the same time, by the same hand. Caradino stayed at my *castello* and painted them both—one after the other.'

Carla's face stilled. 'How nice for them,' she said drily. 'It seems your ancestor kept his mistress…handy.'

But the Count did not rise to her sardonic comment. 'It was quite normal in those times. Nothing exceptional. Both women knew and understood the situation.'

Carla's lips pressed together. 'Knowing and understanding are not the same thing as tolerating and agreeing,' she riposted.

The dark, hooded eyes were veiled. 'Women had no power in those times. And after all,' he went on, 'my ancestor's mistress was *very* lavishly looked after.'

'She's carrying his child,' Carla retorted.

She could feel an emotion rising up in her—one she did not want to feel, but it was coming all the same.

'An excellent way to secure the Count's protection,'

agreed Cesare. 'I believe they had several children, over the years. He was very faithful to her, you know. Surprisingly so for the times.'

Automatically Carla's eyes went not to the mistress of the former Count but to his wife. No sign of fertility there—and in the eyes only that haunting sadness.

Thoughts ran through her head, unstoppable.

How did she feel? How did she cope? Knowing her husband was having children, openly, with his mistress? Yet presumably she, too, must have had an heir, at least, or the line would have died out—which it obviously hasn't?

'But enough of my ancestors—have you seen the other paintings displayed here yet?'

The voice of the man at her side drew her back to the present. She turned towards him. Saw him with fresh eyes, it seemed. Her gaze went past him to the portrait of Count Alessandro, who had been so unconcerned as to have his wife and mistress painted simultaneously.

A shaft of female indignation went through her, as she brought her gaze back to the current Count.

'Not all of them yet, no,' she said. She made her voice purposeful. 'And I really must. I have fifteen hundred words to write up about the exhibition.'

She named the arts magazine she wrote for, as if she was aware that by stressing her professional interest she would diminish her personal one.

'And I must do my duty by all the paintings here!'

She spoke lightly but deliberately. She smiled. An equally deliberate smile. One that completely ignored the question he had asked her only a few minutes ago, making no reference to it.

'Thank you so much, Signor il Conte, for showing me

these fascinating portraits, and for giving me such insight into them. It's always enhancing to learn the origins and the circumstances of a portrait's creation—it brings it so to life! And especially since the artist Caradino is so seldom exhibited.'

She smiled again—the same social smile—signalling closure. For closure, surely, was essential. Anything else would be…

Her mind veered away, not wanting to think of the path she had not taken. The yielding she had not made.

Instead she gave the slightest nod of her head in parting and walked away. Her high heels clicked on the parquet flooring and as she walked she was intensely conscious of his following gaze, of how her shapely figure was outlined by the vivid tailored dress she was wearing. Intensely conscious of the urge overwhelming her to get away. Just…*away.*

As she walked, she sipped at her champagne again. She felt the need of it. Her colour was heightened, she knew—knew it from the hectic beating of her heart.

He desires me—the Conte di Mantegna has looked at me and found me pleasing to him…

Into her head sprang an image, immediate and vivid, conjured out of her ready imagination. That woman in the portrait—the brunette—working, perhaps, in her father's shop, or sweeping floors, or even toiling out in the fields in sixteenth-century Italy… *Il Conte* passing by, seeing her, liking her beauty, taking a fancy to her. Finding her pleasing to him. Lifting her with one beckoning of his lordly, aristocratic hand out of her hard, poverty-stricken life to dress her in a silk gown and place roses in her hands and jewels around her throat, and take her to his bed…

She felt the pull of it—the allure. Had to force herself to remember all that would have gone with it. The price that woman would have paid.

To know that her place in his life was only ever to be his inamorata—*never to aspire to be his wife.*

And as for the Count—oh, he would have had everything he wanted. His pale, subservient wife—his compliant, obliging mistress.

Having it all.

She dragged her mind away, making herself inspect the other paintings, consult her catalogue, interview the exhibition's curator, and then get a few words from the gallery's director, who greeted her warmly, both in her professional capacity and as the stepdaughter of the late chairman of a global hotel chain—a generous patron of the arts himself.

It had been her stepfather who'd first noticed her interest in art as a teenager, and it was thanks to him that she'd studied history of art at prestigious universities both in England and Italy. He'd encouraged her in her journalistic career. It was a career she found immensely satisfying, and she knew herself to be extremely fortunate in it.

Now, with all her notes taken, she was ready to leave. She'd spend the evening going through them, drawing up the article she would write.

As she made her farewells she found herself glancing around. She knew who it was she was trying to glimpse. And knew why she should not be. Cesare di Mondave was far too disturbing to her peace of mind to allow herself to have anything more to do with him.

He was not to be seen anyway, and she told herself she was glad. Relieved. Because to further her acquaintance with Cesare di Mondave would *not* be good sense at all.

Involuntarily her eyes went to the portrait of his ancestor—Count Alessandro, regarding the world in all his High Renaissance splendour, his dark gaze compelling, arrogant. In her mind's eye she saw his wife and his mistress. Two women, rivals for ever, their destinies yoked to the man who had commissioned their portraits.

Had they both loved him? Or neither?

The question hovered in her head, its answer long consumed by the centuries that had passed. All she could know, with a kind of ironic certainty, was that it would not be wise for *any* woman to have anything to do with the man in whose veins ran the blood of Luciezo's Count Alessandro.

It didn't matter that his descendant could have an impact on her that she had never encountered before. That his dark lidded eyes could raise her pulse in an instant… that her eyes had wanted only to cling helplessly, hopelessly, to his sculpted, powerful features, that her hand had yearned to reach towards him, graze the tanned skin of his jaw, brush the sensual swell of his mouth… It didn't matter at all.

Because letting herself get embroiled with the arrogant, oh-so-aristocratic Count of Mantegna would be folly indeed!

She was not, and never would be, like the lush beauty in the Caradino portrait, haplessly dependent upon the Count's continuing desire for her, fearing its demise. Her lips thinned slightly. Nor could she ever be like the woman in the other portrait—oh, she might move in Roman high society, but the Viscaris were hoteliers: rich, but with no trace of aristocratic blood. Carla knew without flinching that when *il Conte* chose a wife, it would be a woman from his own background, with an ancestry to match his.

I would be nothing more than an...an interlude for him.

She walked out onto the pavement and into the warm evening air of Rome in late summer. A low, lean, open-topped car was hovering at the kerb, blatantly ignoring the road signs forbidding such parking. Its powerful engine was throbbing with a throaty husk, its scarlet paint-work was gleaming, and the rearing stallion on the long bonnet caught the light, glinting gold like the crested signet ring on the hand curved around the wheel.

The man at the wheel turned his head. Let his dark, lidded gaze rest on Carla.

'What kept you?' asked Cesare di Mondave, Conte di Mantegna.

CHAPTER TWO

CESARE'S HAND RESTED on the leather curve of the steering wheel. Impatience was humming in him. He appreciated that she had a job to do—this woman his eyes had lit upon, drawn without conscious intent to her dramatic beauty, her voluptuous figure, the extraordinarily dark blue eyes that had a hint of violet in them—but for all that he did not care to be kept waiting.

He'd known who she was before he'd made the decision to approach her—he'd seen her about previously in society, even though the aristocratic circles *he* moved in overlapped only loosely with those of the Viscaris. The Viscaris were, to him, 'new money'—it was a mere handful of generations since the global hotel group that bore the family name had been founded at the end of the nineteenth century. They were newcomers compared to the immense antiquity of *his* family—and Cesare felt the weight of that antiquity upon him each and every day.

It was a weight that both upheld him and imposed upon him responsibilities to his ancestry that others could not understand. A duty that reached far back into the Middle Ages, stretching across all his estates from the high Apennine lands leased as a national park, to forests and vineyards, agricultural land and olive groves, and across all his many properties. Every *palazzo* was a historic monument, including the magnificent baroque Palazzo Mantegna here in Rome, now on loan to the nation and housing a museum of antiquities. And all those estates and properties came with tenants and employees whose livelihood he guaranteed—just as his ancestors had.

Yet at the heart of it all was the ancient Castello Mantegna, the heart of his patrimony. Within its mighty walls, built to withstand medieval warfare, he had spent his childhood, roaming the forests and pasturelands that one day would be his.

Was that something anyone not born to such a heritage could truly understand? The weight of inheritance upon him?

Or did they merely see *il Conte*—a wealthy, titled man who moved in the uppermost echelons of society, with a cachet that many would only envy? And which women would eagerly seek to bask in...

His dark eyes glinted. There had been no such eagerness in Carla Charteris, though he'd made clear his interest in her. He was glad of it—but not deterred by it. For his long experience of woman had told him immediately that the first flare of her violet-hued eyes as he'd addressed her had showed that she was responsive to him. That was all he'd needed to know—their barbed exchange thereafter had merely confirmed it. All that was required now was for her to acknowledge it.

He leant across to open the passenger side door. *'Prego,'* he invited in a pleasant voice.

He'd surprised her—he could tell. Had she really believed that walking away from him would discourage him?

He went on in a dry voice, 'It would gratify me if

you complied without delay, for the traffic warden over there—' he nodded carelessly along the street to where such an individual had recently turned the corner '—would so very much enjoy booking me.' He gave a brief sigh. 'I find that officials take particular pleasure in exercising their petty authority when their target is driving a car like this one.'

He smiled. He could see the conflict in her eyes—in those amazingly dark violet-blue eyes of hers—but above all he could see that same flare of awareness, of desire, which had been in them when he'd first approached her. That told him all he needed to know.

His expression changed again. *'Carpe diem,'* he said softly. His eyes held hers. Tellingly, unambiguously. 'Let us seize all that we may have of this fleeting life,' he murmured, 'before we are dust ourselves.'

His casual reference to her own comment in front of the Luciezo was accompanied by an exaggerated gesture of his hand as he again indicated the seat beside him.

His lashes dipped over his eyes. 'What is so difficult,' he murmured, 'about accepting an invitation to dinner?' His gaze lifted to hers again, and in his eyes was everything that was not in his words.

Carla, her expression immediately urgently schooled, stopped in her tracks on the pavement, felt again that incredible frisson go through her whole body—that shimmer of glittering awareness of the physical impact he made on her.

All around her the city of Rome buzzed with its familiar vitality. The warmth of the early evening enveloped her, and she could hear the noise of the traffic, the buzz of endless Vespas scooting past. The pavement was hot beneath the thin soles of her high heels. While in front of her, in that outrageously expensive car—as exclusive and prestigious as its driver so undoubtedly considered himself to be—the oh-so-aristocratic Conte invited her to join him.

As she had before, in the gallery, she felt the overwhelming impact of the man. Felt even more powerfully the impulse within her to give him the answer that he was waiting for.

Thoughts—fragmented, incoherent—raced through her.

What is happening to me? Why now—why this man of all men? This arrogant, lordly man who is scooping me up as if I were no more than that woman in the portrait—scooping me up to serve his pleasure...

Yet it would be for *her* pleasure too—she knew that with every shimmer in her body as she stood, poised on the pavement, feeling the weight of his lidded gaze upon her. That was the devil of it—that was the allure. That was the reason, Carla knew with a kind of sinking in her heart, that was keeping her here, hovering, just as he was keeping that monstrous, powerful car of his hovering, its power leashed, but ready to be let forth.

His words, mocking her, echoed in her head. *'What is so difficult about accepting an invitation to dinner?'*

His voice—deep, amused—cut across her tormented cogitations. 'You really will need to decide swiftly—the warden is nearly upon us.'

The uniformed official was, indeed, closing fast. But Carla's eyes only sparked deep blue. 'And you couldn't *possibly* afford the fine, could you?' she retorted.

'Alas, it is a question of my pride,' Cesare murmured, the glint in his eye accentuated. 'It would never do for *il Conte* to put himself in the power of a petty bureaucrat...'

Was he mocking himself? Carla had the suspicion he was not…

For a moment longer every objection she had made when he'd first invited her to dinner flared like phosphorus in her head. Every reason why she should give exactly the same kind of answer as she had then—evasive, avoiding the invitation—then walk briskly away, back to the comfortable, predictable evening she'd planned for herself in her own apartment. Making herself dinner, going through her notes in preparation for writing her article. An evening that had nothing, *nothing* to do with the man now waiting for her answer…

And yet—

Her own thought replayed itself in her head. *How dangerous might it be to light a passion that could not be quenched?*

But other thoughts pushed their way into her head. Thoughts she did not want to silence. Could not silence… *Desire and passion will burn themselves out! They cannot last for ever.*

Neither desire nor passion was love.

Yet both were powerful—alluring—speaking to her of what might be between them.

Passion and desire.

The same tremor went through her, the same flush in her skin as when he had first made his desire for her plain, calling from her an answering awareness. No other man had ever drawn from her such an overpowering response.

For a second longer she hesitated, hung between two opposing instincts.

To resist that response—or to yield to it.

The dark, lidded eyes rested on her—holding hers.

With a sudden impulse, impelling her way below the level of conscious decision, she felt her muscles move as if of their own volition. She got into the car, slamming the door shut.

Instantly, as if preventing her from rescinding her decision as much as avoiding the attentions of the parking official, Cesare opened the throttle, pulled the car away from the kerb—and Carla reached for her seat belt, consciousness rushing back upon her in all its impact.

Oh, dear God, what the *hell* had she just done?

I got into his damn car just to save his damn aristocratic pride! So he wouldn't have to endure the ignominy of getting a parking ticket! How insane is that?

Completely insane. As insane as letting Cesare di Mondave drive off with her like this—the lordly *signor* scooping up the peasant girl.

Her chin lifted. Well, she was no peasant girl! She was no poor, hapless female like the one in the portrait, trapped within the punishing limitations of her time in history. No, if she went along with what this impossible, arrogant man had in mind for her—*if,* she emphasised mentally to herself—then it would be what *she* wanted too! Her free and deliberate choice to enjoy the enticing interlude he clearly had planned.

But would she make that choice? That was the only question that mattered now. Whether to do what every ounce of her good sense was telling her she should not do—and what every heat-flushed cell in her body was urging her to do. To resist it—or yield to it. She turned her head towards him, drawn by that same impetuous urge to let her eyes feast on him. He was focussing only on the appalling evening traffic in Rome, which, she allowed, *did* need total focus. She let him concentrate, let herself enjoy the rush that came simply from looking at his profile.

Sweet heaven, but it was impossible not to gaze at him! A modern version of that Luciezo portrait, updated for the twenty-first century. Indelibly graced with features that made her eyes cling to him, from the strong blade of his nose to the chiselled line of his jaw, the sensual curve of his mouth. She felt her hands clench over her bag. Weakness drenched her body. What she was doing was insane—and yet she was doing it.

She felt her pulse leap, and a heady sense of excitement filled her. A searing knowledge of her own commitment. Far too late now to change her mind.

And she did not want to—that was the crux of it. Oh, the lordly Count might have scooped her up just as arrogantly as his ancestor had scooped up the peasant girl who would become his mistress, but it had been *her* choice to let herself be so scooped.

Rebelliousness soared within her—a sense of recklessness and adventure.

I don't care if this is folly! All I know is that from the moment he looked at me I wanted him more than I have ever wanted any man—and I will not deny that desire. I will fulfil it...

Fulfil it with all the ardour in her body, every tremor in her limbs. It was folly—reckless folly—but she would ignite that passion and burn it to the core.

'Take the next left here,' Carla said, indicating the narrow road in the Centro Storico that led down to her apartment, part of an eighteenth-century house. It was a quiet haven for her to write in, and to be well away not just from the buzz of the city but also from the tensions running across the Viscari clan.

Her mother, she knew, would have preferred her to stay on in Guido Viscari's opulent villa, but thanks to her stepfather's generosity in his will Carla had been able to buy her own small but beautiful apartment, taking intense pleasure in decorating it and furnishing it in an elegant but comfortable and very personal style.

However, her thoughts now were neither on the ongoing tensions in the Viscari clan nor on her apartment. There was only one dominating, all-encompassing consciousness in her head…

Cesare.

Cesare—with whom she had just dined, with whom she had conducted, she knew, a conversation that had taken place at two levels. One had seen him being the perfect escort, the perfect dinner companion, conversing with her about her job, about the arts, about the Italian landscape—of which he owned a significant proportion—and about any other such topics that two people making each other's acquaintance might choose to converse about.

He'd asked her a little about herself—neither too little to be indifferent, nor too much to be intrusive. He'd known who she was, but she was not surprised—she'd known who *he* was, though they'd never chanced to meet before.

But there'd been another conversation taking place as they'd sat there over a lingering dinner in the small, ferociously exclusive restaurant Cesare had taken her to—where he had immediately been given the best table in the house, and where they had been waited on attentively, discreetly, unobtrusively but with absolute expertise.

He had nodded at one or two other patrons, and her presence had caused the lift of an eyebrow from one group of women, and a penetrating glance, but no more than that. She had been acquainted with no one there, and was glad of it. Glad there had been no one she knew to witness the second level of the conversation taking place between herself and Cesare di Mondave, Conte di Mantegna.

The conversation that had taken place powerfully, silently and seductively—oh-so-seductively—between him and her, with every exchange of glances, every half-smile, every sensual curve of his mouth, every lift of his hand with those long, aristocratic fingers.

The light had reflected off the gold of his signet ring, impressed with his family crest—the same lion couchant that his ancestor had displayed on his own ring in the Luciezo portrait—and Carla had found herself wondering if it could be the very same ring.

Eventually Cesare's hand had crushed the white damask napkin and dropped it on the table to signal the end of their meal, and they'd got to their feet and made their way towards the exit.

Nothing so crude as a bill had been offered by the maître d'—nothing more than a respectful inclination of the head at their departure, a gracious murmur of appreciation from the Count, a smile of thanks from herself as they left, stepping out onto the pavement, where his car had been waiting for them.

Now, as they drew up at the kerb by her apartment, he cut the engine and turned and looked at her, an enigmatic expression visible in the dim street light.

Her consciousness of his raw physical presence seared in her again. She smiled at him. 'Thank you,' she said, 'for a lovely evening.' Her voice was bright, and oh-so-civil.

She realised she'd spoken in English. They'd gone in and out of Italian and English all evening, for the Count's English was as fluent as her Italian had become in the ten years she'd lived in Rome, though surely no Englishman could make his native language as seductive, as sensual as an Italian male could make it sound?

But English was the right language for this moment. Crisp, bright and utterly unseductive. The polite, anodyne description of something that had been so much more. She reached out her hand for the door release, her body still turned towards him.

A smile curved his mouth, long lashes dropping over his lidded eyes. 'Indeed,' he agreed.

She could hear the amusement in his voice, feel it catch at her, making her breathless, her pulse quicken.

'And after such a *"lovely evening"*...' his amusement was deeper now, his accented English doing even more to make her breathless '...there is only one way to end it, no?'

For an instant he held her gaze in the dim light, daring her to accept, to concede, to do what he wanted her to do—what he'd wanted of her from the first moment he'd set eyes on her.

'Like this,' he said.

His hand stretched out, long fingers tilting up her face to his as his mouth lowered to hers. Slowly, sensuously, savouring. With skill, with expertise, with a lifetime of experience in how to let his lips glide over hers, his mouth to open hers to his, to taste the sweetness within. As soft, as sensual as silk velvet.

She drowned in it. A thousand nerve endings fired as

he made free with her mouth, his long fingers still holding her. And when he had done he released her, drew back his hand, let it curve around the driving wheel.

He smiled. *'Buone notte,'* he said softly.

For a moment—just a moment—she was motionless, as if all the shimmering pleasure he'd aroused in her with only a single kiss had made it impossible for her to move. She could do nothing except meet that amused, lidded gaze resting on her like a tangible pressure.

Then, with a little jolt, she pushed open the car door. Swallowed. In a daze she got out, fumbled for her keys, found them and shakily inserted them into the lock of the outer door of her apartment building. Then she made herself turn to look back at him. Bade him goodnight in a voice that was no longer bright and crisp.

He said nothing, merely inclining his head as she turned away, let herself into the cobbled inner courtyard, shut the heavy outer door behind her.

She heard the throaty growl of his car as he moved off. On shaky legs she went up to her apartment, and only when inside its sanctuary did she feel able to breathe again.

Cesare strolled to the window of his Rome apartment and gazed unseeing out over the familiar roofline. The large plate glass window of the modern designed space was glaringly different from the richly historical interiors of his other properties, and it gave a wide view over the city even at this midnight hour. He did not step out onto the large adjoining balcony; instead he merely continued to stand, hands thrust into his trouser pockets, legs slightly astride.

Was he being wise? That was the question that was

imposing itself upon him. Was it wise to pursue what had been, after all, only the impulse of a moment—following through on a momentary glimpse of the woman who had caught his eye? Following through sufficiently to decide that it was worth spending an evening of his life in her company. Worth considering, as he was now considering, whether to pursue a liaison with her.

There were many reasons to do so. Uppermost, of course, was the intensity of his physical response to her. Unconsciously he shifted position restlessly, his body aware that a single kiss had only whetted the appetite that he could feel coursing through his blood. It was an intensity that had, he acknowledged, taken him by surprise. But was that reason enough to do what he knew his body wanted him to do?

Before he could answer, he knew from long experience that there was another question he must answer first.

Will she understand the terms of our liaison?

The terms that governed his life just as they'd governed all who had borne his ancient name and title. Had been hammered into him by his own dictatorial father who'd constantly impressed upon him his heritage, and yet who'd regarded him as favouring too much the mother whose outward serenity Cesare was sure had concealed an unvoiced regret.

Her husband had objected to her having any interests outside her responsibilities as his *contessa*, and she had confined her life to being the perfect chatelaine, the mother of his heir. His father had taken his son's sympathy for his mother as a reluctance to respect the demands of his heritage, and after his mother's premature death from heart disease, when Cesare was only nineteen, the rift between them had widened without her presence as peacemaker.

But when his father had died, some eight years later, he'd been determined not to neglect any aspect of his inheritance, dedicating himself to its preservation. If his father could see him now, half a dozen years on, perhaps his harsh judgement would be set aside.

The words that he had uttered only that evening, in front of the Luciezo painting of his sixteenth-century forebear, floated in his head.

'Pride in his family, his lineage, his honour—all that he owes his house...'

With the echo of those words his thoughts came full circle back to the woman to whom he had spoken them. Did she understand why he had said what he had about his ancestor—about himself? It was essential that she did. Essential that she understood that, for him, one thing could never change.

In his mind's eye two images formed—the other portraits in the triptych, the Count's wife and his mistress. Separate for ever, coming from different worlds that could never meet.

Four centuries and more might distance him from Count Alessandro and the women who made up the triptych, but for himself, too, his countess would need to share his own background. Not because of any heraldic quarterings she possessed, but because only a woman from the same heritage as himself could truly understand the responsibilities of such a heritage. That was what his father had instilled into him. He had even identified for him the very woman who would make him the perfect next Contessa...

His expression changed and he stared out over the

roofs of this most ancient city into whose roots his own ancestry reached. The lineage of a patrician of Ancient Rome was still traceable in his bloodline.

The woman who would be his Countess was well known to him—and she was not, nor ever could be, a woman such as the one he had embraced a brief hour ago, fuelling in him a desire for satiation that he must not yield to.

Not unless—until—he could be sure she accepted what could be between them. And what could not.

As, too, must he. That, also, was essential…

CHAPTER THREE

CARLA STARED AT her screen. She still had six hundred more words to write for her article, and she was making heavy weather of it. She knew exactly why.

Cesare di Mondave.

He was in her headspace—had been totally dominating it, consuming every last morsel of it, since she'd made it into her apartment the night before, senses firing, aflame.

All through her sleepless night she'd replayed every moment of the evening over and over again—right up to that final devastating moment.

Cesare kissing her…

No! She must not let herself remember it again! Must not replay it sensuously, seductively, in her head. Must instead force herself to finish her article, send it into the impatiently waiting sub-editor at her office.

But even when she had she was unbearably restless, her heart beating agitatedly.

Will he phone me? Ask me out again? Or—a little chill went through her—*has he decided he does not want me after all?*

Face set, she made herself some coffee. She should not be like this—waiting for a man to phone her! She should be above such vulnerability. She was a strong-minded, independent woman of twenty-seven, with a good career, as many dates as she cared to go on should she want to, and there was no reason—no *good* reason!—for her to be straining to hear the phone ring. To hear the dark, aristocratic tones of Cesare di Mondave's deep voice.

And yet that was just what she was doing.

The expression in her eyes changed. As she sipped her coffee, leaning moodily against the marble work surface in her immaculate kitchen, more thoughts entered her head. If last night's dinner with Cesare was all there was to be between them she should be relieved. A man like that—so overwhelming to her senses—it was not wise to become involved with. She'd known that from the moment he'd first spoken to her, declared his interest.

But where was wisdom, caution, when she needed them? She felt her pulse quicken again as the memory of that kiss replayed itself yet again.

With a groan, she pulled her memory away. She shouldn't be waiting for Cesare di Mondave to phone her! Not just because she should *never* be waiting around for a man to phone her! But because she should, she knew, phone her mother—reply to her latest complaint about her sister-in-law's disapproving attitude towards her.

She gave a sigh. Her mother—never popular with Guido's younger brother Enrico and his wife, Lucia—had become markedly less popular after her husband's death, when it had become known that the childless Guido, rather than leaving his half of the Viscari Hotels Group shares to his nephew, Vito, had instead left them to his widow, Marlene. They had been outraged by the decision, and when Enrico had suddenly died, barely a year later, his premature death had been blamed on the stress of worrying about Marlene's ownership of the shares. Since then, Vito had sought repeatedly to buy them from Marlene, but Carla's mother had continually refused to sell.

To Carla, it was straightforward. Her mother *should* sell her shareholding to Vito—after all, it was Vito who was the true heir to the Viscari dynasty, and he should control the inheritance completely. But Carla knew why her mother was refusing to do so—her ownership of those critical shares gave her mother status and influence within the Viscari family, resented though it was by her sister-in-law.

Carla's mouth tightened in familiar annoyance. It also continued to feed her mother's other obsession. One that she had voiced when Carla was a teenager and had repeated intermittently ever since—despite Carla's strong objection. An objection she still gave—would always give.

'Mum—forget it! Just stop going on about it! It's never going to happen! I get on well enough with Vito, but please, please, just accept there is absolutely no way whatsoever that I would ever want to do what you keep on about!'

No way whatsoever that she would ever consider marrying her step-cousin...

Vito Viscari—incredibly handsome with his Latin film star looks—might well be one of Rome's most eligible bachelors, but to Carla he was simply her step-cousin, and of no romantic interest to her in the slightest. Nor was she to him. Vito was well known for liking leggy blondes—he ran a string of them, and always had one in tow, it seemed to her—and he was welcome to them. He held no appeal for her at all.

A shiver went through her. She remembered the man who *did*…who'd made every cell in her body searingly aware of her physicality. Who'd cast his eye upon her and then scooped her up into his sleek, powerful car effortlessly.

She felt the heat flush in her body, her pulse quicken. Heard her phone ring on her desk.

She dived on it, breathless. *'Pronto?'*

It was Cesare.

'But this is charming! Absolutely lovely!'

Carla's gaze took in the small but beautifully proportioned miniature Palladian-style villa, sheltered by poplars and slender cypresses, in front of which Cesare was now drawing up. It was set in its own grounds in the lush countryside of Lazio, less than an hour's drive beyond Rome, and its formal eighteenth-century gardens ideally suited the house.

She looked around her in delight as she stepped gracefully out of the low-slung car, conscious of the quietness all around her, the birdsong, the mild warmth of the late-afternoon sun slanting across the gardens— and conscious, above all, of the man coming to stand beside her.

'My home out of town…what is the term in English? Ah, yes…my bolthole.' He smiled.

He ushered her inside, and Carla stepped into a marble-floored, rococo-style hallway, its decor in white, pale blue and gold.

Into her head came a description for the house that was not the one Cesare had just given.

Love nest…

A half-caustic, half-amused smile tugged at her mouth.

Well, why *not* a love nest? It was a conveniently short distance from Rome, and so very charming. An ideal place for romantic dalliance.

Because that was what she was embarking on. She knew it—accepted it. Had accepted it the moment she'd heard Cesare's deep tones on the phone earlier that afternoon, informing her that he would be with her shortly. Taking for granted what her answer would be.

Was she being reckless, to come here with him like this? Of course she was! She knew it, but didn't care. All her life she'd been careful—never one to rush into passionate affairs, never making herself the centre of any gossip. Yet now, a little less than twenty-four hours since she had stood in front of that Luciezo portrait of Count Alessandro, she was going to do just that.

And she would revel in it! For once in her life she would follow the hectic beating of her heart, the hot pulse of her blood, and respond to a man who, like no other she had ever met, could call such a response from her merely by a flickering glance from his dark, hooded eyes. However brief their liaison was to prove—and she knew perfectly well that it could never lead to anything—she would enjoy it to the full until the passion between them burnt itself out, until her desire was quenched.

A man in late middle age was emerging, greeting the Count with respectful familiarity.

'Ah, Lorenzo,' Cesare answered, in a reciprocal tone that told Carla he showed full appreciation of his staff. 'Will you show Signorina Charteris where she may refresh herself?'

Carla was escorted upstairs, shown into a pretty, feminine bedroom, with an en-suite bathroom that had once, she presumed, been a dressing room. As she looked at herself in the glass, checking the careful perfection of her hair and make-up, retouching the rich colour of her lips, for just a second she felt a qualm go through her.

Should I really go ahead with this? Plunge headlong into an affair with a man like this? An affair that can come to nothing?

But that, surely, was why she was doing it! *Because* it could come to nothing! There could be no future with a man for whom marriage to her could never be an option, and therefore love could never be a possibility—never a danger. She would *not* follow in her mother's footsteps, imagining love could come from an affair.

And that is all it will be—an affair. Nothing more than indulging in the overpowering effect he has on me, such as I have never, never known before.

She could see the pulse beating at her throat, the heightened colour in her cheeks, the quickening shallowness of her breathing. All telling her one thing and one thing only. That it was far too late for any qualms now.

With a quick spritz of scent from her handbag, she headed back downstairs. A pair of double doors stood open now, leading through to a beautifully appointed drawing room with French windows. Beyond, she could see Cesare.

Waiting for her.

At her approach, he smiled, his eyes washing over her with satisfaction.

Yes—he had been right to make the decision he had. This would go well, this affair with this enticing, alluring woman. He had no doubts about it. Everything about her confirmed it. Oh, not just her sensual allure and her responsiveness to him—powerful as it was— but any lingering reservations he might have had about her suitability for such a liaison were evaporating with every moment.

All his conversations with her so far had been reassuring on that score. Though she was Guido Viscari's stepdaughter, she made no special claims on the relationship, which indicated that she would make no claims on the relationship that he and she would share.

Her cool, English air of reserve met with his approval—like him, she would seek to avoid gossip and speculation and would draw no undue attention to her role in his life while their affair lasted—or afterwards. She had a career of her own to occupy her—one that was compatible with some of his own interests—and intelligent conversation with her was showing him that she was a woman whose company he could enjoy both out of bed and in.

She will enjoy what we have together and will have no impossible expectations. And when the affair has run its course we shall part gracefully and in a civilised manner. There will be no trouble in parting from her.

Parting with her...

But all that was for later—much later. For now, the entirely enticing prospect of their first night together beckoned.

His smile deepened. 'Come,' he said, as she walked towards him.

A little way along the terrace an ironwork table was set with two chairs, and there was a stand on which an opened bottle of champagne nestled in its bed of ice. But Carla's eyes were not for that—nor for Cesare. They were on the vista beyond the terrace.

Once more a pleased exclamation was on her lips, a smile of delight lighting her features.

'Oh, how absolutely perfect!'

Beyond the terrace, set at the rear of the villa, a large walled garden enclosed not just a pretty pair of parterres, one either side, but in the central space a swimming pool—designed, she could see at once, as if it were a Roman bath, lined with mosaic tiles and glittering in the sun. Ornamental bay trees marched either side of the paving around the pool, and there was a sunlit bench at the far end, espaliered fruit trees adorning the mossed walls.

Cesare came to stand beside her as she gazed, enraptured.

'We shall try out the pool later,' he said. 'But for now...'

He turned to pour each of them a glass of softly foaming champagne. As she took hers Carla felt the faint brush of his fingers, and the glass trembled in her hand. She gazed up at him, feeling suddenly breathless.

His dark gaze poured down into hers as he lifted his glass. 'To our time together,' he murmured.

She lifted her glass, touching it to his. Then drank deeply from it.

As she would drink deeply from her time with this most compelling of men...

CHAPTER FOUR

THE FIRE WAS burning low in the grate. The long, heavy silk drapes were drawn across the tall windows, cocooning them in the drawing room. Cesare's long legs extended with careless proprietorship towards the hearth from where he sat on the elegant sofa.

The evening had been long and leisurely. Champagne on the terrace, watching the sunset, followed by an exquisitely prepared dinner, discreetly served by Lorenzo in the rococo-style dining room.

Conversation had been easy—wide-ranging and eclectic—and Carla had found it both mentally stimulating and enjoyable, as it had been in the restaurant the night before. As it continued to be now, as she sat, legs slanting towards him, on a silk-covered *fauteuil,* sipping at a liqueur. Coffee was set on the ormolu table at her side... candles glowed on the mantel above the fire. An intimate, low-lit ambience enclosed them.

Their conversation wove on, both in English and Italian, melding Carla's expertise on High Renaissance art with Cesare's greater knowledge of the politics and economics of the time. And then at some point—she could not quite tell when—the conversation seemed to drain away, and she could not think of one more question to ask him.

Her liqueur was consumed, she realised, and she reached to place the empty glass on the low table at her side. As she released it Cesare stretched out his own hand. Let his fingers slide around her wrist.

It was the first physical contact between them that evening, and it electrified her.

Her eyes went to his, widening at the ripple of sensation that his long, cool fingers circling her wrist engendered. His eyes were on her, heavy and lidded.

Wordlessly, he drew her to her feet. Wordlessly, she let him. Still holding her wrist loosely, he lifted his other hand to her face. Those long, graceful fingers traced the outline of her cheek, her jaw. Faintness drummed in her veins and she felt her body sway, as if no longer able to keep itself upright.

Cesare smiled—a slow, sensual smile. As he had done in the car the night before, just before he'd kissed her. Kissed her as he did now—slowly, leisurely, with infinite sensuality, his mouth like velvet on hers...

'How very, very beautiful you are...' The words were a murmur, a caress. His gaze met hers. His mouth drew free. Her lips were still parted, her eyes still wide and clinging.

'Shall we?' he asked.

She did not answer. Did not need to.

She let him take her upstairs, into the bedroom she'd been shown to earlier, the house hushed around them. Then he was slipping the embroidered evening jacket from her, letting it fall to a chair, sliding down the zip of her dress, easing it from her shoulders. His mouth grazed the bare skin between the cusp of her arm and her neck, and she felt her head move to take in the luxury of his kiss. Slowly she stepped away from him a moment, to step out of her dress, drape it carefully on the chair.

As she turned back she saw that he had carelessly shrugged his own jacket free, and was loosening his tie, slipping the buttons of his shirt. Her eyes went to the smooth, hard wall of his chest. With an instinct older than time she stepped towards him, clad only in bra and panties, and the girdle of her stockings. She saw his eyes flare with male reaction. Felt her own fingertips reach to graze with infinite delicacy across the revealed skin of his torso. Saw his shoulders tense, his pupils become pinpoints.

Wickedly, oh-so-wickedly, she let the palms of her hands slide beneath his shirt, around the warm, strong column of his back, craning her head back to smile into his face with invitation and desire.

For one long, impossible moment he held fast, and still she smiled up at him.

Then, as if a limit had been reached, he gave a low growl in his throat and crushed her to him. His mouth came down on hers and now there was no slow, velvet arousing caress. Now there was only male hunger. Raw, insistent.

Fire flamed in her and her hands flattened on his spine, holding him against her as his mouth devoured hers. Arousal seared in her, her pulse soaring, skin heating. She felt her nipples crest, her breasts engorge—felt, with a fierce flare of arousal, his own arousal against her hips. Sensual excitement filled her…a mad headiness possessed her.

Desire, hot and tumid, took her over—took him over. Possessed them both.

He crushed her down upon the bed, upon the heavy satin covers, and the world was lost to her.

And more than just the world.

Carla twirled around her apartment, her body as light as air, her feet almost off the ground. *Cesare!* Oh, the very name, the very thought of him, filled her being, her mind, every synapse of her utterly possessed existence! How she thrilled to say his name, to see his face, his body— that powerful, sensual, perfect body!—in her mind's eye all the time…

She did not need to be with him to see him. He was there in her head, a constant presence, and every beat of her pulse was telling her what he had done to her.

Their first night together had set her aflame—caught her in a maelstrom of sensation and ecstasy that she had never known possible, that had set her alight with a flame that could not be quenched.

They had stayed at the villa for two days, and Carla had simply blotted out the rest of the world. She'd phoned in to the office the next day, on some pretext or other, to say that she was out of communication, and then she'd turned off her phone and given her entire and absolute focus to the man she was with. To Cesare—who had possessed her utterly, body and mind.

Cocooned at the villa, the only person they'd seen had been Lorenzo, for they had not ventured beyond the formal rooms that she and Cesare had occupied or the gardens beyond the terrace—and the joys of the sparkling Roman-style swimming pool. Where swimsuits had not been necessary…

And making love in the water, beneath the stars at

night, had been a revelation of sensual pleasure such as she had never, never anticipated. She had cried out in ecstasy as he'd held her, cradled her to him, and her head had fallen back, her hair streaming out into the water, her face lifted to the heavens, eyes wide with their reflected glory, as her body had shuddered, and shuddered again, in Cesare's strong possession.

Then, finally, as she'd let her head rest against his shoulder, let the water lap gently around them, he'd waded from the pool, wrapped her in the softest towels and carried her indoors and up to the bedroom—to make love to her all over again…

And again and yet again. Waking and sleeping, sleeping and waking, until the morning sun had streamed through the curtains and he'd been smoothing her tousled hair, smiling down at her.

'Breakfast,' he'd said. 'And then, alas, Rome. I have a lunch meeting I can't get out of.'

Carla had gazed up at him. 'And I must phone my editor.'

She'd smiled, lifting her hand lazily to graze the growth along Cesare's chin. If he grew a beard he'd look even more like his ancestor, she'd found herself thinking, amused.

But amusement had not been uppermost in her thoughts. There had been a stab of fear in the back of her mind—one that had returned as they drove back into Rome later in the morning.

Will he want to see me again—or is this all I shall have of him?

The stab had come again, almost drawing blood…

She'd hidden it, though—had known she must. Known with every instinct of her femininity that making any reference to that at all, asking any such question, would be the very last thing that would help to persuade him that he *did* want to see her again—*did* want more, much more, of what had been between them these last two incredible days.

And so it had proved. As he'd dropped her off at her apartment, he had casually wrapped his hand around her nape, drawn her to his mouth for a farewell kiss. But only farewell for the moment.

'I can't do tonight,' he'd said with a smile, his eyes washing over hers with warm intimacy, 'but the following night is clear. Tell me…how are you with opera?'

Carla had smiled in return, not letting the relief show in her face. 'Very predictable, I'm afraid. Verdi and Puccini, fine, Wagner and modern, not fine—'

He'd laughed and let her go. 'How about Donizetti?'

'*Bel canto* I can cope with,' she'd said in answer, and laughed too.

'Good. Can you meet me before the performance? I'll text you where. We can have a drink beforehand, eat afterwards. How would that suit you?'

Anything—anything would suit me! Anything at all!

The words had soared in Carla's head, but she had not spoken them. Again, instinct had told her otherwise. Instead, she had simply smiled.

'Lovely!' she'd said. And then she'd reached for the door catch, letting herself out of the car as it hummed by the kerb. She'd lifted her hand, given a little wave of farewell. 'See you then,' she'd said airily.

Without looking back again she'd opened the doors to the inner courtyard and stepped inside. Then, and only then, had she clutched at her key and given a crow of joy, of pleasure and relief.

Yes! Yes, he wanted to see more of her, wanted more time with her. Wanted her again… As she—oh, as she wanted him…

Cesare! Oh, Cesare—

His name soared in her head again—filling her mind, her being.

Him and only him…

'How's the article coming along?'

Cesare half twisted his head to call back into the shaded bedroom from where he sat, long legs stretched out in tan chinos, lounging out on the sunlit balcony, his city shirt swapped for a knitted polo, feet in casual, handmade loafers.

Beyond, the darkly glinting waters of Lake Garda hid their glacial depths, reflecting the encircling mountains. He flicked open the tab on the beer he'd just taken out of the minibar in the hotel room. As he sipped its cool flavour his sense of ease deepened. The leisurely weekend ahead beckoned him, and the prospect not just of taking his ease, but of spending it with Carla, bestowed a sense of well-being on him.

The time he spent with Carla always did that to him.

I made a good choice in her. She's worked out well— very, very well.

His eyelids drooped a moment as reminiscence played pleasurably in his head and anticipation of the night to come tonight did likewise. Carla might present a cool, composed front to the world, but when they were alone, when the lights went out… Oh, that was a different matter!

He felt his body quicken in memory. Like a struck match, when he reached for her she went up like a sheet of flame. Passion flared like phosphorous, incandescent and searing. Desire, unleashed, scorched between their bodies…

But it was not that alone—outstanding though it was—that had kept their affair going for so long. It had been six months now, and he showed no sign of tiring of her. But why *should* he tire of her, when passion still ran so strongly? And even when it was exhausted she was so very suitable for him—the ideal woman to have an affair with. She made no attempt to cling to him. Indeed, sometimes he found himself irked by her occasional unavailability, when she cited pressure of deadlines. But he respected her for it all the same. Made no demands on her when she was working.

His eyes shadowed for a moment. His father had shown no such respect for his mother—his mother's role had been to be a docile *contessa*, arranging her life only around the requirements of her difficult husband. Even the weakness of her heart condition had not made his father tolerant of what he perceived as any dereliction in her primary duty to be the chatelaine of his estates.

It was not an attitude he would take when he himself married. Of course his *contessa* would need to be completely willing to play her role as his wife, just as he himself would shoulder the myriad responsibilities of his position, but that did not mean she could have no life of her own as well. In fact…

He snapped his mind away. It was inappropriate to dwell on the qualities his wife would have when he was here with a woman who could never have that title.

And who would not want to.

Nothing about Carla Charteris gave him any cause for disquiet in that respect. And for that he was entirely appreciative. So if, right now, he was having to wait for her to finish her article, then wait he would—as patiently as his temperament permitted.

Some ten minutes later, as he was nearing the end of his can of beer, it was rewarded.

'Finished!' came Carla's voice from inside, with a sense of relief. 'All submitted.'

She lifted the laptop off her knees, closing it down, glancing out towards the darkening balcony. She'd been slightly apprehensive in booking this hotel, in case it did not meet Cesare's exacting standards, but its five-star rating was well deserved. Situated at the lake's edge, its luxury was discreet rather than ostentatious, and a weekend here—following on from her trip to Venice to cover the opening of a new gallery, which had conveniently coincided with Cesare's series of business appointments in Milan—should be extremely pleasant.

Pleasant? The mild word mocked her. The time she spent with Cesare was so much more than 'pleasant'! It was—

Incredible—unbelievable—wonderful—unforgettable!

Her expression softened. Had it really been six months since that first night at his elegant little villa outside Rome? Since then they'd stayed there frequently, recapturing each and every time the scorching intimacy that had swept her away then as never before. Could she have experienced such passion with a man who was *not* Cesare? Impossible—just impossible! He dominated her consciousness each and every day, whether she was with him or not.

Yet she tried hard not to show it—instinctively knowing that any sign from her of being possessive would be fatal. It was that instinctive awareness that told her to be sure never to make any assumptions about him, never to ask him when they would next see each other. Never to rearrange her life for him.

I want to reassure him that he is safe with me. That I do not depend on him. That I have my own life, separate from my time with him.

It was an odd thought, and the reasons she was thinking it were skittering in the back of her mind, trying to land. But she would not let them. Instead, she would enjoy to the max the times they *did* have together—such as this weekend.

She padded on bare feet to the minibar, drawing out a miniature bottle of wine and a glass, then headed out to the balcony, sliding her hands over Cesare's broad shoulders, squeezing lightly.

He turned his head, brushing the tops of her fingers with his mouth. The sensation sent familiar little tremors through her, but she only took a seat beside him on the other sundowner chair, gathering the loose cotton folds of the long printed sundress she'd changed into from her formal Venice outfit, and poured her wine.

'*Salute!*' he said lazily, and clinked his beer can against her glass.

She returned the toast and took a mouthful of chilled wine, turning to look out over the view. It really was spectacular, and she drank it in as Cesare was doing.

'It's good to see mountains again—though these are a bit too serrated for my tastes,' he heard himself observing, letting his fingers intertwine with hers.

As he spoke, he found himself wondering why he'd made such a remark to Carla. As a rule, he never talked about his own home—even if it was only to contrast the high peaks of the jagged Dolomites with the lower, more rounded Apennines that were the ever-scenic background to the Castello di Mantegna. The *castello* wasn't a place she would ever see, so there was no point mentioning it.

At the thought, a slight frown flickered across his eyes. He crumpled his beer can, tightening his fingers on Carla's.

'Shall we head down to the restaurant?' he said.

He got to his feet, drawing her with him. His eyes went to her. She looked good—but then she always looked good. Always immaculately groomed, with her fantastic figure on show. Wearing what she did now—that loose dress—she looked different somehow. Still a knockout—always that—but more...*medieval*. Her hair was loose too, waving lushly down her back.

A ripple of desire went through him, but he put it aside. That was for later.

They headed downstairs, Cesare carrying her unfinished glass of white wine for her, and in the dining room, which still caught the roseate glow of the lowering sun, they took a table overlooking the lake.

Cesare's sense of well-being deepened. This was good. It really *was* good. Being here, well away from Rome, from home, from responsibilities and social obligations, just having time to himself with the woman he wanted to be with.

How long will I keep this going? This affair...this liaison?

The question wound through his head as they got on with choosing from the menu. The answer came of its own accord.

While it stays good.

* * *

It had certainly stayed good for the rest of their long weekend together.

A sating, fulfilling night together, a slow, leisurely breakfast the next morning, before hiring a car to explore the lake's circuit, and the following day taking a private launch out onto the water itself, lunching on one of the little islands in the lake.

The weekend passed too soon. And it was with regret that he announced at breakfast on Monday morning that he must leave for Milan again.

Carla nodded. 'And I've promised my mother I'll spend some time with her. I've somewhat neglected her these past months.'

Cesare reached for his coffee. As ever, Carla had made no demur at their parting, and he was glad of it. After Milan he must go home—put in some time there, attending to his affairs. His agenda was crowded—the never-ending maintenance work on the *castello* itself, a controversial wind turbine proposal to evaluate, a refor-estation project to check up on, a request for the loan of artworks to yet another exhibition to decide on.

Maybe he should discuss that last item with Carla—

He pulled his mind back abruptly. No, that would be a bad move. That might set seeds growing that he did not want to see taking any kind of root. Impossible that they should do so.

Quite impossible.

They drove down towards Milan. Cesare would divert via the airport to let Carla catch her flight back to Rome.

As they drew near, he remarked, 'What would you say to a visit to London?' he asked. 'I'll need to go next month.'

Carla considered. 'I'll have to check my diary,' she said. 'I'm not sure what I've got coming up.'

Cesare nodded. 'Let me know,' he replied easily.

'Will do,' she agreed.

She kept her voice neutral, though inside she felt the familiar flutter of emotion that came whenever Cesare indicated that she was included in his future plans.

Short-term future plans, at any rate.

No, she mustn't think like that. What they had was good. Very good. Incredibly good. Fantastically good. But—

I don't know what the future will bring. I just don't know. I don't dare know.

She felt a hollowing inside her as the thoughts rushed into her head. Disquieting suddenly, as they echoed again. *Why* should she not dare know...?

An unfamiliar emotion swirled within her, disturbing her by its very presence. And as her eyes went to him now, that hollowing inside her was still there—that disturbing, unidentified emotion that seemed to deepen, to make her gaze cling to his profile as he drove along the *autostrada*, his dark eyes focussed on the road.

As if aware she was looking at him, he glanced sideways a moment. Instantly she schooled her expression. Not noticing the sudden flicker in his eyes before he spoke.

'Do you *have* to be in Rome today?' he said. 'Why not stay in Milan with me? I'll be busy all day, but surely the charms of the *quadrilatera* would while away the hours away for you!' He spoke lightly, knowing that although Carla was always superbly attired, she was no fashionista obsessed with Milan's famous *haute couture* quarter.

'And, of course,' he added, 'there's always the Da Vinci *Last Supper* to look in on!'

That might tempt her more…

He caught himself—was that what he was seeking to do? Tempt her to stay with him now instead of heading back to Rome?

Well, why not? Why shouldn't I suggest she stay with me tonight and head down to Rome tomorrow? It's a perfectly reasonable suggestion.

But that wasn't the reason for his question to himself—he knew that perfectly well. The reason for the question was why he should object in any way to Carla getting back to her own life. Because he shouldn't object—of course he shouldn't. She was her own woman, with her own life, not in the slightest bit assuming that her life was melded to his—and that was very necessary. Essential, in fact, for their liaison to continue.

So why should I need to remind myself of that?

That question was displaced only when he heard Carla's answer. Her tone was a little more clipped than usual, the quick shake of her head infinitesimal.

'I can't, I'm afraid. I've promised my mother, and I don't want to let her down.'

Was there regret in her voice? Hesitation? As if she were reluctant to turn down his invitation to stay with him longer, issued on an impulse he did not wish to scrutinise beyond wanting their mutual enjoyment. If there was, Cesare couldn't hear it. Could only hear her turning his suggestion down.

Could only feel the nip of…of *what*, precisely? Merely annoyance that he was going to have to do without her until they next met up again in Rome? It couldn't be more than that—he would not permit it to be more.

Making himself give a slight shrug of polite regret, he nodded. 'Ah, in that case, then, no,' he murmured courteously.

The turning for the airport was coming up, and he steered off the *autostrada*. Yet after he'd dropped her off he was again conscious of a sense of displeasure. Even regret for himself, that Carla had not stayed with him when he'd wanted her to, despite her perfectly valid reason for not doing so. He would not wish her to neglect her mother for his sake.

Memory flickered in his mind, and he recalled his own mother. How she had always moulded herself around her husband's wishes, whatever they had been, always at his side, always compliant.

It was something he recalled again as, returning home after Milan, he busied himself with the myriad items waiting for him at the *castello*.

Passing the doors of the trophy room—one of a series of staterooms, including the *galleria* containing priceless artworks such as the Luciezo-Caradino triptych—he paused to glance inside. It was his least favourite room, despite its imposing grandeur, for the walls were thick with the antlers and heads of creatures slaughtered by his forebears and added to copiously by his father.

His own open distaste for his father's predilection for slaughtering wildlife had been frequently voiced to his mother, and he'd known she'd shared his disapproval, yet never had she criticised his father. She had acquiesced in that, as she had in everything to do with him, subjugating her views to his on all matters.

Her perpetually acquiescent attitude had both dismayed Cesare and exasperated him.

Cesare's mouth tightened as he walked on into the

more recent eighteenth-century part of the *castello*, where
the family accommodation was. Every window of the
magnificent enfilade of rooms looked out upon terraced
gardens and dramatic views over the plunging river valley beyond, framed by the soaring upward slope on the
far side that drew the eye to the stony peak of the mountainous summit.

Instinctively, his footsteps took him to the French
windows of the drawing room, and he stepped out into
the fresh air, drinking in the vista all around him. For a
few pleasurable minutes he stood on the terrace in the
breeze-filled sunshine, feeling the customary deep and
abiding sense of possession of this landscape—this was
his home, his domain, his patrimony. And, whatever the
dissensions between himself and his father, he had done
his best—would always do his best—to prove himself
worthy of his inheritance, to shoulder his responsibilities and carry out all the duties of his title and estates.

Including the most critical of all—to establish his new
contessa, so as to continue the bloodline that stretched far
back into the past, to safeguard it for the future. When
the time came to take that step—as come it must, one
day—his choice of wife would be a wise one—that was
essential.

Taking one last deep breath of the crisp, clean air, he
went back indoors, made his way to his study at the fur-
thest end of the enfilade. Although the windows gave
out onto the same spectacular view he'd enjoyed from
the terrace, he schooled himself to turn his attention to
the stacks of paperwork neatly piled by his secretary on
his desk.

Time to get down to work.

A swift perusal of the files and business correspondence enabled him to select his priorities for the morning, and he was just about to open his emails when his eye caught a glimpse of the handwriting on an envelope in the in-tray containing his personal correspondence. For the most part this consisted of social invitations he would sort through later. But the sight of the handwriting arrested him.

He pulled the envelope out of the pile. Stared down at it a moment. It bore an airmail sticker and a US stamp—and Cesare knew exactly who it was from.

It was from the woman he was destined to marry.

CHAPTER FIVE

'DARLING, HOW LOVELY to see you—it's been such a long time!'

Carla's mother's embrace was reproachful, and Carla felt herself wincing guiltily. It *had* been a long time since she'd spent any amount of time with her mother. Their last meeting had been several weeks ago, and only for lunch while out shopping.

'Well, I'm here now!' she answered lightly, exchanging a careful cheek-to-cheek kiss with her mother. 'And I'm in no rush to leave!'

She would stay at Guido's villa for a few days—it would be at least a week before Cesare was back in Rome and she would see him again.

But you could still be in Milan with him tonight if you'd said yes to him!

The reminder was like a little stab. On the short flight down to Rome she'd replayed that brief exchange a dozen times—and a dozen times wished she'd not given him that short, cool answer. Yet at the time it had seemed essential to say what she had.

I was trying to negate that sudden fear I'd had—fear about why I didn't dare think what my future would be with Cesare. Because I shouldn't feel that—I've always known that there is no future with him. Known that I mustn't care that there is no future.

Known, too, right from the start, that if she wanted any time at all with Cesare she must try not to cling to him, try not to want him too much. He had to know she would never have any expectations of him, never make any assumptions.

Never want a future with him longer than he was prepared to give her.

Or she would have nothing of him at all.

Nothing.

The hollow feeling came again, like a crevasse opening inside her. A crevasse into which that same emotion flared again—more than disquieting, deeper than disturbing.

To have nothing of Cesare—how could I endure that?

No—she tore her mind away. She must not think like this! She was regretting not staying with him in Milan, that was all! Regretting insisting on arriving today at her mother's, even though she could, she knew, have postponed her arrival by a day. It would not have made any great difference to her mother, and she'd have stayed on a day longer to compensate.

I turned down Cesare when I didn't need to.

But she knew why she had done it.

It was to show myself that I don't want to cling to him...don't need to cling to him. To show myself how we are simply having a relationship between adults that we both enjoy, that suits us both. And that is all.

'So...' her mother's voice interrupted her insistent thoughts and she was glad of it '...how was Venice? Tell me about this new gallery that's been opened. Where did you stay? At the Danieli or the Gritti?' she enquired, naming two of the city's top hotels.

As she answered, telling her mother about her trip there and the article she'd written, Carla welcomed the diversion—welcomed, too, over dinner, letting her mother run on about her social comings and goings, knowing how much Marlene enjoyed her position in Roman society.

Only when all these had been comprehensively covered did Carla ask, casually, after any news of the Viscaris. Vito, she knew, had been on an extensive inspection tour of his European hotels, and was due back in Rome imminently.

'I do hope, Mum,' she ended, casting a significant look at her mother, 'that when he's back here you'll finally agree to sell him Guido's shares...'

The sooner that was done, the better. It had caused a significant rift in relations with her stepfather's brother's side of the family that had rumbled on ever since her stepfather had died.

But immediately her mother bridled. 'Darling, Guido entrusted those shares to *me*! And he had his reasons.'

Carla gave an exasperated sigh. 'Mum, please don't be stubborn! It makes far more sense for Vito to own the entire shareholding—'

The next moment she wished she'd never mentioned the wretched subject.

Her mother's eyes flared. 'Yes, and he could—very easily! Carla, darling, *why* don't you listen to me on this? It would make perfect sense—would be what I've always dreamt of! It would unite both sides of the family! *And* unite the shareholdings as well!'

Carla threw up her hands. Damn, she'd walked into this one!

'Mum,' she said warningly, 'don't go there! I know you've had a thing about it for ever, but please just accept that Vito and I are simply not interested in each other! Not in the slightest! And whether or not Guido left you his shares doesn't change a thing!'

She attempted to put a humorous note into her voice, to defuse the situation.

'Vito wouldn't look twice at me—I'm not blonde, which is the only type of female he ever falls for, and his flashy film star looks just don't do it for me either. I far prefer—'

She stopped short. But it was too late. Her mother pounced.

'Yes, that's *exactly* what I'm concerned about! Darling, are you *mad*?' She leant forward, her expression agitated. 'Cesare di Mondave of all men! I've been hoping and hoping it would just be a brief fling…or whatever you want to call it! But it's been months now and you are still with him! Have you *no* sense?'

Carla shut her eyes, then flashed them open again. Realising with a wash of angry dismay that giving her mother an opportunity to voice her obsession about her marrying Vito had been the least of it!

During the last six months she'd never mentioned Cesare to her mother—had deliberately kept their relationship out of any conversation. The fact that her mother doubtless knew—for Rome was a hotbed of gossip—was no reason to be open with her mother about it. And not just because it didn't play to Marlene's fantasy about finally getting her together with Vito. But because she knew her affair with Cesare would get exactly the reaction she was getting now.

Emotion stormed up inside her. Anger at her mother, and at herself for walking into this. The last thing she wanted was an inquisition.

'I'm twenty-seven years old—I can handle an affair,' she said tightly.

Her mother's eyes were piercing. '*Can* you?' she said. Her expression changed. 'Darling, it's you I'm thinking of! Affairs can go badly wrong.' She paused again. 'I should know. For me there was no happy ending. And that's what I fear for *you*! There can be no happy ending for you as Cesare di Mondave's mistress—'

Rejection was instant in Carla. '*Mistress?* Of course I'm not his *mistress*!'

Yet even as she rejected the term across her mind seared the memory of that triptych, and the sixteenth-century's Conte's mistress.

I am not that woman—I am nothing whatsoever like that wretched woman! I am not Cesare's mistress, I am his lover, and he is my lover, and we are together by choice, of our own free will, and I'm perfectly happy with that. Perfectly!

She could see her mother backing off, taking another breath. 'Well, whatever you call yourself it doesn't matter. All that matters to me is that you don't get hurt!'

She shook her head one more time.

'I know I can't stop you, but…' she looked worriedly across at Carla, holding her gaze '…promise me that, whatever happens, when it comes to Cesare di Mondave you won't go and do something unforgivably stupid.' She took a breath. 'Promise me that you won't go and fall in love with him!'

There was silence. Absolute silence. And then Marlene's voice again, sounding hollow now.

'Please promise me that, Carla—*please*.'

But Carla could not answer. Could not answer at all…

Emotion was pouring over her like an avalanche. Wiping the breath from her lungs. Suffocating her with a blinding white truth…

Cesare was out on the terrace, hands curled around the cold stone of the balustrade. Above the gardens and the valley the moon was rising, casting its silver glow over the world. His expression was studied.

Francesca.

Francesca delle Ristori—Donna Francesca—daughter of a *marchese*, granddaughter of a duke on her mother's side, daughter of one of his father's best friends, and ideally suited to be the next Contessa di Mantegna.

Ideally suited to be his wife.

He'd known her all his life. Known her and liked her. And what was not to like? She was intelligent—extremely so—sweet-natured, good-tempered, and, as a bonus, beautiful. She had a pale, ash-blonde beauty that would adorn his arm…that some of their children, surely, would inherit.

Into his head, memory pierced. His father talking to him…*at* him…shortly before the seizure that had killed him.

'She'll be the perfect wife for you—if you've any sense at all you'll see that! She's serious, committed and would be an ornament in her role as your mother's successor!'

It was impossible to disagree with his father's judgement. Francesca would, there was no doubt in his mind whatsoever, make a perfect wife, the perfect next Contessa di Mantegna and mother of the future Count.

When the right time came.

If it was to come at all.

His jaw tightened. That, he knew, was the meat of Francesca's letter to him. Was this long-mooted marriage of theirs to take place—or not? A decision was necessary. And very soon.

And that was the problem he had.

It's come too soon.

As the words formed in his head his inner vision blotted out the moonlit valley before him. He was seeing Lake Garda, sunlight bright on its deep, dark waters, the reflection of the jagged mountains in its surface, seeing his arm casually around the woman beside him as they leant against the stone balustrade on the hotel terrace overlooking the vista.

The memory burned tangibly in him—he could almost feel the soft curve of her hip indenting into his, her hand around his waist. More vivid memory came now, of the last time they had made love, her body threshing beneath his, her mouth hungry for his, her passion released, ardent and sensual, so arousing a contrast with her air of English composure when she was not in his embrace.

I don't want to give that up—not yet.

Oh, one day he would marry—of course he would—but his own preference would have been to postpone marriage for some time. For him there was no necessity to do so yet. But his marriage must be a partnership—with his wife an equal partner. Not for him a marriage like his parents'. His wife would not live the life of his mother, shaping herself around his father's wishes, giving up everything else in her life but her role as Contessa. No, Francesca would be very different—and that included her very understandable desire to marry when the time was right for *her*.

And that time seemed to be now.

He could not ask her to delay—not given the information she had shared with him in her letter. Whatever his reluctance to make that decision now, it had to be done.

He stared out over the valley one long, last time. Slowly, very slowly, his thoughts reached their conclusion. Slowly, very slowly, he exhaled, inclined his head.

Decision made.

In the bedroom that had been hers since her teenage days, up until the time she'd moved out to her own apartment, Carla lay in bed, sleepless, staring up at the painted ceiling. Her eyes were huge, distended. Words ran like an endless litany round and round the inside of her skull—like rats in a trap. Desperately seeking escape.

I'm not in love with Cesare! I'm not! It's just passion—desire—that's all! The way it was from the very start! He makes my heart beat faster just looking at him—but that isn't love! I won't let it be love. I won't.

But even as the litany was repeated she could hear another voice speaking.

So why do you fear not knowing how long he'll want you? Why would you fear a future where you have nothing of him any longer? Why have you kept trying to prove to yourself that you have no need to cling to him, no need to want to be with him more than you are? Why did you make yourself turn down his invitation to stay longer with him today in Milan?

She knew the answer to those questions—knew why she did not want to hear them, did not want to answer them. Did not want to face the truth of what had happened. Fear beat up in her, firing through her veins.

It mustn't be love—what she felt for Cesare, what she felt about him. It just mustn't...

I'm not that stupid! Dear God, I'm not that stupid! To have fallen in love with Cesare di Mondave...

But as the dawn came she knew, with a hollowing of her heart, that what her mother had feared—what she herself had guarded against, right from the start—had happened. And in her head, her mother's warning tolled like doom.

'There can be no happy ending for you—'

A fearful coldness filled her.

CHAPTER SIX

CESARE HANDED THE keys of his car to the valet parker and headed into the restaurant. He was running late, and he knew why. Emotions spiked across his mind, troubling and unwelcome. Tonight was not going to be easy—but it had to be faced. He had to say what he had to say, do what he had to do. No escaping it.

And take the consequences.

Emotion struck again—powerful, like a leopard on a leash. His life was privileged—immensely privileged—but the responsibilities that came with it required a price. A price that he did not wish to pay.

He felt the leashed emotion tug again, bringing to his mind's eye the portrait of his ancestor, Count Alessandro, whom Luciezo had captured for posterity.

You had it easier—you kept your privileges and did not have to pay for them at all!

The triptych was testament to that. The Conte di Mantegna—flanked by his wife and his mistress. And he had kept them both—enjoyed them both. Had had to give up neither—give up nothing at all. Paid no price at all for the life he'd led.

Cesare's jaw tightened. Well, that was then, not now, and now, in this current century, no such arrangement was possible. Not with honour. To marry Francesca meant giving up Carla. No other option.

As he strode into the dining room he saw her immediately. Saw how her blue-violet eyes fastened on his, simultaneously felt another, different emotion seize him.

Her crepe dress in a luscious plum colour graced her full figure, her rich, brunette hair was coiled at her nape, and those lustrous eyes, the generous, sensual mouth, would draw male eyes from everywhere. But her attention was only for him. It had always been that way, and he was accustomed to it.

Yet into his head at that thought came another.

I will have to see her lavishing that same unwavering attention on another man—another man who will have her to himself...

The thought jabbed in his mind like a spike being driven in. As he reached her, sat himself down, he found himself lifting her hand and dropping a light kiss on it.

'*Mi dispiace.* I was delayed.'

Her smile was instant, and he could see relief in it. But as he looked into her face he could see more than relief. He could see a sudden veiling of her expression. As if she were hiding something from him.

A moment later, though, her expression was open again, her usual air of composure back in place. 'Long day?' she asked sympathetically, starting to skim down the menu.

'Long enough,' Cesare replied.

For the first time with Carla he was conscious of a sense of deceit—it was discomfiting.

He turned the subject away. 'How have you been? Did you visit your mother?'

She nodded with an assenting murmur, but said no

more. Cesare did not usually ask after her family—and she never asked after his family affairs. It was an invisible line she did not cross.

The sommelier was approaching, and Cesare turned his attention to him. There was a hollow feeling in the pit of his stomach that had nothing to do with hunger.

Or not hunger for food.

I don't want to do this—I don't want to do it but I have no option. It has to be done, and it has to be done now—tonight.

But not right now. Not over dinner. What he had to say required privacy.

And, besides, I want one more night with her—one last night.

He broke off such thoughts as the sommelier returned, filling their glasses. When he had gone Cesare lifted his glass. That hollow feeling came again.

'To you, Carla,' he said.

His eyes were dark, his expression serious. For a long moment he held her gaze. He saw her face whiten suddenly, her eyes distend. Then, like an opaque lens, he saw her expression become veiled.

Slowly, she inclined her head. 'To you, Cesare,' she replied. Her voice was steady, despite the whitening of her face.

She drank, taking a larger mouthful than she had intended. But right now she needed its fortifying strength. The tension from having waited for him so desperately, overwhelmed by the devastating realisation of what she felt for him, had made her feel faint. Emotion was knifing in her. She felt as if she were seeing him for the very first time.

And I am—I'm seeing him with eyes that see what I

*have refused to admit until now—what I have guarded
myself from for six long months, and what has now overcome me. The truth of what I feel for him.*

Weakness flooded through her, dissolving her. Shakily, she lowered her glass to the table, hearing in her head
the echo of his simple, devastating tribute.

'To you, Carla...'

That was all he'd said—and yet within her now she
could feel emotion soaring upwards like an eagle taking
flight from a mountaintop. There had been such intent
in his gaze...such as she had never seen before.

Can it mean—? Oh, can it mean...?

For a second, the briefest second, she felt an emotion
flare within her that she must not feel—dared not feel.
She crushed it down. It was too dangerous. Too desperate.

Instead, she watched him set down his glass, saw the
candlelight catch the gold of the crested signet ring on
his little finger. He never removed it—never. It was there
when he made love to her, when they showered, when
they swam. It was as if it was melded into his skin. Given
to him on his father's death, passed down generation to
generation, one day it would be passed to his son, the
next Conte.

She looked away, back at his face, unwilling to think
such thoughts. Wanting only to drink him in as a thirsty
man in a desert would drink in fresh water, feeling her
heart beating heavily within her breast. The heart that
had so recently, so devastatingly, revealed its truth to her.
The truth that she *must* not show...

'So, how are things in the Viscari family?'

His casual question made Carla start. She dragged
back her hectic thoughts. Collected herself. It was un-

usual that he was even asking, but she made her reply as casual as she could.

'Vito's heading back to Rome. He's been away for weeks, inspecting all the European hotels.' To her ears, her voice seemed staccato, but Cesare seemed to notice nothing about it. She was glad—grateful.

'Do you get on, the two of you?' Cesare's enquiry was still polite as he demolished the piece of bread roll he'd buttered.

He was not particularly interested, but it was a safe topic of conversation. And right now he needed safe topics.

She blinked, taken aback by his enquiry. Focussed on how to answer it. With a fragment of her mind she registered that Cesare, too, seemed on edge.

'Surprisingly well, really,' Carla answered, sounding, with an effort, more composed now. She made herself go on. 'Considering how my mother and his are usually daggers drawn. She and my mother never hit it off…' She gave a sigh.

'That's often the way between sisters-in-law,' Cesare observed drily. Their first course arrived, and he began to eat. 'Vito Viscari has had a lot to knuckle down to, given the successive deaths of both his uncle and his father. It can be tough. I vividly remember—'

He stopped. Talking to Carla about how he'd had to discover—rapidly—just how to fill his father's shoes after his fatal seizure was not wise.

But Carla did not seem to notice his abrupt cessation. She forked her seafood and nodded.

It was getting easier for her to sound normal, to get her hectic heart rate back under control.

'Because of his ridiculously gorgeous film star looks,

people tend to think Vito lightweight—but he isn't at all. I have considerable respect for him,' she said.

Cesare's eyes rested on her a moment. 'And he for you, I hope. After all, you had to contend with arriving in a new country, learning the language, adapting to a new way of life.'

'Vito was very kind to me,' she answered, her voice warming. 'Helped me settle in. Improved my Italian, took me about with him to meet his friends. Warned me off several of them!' she finished with a laugh.

The laugh had sounded quite natural to her ears, and she was again grateful.

Cesare smiled. But he knew it was something of a forced smile. There had been a fond note in her voice, and he had not liked to hear that. Nor did he like to examine *why* he had not liked to hear it.

'Would he have warned you off me?' he heard himself asking.

He'd kept his voice light, deliberately so, masking that slight jab that had come when he'd heard her praising her step-cousin so affectionately—yet he was aware that he had asked the question. *Why* he had asked it.

For all his light tone, he saw her face still. The expression in her eyes changed.

'He would not have needed to, Cesare,' she said quietly. 'I've always known the score with you. Credit me with that much, at least.'

His eyes shifted away, his jaw tightening. Then, abruptly, his gaze came back to her. She was looking at him, again with that veiled expression in her eyes. Impulsively he reached for her free hand, raised it once more to his lips. This was the last night of his life that he would spend with her—he would not stint on his appreciation of her. Of what she had been to him.

What she can be no longer.

He felt again that jab of regret that it should be so. More than a jab. Yet again the words sounded in his head.

Not yet.

But there was no point thinking that—none. He must part with her, and that was all that was possible now. That—and this one last, final night with her.

'I credit you with a great deal, Carla.'

There was emotion in his voice. She could hear it. And inside she felt again that sudden flare of emotion that she had felt when he'd raised his glass to her, let his gaze rest on her with such intent.

She returned his gaze now, as he let go of her hand and it fell to the table. Her breath seemed dry in her lungs.

Why had he said that? Why was he acting the way he was tonight? There was something about the way he was being that she had never seen in him before.

What does it mean?

She swallowed, feeling her cheeks flush suddenly. Dipped her head to resume her meal. Yet through her consciousness her mind was racing. That same swooping sensation was within her. Cesare was different tonight. She could see, could tell—knew with every instinct that something was changing between them. Something profound that would alter everything...

Can it be—can it really be? After all, if I was in denial for so long, if I told myself over and over again I could not possibly feel love for him...could it be that maybe, just maybe, for him it's the same?

The thoughts were barely there, barely allowed, barely shaped into words—for she dared not let them be. Dared not give in to the swooping, soaring inside her as their meal progressed, as emotions swirled and formed and dissolved within her.

How *could* she dare? How could she dare give in to the one emotion above all that she yearned to give in to?

How could she give in to hope?

Hope that he might just feel for me what I now know I feel for him... That—despite everything—he's fallen in love with me too?

'A miracle—a parking space!'

Carla's exclamation was heartfelt. To find a free parking space on her narrow street was, indeed, a miracle. Yet there it was.

Is it a sign—can it be a sign?

She almost laughed at herself for the notion, yet knew with a fragment of her mind that she was not joking at all.

As Cesare expertly parallel parked in the confined space, she could feel yet again her emotions soaring within her. For hope was a bird that, once released, could not be imprisoned again.

Throughout the evening, Cesare's air of particular attentiveness to her had been palpable, that sense of something different about him unmistakable.

Now, as they climbed out of the car and she opened the outer door to let them both into the inner courtyard, his closeness to her was even more palpable.

Upstairs in her apartment she went into the kitchen to set the coffee brewing. Usually when he stayed over with her he settled down on the white sofa, his long legs reaching out, and shrugged off his jacket and tie, happy to lounge with her while drinking coffee, and sometimes a liqueur, before arousal took them both and swept them off to bed.

Tonight, however, he followed her into the kitchen.

'Do you really want coffee?'

She turned. He was standing there, and in his eyes was an expression that wiped all thought of coffee from her mind—all thought at all. An expression that was all too familiar to her. Slowly she shook her head. For one long, timeless moment she did not move, and nor did he. Something flowed between them. Something that took her back to that very first night they'd spent together.

The villa outside Rome, Cesare's love nest, had seen much use in the months since then. But at this moment all she could think of was that very first night.

Warmth beat up in her. Suffusing her skin, flaring out from her core. He stepped towards her, curved his long fingers around the nape of her neck, drawing her towards him. But not into his arms. He held her in front of him while his other hand rested lightly around her waist. His dark, lidded eyes held hers, unfathomable, unreadable.

Turning her bones to water.

She felt emotion rise up in her like a sweeping tide, pouring through her. Her lips parted and there was a low, frail noise in her throat.

'Cesare—' His name was like a whisper in her mouth…an echo deep within her.

The knowledge of what she now knew she felt for him had ripped across her like a revelation and it trembled within her. It was making her tremble again now as the thumb of the hand at her nape reached forward to graze the cusp of her jaw, stroked the hollow below her ear in a soft, sensual caress that sent a thousand feathers fluttering through her veins.

'You are so, so beautiful,' he said.

Slowly, infinitely slowly, as if he were savouring every long moment of its descent, he lowered his mouth to hers. For one long, timeless moment, his kiss was nothing more than a velvet graze along her lips. Then, with a rasp in his throat, he tightened his fingers at her nape, his hand at her waist, and hauled her to him hungrily, ravenously.

As though she were the last meal he would ever eat.

Like a sheet of flame she went up in an inferno of sensation, of passion and desire, white-hot and incandescent. With absolute mastery he possessed her mouth and then, feasting his way down, he swept her up, clamping her against him as he strode from the kitchen, pushing open the door of her bedroom, coming down on the bed beside her.

Clothes were shed, bodies were arching, limbs twining, mouths meeting and melding. Bodies fusing.

Fusing with that same white heat, that same incandescence. She cried out over and over again, her body shaking. The ecstasy he wrought on her was unbearable, meeting for the first time the flood of emotion that poured through her, the knowledge of what it was he meant to her...

The man she loved. Cesare—oh, Cesare—the man she loved.

The knowledge of it, the certainty and the rapture of it, was a possession of her heart and of her soul even as she gave him possession of her body, took possession of his, giving to him all that was within her. It was a glory, a dedication of herself to him without measure, without reserve. An absolute oblation of herself...

And at the end, as wave after wave of shuddering ecstasy and love finally ebbed from her, she held him in her arms, crushing him to her. His dampened skin cooled, his hectic breathing calmed, and she wrapped herself around him, half cradled by him, their limbs tangled and exhausted. She knew, with certainty and utter conviction, that she had never known happiness until this moment. Never known until this moment what love truly felt like.

She held him close against her, smoothed the strong contours of his powerful back. Wonder filled her—and a gratitude beyond all things. He had cried out as the moment had possessed him, as if it had been the very first time they had made love. The intensity of it had shaken her, overwhelmed her.

It could mean only one thing—surely only one thing? His passion for her had been greater than he'd ever shown, his response more searing than she had ever known it to be, his fulfilment fiercer, more burning than she had ever seen before. And now, as she lay with him, his arms around her were tighter than she had ever known.

As if he would not let her go.

As if he would *never* let her go…

As if she were his and he was hers for ever now…

For ever…

Eyelids fluttering, she felt the great lassitude of her body sweep over her, and sleep took her.

She awoke alone. In the bathroom she could hear the shower running. For a few moments she lay, languorous, her mind in a dream state. Wonder still suffused her— like an underground spring filling the receptive earth. Happiness—rich, and full and glorious—ran in her veins like cream. She had never been happier in her life.

Because of Cesare—oh, Cesare, Cesare, Cesare! The world was new-made, new-found. Illumined by love, by joy, by glory.

The shower was cut off. A moment later Cesare was walking into the bedroom, a towel snaked around his hips. He walked quietly, as if not wanting to disturb her. She went on lying there, immobile, watching him through shuttered eyes only just affording vision.

She watched him dress swiftly, surely, fastening his cuffs, knotting his tie—all the tiny, familiar minutiae of the morning. She felt a vague disappointment, for clearly he had an appointment to get to. But then, *she* had to attend an editorial meeting that morning anyway, and a lunch afterwards, so she did not mind him leaving her like this. There would be tonight—and the night after, and all the nights thereafter. The future was stretching ahead of them. She was sure of it, certain of it.

How could it be otherwise now?

Now that I know I love him.

For now, with love pouring through her, she knew, above all, that she could dare to hope.

Whatever it is he feels for me he does *feel for me! I am more to him than I was! I know it—oh, I know it, I know it!*

Give him time—just give him time. Make no demands, be as cautious and as careful as ever. But with time— oh, with time he will come to feel more for me. Whatever might happen...

There were no certainties about him, but there *were* possibilities. Oh, that much she must have faith in. She must and she could—and she did.

Her mother's warnings seemed a thousand miles away—as did her own warnings, issued to herself all her life, all these months with Cesare.

I can believe in my happy ending—I dare to believe in it! I dare to hope! To have faith in my heart...in his...

Her love could make it happen—she needed only hope and faith. And both were streaming through her as her eyes drank him in, her heart overflowing with wonder and gratitude. With joy.

He crossed to the bed, sat down on it, his hand reaching for her shoulder as if to wake her. She opened her eyes—opened them and smiled, lifting her hand to catch his. For a second he let her, then her lowered her hand to the sheet, taking his own away. His face was expressionless.

Out of nowhere, like a knife sliding into her guts, fear gouged inside her.

'Carla, there is no easy way to say this…'

His voice was deep, with a tension in it that cut like a wire through flesh. His mouth was compressed, and she could only stare at him, motionless and frozen, while inside the fear widened into a chasm, swallowing her.

He took a breath, got to his feet. Stood tall and powerful, looking down at her. Remote and distant.

'This is the last time I can see you,' he said. 'In a few days I shall be announcing my engagement.'

He looked down at her. His eyes had no expression in them at all.

'I didn't want you hearing it from anyone else. Roman gossip is vicious.' He paused again, his mouth tightening yet more. 'I want you to know…'

And now, for the first time, there was something in his eyes—something that only plunged that knife into her yet deeper, with a serrated, twisting blade, eviscerating her.

'I want you to know how good these last six months have been. How…very good.'

He turned away. Reached her bedroom door.

'I'll see myself out.'

There was another pause, a whitening around his mouth.

'Look after yourself, Carla.'

Then he was gone, and she could hear him walking across her living room, reaching her front door. For a second, an infinity of horror, she froze. Then, muscles bunching, she hurled herself from the bed like a tornado, tore after him. Naked—completely naked. As naked as her soul.

Her eyes blazed like furnaces. A single word shot from her.

'Why?'

He turned. There was no expression in his face. It was tight and closed as the great oaken doors of his *castello*. Guarding him against all who might invade. He had not let *her* invade. Would not permit her to do so.

He answered her now, his voice steady, unemotional. As it had to be. As it was essential for it to be. He would tell her what he had had to tell himself. Rigid discipline held him to his course, as if he were urgently steering his car out of an aquaplane that would otherwise send him crashing down into a bottomless crevasse.

This had to be done. It had to be said—*had* to.

'You said yourself, Carla, that you've always known the score with me. As I said, I gave you full credit for that.' He took a breath. 'Full credit for understanding *"why"*.' His mouth thinned. 'I have to marry. I've always had to marry. I've always had an…understanding…'

Was there irony in his repetition? He was beyond irony—beyond everything right now except knowing that his only urge was to get away, not to see her standing there, her body naked—the body he had possessed. Still wanted to possess…

'An understanding,' he said, 'for many years. And whilst my…my fiancée…' He said the word as if it were alien to him, in a language he did not comprehend, had never needed to speak till now. 'My fiancée has shared that understanding, she has had her own interests to pursue till now. She's been living in America, but now she needs to decide whether to stay there…or come home. To fulfil the…the understanding…we have always had.'

He took another breath. Every word he was speaking seemed to be impossible to say. It was a clash of worlds and he was crushed between them.

'She's now made her decision, and it is to return to Italy. Therefore…' he swallowed '… I must part with you. I apologise that I could not give you more warning, but…' He took another heavy breath. 'She's flying to Italy tomorrow, to visit her parents, and naturally they will want to hear her decision. And then…' His expression changed again. 'Then they will all be visiting me at the Castello Mantegna, where our engagement will be formally announced.'

She stared at him.

Her eyes were stretched, distended. 'Do you love her?'

It seemed the only question she could ask. The only one in the entire universe.

Her voice was thin, like wire pulled too fine. It grated—grated on him. What place had 'love' in his life? None that he could permit.

A look of impatience, of rejection, passed over his face. 'Love is an irrelevance. Francesca and I are…well-suited.'

For a second—just a second—his eyes searched hers. He took a breath, forcing himself to say what he did not want to say, did not want to face.

'Carla, if you have ever fancied yourself to feel for

me anything at all...' His mouth tightened, his hand on the doorjamb clenching. 'You must know I never invited any such feelings from you—never consciously or unconsciously sought them. I never, Carla, gave you any indication whatsoever that there could be anything between us other than what has been. Acquit me of any accusations to the contrary. We had an affair. Nothing more. It could never have been anything more. You knew that as well as I.'

Long lashes dipped over his lidded, expressionless eyes—eyes that slayed her like a basilisk's lethal glance.

'I must go,' he said.

And he went.

Walked through the door. Leaving her. Closing the door behind him.

The noise seemed to echo in the silence. A silence that spread like toxic waste after the deadly poison of his words to her. That lasted until, timeless moments later, a strange, unearthly keening started in her throat...

'Carla! Open the door!'

Her mother's voice came on her voicemail. Continued loudly.

'I am not leaving here until you do. Just open it!'

Carla heard her, heard the sharp, demanding rap come again on her front door. Her mother would not go—she knew she wouldn't. Her mother's will was unbreakable.

She walked to the door, opened it, and her mother surged in.

Then stopped.

'Oh, dear God,' Marlene said, her voice hoarse.

She stared, horrified, at Carla, and Carla knew why. Her hair was unbrushed, she was wearing a tracksuit, not a trace of make-up. Her eyes were red, cheeks blotched. There were runnels running down from her eyelashes to her chin, where tears had been shed and had dried, shed and dried.

For two whole days.

Her mother's hand had gone to her mouth in disbelief, but now she lowered it.

'So, it's true, then?'

Carla looked at her. 'I take it the gossip has started already?'

Marlene drew in a breath sharply. 'Oh, yes,' she said. 'And *several* of my acquaintances have made absolutely sure I knew about it!'

Carla turned away. Tears had started again—but to what purpose? To what purpose was anything at all?

Her mother was speaking, her voice harsh, vicious, but she paid no attention.

She warned me, and I didn't listen. 'No happy ending,' she told me—but I thought I knew better.

She felt her face convulse, her throat constrict as if a snake were strangling her, its coils thrown around her body, tighter and tighter, crushing the life out of her, the breath.

She felt her mother's arms come around her, but what comfort could they bring? What reassurance? What help?

None. None, none, *none*.

Bitterness filled her, and self-hatred.

No happy ending...

She shut her eyes, resting her head against her mother's shoulder as her mother went on speaking, saying things she might say to a child, patting her back, rubbing it as if she could make her better. But there was no 'better', no happiness, no nothing. Only memories stabbing into her, over and over again, each one eviscerating her, taking out a little more of what she was made of.

Dear God, I thought—I really, really thought—that he was being different that night in the restaurant because he was starting to feel something for me! I thought that there might be possibilities of his returning what I'd just discovered I felt. I actually started to hope...to believe in a future for us...to believe in love between us...

Anguish clutched at her, its icy hand around her heart. Her stupid, stupid heart.

Why did I have to go and realise what had happened to me? Why did I have to discover what I'd come to feel for him? If I hadn't—if I'd still thought it was only an affair and nothing more than that—I wouldn't be here like this now...destroyed...just destroyed.

'You told me...you told me—*no happy ending.*'

She must have spoken. Words must have scraped past her lips. Her voice seemed to come from very far away, from polar regions where icy winds blasted her to pieces.

No happy ending.

She felt her shoulders taken, saw her mother step back from her, still holding her. Carla looked at her face, and what she saw made her stare.

'But what there *could* be,' Marlene said, biting out each word, her eyes suddenly as bright and hard as diamonds, 'is a *better* ending.'

She dropped her hands. The diamond brightness in her eyes was glittering now, her face as hard as crystal.

'There's only one way to do this, my darling girl. Only one! When a man does to you what that...that *swine*... has done to you, there is only *one* thing to do!'

She sat down on the sofa, patted the seat next to her.

'Sit down, Carla, and let me put something to you.'

CHAPTER SEVEN

CESARE'S VOICE WAS warm as he greeted the guests being ushered into the drawing room at the *castello*—the Marchese and the Marchesa and their three adult children—Francesca and her younger brother and sister.

Francesca he'd already met up with, as she'd requested, on her own, when she'd arrived back in Italy. They'd talked, long and in detail, feeling their way forward, reaching a mutual understanding. Now she was here at the *castello* with her family to formalise that understanding.

Their greetings were cordial and affectionate. He'd known her family all his life, just as he'd known Francesca—though he'd seen little of her since she'd gone to the States to do her post-graduate studies four years ago. Only occasional meetings when he'd been out there on business and taken the opportunity to look her up, or when she was visiting Italy from time to time.

There had been no rush—no need to meet up more.

He'd hoped that he could go on like that for a while longer still.

Into his head stabbed an image—he thrust it from him. He'd been thrusting it from him for days now. It was essential to do so. Absolutely essential.

Carla is in the past. I have made my decision. I will not rescind it. I cannot—

Because it would be impossible to do so. Impossible now that Francesca was here, with her family, for the intimate gathering that would result in their formal engagement. The engagement he was entering into entirely of his own volition. His own preference. The engagement that had always been waiting for him. That would now be fulfilled.

Putting Carla behind him for ever.

Greetings over, he signalled that the champagne should be served. His staff were excited, he could see, for this was to be their new chatelaine—the new Contessa. They approved of his choice—and what was there not to approve of? Francesca had visited here often—with her parents, as a child, as a teenager and as an adult.

Now, as she sipped the vintage champagne, Francesca looked tall and serene in a Grecian style off-white gown that matched her ash-blonde hair, her pale, slender beauty—very different from Carla's full-figured, vivid looks.

Carla…whom he would now never see again—except perhaps on rare social occasions if their paths should cross in Rome. But never again would she be what once she had been to him.

I wanted longer with her.

The guillotine sliced down again. Sliced through the thought and the image that formed in his head of Carla at her most alluring. He must not think of her—must *not*. Francesca was saying something to him and he must pay attention to her, ask a question in return. Something about her work that he hoped was not too unintelligent. But her field of research was so rarefied he knew he could only stumble at its edges.

She smiled, giving him an explanation he could understand. Behind her, her father beamed proudly, and her mother bestowed a doting look upon her.

'A doctor of science!' her father said, with pride openly in his eyes. 'And achieved two years before it was expected!'

'Astrophysics!' breathed her mother.

Cesare shook his head ruefully. 'I'm humbled even by the thought of it!' he exclaimed lightly.

Francesca gave a laugh. 'Oh, Ces—you? Humble? You've never been humble in your life!'

'Before *your* intellect, how can I be otherwise?' he rejoined promptly.

His eyes rested on her. She truly was a remarkable woman—extreme intellect, glowing beauty and an ancestry that wound throughout the annals of Italy's history.

She will make an exceptional contessa*!*

His father had been right—irrefutably right—in his judgement of Francesca delle Ristori. Only one aspect had he neglected—and that was what Francesca had needed to discuss with him so deeply.

Cesare had heard her out, given her all the assurances she required, let her choose entirely by herself whether she was going to do as she had now chosen—be his wife. He had assured her that of course there would be no question—none at all—of her having to focus solely on her role as his *contessa* as his mother had. She would join whatever research facility suited her field here in Italy, for as long as she wanted to, and find fulfilment both as his *contessa* and as a research scientist.

Francesca would *not* be the kind of wife his own

mother had had to be—of that he was completely sure. He didn't want that—and nor would Francesca have contemplated marriage to him on any other basis.

He drew her out a little over dinner, and she smiled and mentioned some possibilities of where she might work in Italy.

'I need to see how my doctoral research paper is received,' she said. 'Its reception may determine what offers I'm made, and by whom.'

'I'm sure they will be clamouring for you from all quarters!' he said gallantly.

Francesca laughed, and so did her parents and siblings.

The meal passed in similar convivial fashion. Everyone was pleased. Her parents were highly satisfied—for them, their daughter's marriage to him would ensure she stayed in Italy, and that was their preference. Francesca seemed pleased too, and he was glad of it. Her choice had not been made without inner conflict, but she had made it all the same. And in his favour.

And as for him—well, of *course* he was pleased. How could he not be? How could anyone not wish for Francesca as his bride, his wife, his *contessa*, the mother of his children, the companion of his life, his entire future...

Just as he'd anticipated, all his adult life...

The image he had banished earlier came into his head again, like a spectre haunting him.

Carla...

He sliced it off at source. Asked another question about astrophysics.

The evening ended.

Francesca and her family repaired to the guest quarters.

He would woo her later—do all that was necessary

between them to make her comfortable with him in that respect. Their respective pasts were irrelevant. With the decision made between them, all prior involvements would be severed. Terminated.

That guillotine sliced again.

Ruthless. Lethal. Permanent.

Because it had to be.

Carla stood, her back stiff, her face stiff, talking, sipping mineral water, refusing canapés, posing for photos. Her mother was entertaining—*fare uno mostro*—putting on a show, as she so loved to do.

This time it was for the director of a museum to which some of the choicest pieces of Guido's extensive collection were being donated. Her mother was in her element, Carla could see, being very much the gracious hostess, the generous patroness of the arts.

Across the large salon in her stepfather's opulent villa Carla could see her step-cousin, Vito, only that day arrived back in Rome from his tour of the European hotels, with his mother, Lucia. The latter looked icily furious, the former was visibly 'on duty'.

Carla had said very little to him during the evening. She was not in a talkative mood.

The reception went on and on. There were speeches— her mother's, in careful, laboured Italian, and then Vito stepping forward, clearly intent on representing the official side of the Viscari family. And there was posing for more photos, herself included, standing right next to Vito. The only saving grace was that she would not be writing this up—that would be too nepotistic.

Anyway, she hadn't been to work for days now. Citing a bug...a touch of flu.

Whether anyone believed her or not, she didn't care. She doubted the gossips did. They knew *exactly* why she was out of circulation.

Her mouth tightened.

Francesca delle Ristori—that was what Cesare's bride-to-be was called. The gossip columns were already full of open speculation. And after all, why not? What was there *not* to speculate about?

A vicious light glared in Carla's eyes.

She's the granddaughter of a duke, the daughter of a marchese, *a family friend from for ever—she has long fair hair down to her waist and she has a PhD in astrophysics! Dear God, is there anything she hasn't got?*

But there was only one thing she wanted Francesca delle Ristori *not* to be—only one.

Cesare's fiancée.

The knife thrust again into her guts. Eviscerating her. Her hands clenched at her sides.

People were leaving—finally. From her immobile position she saw her mother and Lucia go through a poisonous little ritual of one up-manship about the evening's success, then her mother was graciously inviting her sister-in-law and Vito to stay and take coffee with her, to hear all about Vito's recent travels. Adding, portentously, that they really must settle the business of Guido's shares...

Immediately, Vito tensed, Carla could see, and exchanged looks with his mother. Then promptly offered to escort his mother to her car, while he returned for coffee. The mention of Guido's shares—half the family shareholding—was a bait Vito would not be able to refuse. How could he? His determination to acquire the shares, giving him total control of the hotel chain as the sole Viscari left, was paramount. The shares her mother had adamantly refused to sell.

Now, walking with punishing stiffness, Carla followed her mother into the drawing room, taking up a stance behind her mother's chair. Vito strolled in, having said farewell to his mother—doubtless sympathising with her for the ordeal they'd both endured, with Marlene queening it over them as Guido's widow.

Well, she didn't care. Didn't care about Lucia's irritation, or Vito's frustration over the shares, or her mother's endless manoeuvrings. She cared only about one thing.

It burned inside her like hell's furnace. Her hand tightened, spasmed over the back of her mother's chair. Her mother was talking, but Carla wasn't listening. Vito was answering, but she wasn't listening to him either. The barbed exchange went on, but she paid it no attention.

Not until the moment came. The moment her mother had planned for, schemed for, hoped for, for so long now. The moment Carla had never in a thousand years thought she would collude with.

As she did now.

She heard her mother talking to Vito, her tone saccharine. 'What could be better than uniting the two Viscari shareholdings by uniting the two halves of our family? You two young people together!'

Silently, she watched Vito's reaction. Saw angry disbelief lash across his face. Didn't care. Didn't care at all. Saw his furious gaze snap to her, demand she answer—demand she shoot down immediately what her mother had just said. Refuse, outright, the preposterous notion Marlene had put forward.

She refused to think of the devastating, demolishing impact on her step-cousin.

The agonising pain of Cesare's brutal rejection had caused a consuming need to hit back at him, to claw around her raw and ravaged heart the tattered, ragged shreds of her own pathetic pride any way she could—no matter who paid the price for it, no matter how vilely it made her behave.

'I think,' she heard herself say, from somewhere very far away, where icy winds scoured all emotion from her, 'that's an excellent idea.'

The next days passed in a choking blur. Carla blanked everything and everyone. Refused to talk, refused to face what she was doing. She was like one possessed by an evil spirit, with the devil driving her.

Vito, getting her away from Marlene, had railed at her disbelievingly. Then he'd done worse than rail. He had realised why she was playing to her mother's obsession. His expression had said it all as the reason for her collusion with her mother dawned on him.

'So that's it—he's finished with you, hasn't he?'

Vito's pity had lacerated her, like thorns scraping her flesh. Then he'd poured acid on the wound.

'To speak frankly, it was always going to end that way. The Conte di Mantegna can trace his bloodline back to the ancient Romans! He's going to marry a woman who can do the same! He might have affairs beforehand, but he'll never marry a woman who—'

'A woman, Vito, who is about to announce her engagement to another man!' The words shot from her as from a gun.

Because that—*that*—was the truth of it! That was the poisonous salvation that her mother had put to her that unbearable morning in her apartment. *That* was how she was going to survive what Cesare had done to her—what she had done to herself. Falling in love with a man who was marrying another woman. A woman so much more *suitable* to be his wife than she was! A woman, so the gossip columns were already saying, who was utterly perfect to be the next Contessa di Mantegna.

As she herself had not been.

Worse than the words in the fawning articles had been the photos of Cesare and Francesca delle Ristori— smiling, elegant, aristocratic, such a perfectly matched couple!

Worse again than that were the photographs of herself and Cesare—taken, so she supposed in her embittered misery, at any time during the last six months at restaurants and art galleries—or of herself alone, the photos that accompanied her articles.

And the prurient, goading words that went with them, contrasting her with Cesare's noble-born fiancée.

One-time constant companion...
Another shapely beauty to adorn the arm of our dashing, illustrious Conte di Mantegna...
Daughter of late hotelier Guido Viscari's English wife, co-owner of the Viscari luxury hotel chain.

Well, it was *that* that was going to save her! Save her from the unbearable humiliation that crushed her, from the mockery of the world—and herself.

You fool—you pathetic fool! To have thought—to have really believed—that that final night with him was the start of something more! That he was feeling for you what you had realised you felt for him! When all along...

Her mind twisted away and the scorpion whips lashed

again. Wielded by the devil that was driving her now, along the desperate path she was taking. But she would take it all the same, and wouldn't care what she was doing to Vito, wouldn't care that he hated her for it, would not *let* herself care.

She would only forge on with it, frantic to cling to the only thing she *could* cling to—getting her own engagement announced to stop the pitying comments, the veiled sneers, the less than veiled gossip, targeting her as the discarded former *inamorata* of the noble Count now set on marrying his noble bride...

Because no one, *no one*, would pity her or sneer at her when she was the wife of one of the most eligible bachelors in Rome! When her husband was the multi-millionaire Vito Viscari with his film star looks, fêted and courted by all, a major European corporate player, and when their marriage had united the ownership of a global hotel chain!

Because if Cesare di Mondave could make a dynastic marriage—well, so could *she*! And her marriage to Vito would show Cesare she cared as little about him as his engagement to the beautiful Francesca delle Ristori showed that *he* cared about the woman he'd spent the last six months with! Show him that their time together had been nothing more than a pleasant interlude for *both* of them, before they'd *both* taken up their destiny—he to marry his aristocratic bride, she to unite the two halves of the Viscari family.

But she *had* to get her engagement to Vito announced formally! She had to make it happen—was desperate for it!

The devil drove her on, his reins steering her remorselessly, unpityingly.

Yet still Vito held out.

Balked at committing to her.

Wanted to reject her—just as Cesare had rejected her!

He had no desire to marry her—just as Cesare had no desire to marry her!

Desperation and despair possessed her, darkening her vision. She *had* to get Vito to publicly commit to her—by *any* means. Any at all—whatever it took.

Carla could see that as plain as day through the dark flames in her vision. Her mother saw it too. Took steps. Rumours flew—were Guido's shares for sale? If so, to whom?

The financial press ran with the story, just as her mother had intended. Rival hotel chains' names were speculated. Nic Falcone, his long-time competitor, was the front runner, keenest to snap up the oh-so-enticing Viscari shares. Yet still Vito would not agree to announce their engagement—now he was saying there was already a woman in his life, an Englishwoman he'd met on his European tour, whom he'd brought to Rome and who was staying at the Viscari Roma.

So Carla paid a visit there. Found the beautiful, long-legged blonde who was so clearly besotted with Vito. Told her that she was no one special—*like I was no one special to Cesare*—that Vito would have finished with her soon enough anyway—*like Cesare did me*—and with every stinging, bitter, galling truth, a knife went into her own heart, twisting in agony. And when Vito turned up, full of angry denunciation of what she'd said, she defied him to deny it—defied him to say she was *not* his fiancée. He could not—not if he wanted her mother's shares, if he valued them more than the tearful woman clinging to his chest, sobbing…

The blonde's despairing sobs tore at Carla, tore at her own throat, but she would not recant her words. Found justification for them in her own misery and torment.

It's better she knows now what's important to Vito— and it's not her!

Just as *she* had not been important to Cesare…

The devil's scorpion whip lashed at her again, driving her onwards as she dragged Vito away, forcing him on along the dark path she was treading, her eyes glittering with desperate fervour. Damning herself and everyone around her.

CHAPTER EIGHT

CESARE STOOD IN the massive fortified gateway that led to the walled courtyard of the *castello*, watching the Marchese's car wind its stately way down the hairpin road snaking into the valley below. Then he turned away, walked back into the *castello*.

The visit of Francesca and her parents had been a complete success, and now she was going with her parents to the family seat in the north of Italy before flying back to the USA to settle her affairs there.

There was no immediate rush for them to marry—the date was set for late summer, and Francesca's mother was intent on enjoying every moment of the lavish preparations. Also, Francesca wanted to see if she could secure a post-doctoral position at a physics department in Italy. When she returned from America, visited the *castello* once more, Cesare would start to take her out and about with him on prenuptial social engagements. Start his personal courtship of her, the woman who would be his bride.

As the woman he had set aside could never be.

Could never be in his life again in any way.

As it always did, the guillotine sliced down in his head. That subject was still not safe. With iron self-discipline— a self-discipline that he seemed to need increasingly now, but which, surely to God, would fade as time passed—he put aside the thoughts he must not have, the memories he must not recall.

He strode indoors, but as he did so, he glanced up the massive oak staircase that led to the upper floor of the staterooms. That floor was dominated by the full-length *galleria*, once the exercise space for the ladies of the house in bad weather, which now contained the bulk of the artworks here at the *castello*.

Including the Luciezo-Caradino triptych.

As if impelled, Cesare felt himself heading towards the base of the stairs. Then, abruptly, he pulled away. No, he would *not* go and look at it. To what purpose? He knew what it looked like. Knew why he wanted to go and look at it.

His expression steeled. His ancestor might have been born at a time when a man could 'have it all', but those times were gone. There could be no honour in thinking otherwise—not a shred of it.

I have made my choice and I will abide by it. Carla is in the past now, and she must stay there. My future is with Francesca. And Francesca has made her choice too—she has, chosen to be my wife.

He walked into his study, sitting himself down at his mahogany desk, ready to catch up on work after several days of entertaining Francesca and her family. His eyes flickered. He had made his choice—Francesca had made hers. But Carla—Carla had not made a choice, had she?

For a moment—just a brief, flashing moment before that guillotine cut down again across his mind—he saw her that final morning.

Naked, stripped bare of everything that she'd thought she had—everything she had presumed.

The guillotine sliced down. Harsh thoughts sliced down with it. It was a harshness that was necessary. Essential. And not just for Carla.

Well, she should not have presumed! He had given her no cause to do so—none! He could acquit himself of that! He had never—not once—given her to think otherwise! And she hadn't needed any such reminder from him! She'd said she'd always known, always accepted the necessary limitations of their time together. That it would be…could only be…for a fixed duration.

To our time together.

That had been his very first toast to her. Right from the outset. And their time together had now ended. That was all there was to it.

Impatiently, ruthlessly, he switched on his computer. It fired up and he flicked to the Internet to check his emails. The home page of a leading financial newspaper sprang up, and there, in lead story position, was a headline that stilled him totally.

He had made his choice, Francesca had made *her* choice, and now it seemed that Carla Charteris, after all, was making hers…

Marriage merger keeps Viscari Hotels in the family—Falcone's ambitions thwarted!

He stared, seeing the headline. Seeing the photo that went with it.

Feeling the jagged emotion, like a serrated blade, knifing into him.

The sonorous music swelled, lifting upwards to one last crescendo before falling silent. The hushed murmurings of the congregation stilled as the priest raised his hands and began to speak the words of the ancient sacrament in the age-old ceremony.

Inside her breast Carla could feel her heart beating like a hammer. Crushing all compunction about what she was doing—what she was making Vito do so bitterly against his will.

Emotion filled her and she felt a low, fine tremble go through her, as if her whole being were about to shatter as she stood there, gowned in white, her face veiled. Stood beside the man who was her bridegroom. Waiting for him to say the words that would unite them in marriage.

That would free her, finally, from the hell in which she lived.

But there were no words. There was only silence.

At her side, Vito stood immobile. He had not touched her since she'd walked stiffly down the aisle, her back aching with tension—tension that had kept her in hell for weeks now. A hell she had dragged Vito into as well.

But she didn't care—could not care. Could only keep going with the desperate remedy her mother had offered her—a remedy that was, she knew with the last fragment of her sane mind, poisoning her.

She *would not* let Vito go. She could not—*dared* not. If she let him go she would plunge down into the abyss. She *had* to marry him—she just had to! She would not be safe until she did. Safe from everything that was devouring her.

When I'm married to him I can be safe! I can be Signora Viscari and have a role to play, a person to be. Being his wife will give me protection.

Her mother thought it was only protection from the

sneers of the world, the gossip and the jibes, that she wanted, but that was not the protection that she so desperately sought. She needed protection from herself.

Without Vito's ring keeping me safe, keeping me here in Rome, keeping my days spent organising my wedding, without all that I'd be terrified...terrified...

Cold snaked down her back. It was terror—the absolute terror that possessed her.

That she'd go to Cesare and beg him...beg him...

Beg him to take her back on any terms—any terms at all!

In her vision she saw again that damnable triptych— the lordly Conte flanked by his pure, perfect wife...and his lowly mistress.

Her stomach hollowed. Once she had thought herself far above comparing herself to the Caradino beauty. In this day and age there could be no such role for any woman. None.

How desperately wrong she had been.

Love makes slaves of us. Strips everything from us. Craves only the object of our heart...

She felt herself tremble again as she stood beside Vito, waiting for him to say the words that would keep her safe. Safe from all that tore at her.

Her mother's cruel description seared in her head. 'Cesare's mistress', she'd called her daughter. And there had been more words too...

'No happy ending.'

Except for Cesare. Cesare with his beautiful, clever, aristocratic bride—the perfect Contessa.

'Do you love her?'

The agonising question she'd hurled at him haunted

her, seared in her head now, as she stood rigid with tension beside the man she was forcing to marry her.

And in her head Cesare's reply came again.

'Love is an irrelevance.'

Her face convulsed beneath her veil. Words tumbled through her head, hectic and desperate.

And it will be irrelevant for me too! I don't love Vito, and his emotion for me is only loathing and bitter hatred for what I've done to him, for the price I'm making him pay to get his family shares back. But when I'm safe—truly safe—I can let him go. In six months...a year...he can get on with his life again. I'll ask for an annulment and release Vito and then he can go and find that blonde of his if he really wants to. He can have it all—the shares, the blonde, everything... It won't be the end of the world for him, for her. They can sort it out between them if they really want to.

As for herself—well, this time around it would be *her* choice not to be married! *She* would be the one to end it!

I'll walk out with my head held high—no one will pity me! No one will think me scorned ever again! And Cesare and his beautiful, nobly born, terrifyingly clever, oh-so-damn-wonderful bride can go on having their wonderful life together and I won't care—I won't! I'll have shown him that I can do very well without him! That I've survived.

As if surfacing from a deep, suffocating dive, she became aware that the silence was lengthening. That Vito was still not saying the words she needed to hear—the words that would rescue her from this hell she was in.

Her head jerked towards him, her eyes distending. Filling with urgency.

Then finally Vito was speaking. But it was not to the

priest. It was to her. His face stark, he was turning to-wards her. Saying words that drained the air from her lungs.

'I won't do this, Carla.'

She heard his words. But they came from a long, long way away. There was a roaring in her head...

'No, Mum—I said *no*!'

Carla's voice was like a knife. Her mother was argu-ing with her, trying to make her go back to Guido's villa with her. But she could not bear another moment of her mother's company.

Raging, shouting, almost hysterical, Carla sat in the vestry, on a hard bench, her nails digging into her palms.

'I'm going back to my apartment.'

How she'd got there she could not remember—one of the wedding cars, she supposed, waiting by the rear en-trance to the church, had taken her away from the avid, buzzing speculation of the congregation. But now she was finally there in her bedroom, standing in her wed-ding dress.

Palest white, like the decor in her apartment. As if she might disappear into it...

A bead of hysteria bubbled in her throat. She fought it down. She must not let it out. She must keep it deep inside her. Must, instead, reach behind her back and with stiff, aching arms undo, hook by hook, the gown she had put on less than three hours ago at Guido's house.

I was so nearly safe—so nearly! And now...

She felt terror beat up in her—had to fight it down. Fight down the cold, sick feeling inside her that was run-ning in every vein like liquid nitrogen.

He jilted me. Vito jilted me. Turned me down. Rejected me. Refused to marry me... Refused, refused, refused...

She felt the hysteria in her throat again, felt her eyes distend, felt pressure in her head as if it might explode. Felt her fingers tremble as the last of the hooks were undone and the heavy, beaded satin and lace gown plummeted to the floor.

She stepped out of it, twisted out of her shoes. God knew where her veil was—she'd torn it from her as she'd gained the vestry, with Vito's arm clamped around hers. If it hadn't been she'd have fainted on the spot. As it was she'd swayed, felt the church whirling around her, and heard a choking noise come from her throat.

She could be glad of that—glad that it had given her a lie to cling to.

'The bride is indisposed...'

Hysteria clawed again. Yes, 'indisposed'—that was what she was.

Not jilted, not rejected, not spurned.

Somewhere in the depths of her head she knew, with a kind of piercing pain, that she had only got what she deserved.

I forced Vito to the altar—behaved shamefully...selfishly.

Desperately.

She walked into the bathroom, yanking on the shower. She stepped under the plunging water, still in her underwear, her hair still pinned into its elaborate coiffeur, soaking herself in the hot, punishing water.

How long she stood there, she could not say. She knew only that it seemed to take an agony of time to peel off the underwear clinging to her streaming wet body—to free herself from the silken mesh of her stockings, push down her panties, yank off her bra, until she was standing there, a mess of lingerie in the shower tray, her hair covering her face, her back, standing there in the scorching hot water, shivering violently...

With shaking hands she turned the water off, pushed the dripping locks from her face, clambered out of the cubicle to seize a towel for her hair, for her body, her feet. She was still shaking, though her skin was red and overheated.

Somehow she made it to her bed. Somehow she thrust the wet towels from her, crawled under the covers like a wounded animal. Somehow, she curled her body, knees drawn up, arms wrapped about herself, her still wet hair damp on the pillow.

She felt the world recede and the blessed mercy of sleep came over her. The oblivion she sought.

CHAPTER NINE

CESARE SMILED AT his hostess, greeting her with a kiss of her hand. He'd flown in from the USA that morning, back from a visit to Francesca—his first as her fiancé.

In America, seeing her for several days in her work environment, as opposed to seeing her as his guest with her family at the Castello Mantegna, she had seemed very...well, *American*...

There, she was not Donna Francesca, she was Dr Fran Ristori—the aristocratic honorific *'delle'* had been abandoned, he noticed—and she was clearly completely at home in the high-altitude intellectual freemasonry of her colleagues.

The conversation at the dinner party she'd given for him at her apartment on campus, to introduce him to her colleagues, had been virtually incomprehensible to him, excellent though his English was. It was his ignorance of astrophysics that had let him down...

But seeing her with her academic colleagues, speaking English with an American accent, so at home in the rarefied atmosphere of her subject, had made him think to ask her again if she were sure of her decision to marry him.

Had she hesitated? If she had, then her words had only negated that hesitation.

'Yes. You've assured me I can be both a *dottore di fisica* and Contessa di Mantegna. That was what I needed to hear. But…' Her clear blue eyes had rested on him. 'What of you, Ces?' She'd paused minutely, then spoken again. 'My spies tell me my arrival was something of an…an interruption for you.'

For the space of a heartbeat he had been silent. Then he had answered. 'What was interrupted is over, Francesca. Be very sure of that.'

Her eyes rested on him again. 'And are *you*?' she'd asked quietly. 'Are you very sure?'

He had felt the beat of his heart, the pulse of his blood. How many beats? Two? Three? More? Enough for him to exert the necessary control to say what he must.

'Yes,' he had answered. 'She is marrying someone else. I wish her well.'

In his head he had felt the serration of that same knife that had stabbed him when he'd learnt of Carla's engagement to Vito Viscari. He'd remembered the jab he'd felt that last night at the restaurant with Carla, when he'd heard that note of affection for her step-cousin in her voice.

Is that why she's marrying Viscari—just as I am marrying Francesca? An old affection, born of long years of familiarity? A marriage of mutual convenience for them both?

So how could he object? What justification was there for that knife blade slicing into his head as he told Francesca he wished her well? He would not permit it to be there. It served no function and had no cause. No justification. No place in his life. Just as Carla now had no place in his life.

Slowly, Francesca had inclined her head. Then, with

a little breath, she had changed the subject. Asked him something anodyne about his flight the next day.

Now, back in Rome, he was attending an evening party, accepting felicitations from friends and social acquaintances. His hostess, he realised with a slight frown, was Estella Farese, who had been present at the restaurant he'd first taken Carla to at the end of the previous summer.

The guillotine sliced down in his mind. He would *not* remember his time with Carla. Would banish it from his memory. Banish everything about it. Looking back was... irrelevant. Choices had been made, decisions taken. Irrevocable decisions—and not just for himself. Carla, too, had made decisions.

Is she married already? Viscari would not have wanted any delay—would have wanted to get those shares safe in his hands as soon as he could.

And that was good, wasn't it? Good that Carla had moved on. And if she'd decided to marry her step-cousin, with his film star looks let alone the fact that he came with a luxury hotel chain—to which *she* was contributing half shareholding—well, that only made Vito Viscari an entirely suitable man for her to marry. Entirely suitable.

So there was no reason—no *good* reason—why he should object to her marriage. Why his jaw should tighten, his eyes harden. Why that same spike of jagged emotion—that serrated blade—should flash across his mind, knifing into him now, as it had when Francesca had put her loaded question to him. The question she had had every right to ask and that he'd had every obligation to answer in the way he had. No valid reason at all. Except...

Except that when I think of her and Viscari—of her and any other man—I want to find her...find her and—

His hostess's voice cut across his thoughts as that serrated blade knifed into him again.

'*Cesare!* How lovely of you to be here!' Estella's greeting was warm. 'Now, do come and tell me—how is dear, *dear* Francesca! *How* delighted I am that you two are finally engaged! We've all had to wait *so* long! *Such* a brilliant young woman.'

She took Cesare's arm, guiding him towards the far side of the salon.

They passed a knot of women, avidly conversing with each other, and they suddenly paused, as if taken aback by his proximity, only continuing as he passed by. Their eager tones, though, penetrated his awareness.

'Jilted! Yes, my dear, I was there! I saw it all! He refused to marry her!'

A titter of unkind laughter followed.

'He wanted the shares, but not the stepdaughter!'

Another voice intervened. 'No, no, it was *she* who balked! She nearly fainted at the altar. He almost had to carry her away. It's my belief...'

The voice dropped, but not so low that it did not reach Cesare's ears.

'...that she couldn't accept Viscari when she might have had—' She broke off.

The first voice came again—spiteful and contemptuous. 'She never had a *chance* of that! How could she? Mantegna has been promised to the delle Ristori girl all his life! Just as their engagement now proves!'

Estella sailed on by, speaking a little louder than she needed to, as if to drown out the gossips' voices. She proceeded to quiz him about his trip to America, about the forthcoming wedding, about whether Francesca would continue with her research career afterwards.

Cesare felt himself go into automatic mode, giving responses almost at random. But inside his head a bomb was exploding in devastating slow motion.

She didn't marry him.

The words repeated in his head. Like a gunshot.

She didn't marry him.

They stayed in his head for the duration of the evening. Were still there as he left, exhausted by polite enquiries after Francesca, and how the wedding preparations were proceeding, and showers of felicitations and congratulations and well-wishing.

There had been no further tactless or untoward remarks about what was clearly sending the gossips into overdrive.

A jilting at the altar! A fainting bride! A mother in hysterics! *Two* mothers in hysterics! And all of Rome to witness it!

Back in his apartment, the words were still there, ricocheting around inside his skull. He strode across the room, pulled open the drinks cabinet. Fetching a bottle of whisky, he poured a hefty slug. He knocked it back in one.

She didn't marry him.

Then, with a rasp, he pushed the whisky bottle away, relocked the cabinet. He went into the room he reserved for his office. He needed distraction. He would check on his affairs.

Grimly, he turned on his PC, letting it fire up. So what if she didn't marry Viscari? What was it to him? Nothing—nothing at all! *She* was nothing to him! He'd made his decision—put her aside. Finished the affair. *Finished it!*

He'd had no choice to do otherwise. No choice at all.

I could not have them both—those times are gone.

His mouth contorted and he rubbed his hand across his face—a rough gesture, as if he could wipe out what was inside his head.

Two images formed in his vision.

Francesca delle Ristori—the woman he was going to marry.

Carla Charteris—the woman he had put aside to do so.

Carla...

And, like a sluice gate opening, a dam breaking, all the images that he had kept out of his head since the moment he'd walked out of her apartment stormed in upon him.

More than images...worse than images.

Memories—vivid, tangible, indelible.

Carla swimming with him at midnight in the pool at the villa in Lazio, their naked bodies glistening in starlight.

Carla, her limbs wound with his, spine arched as she cried out in his arms.

Carla smiling at him across the dinner table, telling him something about Luciezo, or Tintoretto, or Michelangelo—some detail of art history he did not know— while he set it in historical context and they discussed the implications of it.

*Carla shaking her hair free as he drove along the au-*tostrada *towards the villa in Lazio, taking their time off together, looking forward to nothing more than easy, restful, peaceable days together—to sensual, passion-fuelled nights...*

Memory after memory.

Nothing more than memory now. Now and for ever—for the rest of his life.

As it must be.

Desperately, urgently, he made his thoughts fly across the ocean, back to where he'd left the woman who was going to be his *contessa*, his destined bride, the woman who was right for him in every way. But Francesca's image would not come—would not be conjured. Instead dark hair, blue-violet eyes, that rich, sensuous mouth that could smile, or kiss, or gasp in passion at its peak…all occluded his vision.

She didn't marry him.

The words came again—sinuous now, soft and dulcet, weaving in and out of his synapses. He felt his blood quicken, let memory ripen in his thoughts.

More than memory.

He shifted restlessly in his chair. It had been so long… so long since he had set her aside. Yet she was here—so close. Across the city—a kilometre or two…no more than that. How often had he gone to her apartment in those six months that had been their time together? How often had his hands closed over her shoulders, drawing her lush body to his as his mouth lowered to her parting lips, tasting the delectable sensual nectar of her kiss, deepening to heated arousal…?

Carla—with her blue-violet eyes, her rich mouth, her full breasts and rounded hips—with the dark, lustrous hair he'd loved to spear and tangle his hands in as he spread her body out on the bed for himself to caress, possess…to take and be taken while flames of passion had seared them both—Carla… Ah, Carla, who was only a dozen rooftops away…

Carla, whom he had set aside to fulfil his responsibilities to his name, his house… Carla, who could never be more to him than what she had been—and to have been that was…

Carla, who had thought to marry a man who was nothing to her! Merely for the reallocation of a handful of shares.

His mouth twisted. He had told himself she was entirely entitled to marry Viscari, had made himself applaud it—be glad of it. Glad that he could set her aside knowing she would be making a future for herself as her step-cousin's wife. Telling himself that her marriage made sense, was entirely suitable—just as his own was.

He could tell himself all he liked.

It was a lie. A barefaced lie to hide the truth of why she had taken such a step.

That was not why she'd walked up the aisle towards Vito Viscari! She'd done it for one reason and one reason only and he knew it—knew it with every burning fibre of his being.

She did it to punish me—because of what I did to her. Because I put her aside…put her out of my life.

That was the reason—the only reason.

Emotion reared up in him—savage, powerful. Fuelling the memories surging through his head. Impelling him from the room, from the apartment.

To one destination only.

Carla swayed, her body racked with pain. Her mind more so. Twenty-four hours—had it really been only twenty-four hours? Twenty-four hours since she had collapsed into the blessed oblivion that had blotted out the horrors of the afternoon before?

She clenched her hands, feeling her painted nails

digging into her palms. She welcomed the pain. She deserved it. Deserved it for being the cretinous, contemptible fool that she had been.

To think I could get him to marry me! To salve my shattered pride! To let me outstare the world—outstare the man who threw me aside as if I was less than nothing to him!

Mortification filled her—and self-contempt. And bitter, bitter remorse.

She deserved what Vito had done to her. Deserved his refusal to be blackmailed into saving her stupid, stupid face. Deserved everything.

She trailed into the kitchen, filled the kettle. She would drink tea and force herself to eat, despite the sickness in her stomach.

The future stretched ahead of her—empty and bleak.

She would leave Rome. She must. And her mother would be leaving too. No doors would be open to her now—Lucia Viscari would ensure that. For who would receive a woman who had sold her own husband's legacy—half the entire company—to his business rival, just to punish the man who had jilted her daughter at the altar? No, Marlene would leave for Spain and she would go with her. What else could she do?

The doorbell jangled, making her start. Dear God, not her mother again, surely? She had left only a few hours earlier, her fury at Vito's behaviour venomous, her vengeance upon him ruthless.

Carla had tried to stop her.

'Do you blame him, Mum? *Do* you? I behaved despicably to him! None of this was his fault, and yet I made him take the fall for it! And if you sell those shares to Nic Falcone you will have behaved as badly! Sell them to Vito—like he's implored you to do ever since Guido died!'

But Marlene had been deaf to Carla's pleas. Driven by maternal rage at her daughter's humiliation. There had been nothing Carla could do.

The doorbell came again—insistent now.

She put the kettle down, trailed to the door. Opened it.

Cesare walked in.

Shock, like a seismic wave in slow motion, detonated within Carla, hollowing her out, draining the breath from her body. Faintness drummed at her and she clung to the door frame for support.

He took it from her, closed it. Turned to her.

There was a blaze in his eyes. A black fire.

'Get out.' Her voice was faint, and very far away.

He ignored her, walked past her into her sitting room. His eyes came back to her as she stepped inside. She clutched her dressing gown to her, as if it might support her.

'I said get out,' she said again.

He looked at her. That black fire was still in his eyes. 'Were you really going to marry him? Did you truly intend to go through with it?'

'Yes!' she answered, her voice a searing hiss.

Emotion was knifing inside her. To see Cesare *here*, in her apartment, a handful of metres away from her…

His mouth tightened like the line of a whip. 'They can't decide, the gossips, quite what happened yesterday. Whether he threw *you* over or you him.' He paused. 'So which was it?'

She gave a laugh. A savage, vicious laugh.

'Which do you think, Cesare?' Her face convulsed. 'I should be used to it, shouldn't I? Being thrown aside!'

She took a shuddering breath. Lifting her chin, her eyes flashing like daggers, she clutched the material of her robe across her breasts, as if keeping him at bay. But she didn't need to keep him at bay, did she? He didn't want her...he would never want her again.

She slashed a hand through the air. 'So get out, Cesare! Get out of my apartment and out of my life—just *get out*!'

He stood motionless while she hurled her diatribe at him. Then, when all the fury of her words was spent, he stepped towards her.

'Get out...' she said again. Her voice was hoarse.

She should move...she should retreat. Flee. Barricade herself in her bedroom.

She could not move.

'You should not have tried to marry him,' said Cesare. His voice was strange.

There was a choking sound from her throat, but she had no words to answer him. He did not need any.

'When I saw that photo of you, that announcement in the financial press, I—' He stopped. Could not continue.

Emotion welled in him. Dark and blackening. Somewhere, far across the Atlantic Ocean, was the woman he was supposed to marry. While here...

'You should not have tried to marry him,' he said again.

From the depths of his mind he tried to conjure Francesca's face. But she was not there. He tried to say her name in his head, but he could not. That guillotine had descended across his mind, cutting him in half. There was a woman's name he needed to say—

The name of the woman who stood before him.

Her eyes were huge in her face, her hands convulsing on the silk of her robe. A robe he knew well. Raw silk, peacock-blue, shot with violet like her eyes. He'd said as much to her once as he'd slid it from her naked body, letting it pool on the floor.

He stepped towards her, reaching out his hand for the shoulder of her robe, letting his fingers slide over its silken surface. He felt her body shudder beneath his touch. Saw her close her eyes as if to shut him out, her long lashes wet.

'Carla...'

He said her name—the name he needed to say. Felt his hand fasten on her shoulder, his other hand graze down the edge of the material across her collarbone. Her delicate, intricate collarbone... The pale satin skin below yielded to his touch. And only to his.

No one else's! No other man should touch her.

His blood pulsed like a hammer in his veins. He could not do without her. Not tonight.

Memory drummed across his mind. *This* was why he was here. To make those memories real again.

He lifted her chin, cupping it with his fingers. Her eyes flared open. There was terror in them—and more than terror.

'Don't do this...' Her voice was faint.

He shook his head. 'Then tell me to go,' he said. 'You've said it to me over and over again. Say it to me now. Say it, Carla—tell me to go. To get out of your life.'

She could not speak. Could only stare.

'Tell me to get out, Carla.'

His voice was a harsh, raw husk, his mouth twisting as he spoke, his eyes spearing hers. A pulse throbbed at his throat and his long fingers plunged into her hair, indenting into her skull. Holding her for himself...*only* for himself...

'Tell me to get out,' he said again, one final time.

But she could not. She could do nothing. Nothing at all. Could only feel her lips part, helpless, hopeless as, with a rasp deep in his throat, he lowered his mouth to hers, grazing it, taking his fill.

'I want one last time,' he said, his voice still a husk, his eyes still burning with that black fire. 'One last time, Carla. One last time to show you why you should not have agreed to marry another man. *Any* other man—'

He grazed her mouth with his again, his hand slipping the silk from her shoulder, exposing a single breast.

'So tell me to go, Carla…or tell me to stay…or tell me nothing at all.' His hand moved, to cup the lush curve of her breast, so rich and ripe, to feel its crest peak and bloom within his palm,

And then the time for speaking was done. With a surge of his blood, he opened her mouth beneath his, his hand tightening at her breast, kneading the soft, aroused flesh.

A moan escaped her throat. Helpless. Hopeless.

She could not speak, could not protest. She could do only what every part of her body, her being, wanted… craved her to do.

Her hands snaked around his back, hauling him to her, crushing his hips into the cradle of her body, feeling her body surge, his body answer hers.

And then the black fire took them both…

Carla moved slowly, as if emerging from paralysis. Consciousness seeped through her. For a moment she lay there, motionless. At her side, his limbs heavy upon her, Cesare slept. His face was in repose, and for a long, timeless moment Carla looked upon it.

Behind her eyes, thoughts ran.

There was a sickness inside her.

Slowly, infinitely slowly, she began to move. He did not stir. Weak with gratitude for that one small mercy, she slid from the bed. Silently, desperately, she found clothes, crept from the bedroom, forced unwilling limbs into them, found her handbag, her keys.

The morning light was dim—dawn barely broken. Her heart was pounding…the sickness was overwhelming her. She stepped forward, as if impelled by a power she could not resist.

At the door of the bedroom she halted. Her eyes, stricken, went to the figure lying in her bed, sprawled across it, the strong planes of his muscled back delineated in the dawn light. Emotion, like a wolf, leapt in her throat to devour her. Her hand was pressed to her mouth, and a sound that might have been a sob was stifled before it could be born.

Then, as if it required all the strength in her body, she turned away.

Left the apartment.

Left the city.

Fled for her very life.

CHAPTER TEN

THE SPANISH SUN was warm on Carla's bare arms and legs as she sat on the terrace of her mother's huge, newly purchased villa on this most exclusive stretch of the Costas. It seemed a lifetime ago since she had been in Rome. Yet only a handful of months had passed since she'd fled like a wounded creature.

A haunted expression filled her eyes. Then, deliberately, she picked up the newspaper at her side, turning, as she often did now, to the financial pages.

Her expression tensed. Yes, there was another news item—small, but immediately eye-catching to her—about Viscari Hotels. Something about yet another fraught board meeting, now that Nic Falcone was co-owner of the whole company and helping himself to the pick of Viscari Hotels across the world, dismembering Vito's inheritance piecemeal.

Guilt, familiar and shaming, fused through Carla. Guilt and remorse.

How could I have done that to him? How could I?

But she knew how—knew, even as the hot Spanish sun beat down on her, how her whole being had writhed in the torment of Cesare's rejection of her, in the humiliation of knowing that she had only been exactly what her mother had feared she was.

Nothing better than his mistress. To be set aside the moment his aristocratic bride beckoned!

She closed her eyes, fighting the emotion that swept up in her. What good was it to remember? Cesare had treated her by his own rules—and it had been she who had been the fool! A fool to fall in love with him—a fool ever to think she could have her happy ending…that Cesare could return her love for him…

She felt her stomach churn again. And the worst fool of all to have let him into her apartment that last, disastrous, fatal night after Vito's jilting of her. Fool upon fool!

And now…

Her hand dropped the newspaper, slid across her stomach to ease the nausea that bit there.

Dear God, how great a fool she was!

'Carla, darling, there you are!'

Her mother's voice was a welcome distraction as Marlene emerged out of the villa. She paused, surveying her daughter.

'How are you feeling this morning?' she asked carefully.

Carla stood up. 'I'm OK, Mum.'

'*Are* you?' Marlene's eyes worked over her, concern in their expression.

She was about to say more, Carla could tell, and she needed to stop her. She picked up the newspaper.

'There's another piece in here about Viscari and Falcone,' she said.

There was reproof in her voice, and she could see her mother's colour heighten.

She held up a hand. 'Mum, don't say anything—we're

never going to agree on this. But I did treat Vito appallingly.' She took a breath, saying what she had resolved. 'I'm going to go to Rome. I have to see him—to…apologise. And also,' she carried on, still not letting her mother speak, 'I want to put my apartment on the market.' She paused. 'I'm never going to live in Italy again, so there is no point owning it. And besides—'

She halted. She would not tell her mother that she intended to do more than merely apologise to Vito. Since her mother had profited hugely from selling Guido's shares to Vito's rival, she would make what amends she could by gifting the proceeds from the sale of her flat—bought, after all, with Guido's legacy to her—to Vito. He could use it to help fund his financial recovery. Pittance though it was, it was the only thing she could think of doing.

'Darling…' Her mother's voice was openly worried. 'Are you sure you want to go back to Rome? I mean—'

Carla shook her head. 'No, I don't want to—but I must.'

It was what she'd kept repeating to herself—right up to the grim moment when she bearded Vito in his office in Rome.

The ordeal was gruelling. From the moment she arrived she could feel eyes on her—curious…openly hostile.

Vito himself was stone-faced as she made her stumbling, tight-throated expression of her remorse.

'I'm desperately sorry, Vito, and deeply ashamed of myself. I let my own misery over Cesare consume me. It made me behave vilely to you—and…' she swallowed '…to…to your girlfriend.' She paused again, uncomfortable. 'I hope... I hope you were able to make it up with her after...well...since then.'

A bleak look passed across his face. 'That wasn't possible,' he said.

Carla felt guilt bite at her again. 'I'm sorry,' she said. 'Would...would it help if I...if I went to see her? Apologised for what I said...what I did?'

The bleak look came again. 'I have no idea where Eloise is. She's vanished. I've been trying to find her since—' It was his turn to break off.

'Oh, Vito, I'm sorry!'

Carla's voice was even more apologetic, her guilt ever deeper. There had been something in her step-cousin's voice that she recognised in herself—a bleakness that matched her own.

Her face twisted. 'I didn't realise she was so important to you... I mean, you usually—' She broke off again.

Vito looked at her, his eyes strained. 'Yes, I know. I *do* usually have some long-legged blonde on my arm,' he said, echoing the words she'd used. 'But Eloise—'

He broke off again, and now Carla *knew* she could see something in his drawn face that she recognised only too well. Vito's dark eyes looked at her with a nakedness in them that smote her.

'Eloise was different. I wanted so much to spend time with her—to discover if...if she was the one woman I'd ever met whom I could—'

He broke off again.

'And now I'll never know,' he said.

The bleakness in his voice broke Carla. Impulsively she stepped forward.

'Vito—let me help! Please let me help you find her. There must be a way—there *must*!'

He looked at her. 'How? She won't answer my texts or my calls. I don't have any address for her in London, where she lives, because she works as a nanny. I've had investigators checking nanny agencies, but nothing—absolutely *nothing*! She's vanished!'

Frustration and pain were clear in his voice. Carla felt her mind racing. An idea was forming in her mind.

'Vito—listen. Even if *you* can't find her—and neither can your investigators—maybe…maybe the press can!'

Vito looked at her blankly. Carla felt words tumble from her in her desperation to make amends—any kind of amends—to the step-cousin she had treated so shamefully.

'Vito, I'm a journalist—I know how the press works. What about this? I'm fairly friendly with the features editor on one of those glossy international celebrity magazines. She loves it that I know loads of the people she likes to put in it, especially you! I've always been very discreet, but this time—'

Swiftly she outlined her idea.

Vito looked at her. For the first time the lines around his eyes seemed to lighten. 'Do you think it has a chance?' he asked.

Carla looked at him. 'It's worth a shot, isn't it? A centre spread of you, with a glamorously romantic photo of you both, and a headline asking, *"Can you find my beautiful Eloise?"* Those glossy celebrity magazines have a *huge* readership!'

'Can you set it up for me? A meeting with this features editor?' There was sudden urgency in Vito's voice.

Carla smiled. The first time she'd smiled for a long time. If this was some way to make amends to Vito, however belated, she would do it.

'I'll phone her now,' she said.

Five minutes later she put the phone back on Vito's desk.

'She almost bit my hand off,' she told him.

She could see her step-cousin's eyes flare—fill with hope.

He got to his feet, came round to her. Took her hands. 'Thank you,' he said.

Emotion welled up in her. 'Oh, Vito, don't thank me! Not after what I did to you! I can never forgive myself— *never*! I was just so…so twisted up inside. So—'

She broke off again. Half turned away. But Vito did not let her go. Instead he put his arms around her, hugged her tightly. She felt tears prick at her eyes.

Then, abruptly, Vito stood back from her, looked at her with shock in his face.

'Carla—' There was disbelief in his voice.

Too late, she realised why. She stepped away, disengaging her hands.

'Cesare?' Vito's voice was hollow.

Colour stained her cheekbones. 'After…after you refused to marry me he…he turned up at my apartment. It was—'

'Does he *know*?' There was a steely note in Vito's voice.

Violently, Carla shook her head. 'No! And he mustn't! Vito—he *mustn't*!'

Vito's brows snapped together, giving him a quelling appearance. 'He must know *at once*!' he retorted. 'Before he goes any further with his engagement!'

Carla caught at his sleeve. 'No! Please, Vito! I couldn't bear it!' There was panic in her face.

For a moment his quelling expression held. Then, abruptly, it vanished.

'I understand,' he said. His voice changed. 'Carla, look...now that we've made our peace with each other I think we should show Rome that the family rift...is no more.'

He held up his hand decisively. 'I know that the gossips couldn't decide just why our wedding never took place, but I want to show them that whatever has happened since—' he did not spell out what her mother had done '—you and I, at least, are friends. So I think we should be seen out socially, while you're here in Rome, to confirm that.'

She looked at him uncertainly. 'If...if you want,' she said.

How could she refuse anything that Vito asked of her, given how badly she had treated him? Socialising in Rome might be the most gruelling ordeal she could imagine right now, but she must face it for Vito's sake.

And if I fear I might see Cesare—well, why should I? Viscari circles don't usually overlap with his, and anyway Cesare's probably in his castello *planning his wedding...*

She felt the nausea bite again—and something worse than nausea. Much, much worse.

'Good.' Vito nodded. He smiled. 'How about tonight?'

She paled. 'Tonight?' she echoed faintly.

Vito quirked an eyebrow. 'You have something more pressing?'

Slowly she shook her head, realised that in all conscience she could not refuse.

That evening, as she stood staring blankly at her reflection in the mirror, she knew the last thing she wanted was to go out into society—even though she owed it to Vito. So, ignoring the knots in her stomach, she threw one last glance at herself, reassured by the dark indigo evening gown, generously cut—nothing clinging or curvaceous now—and her immaculate hair and make-up.

Her phone buzzed to tell her that Vito was waiting for her in his car below, and she left her apartment.

She had spent the afternoon with estate agents and her solicitor, booking a removal company to transfer her possessions to her mother's house. She would tell Vito this evening that she was going to hand him the proceeds of the sale—it wasn't much, compared to the loss he'd suffered, thanks to her mother, but it was all she could do.

She paid little attention to where he was taking her, but as they walked inside an ornate *palazzo*, the venue for the fundraising reception for a *museo di antiquity* that Vito was attending, she suddenly froze.

Her hand clawed on Vito's sleeve. 'This is the Palazzo Mantegna!'

He glanced at her. 'I know,' he said. 'That's why I brought you here—Cesare will be here as one of the *museo*'s patrons.'

Desperately, Carla tried to pull away.

But Vito's hand clamped over hers. 'Carla—he has to know. He *has* to!'

A drumming filled her senses.

Cesare was talking to his fellow *museo* patrons, but for all his polite conversation he had no inclination to be there. His mood was grim.

Francesca was still in America, vacating her apartment, making ready to move back to Italy and become his *contessa*. He was glad of her absence. How could he face her after what he had done? Committing an act of folly so extreme he could not now believe that he had done it.

Folly? Was that what it had been? That final, self-indulgent, devil-driven night with Carla? The sour taste of self-disgust filled him. Of shame.

I went to her with my betrothal ring on Francesca's finger! And yet I presumed to accuse her of being prepared to marry another man! As if she had betrayed me... spurned me for another man.

In that one shameful night he had behaved unforgivably to the woman he'd undertaken to marry *and* the one whom he could never marry. Could never again possess. Could never again see, or have anything to do with.

She is lost to me for ever.

As he said the words, he felt something twist inside him, as if the point of a knife had broken off, stayed in his guts. It would stay there, lodged for ever. Scar tissue would grow around it, but it would remain for all his life. A wound that would not heal...

'Signor Conte—'

He was being called to the podium to make a short speech. The moment he'd done that he'd leave. Tomorrow he'd head back to his *castello* and ready it for his future bride.

He felt his mind veer away. Contemplating his wedding—his bride—was not what he wanted to do. Memory sifted in his mind. It had been a function similar to this—the opening of that exhibition he'd lent the triptych to—where he'd first had his interest caught by Carla Charteris.

He could see her now instantly, in his mind's eye, her figure sheathed in that cobalt blue cocktail dress, her svelte brunette beauty immediately firing his senses. Calling to him…

His gaze flickered blankly over the throng of guests milling around in the palatial hall of his ancestors' former residence in Rome.

Flickered—and stilled.

No—he was imagining it. He *must* be. It could not be—

Without volition he was walking forward. Striding. People were stepping aside for him.

She had seen him. He saw it in her paling face, her distended eyes. Her hand was clutching at the sleeve of the man with her.

Viscari! With an inner snarl that came from some deep, primitive part of him, Cesare felt jealous rage spear up inside him as he reached the couple.

He could see Vito Viscari step forward slightly, as if to shelter Carla, whose face was still bleached and stark. Then, with a little breathless sigh, she started to crumple.

There were voices—deep and masculine, angry and agitated—penetrating her brain. Her eyelids flickered feebly, and she became aware that she was perched dizzily on a chair in a small antechamber—and that Vito and Cesare were standing over her.

'Are you all right?' Cesare's demand was stentorian, his face grim. The question was directed at her—he was ignoring Vito totally.

But it was Vito who was answering for her. 'No,' he said tersely, 'she is not.'

Carla's heart was hammering, the blood drumming in her ears.

Cesare's gaze snapped to Vito. 'What is wrong?'

Vito started to speak, but Carla reached for his arm.

'Vito, no! *No!*' Terror was in her now. She had to stop him—she *had* to!

But the expression on Vito's face was one she'd never seen before. Angry—stern. He was squaring up to Cesare, who was glaring at him, his face dark and closed.

Vito's chin lifted. He paid no attention to Carla. 'Your marriage plans are going to have to be altered,' he said to Cesare. 'Carla is pregnant.'

Cesare's car speeded along the *autostrada* heading into the Lazio countryside. At his side, Carla sat silent. Memory was biting like a wolf in her mind. How she had sat beside Cesare like this that first weekend together as he'd sped her towards his beautiful little rococo love nest.

I thought I could handle an affair with Cesare. A civilised, sensual affair, for the mutual enjoyment of both of us.

How utterly, totally wrong she had been. How incomparably stupid. Folly after folly! All compounded by the single greatest folly she had committed.

To have fallen in love with him. Cesare di Mondave, Conte di Mantegna. A man who would never marry her.

Except—and that wolf bit again, in her throat now—now that was exactly what he was prepared to do.

The irony of it was agonising. Unbearable. As unbearable as the words she had heard her step-cousin uttering last night. And Cesare's explosive outburst… Vito's coldly terse assurance.

Both of them had ignored her until a moan had come from her lips, and then suddenly they'd both been there, bending over her.

She'd pushed them both away, struggling upright.

Cesare's arm had come around her instantly, but she'd pulled herself free. Her head had been pounding, her heart racing.

'Leave me alone! Both of you!'

A look had been thrown between Cesare and Vito. Cesare had said something to Vito she had not been able to hear, hearing only the grimness in his voice. Then Vito had nodded.

'Be sure you do,' he'd said, in that same terse voice.

Then Cesare had looked at Carla. His face had been unreadable. He'd seemed a thousand miles away. A million.

'All the necessary arrangements will be made,' he said to her. 'I will fetch you tomorrow. Until then—'

He'd exchanged one more look with Vito, and then he had gone. It had been Vito who'd seen her back to her apartment, talking to her—*at* her—all the way. She'd said nothing, her mouth tight, compressed. Right up until Vito had seen her into her apartment.

Then she'd turned to him. 'I am not marrying Cesare,' she'd said.

Vito had said nothing. And then—'He has given me his word that he will. For now, that is enough.'

He'd left her, and this morning Cesare had arrived. She'd seen his eyes moving around the apartment and had known that he was remembering the fatal night he'd forced his way in, daring her to make him leave.

And now he's reaping the consequences.

She'd wanted to laugh, hysterically, but had silenced herself. Almost wordlessly he'd ushered her down to his waiting car and she'd gone with him, her suitcase packed.

She'd wanted to go back to Spain, to her mother, and yet here she was, in Cesare's car, going back to the place that had once been a place of bliss for her. Now, it was evident, it was going to be the scene where Cesare di Mondave steeled himself to offer to marry his former mistress who'd so disastrously got herself pregnant.

'Is it cool enough for you? I can turn up the air conditioning.'

Cesare's voice interrupted her bleak thoughts. His tone was polite. Distant.

'Perfectly cool, thank you,' she answered, her tone matching his.

He drove on in silence.

At the villa, Lorenzo was there to greet them, as he always had been. Carla was glad of his presence—it insulated her from Cesare.

Yet as lunch was served, and Lorenzo departed, suddenly she was alone with Cesare again. She watched him reach for his wine glass. Then set it down, untouched. He looked across at her from the head of the table to herself at the foot. His face was still expressionless.

It hurt her to see him. Hurt her eyes to take in the features of his face, which had once been so familiar to her—so familiar that she could have run her fingertips over its contours in the dark and known it to be him out of all the men in all the world.

And now it was the face of a stranger. She could not bear it…

But bear it she must. Must bear, too, the words he now spoke to her.

'Would you have told me that you were pregnant had your step-cousin not intervened?' he asked. His words were staccato.

Carla looked at him. 'No,' she said.

Something flashed in his eyes, but all he said was, 'Why not?'

She gave a shrug—the tiniest gesture. 'To what purpose? You were engaged to another woman.' She paused. 'You still are.'

The dark flash came again. 'You must leave it to me to communicate with my...my former fiancée,' he said heavily. His mouth was set. 'You will understand, I am sure, that this will not be easy for her. This situation is nothing of her making and I must do all that I can to make it as comfortable for her as I can.'

She watched him pick up his wine glass again, and this time he drank deeply from it. His unreadable gaze came back to her.

'Once I have spoken to Francesca—and out of courtesy also to her parents—our betrothal will be formally announced. Until that time I would be grateful...' he took a breath '...if you would be...reticent about our engagement.'

Carla did not answer.

He went on. As if he were forcing himself. 'And for the same reason I would ask you to stay here, in the villa, until I am free to become formally betrothed to you.'

Her answer was a silent inclination of her head.

For a long moment Cesare let his gaze rest on her. Emotions were mounting in his chest, but he kept them tightly leashed. It was essential for him to do so. He watched her pick up her knife and fork and start to eat. She did not look pregnant. But then, she was scarcely into her second trimester.

He felt his insides twist and knot.

She carries my child! A child she would never have told me about! I would have married Francesca—had children by her, a son to be my heir—while all along Carla would have been raising another child of mine, born outside marriage.

For a second—just a second—images flashed in his head. His ancestor, Count Alessandro, flanked by the two women in his life. His wife—the mother of his heir—and his mistress, her body rich with his bastard child.

That will not be me! Never.

Inside, he felt his leashed emotions lash him, as if trying to break free, but he only tightened the leash on them. It was not safe to do otherwise. He must ignore them, focus only on the practicalities of what must happen now. His world had just been turned upside down and his task was to deal with it.

Blank out everything else.

Blank out the memories that assailed him of how often he and Carla had retreated here to the villa to have private time together, relaxing away from their work, their busy lives. Private…intimate… Enjoying each other's company, in bed and out. Enjoying their affair.

An affair he had ended because it could no longer continue—because of the commitment he had to make to his family responsibility, to the woman who had expected to marry him all her adult life.

The commitment that now, because of his own insane behaviour the night he'd gone to Carla's apartment, driven by demons he had not known possessed him, he had to set aside. A commitment overridden by a new, all-consuming commitment. To the child Carla was carrying.

Only to the child?

The question was searing in his head, but he must not let it. Not now—not yet.

Once more he yanked at the leash on his emotions,

tightening his grip on them, and let his eyes rest on Carla, so pale, so silent.

Across the table she felt Cesare's tense gaze on her. How often had she eaten here with Cesare in the months they'd spent together? Taking their ease—talking, smiling, laughing—their eyes openly entwining with each other, the air of intimacy between them as potent as their glances.

Yet now it was as if they were each encased in ice.

What can we say to each other? What is there to say? How can we ever speak to each other as we once did? Comfortable, companionable...

'Are you well in the pregnancy?' Cesare's words, still staccato, interrupted her bleak, unanswerable questions.

'Perfectly,' she answered, her tone of voice echoing his. 'Some nausea, but no more than that. It will ease as I go into the next trimester.'

He nodded. 'I'm glad to hear it.' He paused again. 'I'll book an appointment with whatever obstetrician in Rome you choose. And perhaps it would be sensible to book you into a delivery clinic before long.'

'Thank you,' she answered. She tried to think of something else to say, and failed.

'Have you had an ultrasound yet?'

Another stilted question. Only highlighting the strain between them.

She shook her head, answering no just as stiltedly.

'Perhaps we should book one. Are there any other tests that need to be done?'

'I'll speak to the doctor, but it should all be very straightforward.'

He nodded. 'Good.'

Good? The word echoed in Carla's head, mocking her.

'Good' was a million miles from what it was. She felt nausea rising up in her throat and had to fight it down. She had just told Cesare she was coming out of morning sickness, but this nausea didn't come from her body, from her pregnancy.

It came from a source much deeper inside her.

Stolidly, she ate her way through the rest of the meal.

Painstakingly, Cesare kept a limping conversation going, talking about her pregnancy, asking questions she could scarcely answer.

When the meal was over they repaired for coffee to the terrace, underneath a shady parasol, catching the lightly cooling breeze. Out in the beautiful walled garden the sun sparkled off the water in the pool.

'How much exercise can you take?' Cesare asked.

'As much as I like, really. Swimming is the best— especially as I get closer to my due date,' she answered.

Her eyes went to the pool. So did Cesare's.

Is he remembering too? Remembering how we swam stark naked beneath the stars?

Emotion gripped her, like a knife sliding between her ribs.

Without thinking, Carla reached for the silver coffee jug, pouring black coffee for Cesare as she had done a hundred times before, handing him the delicate porcelain cup and saucer with its silver crested coffee spoon. He sketched a constrained smile of thanks and took it, sitting back in his chair, crossing one long leg over the other.

Absently, he stirred his coffee. Then, abruptly, he looked across at her as she poured hot milk into her own coffee.

'We can make this work, you know, Carla. We just

have to…to set our minds to it.' There was resolution in his voice, determination in his expression.

She lifted her cup to her lips, took a sip, then lowered it. She looked across at him. Her eyes were bleak. Negating his resolve.

'How can we?' she said. 'You'd be marrying your mistress. How can that ever work?' Her voice was tight—so tight it must surely snap, like wire under unbearable tension.

'You were never my *"mistress"*!' The words came from him like bullets. Automatic, instinctive. 'Do not paint yourself as such! We had an affair, Carla—a relationship. It was simply that—' He broke off.

She shut her eyes. Took a ragged breath. She would finish for him. Tell the truth that had always been there, right from the start—the truth that was not her fault, nor his, but that had always set the terms of their relationship.

'It was simply that marriage to me was never on the cards for you—and it still doesn't have to be, Cesare! I'm perfectly prepared to stay stashed away in Spain with my mother. I'll never show my face in Rome again! If you want to pay towards the child's upkeep, you're welcome—but I don't need your money. I'll sign any document you like never to make a claim on your estate, or your heirs.'

She fell silent. Breathless. Inside her there seemed to be a knot—a tight, hard knot that was getting tighter and harder every second. She kept her eyes on Cesare. Fixed. Resolute.

I have to say this—I have to do this. He must hear from me that I do not want this marriage.

She felt a crying out in her heart.

Not a marriage like this! Oh, not a marriage like this!

Across her heart a jagged knife seemed to be dragging its serrated blade. Had she ever had such insanely impossible hopes that he might be falling in love with her? That last evening of their affair, when he'd been so different, she'd thought—dear God, she'd really, truly thought—it might be because he was recognising what she had come to mean to him!

The jagged knife drew her heart's blood from her. But now all she was to him was a burden. An obligation. A duty he must fulfil.

For a moment—an instant—she thought she saw emotion flash darkly across his face. Then it was shuttered.

'That is out of the question,' he said.

He drank his coffee, jerkily lifting the cup to his lips, precisely setting it back down, as if every muscle were under tight control.

He looked across at her. 'Once,' he said, 'it might have been acceptable to have a…a second family, an informal arrangement.'

Into his head flashed that Caradino portrait of Count Alessandro's mistress, the mother of his illegitimate children, her swollen belly. He thrust the image from his head.

'But that is out of the question these days!' His voice was a snap—a lock to shut out any other possibility.

It did not silence Carla. Her violet eyes flared with emotion. 'It's just the opposite!' she retorted. 'There is no longer any social opprobrium in having children outside marriage. We don't have to go through a marriage ceremony just for appearance's sake! Not like—'

She broke off. A crushing sense of fatalism paralysed

her. Words, unsaid, scars inside her head, played themselves silently.

Not like my parents had to...

Cesare's shuttered expression did not change. 'No child of mine will be born outside marriage,' he said.

There were lines around his mouth, deep-scored. Carla stared at him, a stone in her chest. Then Cesare went on speaking, crossing his legs as if restless yet forced to sit still. Forced to endure what he was enduring.

'When we are in a position to formally announce our engagement,' he said, his voice coming from somewhere very distant, 'you will come to the *castello* and take up residence there. We shall be married in the chapel and—'

'No!' Once again Carla's defiant voice cut across him. Her chin went up and her eyes were burning violet. 'There will be only a civil ceremony. Nothing more. That way...' She took a ragged breath. 'That way we can divorce, without impediment to your future marriage.'

His brows snapped together. 'What are you saying?' he demanded.

'What has to be said! Oh, Cesare, if this is something we really have to do, then in God's name let us do it so that it does the least damage possible!'

She ran her fingertips over her brow. She was hot suddenly, despite the shade, hot and breathless. How could she sit here with Cesare in this dreadful mockery, this travesty?

Her voice dropped. 'Cesare, we can't do anything else. A civil marriage to legitimise the birth, and then a civilised divorce.'

He was looking at her. 'If you bear a son, he must be raised to his heritage,' he said.

She looked at him. 'Let me pray for a girl, then—

that would solve everything, wouldn't it, Cesare? A girl who can grow up with me and leave you free to marry the woman you want to marry and have your heir with. Wouldn't that be the best? *Wouldn't* it?'

He was looking at her, a strange expression on his face. She could not read it—but not because it was shuttered. Because there was something in it she had never seen before.

'Is the thought of marriage to me so repulsive to you, Carla?'

She dropped her eyes. She had to. What could she say?

It would be unbearable! Unbearable to be married to you...loving you so much and yet being such a burden to you! Someone you don't want—who is forcing herself on you simply because she's carrying your child!

She swallowed. That jagged knife was in her throat now. She forced her eyes back to his, reaching for her coffee, making herself drink it.

'No more than it is repulsive for you to marry me,' she said, her voice low.

His gaze was on her—that strange, unreadable gaze that she could not recognise.

'I don't see why it should be repulsive at all,' he said slowly, his eyes never leaving her. He took a breath. 'After all, our time together showed we are, in fact, highly compatible. Neither of us were ever bored in each other's company.'

As he spoke memory flickered in his head. Not of Carla, but of the dinner party with Francesca, in the USA, with all her physics colleagues talking about things he had not the faintest comprehension of. With Carla it had been quite different—

At the choking point of their leash, he could feel his

emotions straining to be free. Unleashed. One, at least, he *could* set free, granting him release.

His long lashes dipped over his eyes, clearing them, leaving them with an expression that Carla recognised only too well, that drew from her a tremor that was deep inside her.

'And sexually, of course, we are highly compatible.'

His gaze rested on her, only momentarily, but for long enough to send colour flaring out into her heated cheeks. She tore her gaze away, clattered her cup back on its saucer, stared out over the sparkling azure water of the pool, suddenly longing for its cooling depths.

The blood was beating in her veins, hot and hectic. Cesare was speaking again, and she heard his words, heard the sensual languor in them that only heated her blood the more.

'You must let me know, Carla, when it is safe for us to resume physical closeness. I know that in the early months it is not advised, but—'

She pushed back her chair, scraping it on the stone. 'I… I need to lie down!' Her voice was high-pitched, and even as she said the words she felt her colour mount.

He was on his feet too, his emotions back under control, back on their leash. 'Of course,' he said. 'You must rest.'

He glanced at his watch. Then back at Carla. Carla, the woman for whom, for all the complications and confusion and complexity, he felt one emotion that was very, very simple.

Desire.

He had desired her the moment he'd set eyes on her. He desired her still. That was undeniable—*that* was the emotion he knew he was safe with.

But not at this moment. Indulging it at this early stage of her pregnancy was out of the question, he knew, and for that one reason he must take himself off—let alone for all the other reasons assailing him.

'If you will permit, I will take my leave of you. I'm afraid I must return to the *castello*. I will be away, I fear, for several days. There is a great deal to be sorted out.'

Was there grimness in his voice? Carla looked at his shuttered expression. She was sure there was—and knew the reason. What else could it be for him but grim to perform the unwelcome task of telling his fiancée she'd been usurped by the extreme inconvenience of his former mistress becoming unexpectedly pregnant, requiring a swift marriage to satisfy the exacting terms of his sense of self-respect and familial honour?

She felt bleakness go through her. A sense of unreality. Yet this was real—all too real. That jagged blade drew across her heart again, sending a shot of agony through her. To have her heart's desire—marriage to Cesare— and yet for it to be like this was a travesty. An agony.

How can I do this? How? Cesare is forcing himself to marry me—just as I tried to force Vito to marry me. Is that all I'm good for? Forcing men to marry me?

A bead of hysteria bubbled in her throat. She swayed. Instantly Cesare was there, his hand strong under her elbow, steadying her. She felt his hand like a brand upon her.

'Are you all right?'

There was concern in his voice, and his eyes flickered to her abdomen, where only the slightest curve of her figure indicated her pregnancy. It was hardly visible yet—it had taken Vito's bear hug to reveal it to him, as he felt the swell below her waistline.

Vito, whom she had sought to use as a sticking plaster over her broken heart. Broken by the man her pregnancy was now forcing her to marry. Unbearable—just unbearable!

She turned her head to him, her eyes wild. 'Cesare, I can't make you marry me like this! I can't face another unwilling bridegroom! I forced Vito to the altar, using the threat of my mother selling his uncle's shares to Falcone, because I felt so...' She swallowed, finding a word that she could use to Cesare. 'So humiliated.'

She stepped away, taking a huge and painful breath, making herself look at him, her expression troubled, stricken.

'*So* humiliated, Cesare.' She watched his face close up, but went on all the same. 'I tried so hard while we were together—to be the woman you wanted me to be. I never pushed our relationship, never made demands on you.' She paused, remembering the dreadful, hideous moment when he had told her he was leaving. 'And I know you told me you'd never given me reason to expect anything more than what we had. But all the same, when you left me—'

She broke off, her throat thickening. Nearly—so nearly—she had blurted out what she must never, never tell him! What would be the ultimate humiliation for her. The ultimate burden on him.

He must never know I fell in love with him! Never!

He stepped towards her, then halted. There was something in his face again—that same look she had not understood before. Did not understand now.

'I was brutal to you that morning,' he said. There was reproof in his voice. Harshness. But not for her. 'Unforgivably so. But it was because—'

He frowned, and she saw him making his next words come, making himself hold her gaze.

'It was because I did not want to part with you,' he said. He shifted restlessly, altering his stance. 'I didn't want to end our relationship. But my hand had been forced. Francesca needed a decision—'

She saw his hand lift, as if he would reach for her, then drop again. She felt emotion welling in her, but did not know what, or how, or why.

'I had to give you up—and I was not pleased to have to do so. I knew I had to make the ending—swift. I never meant...' His eyes rested on hers. 'I never meant for you to feel what you said you felt.' His voice dropped. 'I never meant for you to feel humiliated by my rejection.'

He shook his head slowly, as if clearing it of things he had never thought about. His eyes fixed on hers again.

'I always respected you, Carla. Always. I still do. And if...' He took a heavy breath and she watched the breadth of his powerful chest widen with it. 'If I have seemed... distant, then think only that this has been a shock to me. Less than twenty-four hours ago...' his voice changed '... I saw my life, my future, quite differently from now.'

'I'm sorry,' she said, her voice low. 'So sorry for what has happened.'

'Don't be! It is not of your making. I take full responsibility! My behaviour that night—when I learnt you had not married Viscari—was unforgivable! No wonder you fled from me!' He paused for a moment, his face working. 'But if you had not fled before I woke, then perhaps—'

He stopped, as if silencing himself. His expression changed again. 'This is not the time for further talk,' he said.

He was finishing their discussion, she could see.

'We will have leisure for that ahead of us. For now—well, America is waking up, and I cannot in all conscience delay contacting Francesca.' He glanced at his watch, all businesslike now. 'So I will take my leave of you—for now. I will phone you this evening.'

She nodded wordlessly, and started to walk back indoors. Cesare fell into place beside her. Side by side—yet separate.

Her eyes went to the pair of elegant silk-upholstered sofas by the fireplace.

That's where he first started to make love to me. The night that he carried me upstairs, began our affair. Made me his.

But he was never hers. *Never.* Not even now, when he was forcing himself to marry her for the sake of the child she carried. The as yet unreal being who would become, as the months yielded to each other, so very, very real. Binding them to each other with an indissoluble bond, even if she were to divorce him and he was to marry—belatedly—his aristocratic Francesca.

This child will bind us to each other for ever. With him wishing it were not so and me...me haunted by what can never be. I can never be the woman he loves.

Into her head came the images on that triptych—the paintings that had catalysed their affair so many months ago. The Count flanked by the two women in his life. The peasant girl, gowned in red silk, who could never aspire to be his wife. And his pale, haunted wife, dutifully married, bonded for life, whether or not she had ever wanted to be.

I've become them both. The mistress he kept for his bed and the wife he married for duty, for a legitimate heir. Neither woman was happy. How could they be?

The bitterness was in her throat. Her heart.

They reached the cool, marbled hallway.

'Shall I see you up to your room?'

Cesare's voice penetrated her dark, bleak thoughts.

She shook her head. 'No—it's fine. I remember the way.'

She hadn't meant to sound sarcastic, and hoped she hadn't. Cesare did not seem to notice anyway. He only nodded.

He took her hands, holding them lightly but in a clasp she could not easily pull away from. His eyes looked into hers.

'Carla—I'm… I'm sorry. Sorry for so much. But however…however difficult things are to start with, you have my word that I will do my best—my very best—to be a good husband to you.'

His gaze held hers, but she found it hard…impossible…to bear it.

'I have said that we can make this work, and we can.' He took a breath. 'We can have a very civilised marriage. If we do divorce, at some later date—well, that is not for now. It is for then. And it may not come to that.'

For a moment it was as if he might say something more. She saw a tic in his cheek—indicating, she knew, that he was holding himself in strict self-control.

She drew back her hands. 'Cesare—go. There isn't anything more to say.' Her gaze slid away, not wanting to meet his. Heaviness weighed her down.

Be careful what you long for.

The warning sounded in her head. Once she had longed to become Cesare's wife—but not like this. Oh, not like *this*!

'Very well—I will take my leave, then.'

He did not make any gesture of farewell. Once, long ago, he would have dropped a swift, possessing kiss upon her lips, as if it were the seal of possession for their next time together. Now she was carrying his child, and that was seal of possession enough.

Except that I am a possession he does not want...

'Goodbye, Cesare.'

She did not say any more. What *could* she say? She'd said everything that could be said. Now they were simply bound to the motions they would need to go through.

She stepped back, waiting for him to leave. But suddenly, impulsively, he took her shoulders, dropped onto her forehead a brief flash of his lips. She felt his hands pressing on her shoulders, the shock of his mouth on her skin.

'We *can* make this work, Carla.'

There was intensity in his voice, in his eyes, pouring into hers. Then he was releasing her, striding away, throwing open the doors and moving out into the sunshine beyond to climb into his car and drive away.

Carla stood, listening to the engine fade into the distance. She walked forward to close the doors. Then slowly, very slowly, went upstairs.

How could they make it work? *How?*

Impossible...

CHAPTER ELEVEN

WITH SURE, SWIFT STEPS, Cesare headed down the winding pathway through the ornamental gardens below the elegant south-facing frontage of the *castello*, down into the deep valley where the narrow river rushed noisily over the boulders and rocks in its bed.

His stride was purposeful. He knew he should be contacting Francesca, but he could not face it—not yet. Instead he was doing what he had so often done as a boy, when he'd been seeking distance from the father he'd never been able to get on with.

By the river's edge he settled himself against an outcrop of rock in the late-afternoon sun, overlooking the tumbling water, fresh and cold and clean. Here, so often in his boyhood, he had found refuge from his father's admonitions and reproofs in watching the wading birds darting, in lying back on sun-warmed stone, hearing the wind soughing in the forest trees. Feeling the deep, eternal bond he had with this domain—the land that was in his blood, in his bones.

How many other Mondave sons had done likewise over the centuries? Waiting to step into their father's shoes, to take over the birthright to which they had been born?

And now, already, another son might be preparing to be born.

Out of nowhere the realisation hit him. Stilling every muscle in his body.

She carries my child! Perhaps my son—my heir!

The arc of the sky seemed to wheel about him and he took a shuddering breath. She was not the woman he had thought he would marry. In a single night, with a single act of tumultuous consummation, he had changed his own destiny. He felt emotion convulse in him. Carla—*Carla* would be his wife. Not Francesca. Carla carried his child. Carla would become his *contessa*.

He could feel the blood beating in his veins. Memory flashed through him—memory after memory. All the nights, all the days he'd spent with her. The sensual intensity of her body in his arms. The casual companionship of their times together.

I did not wish to part with her when I did.

He had told her that truthfully. Admitted it to her—to himself.

Yet into his head came her bitter words to him. 'You'd be marrying your mistress.'

His expression stilled, becoming masklike. Distant.

Is this what I want?

But what did it matter? His own desires were irrelevant. They always had been.

He had changed his own destiny. And now he had no choice but to marry Carla and set aside the woman whom he had always cast in the role of *contessa*. In his inner vision, the portraits in the triptych imposed themselves. The two women—the mistress and the wife—flanking his ancestor. The ancestor who had never had to change his own destiny.

He had them both—the mistress and the wife.

His eyes, as he gazed back towards at the *castello*, were suddenly grave. His destiny was to continue the ancient lineage of this house.

Always I've had to follow the path set out for me— first my duties to my inheritance, then my duty to marry Francesca, and now I am set by my honour to marry Carla, who carries my child. Choice has never been a possibility.

Slowly, his expression still grave, he got to his feet, made his way back to the *castello*, let himself into the drawing room. Walking through it, he moved out beyond into the state apartments, up the great staircase to the *galleria* above. Knowing just where he was going—and why.

The triptych at the far end was waiting for him. He walked up to it, looked into the face of his ancestor. *Proud*, Carla had called him, and he had taken her to task for it. She had not liked him, his ancestor, had seen only self-satisfaction, an overweening consciousness of his own sense of superiority as a man above others, taking whatever he wanted from life and paying no price for it.

Cesare's eyes went to the pale blonde woman to his ancestor's right. The woman he had married. *Chosen* to marry. Fingering her rosary, she had her prayer book on her lap, a poignant air and an expression of otherworldliness. As if she longed to be elsewhere. As if the sorrows of her life were too great to bear.

His eyes slid away to the other portrait—the other woman, his mistress. *Chosen* to be his mistress. The rich satin gown, the heavy jewels draped over her, the roses in her lap, a symbol of passion, and the ripe swell of her belly. The expression in her eyes showed her consciousness of her illicit relationship with his ancestor.

His ancestor had been free to choose them both. To pay no price for either.

Again Cesare's eyes slid away, back to the portrait of his ancestor. Saw the long-fingered hand, so like his own, closed over the pommel of his sword. His eyes went upwards to the face that Luciezo had preserved for all posterity. For *him*, his descendant, to look upon and contemplate.

For the first time, as he stood there, so sombrely regarding his ancestor's face, he saw something in those dark, brooding eyes—a shadow around the sculpted mouth…a tightness. A tension. As if his gilded, privileged life had not been entirely to his pleasure. Not entirely what he'd wanted…

Across the centuries that divided them Cesare's eyes held those of his ancestor. As if he would divine his innermost thoughts. Drill across the centuries to see inside the man whose blood ran in his veins.

A tightness shaped itself around his own mouth—a tension.

Abruptly, he turned away. Walking with rapid strides, he moved back down the lofty length of the *galleria*, descending the stairs with clattering heels. He walked into the library with its vast array of shelves, its acres of tomes inset.

His archivist was there, working on some research project or other requested by some university's history department. He started as Cesare walked in, and got to his feet.

'Tell me, are there any personal diaries or journals from Count Alessandro—the one Luciezo painted for the triptych?' Cesare asked without preamble.

His archivist blinked. 'I would need to check…' he answered uncertainly.

'Do so, if you please. And anything that you find, have sent to my office. Thank you.'

Cesare took his leave briskly, wondering to himself what impulse had made him make such a request—wondering what he had glimpsed in his ancestor's impassive face.

He pulled his mind away. He had no time to brood further. He must phone Francesca. That could not be postponed any longer.

His brows drew together. Was this really something that could be said over the phone? Telling her that he could no longer marry her? His frown deepened. He owed her more than that, surely—more than a cursory phone call.

I have to tell her to her face—I owe her that courtesy, that consideration, at least.

He would be changing her expected destiny, just as his was now changed.

He gave a heavy sigh, sitting himself down at the desk in his office, calling up airline websites, seeing when he could fly out.

He would have to tell Carla what he was doing. She would understand. He would be away a handful of days—no more than that, allowing for time differences across the Atlantic. Then he would return and announce his engagement to Carla.

Carla lay in bed, listening to the dawn chorus. She had scarcely slept. She had spent the remainder of the previous day, after Cesare had left, lying on her bed, sleepless, and then restlessly going down to the pool, immersing herself in the cooling water.

As she'd worked her way up and down in a slow breaststroke she'd felt a kind of numbness steal over her. It had lasted through the evening, through dinner—served with Lorenzo's usual skilful unobtrusiveness—and even through the phone call that Cesare had dutifully made.

Conversation had been awkward—how could it have been otherwise?—and after enquiring how she was, and how she had spent the rest of the day, his voice constrained, he had informed her in an even more constrained fashion that he would be flying to the USA the next day to see Francesca.

She had been understanding of his reasons—but as she'd hung up she'd felt a wave of guilt go through her.

He didn't ask for this! He didn't ask for me to present him with my pregnancy, turning his life upside down as it has!

And the woman who'd thought she would be marrying Cesare—*her* life was being turned upside down as well. Ripped out from under her.

By me—by my giving in and agreeing to marry Cesare. Who feels he has no choice but to marry me.

Just as she had tried to force Vito to marry her. Making him do what she wanted. Ripping up his life. Ripping up the life he had been planning to make with that blonde English girl he was now so urgently seeking.

She closed her eyes in misery.

Haven't I done enough damage to people? Do I have to ruin Cesare's life too—and his fiancée's?

The knowledge hung darkly, bleakly inside her.

Silently, she ran her mind back, thinking of the father she could not remember—had scarcely known. For the first time she thought of how he must have felt, told that he had to marry a woman he did not love because she carried his child. Had he had other plans? Other dreams?

Dreams that had been smashed to pieces? Of a life he'd wanted to live and that had been barred to him?

Just as her pregnancy was barring Cesare from having the life *he* wanted. Requiring him to do his duty, take *her* for his wife instead of the woman he wanted to marry.

A cry sounded in her head.

I don't want to force Cesare to marry me!

She felt her heart constrict. Memory poured in around it.

I had my happiness here—as much as I could ever have with Cesare. I knew from the start it was all I could have with him. That he could never be mine—not the way I came to long for him to be.

She felt her eyes distend, looking back into the past, the days and nights she had spent with Cesare. Then looking into the future she had now committed herself to—becoming his wife, his *contessa*, but not the one he had chosen of his own free will.

I can't do this to him.

With a sudden impulse she threw back the bedclothes, her hand automatically easing across her abdomen as she got up. Inside—invisible, almost intangible—new life was growing.

She felt her throat close with sudden, overpowering emotion.

This is Cesare's gift to me. Not his heart, but his child. And it will be enough.

With swift, resolute movements she dressed, re-packed her case, headed downstairs. She needed to find Lorenzo—needed him to summon her a taxi to the airport. Needed to do what she knew she must do—set Cesare free.

* * *

With heavy tread Cesare walked down the ornate staircase to the *piano nobile* of the eighteenth-century section of the *castello*. He was booked on a flight to the USA, and his helicopter pilot was on standby now to fly him to the airport. He'd emailed Francesca last night, to let her know of his impending visit—but had given no indication of his purpose. It would be a shock to her, what he must tell her, but it was one he had no choice but to inflict.

Yet again, as it had done the previous afternoon, across his mind flashed the image of that Luciezo portrait. The ancestor who had had complete freedom of choice in his life. He ejected the image. What was the point of thinking about his forebear? His own life afforded no such freedom of choice.

Abruptly he went into his office, snapped on his laptop, dragging his mind back to the present and all the difficulties that enmeshed him. He must check to see if Francesca had replied to his email. She had—but it took him a moment to steel himself to open it. The enormity of what he was going to have to do to her weighed upon him. She did not deserve it.

Yet nor does Carla deserve to have to marry me. She made it clear enough to me yesterday how reluctant she is!

And he—what did *he* feel about it?

He veered his mind away. That was a path he did not wish to follow. Not now. Not yet. First he must smash up Francesca's life.

He clicked open her email. Made himself focus on what she had written. For an instant, her words blurred, then resolved.

He started to read.

My dearest Ces, your email has been a catalyst for me. I have something I can no longer delay telling you.

He read on, disbelievingly.

Then, as the full impact of what she had written hit him, he sat back, his chest tight. Slowly he reached to close down his laptop. He would reply—but not yet. For now he could only sit there. Taking in what she had written. Taking in the implications.

A discreet knock sounded on his office door. At his abstracted permission to enter, his archivist came in.

'The papers you asked after yesterday,' he said, placing a leather-bound folder in front of Cesare. 'This is Count Alessandro's private journal.'

Cesare thanked him, his manner still absent, his mind still elsewhere. Then, as if to shake his thoughts from him, he reached for the folder and opened it, bringing out a marbled notebook, its pages mottled with age, covered in thin, flowing script. Sixteenth-century Italian, difficult to decipher.

But across the centuries his ancestor's words reached to him. And as he read a frown started across his face. He read on in silence, his expression sombre. Then, at last, he lifted his eyes from the page, from the ink scored so deeply into the antique paper, as if reverberating still with the vehemence of his ancestor.

For a long while he sat. Feeling emotion swirl deep within him—turbid, inchoate. Making sense of what he'd read. Seeing, too, the printed words on his screen—Francesca's email—melding with the antique script in front of him.

Then, with a sudden intake of breath, he pushed back his chair. He needed to stand down his helicopter pilot. And he needed to drive back to Lazio.

He was halfway to the door when he felt his phone vibrate in his jacket pocket. He pulled it out, glanced at the screen.

A voicemail.

From Carla.

He stilled. Pressed 'play'.

And everything in his world changed again...

CHAPTER TWELVE

CARLA WAS SWIMMING—slowly but steadily ploughing up and down the length of the pool at her mother's villa. Had it really only been a week since she'd made her decision to set Cesare free?

As she climbed out of the water she felt a familiar tightening of her chest—an ache of emotion burning within her. Regret? Could it be that? Regret at having walked away from the one chance she would have to be part of Cesare's life?

No—marriage to Cesare like that would have been unbearable! She had told him so, and it was true. True, true, *true*. So that was what she must hold to—all that must guide her now. However hard it was.

'Darling, are you all right? You mustn't overdo it.'

Marlene's voice was concerned as she hurried forward with an enveloping towel, draping it around Carla's wet back.

Carla smiled her thanks, taking a seat in the sunshine while her mother fussed about her. Her mother had been fussing…hovering…ever since she'd arrived back from Italy. And as she'd heard her daughter out Carla had seen the reaction in her face.

'He's offered to *marry* you?' she'd said.

Her eyes had worked over Carla. Then slid away into her own past.

'The decision must be yours,' Marlene had said slowly. 'But for my part I think it's the right one—the decision you've made.' She'd paused a moment before continuing. 'Marrying your father was the worst mistake I made. I'd hoped it would make him love me. But it did the opposite. He married me because of pressure from his father, who held the purse strings and did not want any scandal. But when his father died—you were only a toddler—he took off.' She'd paused again. 'When he was killed in that car crash there was a woman with him—and he'd just filed for divorce.'

She'd looked at her daughter, her eyes troubled.

'I ruined his life—and marriage brought no happiness for me either.' She'd taken a breath, exhaled sadly. 'No happy ending—for me *or* for him.'

No happy ending...

The words hovered in Carla's mind. Her mother's sorry tale only confirmed the rightness of her decision to leave Italy, to tell Cesare in that solitary voicemail that it was all she could face doing—that she preferred single motherhood to forcing him to marry her instead of the woman he wanted to marry.

'Go back to her, Cesare, and make the marriage you have always been destined to make. I don't want to be the one to part you from her—not for any reason. She is the woman you chose for your wife, not me. The time we had together was very...very special to me. But it is over. I wish you well. This is my choice. Please do not try and dissuade me from it.'

She had had no reply. Knew that she must be glad she

had not. Knew that she must be glad she had set him free. Must bear the pain that came with that.

To have nothing of him... Nothing—just as I had when he left me—nothing of him.

Yet as she sat sipping at her iced fruit juice, feeling the Spanish summer heat warm her damp limbs, her hand slipped to curve around the swell of her abdomen.

No, not nothing. This is Cesare's gift to me.

And memories—memories that she would never lose. *Never!*

Cesare reaching for her, taking her mouth with his, slow and seductive, arousing and sensual, taking his fill of her as her hands stroked his smooth, hard body, glorying in the feel of it beneath her exploring, delicately circling fingertips.

Cesare, his body melded with hers in the white heat of passion, desire burning with a searing flame, until she cried out, her body arching in ecstasy, the ecstasy of his possession...

A possession she could never know again.

She felt that ache form in her chest again, around her heart. An ache that would never leave her. Could never leave her. The ache of a broken heart that could never mend. She could never have the man she loved, loving her in return.

No happy ending...

Cesare walked up the wide, imposing staircase to the panelled, gilded *galleria*. Along the walls priceless Old Masters marched on either side. But he did not look at them. He went only to the far end of the long room. Stood before the triptych, letting his eyes rest on the three portraits, thinking of their tangled, entwined lives.

Once he had thought he knew them...presumed to know them...these three people from so long ago. Thought to know his ancestor, whose blood ran in his veins. The ancestor who had been free to choose, flanked by the women either side of him. The woman he'd chosen for his wife. The woman he'd chosen for his mistress.

Free to choose.

Abruptly, he turned away. Nodded at the two men waiting patiently at the entrance to the *galleria*.

'You can remove it now,' he told them.

Without a backward glance, he walked out of the room.

His expression was unreadable. But emotion was heavy within him. Weighing him down. In his head he heard, over and over again, as he had done since he had first listened to her voicemail, Carla's farewell to him.

'This is my choice. Please do not try and dissuade me from it.'

Behind him he heard the sounds of the triptych being taken down, dismantled. Packed up.

He walked on, face set.

Carla was breakfasting with her mother. The weather was cooler today now, and she was glad. Glad, too, that by the time she was in late pregnancy she would be cooler still.

As it did so often, her hand glided protectively over her abdomen. Her thoughts were full. She must stay calm, serene. Let no agitation break through—no emotion or trauma. She had chosen this path—single motherhood—over a tormented marriage to Cesare. It had been the right choice to make.

Her expression changed. Vito was appalled that she was not going to marry Cesare, but she remained adamant. She would not be swayed. And, for himself, Vito had finally found a ray of hope in his search for the woman she had caused to flee. She might have been located at last. She wished him well—hoped that he would find the happiness he sought.

As for herself—well, happiness was beyond her now. Cesare had accepted her decision. She had heard nothing more from him.

I grew up fatherless, and my child will too. But it will have me, and my mother, and safety and love, and that is all that really matters.

That was what she told herself. That was what she must believe. As for Cesare—well, he would marry his *marchese*'s daughter and live the life he had always planned.

And I will have his child—his gift to me.

It was more than she had ever hoped to have of him. She must be content with that. In time her battered heart would heal, and Cesare would have no place in it any longer.

A sliver of pain pierced her, but she ignored it. Soon, surely, it would cease. The ache in her heart would ease. It must.

It *must*.

'The mail, *señora*.'

Her mother's maid was placing a stash of post on the table, breaking Carla's painful reverie. Idly, she watched her mother sort it, then pause.

'This is for you,' she said, holding up a bulky envelope, her expression wary.

Carla felt herself tense—the stamp was Italian, the dark, decisive handwriting instantly recognisable. Steeling herself, she opened it, taking out several folded papers.

It will be some sort of legal document I have to sign, foregoing any claim on his estate for the baby, or a contract making me a maintenance allowance or something.

But as she unfolded them she gasped. It was neither of those things.

'Darling, what is it?' Marlene's voice was immediately alarmed.

Carla stared, then looked blankly across at her mother. In a hollow voice she spoke. 'It's from a secure art vault in Rome. It tells me...' She swallowed. 'It tells me that the Luciezo-Caradino triptych is now in storage. That it is being held in trust—for...for...'

Instinctively her hand went to her ripening abdomen, her eyes distending. She dropped the letter, seized up the piece of paper with Cesare's handwriting, and the third folded document.

'Mum, I—I—'

She could say no more—only got to her feet, stumbling slightly as she walked away, past the pool, to find the bench underneath the shade of the bougainvillea arbour, overlooking the beach.

She sat down with trembling legs. Opened Cesare's letter to read it. The writing came into focus, burned into her retinas—Cesare's words to her.

I have made this bequest to you not only for the child you carry but as a token—a symbol of what is between us. To understand why, I ask you to read the enclosed. It is a typed transcript from the personal diary of Count Alessandro, who was portrayed by Luciezo.

Read it now, before you read more of this letter.

She let the page fall to her lap, then unfolded the transcript with fumbling fingers. Made herself read it. The Italian was old-fashioned, with some words she did not know. But as she read she felt the world shift and rearrange itself.

Slowly, with a hollow feeling within her, she set it aside, picked up Cesare's letter again. Resumed reading.

It was brief.

I will not make the mistake he made. Whatever decision you now make, know that I am not my ancestor.

It was signed starkly, simply, with his name: *Cesare*.

Carefully—very, very carefully—her heart hammering in her chest, she put the papers back in the envelope. Then she went up onto the patio, where her mother was anxiously looking for her.

Marlene started to get to her feet, but Carla stayed her.

'I have to go to him,' she said.

Her voice was strange. Hollow. Her heart was filling with an emotion she could feel overwhelming her, drowning her.

The hire car ate up the miles, racing along the *autostrada* across the lush countryside of Lazio as she snaked ever upwards into the mountainous terrain, gaining at last, as darkness fell, the mighty stone entrance to the massive bulk of the Castello Mantegna.

I will not make the mistake he made.

Slowly, she made her way to the gate, looked at the walls of the *castello* louring over her. A postern door was set into the towering iron-studded gates, with an ancient metal bell-pull beside it. And a more modern intercom and surveillance camera.

She pressed the buzzer, giving her name. There was silence—complete and absolute silence. No response at all from within that stony fastness.

Her head sank. Defeat was in the slump of her shoulders.

Fool! Oh—fool, fool, fool!

The words berated her, like blows.

'Signorina! Prego—prego!'

The man at the now open postern gate was in the uniform of a security guard—which, Carla realised dimly, given the value of the artworks within, even without the priceless triptych, made sense. He was beckoning her frantically.

Heart in her mouth, she stepped inside, through the gate into the vast, cobbled courtyard within. The guard was apologising fervently, but her eyes were darting either side to the ranks of former stables, now garaging, and the old medieval kitchens, now staff and estate office quarters. Both wings were utterly dominated by the huge mass of the *castello* itself, rising darkly ahead of her.

Dusk was gathering in this huge paved courtyard, and security lights were coming on as she was conducted across it to a pair of palatial iron-studded doors that were being thrown open even as she spoke. Inside, she could see a huge, cavernous hall, brilliantly lit with massive candelabras. And across it, striding rapidly, came the figure of the man she had come to brave in his mountain fastness.

Cesare di Mondave, Conte di Mantegna, lord of his domain...

Faintness drummed at her. The effects of her early start that morning—after a night in which the hours had passed sleepless and tormented with confusion, with emotions that had pummelled through her mercilessly, relentlessly—the drive to the airport, the flight to Rome, the disembarking, the hiring of the car, the journey here. Exhaustion weighed her down like a heavy, smothering coat. Her nerves were shattered, her strength gone.

She sank downwards.

He was there instantly, with an oath, catching her. Catching her up into his arms, even though she weighed more now than she had ever done, as her body ripened with its precious burden. But as if she were a feather he bore her off. She closed her eyes, head sinking onto his shoulder. Feeling his strength, his warmth, his very scent…

Cesare.

His name soared in her head, fighting through the clouds, the thick mist that surrounded her. He was going through doorways, up a marble staircase, all the while casting urgent, abrupt instructions at those whose footsteps she heard running. There were anxious voices, male and female, until at the last she was lowered down upon the softest counterpane. She sank into it and her eyes fluttered. She was lying on a vast, ornate four-poster, silk-hung, and lights were springing up everywhere. Cesare was hovering above her, and there was a bevy of people, so it seemed, behind him.

'*Il dottore!* Get him here—now!'

There was command—stern, urgent—in that deep voice. Obedience in the one that answered it.

'*Si! Si!* At once—at once. He is summoned!'

She struggled upright, emotion surging through her

again, past the tide of faintness. 'No…no… I don't need a doctor—I'm fine… I'm fine.'

Cesare looked down at her. The room, she realised, was suddenly empty. There was only him, towering over her.

'He is on his way, nevertheless,' he said.

There was still command in his voice. Then his expression changed. His gaze speared into hers, and in his face Carla saw something that stopped the breath in her body.

'Why did you come? Tell me—*Dio mio*—tell me!'

She had never heard him speak like that—with so much raw, vehement emotion in his voice. She felt an answering emotion in herself, yet dared not feel it…*dared* not.

Her eyes, so deep a violet, searched his, still not daring to believe.

Slowly, falteringly, she spoke. 'When you wrote…*what* you wrote—I read… I read Count Alessandro's words… and then yours…'

Her voice was strained, her words disjointed. Her eyes searched his. She still did not dare to believe. This was the man prepared to marry her out of duty, out of responsibility. So how could he have written what he had? *Why?* Once before she had allowed herself to hope—hope that his feelings might be starting to echo hers…the very night he'd told her he was leaving her. Destroying her—

So how could she dare to hope again? *Could* she dare? She had to *know*.

'Cesare, why…why did you write what you did? That you would not make the mistake he did?' Her voice was faint, low. Yet her eyes were wide, distended.

That same vehemence was in his face—the same emotion that was stopping the breath in her body, that she had never seen before in it. It had not been there—not once—in all the time she'd known him.

His eyes burned into hers. 'You read his words,' he said. 'He married his *contessa* from duty, from expectation. Yet she never wanted to marry him. Never wanted to marry at all. Her vocation was to become a nun. But her family forced her to marry, to do her duty, to bear his children as a noblewoman should do. And he—Count Alessandro—he did as a nobleman should do: protective of his honour, taking pride in his ancient name. He did not love her, his *contessa*—that was not relevant.'

In Carla's head she heard again what Cesare had said when he had informed her he was intending to marry—that loving Francesca, his intended wife, was not 'relevant'. As she remembered, as she gazed at him now, still not daring to believe, she felt the same emotion that had brought her here, to his ancient *castello*, driven by an urgency that had possessed her utterly.

'And yet...' She heard the fracture in Cesare's voice. 'And yet there was a woman he *did* love.' He paused, his eyes still spearing hers. 'It was his mistress. The mistress he had taken from desire, whom he had never thought to marry. It was his mistress with whom he spent his hours of leisure. And it was the family he had with *her*—for babies were impossible to stop in those times, as you know—that he loved. Not the solitary son he had with his *contessa*—the son who grew to manhood hating the father who so clearly had no time for him, no love. Just as he had no time, no love, for the son's mother, the Contessa.'

Abruptly he let go her hand, got to his feet. Thrusting his hands into his pockets, he strode to the windows overlooking the valley beyond. He spoke with his back to her, gazing out at the night beyond the panes of glass, as if he could see into it, through it, back into a past that was not the youth of Count Alessandro's heir—but his own youth.

'My father had no time for me,' he said.

His voice had changed. Thinned. He was speaking of things he never spoke of. But now he must.

'He thought me oversensitive! Unlike him, I did not think that being a brilliant shot, a hunter of game, of wildlife slaughtered to hang as trophies on his walls, was a worthy accomplishment, fitting for my rank. He despised me for what he called my squeamishness. Judged me for it. Condemned me. Openly told me I was not up to being his heir.'

He was silent a moment, and his lips pressed together. Then he went on.

'When he died I determined to prove myself—to prove him wrong. Oh, I still never took to his murderous love of slaughtering wildlife, but I immersed myself in the management of all the heritage that had come to me—the enterprises, the people in my employ, the tenants and clients, all those whom the estates support and who support the estates. I did my duty and beyond to all that my name and title demanded and required of me. I gave his ghost, the ghosts of *all* my ancestors, no cause at all to think me lacking!'

He turned now, looking back across the room to the figure lying propped up against the pillows on his bed, to the swell of her body visible now in the lamplight limning her features. He felt emotion move within him as he spoke on.

'And the final duty for me to discharge,' he said, his

voice grave now, and his expression just as grave, 'was to marry. The final duty of all who bear my name and title is to marry and create a successor.'

His eyes shifted slightly, then came back to Carla. Her eyes were fixed on him, her face gaunt now.

Cesare took a breath. 'My father always approved of Francesca—always identified her as the ideal woman I should marry. She was suitable in every way—and he told me I would be fortunate indeed if she would agree to the match.'

He shut his eyes again, his face convulsing, then opened his eyes once more. Let his gaze rest unflinchingly on Carla.

'And so she would have been.' He stopped, his jaw tightening. 'If I had not met you.'

There was silence—complete silence.

'But when Francesca wrote to me, told me she had gained her doctorate earlier than she'd expected, she said she would need to choose between staying on in the USA and coming home to marry me.' He paused, his eyes looking inward, his mouth tightening. 'My first reaction to her letter should have told me.' His face twisted. 'Told me that I had changed profoundly. For my first reaction was immediate.' He paused. 'It was to cry out in my head, *Not yet!*'

His gaze came back to Carla.

'Instead—' He took a heavy breath. 'Instead I told myself how *ideal* marriage to Francesca would be. How entirely suited she was to be my wife…how well she would take on the role of my *contessa*. She knew all that it would entail and, unlike my own mother, who made being her husband's wife the sole reason for her existence, Francesca would continue her academic research here in Italy. When she gave me her decision I knew there was only one thing for me to do.' He paused again, and when he spoke his voice was heavier still. 'Remove you from my life'.

She had shut her eyes. He could see it—see how her fingers on the counterpane had spasmed suddenly.

His voice was quiet now, and yet she could hear every word as clearly, as distinctly as the space between them would allow.

'But there was a place I could not remove you from. A place I did not even know you had come to occupy.'

She could hear him now, in the darkness of her blinded vision.

'A place, Carla, where you will always be. That you can never be removed from. *Never!*'

The sudden vehemence in his voice made her eyes flare open. She could see his gaze burning at her.

'I did not know you were there, Carla! I did not know it even when I was filled with jealous rage—a rage I knew with my head that I had no right at all to feel. Yet it tore me apart all the same! When I heard that you'd become engaged to Vito Viscari—' His voice twisted. 'Madness overcame me that night I came to your apartment, blackly rejoicing that he had not married you.' His expression changed again, became gaunt and bleak. 'Even when Viscari told me that you carried my child—even then, Carla, when I knew we would marry, *must* marry, even then I did not realise.'

He stood still, hands thrust deep into his pockets, looking at her across the space that was between them.

'All I could think was how I'd never been permitted to choose—how first it had been my *duty* to marry Francesca, if she would have me, and then…' he took a ragged breath '…it became my *duty* to marry you instead.'

She shut her eyes for a moment, feeling the bleakness she had felt at knowing she was forcing Cesare to marry her. But he was speaking still, his voice changing yet again.

'When I came back here I found myself seeking out that Luciezo portrait—thinking how my ancestor had been free to choose whatever he willed, as I had never been. And yet—'

He broke off, his face working. Carla's eyes were on him again, wide, distended, and her throat was tightening.

'Yet when I read his journal…' He exhaled slowly, his eyes never leaving hers, filled with a darkness that chilled her suddenly. 'When I read his final words, then—'

When he resumed, his voice was raw.

'He cursed himself—cursed what he had done, the choice that he had made in marrying a woman he could not love. He had blighted his whole life—and the lives of both his wife and his mistress, condemning them all to unhappiness. It was a mistake that could never be mended—*never*!'

Carla felt her own face work, her throat close.

Words burst from her, pained and anguished. 'That is what I felt *I* would do if I married you! It would be as if I had become *both* those Caradino portraits—the pregnant mistress becoming the unhappy wife!'

Her fingers clenched again, spasming.

'I knew you didn't want to marry me! How could you, when you'd chosen another woman to marry, had set me aside as you had? How could I condemn you to a loveless marriage to me—condemn you to a marriage you'd never wanted?'

Her voice dropped.

'How could I condemn *myself* to it? Condemn myself to the kind of marriage my own mother made—and bitterly regretted. Just as my father regretted it. And…' Her throat closed painfully. 'Just as you would regret it too. Regret a loveless marriage—'

She broke off, emotion choking her voice. Her eyes closed, and it was as if she could feel sharp shards of glass beneath her lids. There was a sudden dip in the bed—the heavy weight of Cesare jackknifing down beside her. His hand closed over hers, stilling its clenching.

Her eyes flared open, diamond tears within.

Emotion was in his face, strong and powerful, sending a sudden surge to her pulse, a tightening of her throat. There was a searing in her heart against what he might say next.

'It would not be loveless.' Intensity infused his voice. 'It would *not* be loveless,' Cesare said again. 'When I read Alessandro's cry of despair and remorse for the mistake he had made, the mistake that could never be amended, I knew—finally *knew*—what I had blinded myself to! I realised, with a flash of lightning in my eyes, that I could leave you, or you could leave me, and it would make no difference—none at all. For you were lodged in that place from which you could never be removed.'

He paused. Eyes resting on her. The truth was in them, as he knew it must be now.

'In my heart, Carla. Where you will always be. *You* are the woman I would choose for my wife. Whether you carry our child or not.' He took a breath. 'I would choose *you*—because I love you.'

She heard his words—heard that one most precious word that was more to her than all the world—heard it and felt her heart fill with an emotion she could scarcely bear. Did she see the same emotion in his eyes?

She felt Cesare's strong hand press down on hers. Another ragged breath broke from him.

'*That* is what I wanted you to know. *Needed* you to know. You may not love me, Carla, but I *needed* you to know my heart. So that whatever choice you make now—whether to marry me or not—you know that you are in my heart for all time. And that you always will be.'

He took a shuddering breath. Poured all that he was into his next words.

'The choice is yours—it always will be—but if you feel…if you *can* feel even a fraction of what I feel for you, will you accept my hand, my heart, my life, my love?'

Carla felt her hand move beneath his. Curl into his. Hold his fast. Those diamond tears were still glittering in her eyes and she could not speak. She started to lift her free hand and in an instant he had caught it. Raised it slowly to his lips.

She saw his expression change, grow sombre again.

'Alessandro is dust,' he said. 'As are his wife and the woman he loved. For them all, his regret, his remorse, came too late. But we—' And yet again he broke off as strong emotion worked in his face. 'We live *now*—and we can make our future what we will. We can seize it, Carla—seize it and make it our own!'

His hands pressed hers.

'My most beloved *preciosa*, will you accept my hand in marriage? Will you stand at my side all my life, as my beloved wife—my *contessa*? Will you give me the priceless gift of your heart, your love? Will you let the precious child within you be the proof and symbol of our love, our life together? Will you be…' his voice caught '…in one person, both my wife and the woman I love?'

His voice changed, became overwrought with emotion.

'Will you unite the triptych—not, as you feared, as an unhappy mistress becoming the unhappy wife, but in the way it *should* have been united? So that there is no division between wife and love—united in the same woman. United in *you*.'

She felt her heart turn over and fill to the brim with a joy she had never thought to feel.

Cesare, oh, Cesare—my Cesare!

He leant forward to kiss her tears away, then kissed her mouth. Her fingers clutched his as he drew away again.

'I tried not to fall in love with you,' she said, her voice low and strained. 'Right from the first, when we began our affair, I knew that that was all it could ever be. I knew all along there could be no future for us. That one day you would set me aside to make the kind of marriage I knew you must make. But I could not stop myself. I fell in love with you despite my warnings to myself. And when you ended it… I went into a kind of madness.'

Her face shadowed.

'I behaved despicably to Vito. I nearly ruined his life. That's why—' She took a ragged breath. 'That's why I realised I could not ruin your life when you did not love me. When you wanted to marry Francesca—'

She broke off, her expression changing suddenly.

'*Francesca!* Cesare—?' Concern was open in her voice.

He smiled. A wry, self-mocking smile. 'Francesca,' he said, 'has gone to California! It seems,' he went on, half rueful, half relieved, 'that she, too, did not wish to make a loveless marriage—or any marriage at all! She wrote to tell me that out of the blue she has been invited to join an ultra-prestigious research team on the West Coast, led by a Nobel laureate, and it is her heart's desire to take up the post. She is beside herself with excitement, and knows I will understand why she cannot marry me now after all.'

He smiled again, and Carla could see relief in it, as well as a self-deprecating ruefulness.

'Astrophysics is her love—not being my *contessa*!'

Carla's expression changed. 'Count Alessandro's wife wanted to be a nun…' she mused. 'That was *her* true calling.'

Cesare nodded, seeing the analogy. 'And scientific research is calling Francesca. For which—' he dropped a kiss on Carla's forehead '—I am profoundly grateful.' He smiled again. 'You will like her, you know, if she makes it to our wedding. But you will have to accept that you won't understand much of what fascinates her so.'

The wry look was back in his face again, and then his expression altered a little, and he frowned slightly.

'Maybe that was a warning to me—the fact that I found it hard to communicate with her about her work. Although I know she would always have discharged her responsibilities as Contessa, her heart would not have been in it. I think,' he said, 'it took our betrothal to make her realise that what she had grown up with—the expectation she'd always had of what her future was to be—was not, after all, what she wanted.' His voice grew sombre again now. 'Just as did I.'

He paused, his eyes holding Carla's. Then went on.

'I do not ask forgiveness for what I did to you—only

for…understanding. If you can bring yourself to give me that, then—'

She did not let him finish. 'I give you both, Cesare—I understand *and* I forgive! From my heart—believe me!'

Her voice was broken with the urgency of what she said.

His expression changed again, lightening now, and he slid the palm of one hand across her abdomen, catching his breath as he felt the ripening curve of her body. For a moment he closed his eyes, almost unable to believe that this moment had come. A great peace had come upon him, filling his every cell, suffusing his body—his mind and his soul.

He leant towards her, his lips brushing hers, and Carla met them, her eyes fluttering shut as if to contain the immensity of the joy within her. His kiss was warm and deep, and in it were the seeds for a harvest of happiness she would reap all her life.

'My dearest heart,' Cesare said. 'My dearest love.'

He kissed her again—tenderly, cherishingly—this woman he loved, whom he had so nearly lost. Who would now be at his side and in his heart all his life.

For a long, long moment they simply held each other, feeling the closeness of their hearts, feeling the peace of love envelop them. Unite them.

'*My* Cesare,' she whispered.

For now he *was* hers—truly hers—and all her hopes had been fulfilled, all her fears and losses had gone for ever.

Her fingers slid around the strong nape of his neck, splaying into his raven hair. She knew he was hers and she was his. For all time—now and far beyond mere time.

There was the sound of a knock upon the door, the door opening. Cesare's steward announced the doctor.

Cesare glanced at Carla. She had a look of dazed happiness on her face that made a smile curve at Cesare's mouth. Maybe the doctor was not needed. But the woman he loved carried a gift for them both that was infinitely precious.

After greeting the doctor, he left him to his examination and, out in the hall, gave instructions for the best vintage champagne in his extensive cellars to be fetched. Then, in time-honoured fashion he paced outside the bedroom door, until the doctor emerged.

'Well?' He pounced immediately.

The doctor nodded. 'Quite well,' he pronounced. 'Fatigue and an excess of emotion, that is all.' He cleared his throat. 'Would I be presumptuous,' he asked, his eyes slightly wary, 'in offering you, Signor Conte, my felicitations?'

Relief flooded through Cesare. He met the doctor's eyes. 'You would not,' he said decisively.

He spoke deliberately. His steward had returned, ready to show the doctor out. The words Cesare had spoken would be all his steward would require. Within ten minutes every person in the *castello* would know that a different chatelaine from the one they had been expecting would now be in their future.

His heart, as he went back into his bedroom, was soaring. Carla possessed the one attribute that was all he needed in his wife.

She is the woman I love—and will love all my days.

And he was the man she loved.

What else could matter but that? *That* was what his

ancestor Alessandro had taught him, through his own heart-wrenching regret.

I will not make the mistake he made.

The words seared in his consciousness again as he swept Carla—the woman he loved—into his arms.

'The doctor tells me all is well.'

His eyes were warm—so warm—and Carla felt her heart turn over. Could she really be this happy? Could she truly be this happy? And yet she was.

This is real, and it is true—it is not my mere hopes and dreams!

Wonder filled her, and then pierced even more as Cesare drew back and with a sudden movement did what she had never seen him do before. He took from his little finger the signet ring engraved with the crest of his house, which he *never* removed—not for bathing, or swimming, or for any reason—and then reached for her hand again.

His eyes went to her. 'For my *contessa*,' he said, and slid the ring, still warm from his skin, onto her finger.

Then he closed his hand over hers, knuckling her hand under his. He smiled.

'There's actually a signet ring specifically for the Contessa,' he said. 'My mother wore it always from her wedding day. But for tonight, my dearest love, as we celebrate this moment, wear my ring, which I have never taken from my finger since the day I placed it there—the day my father died.'

She felt her throat catch. So simple a gesture—so profound a meaning. She felt tears well in her eyes again. His hand tightened over hers.

'No more tears!' he commanded. 'I will not permit it!'

Her face quivered into tearful laughter. 'There speaks *il Conte*!'

'Indeed he does,' he agreed, patting her hand.

He dropped a kiss on her forehead, then started to draw her to her feet.

'If you feel ready, *mi amore*, can you face my household? My steward will now have informed everyone of our news, and I have ordered champagne to be served in the salon. One glass, I am sure, will not harm our child.'

He helped her stand up, and walked with her to the door.

'And then I am sure you will wish to phone your mother, will you not? I hope she will be glad for you now that she need have no fear that you are repeating her own experience of marriage, and now that she knows how much I love you.'

His expression softened, and Carla felt again that wash of bliss go through her.

Then another emotion caught her. She halted.

'Cesare—my mother is…controversial,' she said uneasily. 'When she sold Guido Viscari's shares after Vito refused to marry me, Lucia ensured she became *persona non grata* in Rome—'

'I think you will find,' replied Cesare, his voice dry and edged with hauteur, 'that as my mother-in-law, and grandmother to my heir, she will find *no* doors closed to her—in Rome, or anywhere else!'

Carla smiled. 'Thank you,' she acknowledged gratefully. 'Though I know she means to live in Spain now, which makes things easier all round.'

'She will visit here whenever she wishes,' Cesare ordained. 'Starting with our wedding. Which—' he glanced at her speakingly, his eyes going to the slight swell where their child was growing '—I would ask to be as soon as possible.'

She looked at him, her eyes glowing with love. 'I would marry you tonight! You need only send for your chaplain!'

His hand stilled on the handle of the door before he opened it. 'Before, you wanted a civil ceremony only.'

Carla shook her head vigorously. 'Cesare—now I will marry you in your chapel here—before God and all your ancestors. I want our marriage to last all our lives and for all eternity, for that is how long I will love you!'

She leaned into him, resting her head against his shoulder, feeling his strength, his presence, his love for her. Her hand entwined with his, the gold of his signet ring indenting her finger, their hands meshing fast, indissoluble. She felt his hand tighten in return, heard the husk in his voice as he answered her.

'And it is how long I will love *you*,' he promised her.

He took a breath, resolution in his stance as he opened their bedroom door. Beyond was the wide landing, the marble staircase sweeping down to the hall, and waiting there, he knew, would be all his household. Beyond he could see the salon doors thrown wide open, brilliantly lit, and champagne awaiting them all.

He stepped out with Carla, leading her to the head of the stairs. And as they paused for a moment, looking down, applause broke out below. He turned to Carla, raised her hand to his lips, then smiled at her, with a smile as warm as the love in his heart.

'Ready?' he murmured.

'Quite, quite ready,' she answered.

And at his side—as she would always be now—she went down with him to take her place as the woman he would marry, the woman he would love all his life—his wife and his own true love. One and the same.

* * *

The metre-thick stone walls of the castello's *chapel seemed to absorb all the low murmurings of the small, select congregation, which stilled as the priest—Cesare's chaplain—raised his hands and began to speak the words of the age-old sacrament.*

Inside her breast Carla could feel her heart beating strongly. Emotion filled her—and she felt a low, fine tremble go through her as she stood there, her cream lace gown moulding to the fullness of her ripening figure. Stood beside the man who was her bridegroom. Waiting for him to say the words that would unite them in marriage—as they were already united in love, each for each other, and both of them for the child who would soon be born to them, who would continue the ancient family of which she was now an indissoluble part.

* * * * *

If you enjoyed
CARRYING HIS SCANDALOUS HEIR
why not explore these other stories
by Julia James?

CAPTIVATED BY THE GREEK
A TYCOON TO BE RECKONED WITH
A CINDERELLA FOR THE GREEK

Available now!

WE'RE HAVING A
MAKEOVER...

We'll still be bringing you the very
best in romance from authors you
love...all with a fabulous new look!

Look out for our stylish new logo, too

MILLS & BOON

COMING JANUARY 2018

MILLS & BOON®

EXCLUSIVE EXTRACT

Leonidas Betancur was presumed dead after a plane crash, and he cannot recall the vows he made to his bride Susannah four years ago. But once tracked down, his memories resurface – and he's ready to collect his belated wedding night! Susannah wants Leonidas to reclaim his empire and free her of his legacy. But dangerously attractive Leonidas steals her innocence with a touch… And the consequences of their passion will bind them together for ever!

Read on for a sneak preview of Caitlin Crews' next story
A BABY TO BIND HIS BRIDE
One Night With Consequences

There was a discreet knock on the paneled door and the doctor stepped back into the room.

"Congratulations, *madame*, *monsieur*," the doctor said, nodding at each of them in turn while Susannah's breath caught in her throat. "The test is positive. You are indeed pregnant, as you suspected."

She barely noticed when Leonidas escorted the doctor from the room. He could have been gone for hours. When he returned he shut the door behind him, enclosing them in the salon that had seemed spacious before, and that was when Susannah walked stiffly around the settee to sit on it.

His dark, tawny gaze had changed, she noticed. It had gone molten. He still held himself still, though she could tell the difference in that, too. It was as if an electrical current ran through him now, charging the air all around him even while his mouth remained in an unsmiling line.

And he looked at her as if she was naked. Stripped. Flesh and bone with nothing left to hide.

"'Is it so bad, then?" he asked in a mild sort of tone she didn't believe at all.

Susannah's chest was so heavy, and she couldn't tell if it was the crushing weight of misery or something far more dangerous. She held her belly with one hand as if it was already sticking out. As if the baby might start kicking at any second.

"The Betancur family is a cage," she told him, or the parquet floor beneath the area rug that stretched out in front of the fireplace, and it cost her to speak so precisely. So matter-of-factly. "I don't want to live in a cage. There must be options."

"I am not a cage," Leonidas said with quiet certainty. "The Betancur name has drawbacks, it is true, and most of them were at that gala tonight. But it is also not a cage. On the contrary. I own enough of the world that it is for all intents and purposes yours now. Literally."

"I don't want the world." She didn't realize she'd shot to her feet until she was taking a step toward him, very much as if she thought she might take a swing at him next. As if she'd dare. "I don't need you. I don't *want* you. I want to be free."

He took her face in his hands, holding her fast, and this close his eyes were a storm. Ink dark with gold like lightning, and she felt the buzz of it. Everywhere.

"This is as close as you're going to get, little one," he told her, the sound of that same madness in his gaze, his voice.

And then he claimed her mouth with his.

Don't miss
A BABY TO BIND HIS BRIDE
By Caitlin Crews

Available January 2018
www.millsandboon.co.uk

YOU LOVE
ROMANCE?

WE LOVE
ROMANCE!

For exclusive extracts, competitions
and special offers, find us online: